Blood Call

Science
Fiction
Saint-L

BLOOD CALL

LILITH SAINTCROW

orbit

www.orbitbooks.net

Copyright © 2015 by Lilith Saintcrow
Excerpt from *Trailer Park Fae* copyright © 2015 by Lilith Saintcrow
Excerpt from *The Girl in 6E* copyright © 2014 by A. R. Torre
Cover design by Wendy Chan
Cover photos © Shutterstock
Cover copyright © 2015 by Hachette Book Group, Inc.

Orbit
Hachette Book Group
1290 Avenue of the Americas
New York, NY 10104
www.orbitbooks.net

Printed in the United States of America

First edition: August 2015

10 9 8 7 6 5 4 3 2 1

Orbit is an imprint of Hachette Book Group.
The Orbit name and logo are trademarks of Little, Brown Book Group Limited.

The Hachette Speakers Bureau provides a wide range of authors for speaking events. To find out more, go to www.hachettespeakersbureau.com or call (866) 376-6591.

The publisher is not responsible for websites (or their content) that are not owned by the publisher.

ISBN: 978-0-316-34360-2

Chapter One

Thin winter sunlight spilled through a window, a square of anemic gold on blue carpet. He stared, turning the knife over in his hands and watching the bright gleam of the blade.

Spent a lot of time doing that, these days. Retirement wasn't boring—once a man got old enough, he learned to like it when bullets weren't whizzing overhead.

A faint sound broke thick silence.

He'd fooled himself into thinking he'd heard it so many times, the actual event was a dreamlike blur. Then the phone buzzed on his desk again, rattling against the leather cup that held two pens and a letter opener.

It was *the* phone. He'd had the number transferred to a newer one, just in case, and the bill was paid automatically every month from an account that never went dry.

Just in case. It was silly, it was stupid, it was probably a wrong number. The ID started with *1-89,* and that meant a pay phone.

Definitely a wrong number. Still…Josiah Wolfe dropped the knife and snatched up the slim black plastic case, hit TALK with a sweating finger.

"Hello." No betraying surprise in the word. His hands were steady. *It's just a wrong number. Someone hit a nine when they should have hit a six, a two when they wanted to hit five. Don't give anything away.*

Her voice came through. "Jo? Josiah?" A staggering gasp, as if she'd been punched in the stomach.

His knees had turned to water. Sweat sprang out on his lower back, under his arms, in the hollows of his palms. Was he dreaming?

Pinch me. No, don't. Let me sleep. He managed to speak. "Anna." *I still sound calm. Jesus God, thank you.*

Wait. Is she crying?

The thought of her crying made his chest feel hollow and liquid.

"I wasn't…" Another one of those terrible gasps. Was she trying to catch her breath? Drunk? Was that why she was crying? "I wasn't sure you'd answer. Or if the number was even s-still good."

He had to drop down into the chair. His legs wouldn't hold him up. "I told you it would be." *When you left me.* The words burst out, hard little bullets, surprising him. "I keep my promises."

He almost winced as soon as it left his mouth. That was like waving a red flag in front of a bull; she might have a sudden attack of good sense and hang up. *Keep her talking, idiot. Keep her on the line.*

Finally, after three years, Anna had called him.

There is a God. Thank you. Thank you so much.

Another deep ragged inhale, as if bracing herself. She sounded like she'd just paused during a hard workout, sharp low gasps. He heard city noise behind her. Cars, the imperfect roar of traffic, and the sound of cold wind. Where was she?

"I d-didn't know." Her voice broke, and he was now certain she was crying.

Warning bells were ringing. It wasn't like Anna Caldwell to cry, especially on the phone with the man she'd sworn at, slapped, and dropped like a bad habit three years ago when she'd found out what he did for a living. It doubly wasn't like her to be at a pay phone, especially on a winter day that, while sunny, was only in the thirty-degree range. She felt the cold acutely; she slept with a blanket on all but the stickiest of summer nights.

It especially wasn't like her to sound so terrified, she was stuttering.

"I d-d-didn't th-think this n-number would w-w-work, b-but I h-had to..." She broke down again, hitching sobs thin and tinny in his ear.

This isn't good. "Anna. *Anna.*" He used his calm-the-waters voice, nice and low but sharp, to grab her attention, cut off the panic. "Where are you, baby? Tell me where you are."

It worked. She took a deep breath, and he could almost see her grabbing for brittle calm, the way she'd done right before she'd walked out on him. That little sound, and her green eyes going cool and distant, her shoulders drawing back—he could picture it clear as day, even now. "I'm on the corner of Maple and Twentieth, in an awful ph-phone booth. I'm cold and I think I'm still wet from the p-pond and I'm scared, and I need your help. I *need* your help."

He was already moving, taking the small pad on his desk and making notes. *Pay phone. Maple and 20th. Pond.* "Stay put. I'm coming to get you."

"I d-didn't know who else to call," she whispered, and the most amazing thing happened.

Josiah began to get a hard-on. He still remembered the way her hair smelled. Still remembered the taste of her sweat, and her low, throaty moan at delicious intervals.

Jesus. Three years, and the woman still managed to turn him on.

"I'm in trouble," she whispered into the phone, as if afraid someone might hear. "Bad t-trouble."

So you called me. "Maple and Twentieth." He was already scooping up his car keys and his black hip-length jacket. His legs shook, but they would carry him. Of all the scenarios he'd played out in his head over the years, he hadn't ever dreamed this one up. "You're outside?" *Idiot. She said a phone booth. You can hear the traffic behind her. Is she at a gas station? Good for a grab, someone could just take her right off the street.* "I'm on my way."

"No!" She practically yelled, and he stopped dead, inhaling sharply and closing his eyes.

Focus, Josiah. Control is everything.

Calm returned, the killing quiet. Anna was in trouble, and he had to be cool and collected. *Get her locale, get in, and retrieve her. It's that simple.* He opened his eyes and got going again, placing each foot with precision.

"No," she repeated, as if he'd argued. "It's not…it's not safe. The Blake, in the foyer. Come in on the…the east side. Through the revolving doors."

The Blake Hotel was less than three blocks from Maple and Twentieth. It had three exits and usually a clutch of tourists taking in the old-fashioned foyer with its crystal chandeliers, ancient wainscoting, and red velvet upholstery. In other words, a security nightmare. He'd done a few jobs in the Blake, none serious. Just deliveries, a long time ago.

4

Don't foul your own nest was a good maxim to follow.

"It's not safe?" The question was out before he could stop himself. Even worse, it sounded cynical. Condescending. As if he suspected her of setting him up.

Nobody in the gray knew about him and Anna. He'd kept that secret successfully, at least. Of course, in this business, it was hard to be sure.

"I think they're still f-following me." She was whispering again. "If you see someone…oh, God. *God.*"

A cool bath of dread began at his nape and slid down his sweating back. *Just what kind of trouble are you in, baby?* He didn't want to waste time asking. "Anna. Calm the fuck down and breathe, I'm coming to get you. The Blake. I'll be there in twenty."

Hitching sobs, again. "I d-didn't know w-who else to—"

Yeah. Who else could you call if you were in trouble? "Get to the Blake, get inside, and put your back to the wall. Warm up. I'm coming to get you." He was already on the stairs on his way to the garage, thankful that it was Hassan's day off and Wilhelmina was in the kitchen; nobody would see him leave. "Hang up and get moving, baby."

"Oh, God…" She sucked in a sharp hissing breath. "The car. That goddamn black car."

What the hell? "What black car?"

Too late. She'd hung up, or had run out of time on whatever change she'd dropped into the phone. Unless she'd used one of the newer ones with credit card readers. No, she was too smart to do that, if she was in trouble bad enough to call him. She was too goddamn smart for her own good.

The wonder was that she'd found a pay phone at all. They were a vanishing breed.

Great. Now his heart was hammering and he tasted copper, as if he was under fire. He shrugged into his coat and checked his watch, habitually noting the time, and slipped the cell into his left-hand pocket. There were a couple of prepaid ones each in the cars, nice and disposable. His shoes made no noise on the stairs; he avoided the creaky spots out of habit as well. He made it to the garage, chose the blue BMW because it had a 9mm and ammo in the concealed compartment, and it would blend in around the Blake.

He'd never expected her to call.

Then why did you keep the phone, Josiah? The garage door went up, and the engine roused itself like a sleepy cat. Willie's little red sedan, the sleek gleaming SUV, and the dirty, primer-spotted Taurus sat in their accustomed places, watching with blank, dead headlights as he pulled out.

What kind of trouble was she in? Trouble so bad she would call *him,* of all people.

I don't care.

The sun struck him fully, and he slid a pair of shades on. Frost still glimmered in deeper shadows where the light didn't hit until afternoon; the roads would be treacherous. He flipped the radio off, and felt the little subconscious *click* inside his head that meant he was thinking clearly again.

She's called me. She needs my help.

All right. This time she's not getting away.

Josiah Wolfe smiled as he drove.

Chapter Two

She'd wanted to warn him about the black cars, but she'd run out of change and she didn't dare use her bank card *or* her beloved iPhone. Who knew what they could trace? They might think she was dead.

I certainly hope *they think I'm dead. Everyone else, too.* Maybe nobody else would…die…if they all thought she was gone.

Anna shivered, glancing nervously at the gas station. She looked like hell; she hadn't combed her hair and she was still wet to the knees from the goddamn pond; her makeup was probably running and blisters starting inside her shoes. Heels were *not* the best way to escape men with guns and walk for miles, ending up in a phone booth that smelled like someone had used it for a urinal. Vivian at Fillmore West would be furious, thinking Anna wasn't even bothering to show up to her own showing; Tasha would be heartbroken. She'd missed drinks with Robbie and Tor; they would be perplexed and hurt.

Also, she was beginning to run out of ideas.

Not only that, but she'd stood and stared at the phone for a little while, zoning out. The numb glazed calm echoing inside her head and chest *had* to be shock. Nobody could be as calm as she was right now after seeing what she'd seen.

Eric…oh, Eric…

She pushed the thought away, shoved the door open, and stepped into a light breeze knifing up from the lake's faraway, innocent baby-blue shimmer. Her black canvas purse strap dug into her shoulder; the purse itself was freighted with the files they presumably wanted to kill her for. Pale winter sunlight poured down on a convenience store parking lot, weeds poking up through cracked concrete and graffiti tangling on a wall over a huge dumpster around the back. The booth was at the very edge of the lot, and she stepped over two broken syringes as her weary body started to shiver again, reminding her that she'd run away from George Moorhouse's lovely split-level wearing only a gray business suit with a thin jacket over a silk shell, a knee-length skirt, and a pair of nylons that were definitely the worse for wear now. She'd had a long black scarf, but she'd lost it in the mad scramble to get *away,* hearing bullets *pockpockpock* into the freezing earth behind her.

A car horn blared. *"Hey, baby! You sellin'?"*

Anna, yanked back into the present, whipped the guy in the chopped-down Cadillac the finger. *I look like a hooker? Or you're just an asshole.* The Caddy zoomed off, the kids inside laughing, and she choked back another black wave of desperation masquerading as hilarity. Little jackasses in mama's car. *What a way to get propositioned.*

She had to wait, shivering and shifting her purse from shoulder to shoulder, for the light at the corner of Fifteenth and Verne; she hadn't told Josiah *exactly* where she was, for no other reason than the instinctive caution of a hunted animal.

I'm doing pretty well. At least I'm still alive. And he might help me.

At the thought of Josiah, she shivered again. She crossed her arms and stared at the red DON'T WALK sign, willing it to change.

For a horrifying second, she'd thought she'd forgotten his number. Then her brain had kicked into gear and she'd dialed, hoping, praying, begging God. After the last four days, she seriously doubted she could do anything else but pray.

I don't have anywhere else to go. And he…knows about this sort of stuff.

That's why you dumped him.

Her stomach growled, reminding her that she hadn't eaten since yesterday afternoon. The wind was going straight up her skirt. She was down to ten dollars in cash and a purse stuffed full of incriminating paperwork she hadn't even had a chance to *look* at yet. Tears burned under her eyelids. *Eric. God, Eric.*

Don't start. You already look strange; you start sobbing on a street corner and someone will call the cops, and you'll be dead before you know it.

A molten tear trickled down her cheek. She swiped it away with the back of her cold hand, swallowing the sudden lump in her throat.

The nightmare rose behind her eyes again: Eric's head tilted back and the gruesome smile of the gash in his throat leering at her, the terrible stink and the *heat;* someone had turned the thermostat up and it had been tropical in the bedroom office. They'd stuffed a ball of paper in his mouth, probably one of the scattered pieces always strewn around his offices like confetti. They had torn his place apart, probably looking for the folders she had in her purse right now.

The files Eric had asked her to keep safe, because he thought his place might be burgled. *One thing, Annie,* he'd said, laying his hand on her shoulder. *If my house is tossed, I'm not calling the police. You get me?*

She came back to herself with another jolt. The DON'T WALK sign was flashing; had she missed it?

Her high heels clattering, Anna bolted across the street and took a right. A stitch slammed up her ribs, forcing her to slow. A short Latino man walking his dog gave her a curious look but stopped outside a bakery, which was sending out a tantalizing smell into the chilly air. It would be break time at work, leaving the desk to Alan so she could run out for her morning latte. Hunger cramped as fiercely as the stitch in her side.

Don't stop, and don't spend any money. If he doesn't show up you're going to need every penny.

Yeah, like ten bucks is going to get me very far.

When she could walk again, she set off toward the Blake. The buildings were getting higher on either side, breaking the force of the wind, but they also blocked the sunlight. There wasn't much of a crowd at this end of Verne Street. Nearer the Blake, there would be well-dressed people out for shopping or the tourist attractions; the museum was up a few blocks and the opera hall a short cab ride away.

Could you hide out in a museum? Now *there* was a thought.

Anna's arm clenched, keeping the black canvas purse tight against her side. She swiped at the icy tears on her cheeks, willing herself to keep moving steadily. *If I could get away from armed men, I can do this. I'm going to make them pay, dammit.*

She had never even *dreamed* she would ever dial Josiah's number again. She racked her brain for alternatives one last time as she walked, her heels clicking against the pavement and her teeth clenched to stop them from chattering, her head held high.

There was nothing else she could do. Eric and George had both warned her not to go to the cops, and she didn't know anyone else who was likely to have even an *idea* of how to handle this. She was a temp; nobody at the office would miss her or think anything of her sudden absence. Her few friends and fellow artists were good people, but you couldn't ask someone whose last installation had been all Plexiglas cocks and red Jell-O vulvas to risk taking a bullet over this. Tasha would hide her, but how could Anna ask her best friend to take that sort of risk?

There was no one, now.

Nobody except the man she'd walked out on. Less than a week before their planned Las Vegas elopement, as a matter of fact. She had gone on with her life and her art, and done her best to forget him.

No matter how much it hurt.

Her hair fell in her face, tendrils of dark brown she wished she'd had a chance to dye. Maybe blond. She'd look bimbo-licious as a blonde, but it might be enough to throw someone off.

The walloping unreality of the last four days hit her again. *I've called Josiah.*

He'd sounded unsurprised. Calm, as usual. *I'm coming to get you.* As if she'd been stranded at a bar or with a flat tire somewhere. Even, casual, and completely confident.

For a killer, she supposed, an ex-girlfriend calling at ten in the morning with a crazy story and a hysterical demand to help must be small potatoes.

Can you just focus on getting to the goddamn hotel? You don't have anyone else you can trust right now. Tasha knew a woodcarver who happened to be a cop; she'd probably want to go to him—and end up shot.

Don't trust the police, Eric and George had both said.

Anna walked along at a good clip, each step hammering into her sore ankle, her busted-up knee—scraped from falling into the ornamental pool; she'd erased most of the skin on her kneecap with that move, but it had saved her head from being turned into hamburger—her aching hips, and finishing up by stabbing into her lower back with a bar of fire. As she got closer to the hotel, crossing Verne Street and cutting up Eighteenth, she started running her fingers back through her hair, trying to straighten it. Maybe she had a comb in her purse?

She wasn't going to be able to talk her way past the doorman. Which was why she'd asked Josiah to come in the east door; she could catch him on the street outside if she was lucky.

I wish I could take my nylons off. That would be even colder, though. She shivered at the thought.

The crowd thickened. One of the great things about living in the city was the way everyone minded their own business—or at least, pretended to. She got a few curious looks, but not many. At least she didn't have blood or muck splashed on her; she had avoided the worst of the gunk in the pool, and a scrubbing with paper towels in the gas station restroom had worked whatever wonder it could.

She no longer looked like Anna Caldwell, secretary by day and mild-mannered freelance artist. No, she probably looked like a mad Lady Macbeth.

Or just possibly like a woman on the run in a nightmare that just kept getting worse.

Go figure; she was running for her life and worrying about if she should have tried to find a comb in the restroom, too.

She sped up. Her heels clickety-clacked, traffic buzzed, and her head began to feel too big for her narrow stem of a neck.

Don't you dare pass out.

She finally glimpsed, with a swimming delirious relief that bordered on the crazed, the carved white marble façade of the Blake rising up, catching a reflection of morning light from the mirrored skyscraper opposite and glowing like heaven's doors. Anna let out a little sigh, chopped into bits by her chattering teeth. She must have been walking without paying attention, because her cheeks were still icy-wet and she didn't remember the blocks between here and the bakery.

Wake up. Look around, look for that goddamn black car. She clutched her purse to her side and clamped her teeth together. Stared at the hotel up the street. This was the south side; she would have to cross the street twice and go around the corner to get to where she could see the revolving door.

What if he'd gotten here before her? Or not come at all?

She almost moaned in dismay. Just because his cell phone number was still good didn't mean that he'd forgiven her for walking out on him, or for what she'd called him the last time she saw him, or...

Though she was perfectly justified, she reminded herself. Perfectly.

Oh, God. I'm going crazy. Please help me.

She swiped at her frozen cheeks with her jacket sleeve, shivering so hard she imagined her hands blurring like a cartoon character's. She had to get inside, one way or another. If she stayed on the street she'd freeze to death.

Josiah. The thought of him, tall and dark-haired and utterly imperturbable, was oddly comforting. Like putting her head down on his shoulder and being certain she was safe; a feeling she hadn't had since before that last, volcanic fight.

He'd said he was coming to get her. She certainly hoped so, because she was out of options. Her last great idea had ended up with Eric's editor shot and Anna herself running for her life. She had precious little left to lose.

I'm just going to have to hope he still feels something for me. She swayed, a funny feeling of her head getting too big and stuffed with cotton wool making the world blur. The cold was working its way in through her skin; she was almost too tired to shiver. *I can pay him, I've got savings left over from Mom's inheritance. That's what he always worked for before, money. And lots of it, if his apartment was any indication.*

She flinched at the turn her thoughts were taking, and almost tripped. Her left foot slid oddly inside her shoe. Something warm trickled down her heel.

I am a total fucking mess.

Her vision blurred. Eric's throat with its horrible necklace of a bloody smile rose in front of her again. She cast a nervous glance at the milling crowd on the sidewalks, the cars crawling through downtown traffic, and took hold of her rapidly thinning courage with both mental hands.

Get into the hotel. Have a goddamn nervous breakdown later.

Chapter Three

He hated to use the valet parking—too easy to get caught without wheels—but he gave the pimple-faced Hispanic kid a twenty and told him to keep the car handy. That might make up for it. He was in a hurry, which a professional should never be.

Where are you, Anna? Just be safe until I can spot you, baby. That's all I ask.

He came in the south entrance and cased the lobby, realizing that he'd been a stupid jackass. He hadn't even asked what she looked like now, if she'd dyed her sandalwood hair or would be wearing shades.

The chandeliers overhead glowed. Soft carpet muffled his footfalls as he drifted through the lobby, just a guest, just an anonymous face. Inconspicuous, chameleonlike, blending in. There were a few short, slim women, but none of them moved like her or had her habit of tilting her head slightly as if listening to a sound nobody else could hear. Her habit of being instantly visible, at least to his eyes, in a crowd. It was the way she carried herself, head high and shoulders back, all those childhood dance lessons.

She had such beautiful fucking posture.

Keep your mind on business. He made one more pass. No, she wasn't in here, unless she was hiding behind a potted palm or the bar. The bar looked good—chrome and glass, not trying to blend in with the 1920s décor of the rest of the lobby. A couple of shots of something eye-wateringly strong would go down really well right now.

The revolving door on the east side began to move again. He'd checked out each arrival up to now; none of them was the woman he wanted to see.

Maybe it had been a practical joke. Those weren't her style, though.

She said she was only three blocks away from here.

His heart threatened to stop.

She stumbled free of the revolving door, her heels clicking against the marble flooring; she headed for the carpeting with quick little mincing steps, limping slightly.

She still had that beautiful fucking posture. He could still pick her out of a crowd, out of *any* crowd.

Anna's long pretty brown hair was slightly mussed, as if air-dried and finger-combed. Her gray tailored suit might have been crisp a couple of days ago. Only good tailoring and quality material kept it from looking rumpled now. Her nylons were visibly ragged and she wore a pair of very nice black heels marred with traces of mud. No coat, and her lips were almost blue with cold. She clutched a large black canvas purse to her side, and her gaze swept around, a deer-in-the-headlights look that gave Josiah a *very* bad feeling, right down low.

Right next to the sensation of being punched in the gut by how beautiful she still was. Underneath both was the lead bar of arousal, way down deep.

There was a bruise on her right cheek, a nasty dark one that only accented her otherwise flawless skin. She bit her lower lip gently, vacantly, and he was suddenly shaken with memory.

God, he used to love that lower lip of hers.

Still did. The thought of tasting that lower lip himself made him uncomfortably aware that he hadn't lost his earlier hard-on. No, he still had a bad case for her.

Well, call the goddamn newspapers. I knew that.

It wasn't going to be long before a hotel employee noticed her. Josiah detached himself from his holding pattern and strode toward her, peripherally aware of everyone else in the lobby. Nobody had observed her yet, thank God.

Just him. And he wanted to keep it that way.

She stared, her gaze flickering through space, looking for something invisible. Her pupils were wide and dark, the intermediate stage of shock visible to trained eyes.

Josiah shrugged out of his coat and took the last few steps, his shoes soundless as the flooring switched from carpet to marble. "Anna." He had to get her away from that goddamn door. "Hey, baby."

She blinked up at him, and sighed. It was such a relieved sound that his heart squeezed in on itself.

She put her arm out like a child, letting him slide the coat on. But she didn't take the purse off her shoulder. Fortunately, his coat was big enough to hide it. She was short; he used to rest his chin atop her head and close her in his arms, feeling like he could shut out the entire world as long as he had her sheltered by his body.

Her gaze swung up to meet his through layers of shock. Green eyes, the pupils wide and dark, swimming with tears. *Jesus Christ. What the hell's going on?*

"Josiah?" She sounded even more terrified than she had on the phone.

"Come on, let's get you out of here. How far did you walk in that getup?"

"A long way." She shuddered, and he scanned the hotel lobby one more time. The doorman outside was occupied with a fat, expensively dressed woman with two brightly wrapped packages and a little yapping dog; that was probably how Anna had slipped past. "Jo—Josiah. I want to hire you."

Jesus. Have you lost your mind, woman? "Shut up." He got her under his arm and started for the south door. "Walk with me. Put your head on my shoulder." *So we can just be a guy and his girlfriend. Try to act normal. Blend in. Good luck, though, with that bruise. Looks like someone popped her a good one.*

Anger rose, smothered by his training. She leaned into him, resting her head on his shoulder. He set off, automatically shortening his stride so she could keep up. It felt natural; after all, he'd spent a long time walking with her.

A long time afterward remembering what it was like, too. Sinking into memory the way a drowning dinosaur sinks into tar.

She smelled like outside, like the cold wind. How long had she been out there without a coat? Little shivers raced through her, but her teeth weren't chattering. He'd seen that before, in men too cold and tired to do much but lie down and wait for death.

He slowed, his arm tightening around her. He was going to have to take the chance of the doorman on the south side, not to mention the valet, remembering them. A woman with a bruise on her cheek and a man who came here alone but left with company. With any luck they'd think he was retrieving a battered girlfriend or make some other assumption. The Blake had a reputation for being discreet, but the risk still made him nervous.

It took less than five minutes to get her into the passenger side of the BMW. The spotty-faced kid valet closed her in, accepted another ten from Josiah with a wink, and held his door, too. The car was still warm; Josiah turned the heater on full blast, made sure she was buckled in, and crept forward past a big silver SUV being unloaded, the owner fussing at the bellboys while his thick-hipped wife stood and looked miserably cold.

Anna's teeth chattered. The heater was turned up all the way. She still smelled like cold wind, but there was another smell. Dirt, damp, wet moss.

And the acrid odor of violence.

He checked the rearview mirror, pulled out into traffic, and pointed them toward the freeway. He was going to drive for a little while, get her warmed up, and make sure nobody was tailing her. Ridiculous, maybe...but he didn't like the feeling he was getting; a little caution was in order.

And he knew all about caution, didn't he.

So why was he involving himself in whatever trouble she had?

We have unfinished business. And because she called me. Me.

He heard a soft sigh, and was gratified to find out her teeth had stopped clicking. She slumped into the leather bucket seat, her eyes closed, her lips still a little blue but recovering nicely. The bruise on her cheek glared at him. Who'd hit her?

Whoever it was would get repaid with interest, if Josiah had anything to say about it. Despite knowing better, he opened his mouth. "How long did you walk?"

Another weary sigh. "A long goddamn way."

I can't work if you don't give me specs. "What's going on, baby?" Nice, casual, even. No pressure.

She made another soft little sound, a helpless moan that was all too familiar. And damned if that didn't make every muscle in his body tighten a little.

"I want to hire you." Then, the crowning absurdity. "I have money. Left over from Mom's inheritance."

He almost drove off the road. Recovered, hit the freeway on-ramp, and accelerated. "Anna…" He stopped right there. *"I want to hire you"? After slapping me, swearing at me, and walking out on me? Three fucking years, and now you want to "hire" me? Jesus Christ in a fucking sidecar.* "What the fuck are you talking about?"

"I want to hire you," she repeated stubbornly. "I want you to kill someone for me."

It was a damn good thing he didn't steer off the road again. *Wonderful. She's lost her goddamn mind. And so have I.*

Chapter Four

He was quiet for a long time. Anna opened one eye, despite the fact that every particle of her body had taken on lead weights. Welcome warmth bathed her, the heater blasting away.

Josiah drove, his hazel eyes slightly narrowed. There was more green in his irises today, either because of what he wore or because he was agitated. She'd be willing to bet on both.

He looked just the same—long nose, mouth relaxed and even, his cheekbones marvels of architecture. His dark hair was a little shorter, but still cutting-edge fashionable; he wore a dark blue cable-knit sweater and a pair of designer jeans. He was still deceptively quick and graceful for such a muscular man. A heavy silver watch glimmered on his left wrist. He'd shaved this morning but a shadow clung to his chin; he got his five o'clock stubble earlier than most.

Anna remembered what it was like to run her fingertips along his jaw, to touch his cheek and feel him shudder over and inside her, muscle flickering as he spent himself. It had always been so touching, to have him helpless in her arms, shaking with the last few moments, a softness she saw nowhere else in his life. She'd wondered what made him so serious all the time, done her best to cheer him up, show him someone cared about him...that is, until she'd found out *why* he was so goddamn serious.

When she'd found out exactly who he was. *What* he was.

"You want to hire me." His tone was flat, but she saw the tiny change in his face as his jaw tightened. That was often the only mark of frustration or anger he would allow himself. The subtle shifts in eye color didn't count.

Paper crackled in her purse as she shifted. The leather was deliciously warm and buttersoft; he had pressed a button and now the seat itself was warming up. Pure luxury. Just hearing him breathe next to her made her feel safe. Her knees had almost given out when he'd stepped close, surrounding her with his coat and the smell that had always whispered *everything's okay*.

He continued in the same even tone. "Let me see if I get this straight. You want to hire a filthy fucking murderer you walked out on. Oh, yes. And how could I forget that last little parting shot? *It makes me sick to think you ever touched me.* Yeah, that was it. And now you want to *hire* me?"

To give him credit, he didn't sound angry. It was the same flat, reasonable voice he'd always used during their infrequent arguments, as if he didn't care one way or the other.

It might have made her flinch, but she was far too exhausted. *It just about killed me to walk away from you*, she wanted to say. *I spent every night after just trying to get through until morning without calling you. How do you think I felt, finding out that you'd hidden that from me, of all people? If you just would have told me...*

What did that make her? She would have been more than

happy to stay with a goddamn murderer if he'd just been honest with her. And now she was perfectly prepared to do whatever she had to.

For Eric in his shattered apartment, with his throat cut open and his swollen hands handcuffed to the chair. She would fight for her brother, the way he'd always fought for her. Even if it meant spending her last penny on this man, to pay for something she could barely admit to wanting.

"You work for money, don't you? I have some. Isn't that how it works?" Her voice broke. She closed her eyes. She was so *tired*.

"No. That's not how it works."

She let out a sharp breath, not believing he'd refused her so quickly. "Jo—"

"Even a filthy fucking murderer is allowed some discretion in the type of jobs he takes." The car slid smoothly forward, engine purring and the heat bathing her, working in toward her frozen core. Her fingers were swelling like sausages. The wetness inside her shoe was still chilly, but her feet weren't numb anymore.

So tired. For the moment, she was warm and at least partly safe. "What do I have to do?" Her throat almost refused to let the words out. "To convince you. How much do you want?"

"It's not a question of money. How long were you out in the cold?"

Three days. I ran out of Eric's apartment with my purse and my coat, and lost my scarf escaping the men who gunned down George. I haven't slept, I've barely eaten, and I'm out of my goddamn mind. "How much?" she persisted. "How much will it take to buy you, Josiah?"

"You can't afford it. How long were you out in the cold, Anna?" That same ultra-reasonableness. God, it was annoying.

23

Ten minutes in his company and she was already remembering why she'd walked out.

As if she'd ever stopped thinking about it. Ever stopped thinking about *him*.

Oh, for God's sake. "Pull over."

"What?" One point for her; he sounded startled.

"You heard me." She tried for furious, settled for sounding exhausted. "Pull the fuck over. I called you because I have nowhere else to turn. If you don't help me I'll be dead by morning. I'm in deep goddamn trouble and people have already *died* and I don't know what else to do. If you won't help me…"

It was a good speech. Movie-worthy, even. She seriously doubted she could get out of this nice warm car and hike down the freeway in her heels. Any of her friends might hide her, but they would end up like George, their heads evaporating with that sickening sound. Eric and George had both warned her not to go to the cops.

I'll figure something out. If he won't help me, I'll do something, anything, whatever I can.

Josiah was silent for a long moment. Then he reached over and turned the heater down a notch. "What's going on?" He didn't sound flat anymore. He sounded, instead, thoughtful.

Relief slid through her, turning her legs into wet noodles and her arms into heavy weights. "You'll help me?"

"I didn't say that. I asked you what was going on." He sighed. "How many people are dead?"

She swallowed. Her stomach growled, reminding her that she was hungry. "F-four. That I know of."

"And you're just calling me *now*?" Point two for her; he actually sounded shocked.

"*I* didn't kill anyone." The darkness behind her lids was soft and deep, and she was warm for the first time in a long time. "And I...I've just been running. I haven't had a chance to think for days."

"What about your brother? What the hell is the hotshot journalist doing? I thought digging up dirt and bailing you out of trouble was his specialty."

He sounded so *disdainful*. Tears rose in her throat again, and this time Anna was too tired to push them down. The blackness behind her eyelids became less welcoming and more full of nightmare images. Salt water, hot instead of icy, slid down her cheeks. "Eric's d-dead, Josiah. Whoever killed him is after me."

Then she broke down and sobbed without restraint, burying her face in her hands. She heard him shifting in his seat. He laid an unopened box of Kleenex in her lap and didn't say anything.

Anna cried until she was exhausted, until the fatigue swallowed her whole and the sound of the car wheels rocked her into a thin uneven sleep. Josiah didn't pull over. He just kept driving.

Chapter Five

She was asleep; she wasn't built for this type of excitement. Anna was part of the normal world Josiah had left behind so long ago, he barely remembered what it felt like. Nine-to-fivers with wives and jobs they hated, going from one day to the next in a sleepwalker's daze. Not like his own world.

Funny, when he thought of it that way it almost seemed reasonable.

Her eyelashes flickered a little and every once in a while she made a small hurt noise, pulling the purse closer to her side, only relaxing once she heard paper shift and crackle.

I am an idiot.

Why couldn't he have told her he was happy to see her, glad she was safe? No, instead he had to be a complete asshole. If Eric Caldwell had stumbled on something that killed him, it wasn't like him to drag his sister into it. He was fanatically protective of little Anna, real big-brother material.

After all, he'd been the one who had, in his well-meaning protectiveness, dug up that goddamn file on Josiah. Which, sometimes in his blacker moments, Josiah could have easily killed him for.

Now someone else had done it.

And here was Anna in the passenger seat, sleeping and shaking and obviously terrified out of her mind. What had she seen? What had Eric stumbled onto?

He hoped it wasn't anything to do with the Torrafaziones. The Mob wasn't his cup of tea, for all that he had done plenty of *tandas* in that arena.

They were too sloppy, and too quick to believe in the "shoot-everything-that-moves" style of problem solving. Just like the fucking Russians, come to think of it. It was getting harder and harder for a respectable freelance businessman to make it, and even worse for a liquidation agent.

Good thing I'm retired, right? He turned onto his street, no tail behind him. He was clean, Anna was clean, and he had her sleeping in his car.

She still smelled a little like gunfire. What the hell was going on?

Eric stumbled over something, got himself liquidated. Then someone else—she said, three other people. Now she's running scared, and she has something explosive on her. Paper. Something in that purse.

It should be relatively easy to get the incriminating paperwork off her and to whatever necessary legal quarter. He had methods; after that it just became a question of keeping her undercover long enough to get whoever was chasing her in a lot of trouble and looking somewhere else.

But here she was. In his car. She'd called *him,* she had nowhere else to go and nobody else to rely on.

In other words, here was a second chance for him to get his

hooks in Anna Caldwell. This time he would have some leverage to keep her with him for a good long while.

An ordinary man might feel a qualm or two about thinking along those lines, wouldn't he.

The gate rolled aside when he pressed the button, and he eased the BMW up the paved drive.

So she had money. What would she do if the price was steeper than plain cash?

He'd been an idiot to let her get away, but what could he have done? Stalked her? It had very nearly killed him to simply let her go, to keep the phone number and quietly endure day after day.

Now, cruel and calculating as it was, his patience had paid off.

She was vulnerable. Exhausted. Looking to him for safety, for guidance. It was a perfect fucking situation, one in which he could regain everything he'd lost three years ago. Easy as one-two-three.

You bastard.

The garage door opened smoothly, and he backed into the spot left open for the BMW. Hassan's motorcycle was still gone, and now Wilhelmina's little red sedan was, too. Willie must have gone shopping.

He was all alone, for the moment.

With Anna.

The bruise on her cheek taunted him. As soon as he cut the engine her eyelids fluttered more, and she came awake with a jolt, sitting straight up in the seat and staring wildly around.

Before he could stop himself, he reached over and took her shoulder, firmly. "It's okay. Everything's all right." *I'm here,* he wanted to say, stopped himself.

He could think it all he wanted to. *Don't worry, Anna. I'm here.*

Anna swallowed dryly, peered through the windshield at the closing garage door. Thin winter sunlight died in stages, and the car began to tick and ping as metal cooled. She darted a quick glance at him, her mussed hair falling in her face, and Josiah told himself that he needed to be calm, be cool, and think about things before he did them.

Yeah. Like that had ever worked, with her.

"Get out of the car." The words were harsh. "Let's go upstairs."

She licked her lips, green eyes wide and wary, and he wished he didn't remember what it was like to taste her mouth, what it was like to slide the strap of her tank top down and kiss the soft upper slope of her breast under her collarbone. It disarranged the inside of his head when he remembered things like that.

"You've changed your mind?" She made another little movement, pulling the purse into her side.

I wonder what she's got in there. "What?"

She had dark circles under her eyes, and that bruise looked fresh. She also looked like she'd lost a little weight. Even so thin, she had a curve to her hips. "About me hiring you. You'll take the job?"

He took the plunge. "Maybe. When you find out what I'm going to charge you, you might change *your* mind."

"I can pay you. I have the inheritance, in savings."

Does she have any goddamn idea how naïve she sounds? "Who said I wanted money? Come on. Get out of the car."

She didn't demur. She just obediently reached for her door handle and tugged on it, then stared in confusion when it didn't open. It took her a second to figure out how to unlock it; she moved like she was drunk. Or sleepwalking.

He opened his own door, took a deep breath of the smell of oil and metal that meant automobiles. It was a good smell, one he liked. Right next to her beautiful hair and the perfume she used to wear. What was it?

It bothered him. Normally, that was the type of detail he was able to recall with absolute clarity.

She stood at the car's back end, hugging herself and looking absurdly small in his coat. He could also make out, now that he had leisure to study her, dried mud along the hem of her skirt and a dark patch on one knee; a ladderlike run stretching up and down from it. Her eyes were huge, and she swayed on her feet. Shock, and she'd been too cold. He needed to warm her up, feed her something, and get some information out of her.

First things first. Time to calm her down. Josiah put his arm over her shoulders, pulling her close into his side. "Better?"

She swayed a little. "What is it you want?"

Persistent, just like always. He pushed her toward the small stairs leading into the utility room. From there he could get her through the house and up to his bedroom. "Start moving, baby. One foot in front of the other."

Her heels clicked on the concrete. She winced each time her left foot came down. He helped her as she hobbled, damn near carried her up the steps, and opened the door. Got her into the utility room, next to the washer and dryer. The good smell of fabric softener and clean laundry folded around them.

"Let's get those shoes off." Josiah took his arm away and bent down. "Left foot first. Lift up…there. Holy *Christ.*"

Her shoe was full of blood. The back of her heel was bleeding, trickling down from the Achilles tendon. She'd rubbed right through the nylons and her skin; the ragged edges told him it had blistered and then been worn away. How long had she walked in these ridiculous shoes?

I should have noticed that. The thought of her struggling to walk with a shoe full of blood made him unsteady. And explosive, like the job he'd taken right after losing her.

He didn't want to think about that. He had not been professional on that run, even after Hassan saved his life. The only thing that finally snapped him out of it had been the thought of her calling the number and getting a disconnected signal.

As coping mechanisms went, it hadn't been the best. Still, it had kept him alive.

"Ouch." She sucked in a breath. Her entire foot was wet with blood, her left ankle was swollen as if sprained, and she teetered in her right shoe.

Josiah dropped the bloody left shoe and stood up in a rush. In half a moment he had her in his arms, picking her up and kicking the door to the garage closed behind him. She wasn't deadweight, but she was perilously close; she put her head on his shoulder and her purse hung limply off to one side, under his coat. "Josiah," she murmured. "What is it you want?"

Jesus. "Shut up." He didn't have the breath for saying much else, so he carried her through the utility room and the kitchen, down the long hall past the dining room, and into the softly lit parquet foyer. Up the stairs, he wasn't gasping but he was damn glad when he reached the top. He carried her down the hall, barely glancing at the Dürer print on the right-hand side. The door to his bedroom loomed; he pushed it open with his shoulder and stepped inside, kicked it shut.

Familiar shapes met his gaze like strangers. Hardwood floor, the Persian rug in front of the fireplace, the leather couch where he spent most of his nights, and the bed from the old apartment, with its mission-style headboard and plain white down comforters—it all looked a little off-kilter. He'd left the closet door open halfway, and the gun on the nightstand was the only thing that didn't look weird. A small desk with the laptop on it stood in front of the window, and the antique armoire hunched in its corner, glowing mellow with furniture polish and reflected sunlight from the window.

He had Anna in his arms again. At last.

"Kick your right shoe off," he said, and she did, hissing a little with pain as she used her slick, wet left toes to do it. "Why didn't you tell me you were fucking bleeding, Anna?"

"I didn't know." Her eyes were open, but thoughtless. She was going deeper into shock. She shivered, a small animal caught in a trap.

"I'm going to set you down on your right foot. Lean against the wall. We're going to get those damn nylons off."

"S-sounds good." The paper in her purse made a collection of odd noises as he carefully, gently, let her down to perch on one foot, leaning against the wall next to her door. "What are you going to charge me, Josiah? I *need* your help. Please. I'm begging you."

Christ. She just didn't know when to shut up. Did she think he would bring her home if he wasn't intending to at least keep her hidden?

He slid his hand under her skirt, up over the outside of her thigh. Her skin was cool, too cold. Her nylons were ragged, but he managed to look over her shoulder, grit his teeth, and get his fingers worked into the waistband. She wore panties underneath; he worked his other hand under the goddamn skirt and got the other side, tugged. The nylons didn't want to come free, but he managed. She shimmied her hips a little to help him and his breath caught in his throat. *Goddammit.*

He was only a man, after all.

"Josiah?" She sounded very young, and very frightened. "Please help me."

Oh, I'm going to help you, all right. A man who could only take so much. He got the nylons and panties down to mid-thigh, shoved them a little farther—and then, deliberately, he ran his fingers up the inside of her thigh.

She was as soft as ever under his touch, and she tensed, a slight gasp suddenly very loud in the quiet room.

"Relax, Anna. I'm not going to hurt you." He sounded strange even to himself as his fingers slid up even farther, finding a nest of delicious warmth after all.

He hadn't lost his touch, knew just what she liked; some things didn't change. His finger slipped between delicate tissues, and he found out she was damp. He concentrated on his work, and in another few moments, she was flat-out wet, and her hips made that slight betraying motion that told him he had her full attention.

It had been a long, long time, and she was just like alcohol, turning everything fuzzy. Impairing him. God help him if he didn't want to just tear enough clothes off to make it work, and take her here against the wall.

He settled for working one finger up inside her, settling the heel of his palm against her mons. She was hot and slick, and all he wanted was to feel it again, feel *her* again.

Feel alive again. One way or another.

He still stared over her shoulder, fixing his attention at a point on the white-painted wall. "You want to know what I'm charging you?" he whispered, almost in her ear. His hand tensed, and she shuddered. Her breathing came quick and light. "I've gotten a little lonely since you dumped me, baby. I'll take payment like *this*—" He stroked her, just the way she liked it. Her hips jerked forward, and her breath was hot against his cheek. "As many times as I want. And you'll act like you like it, Anna. Got it?"

She was impossibly tight, velvet closing around his finger, and he damn well wanted to peel the rest of her wrinkled clothes off and throw her onto the bed. Because now, under the smell of fresh air, she smelled like herself again. Like sunlight and warm satin flesh, and a trace of her perfume.

Jasmine. An odd relief swamped him. *And that soap of hers. Yeah. Whatever soap she uses. I can't remember.*

"Josiah." Her whimper brought him back from the edge with a jerk. She was shaking, tears slicking her flushed cheeks, and whispering his name like a rosary, over and over again.

She no longer looked cold.

Good sense and sanity returned. *What the fuck am I doing?* His finger eased free. *Jesus. Jesus Christ.*

Noiseless sobs shook her. Her eyes were tightly shut, and self-disgust welled up hot and acid, bubbling in his throat. The destroyed nylons were around her knees, and he saw the hideous scrape on her leg again. She must have hit something hard; it was crusted with blood and she made a small hurt sound as he knelt and pulled the sticky little fibers away. Her left foot dripped a single drop of blood onto the floor, and he began to feel light-headed.

"Jesus. You're in bad shape." He sounded shocked even to himself. *What did I just do to you? Good God.*

Her eyes were shut. She sobbed, but the sounds began to

mutate until she was laughing, forlorn little hitching gasps that tore at his heart. When he finally carried her into the bathroom to clean her up, the laughter trailed off and she simply stared, glassy-eyed, into the distance.

And Josiah was, for once, ashamed of himself.

Chapter Six

He washed off her left foot, bandaged the bloody mess on her heel and dabbed at the crusted scab on her knee, gave her ibuprofen and water to help with the swelling in her ankle—*don't think you want ice for that right now,* he said—and handed her a warm washcloth so she could scrub at her aching face. He had a wide-toothed comb to drag through her hair, and he finally helped her struggle out of her dirty clothes and into one of his sweatshirts, navy blue and far too absurdly big for her. Afterward, he half-carried her to the bed, lowering her down in welcome softness, and pulled the covers up over her while she clutched her purse to her chest.

Everything hurt. She could still feel his breath against her ear, and his fingers on the inside of her thigh, inside *her.* Maybe he wanted to get back at her, fuck her and leave her.

She supposed she should be grateful. He'd always been considerate before; she had, quite frankly, never *had* a lover so attentive. At least he wasn't going to be violent about it.

Hopefully.

"I'm going to get you some lunch. When did you last eat?"

His eyes had gone dark and thoughtful as he leaned over the bed. She knew that look; she used to wake and find him watching her as if she was a map of a foreign country. Or a complex, difficult math problem.

What man watched his girlfriend sleep, sometimes sitting up in bed with his chest bare and his eyes dark? Sometimes he would be fully dressed, sitting in the chair next to her bed because he didn't take her to his soulless little apartment up in the penthouse, with its chrome and glass. She'd only been there twice, once to see it and once after she'd seen the file on what he did for a living.

Josiah had never seemed very comfortable anywhere, always watchful and serious. The only times he relaxed were usually in her bed with her head on his shoulder, both of them laughing quietly at some story she told about her daily work.

He'd never mentioned his own days much.

"Anna?" He reached over as if he wanted to touch her face, and she flinched despite herself. *As many times as I want. And you'll act like you like it.*

He froze.

If that's what you want, that's what I'll pay. "Okay." The words felt strange, filling her throat oddly. "As many times as you want. It's a deal."

Serious again, his eyes narrowed. Three years since she'd watched his face to decipher the emotions crossing it; but she still recognized a flash of annoyance. *I must have spoiled his day by calling.* She was instantly rewarded with a jolt of nausea right under her breastbone. "It's a deal," she repeated, as the heavenly softness and warmth closed around her, dragging at her arms and legs. "I'll do whatever you want. I have nowhere else to go."

"When was the last time you ate?" He was well and truly

irritated now, his eyebrows coming together and his mouth turning down at the corners just a little bit.

Still, the warmth was so wonderful, and she felt safe. She had never understood what a precious feeling that was. As if everything were normal again, and she could fall asleep, and wake up with the phone ringing and Eric's voice, irritable and deep in her ear. *You're about to be late for work, Annie. Jesus, why can't you get an alarm clock?*

Because I can always depend on my brother to wake me up, she would reply, and listen to him swear good-naturedly. He'd always been a morning bird, even in college.

She drifted away into deep darkness, her knee and ankle and lower back burning bars of strangely muffled pain, the tender place between her legs throbbing. She sighed. "Josiah?"

"I'm here." He took her hand. Warm, callused fingers held hers carefully. The feeling of safety was so intense she felt the last few vestiges of fear drain away. "Who hurt your brother, baby? You tell me."

"It's big," she heard herself murmur. "The black cars…"

"What car? Who shot at you?" He said it very softly. Something soft touched her cheek. His fingers? Or his lips? She couldn't tell. She had never wondered at how rough his fingers were. "Anna? Talk to me. Who shot at you?"

"Josiah…" She wanted to explain, but she was so tired. Instead, she fell into a black hole, her arms tight around the purse with its paper inside, the files Eric had told her to get.

I did what you wanted, Eric. Now let me rest.

Anna slept.

Chapter Seven

That night, Josiah watched her sleeping.

How many nights had he spent gazing intently at her face as she lay next to him, warm and trusting, both of them breathing in the wonderful lived-in smell of her small, cheap apartment? She temped all over the city, but her real work was creation, and it showed. Art books scattered everywhere, paintings crowding the walls, her work table always full of pens and pencils and paper, a secondary work table with a sleek computer and an electronic pad, her portfolio always at the ready, her kitchen table full of whatever she was interested in lately. He still remembered her painting ceramics. Each of her dishes was different, decorated with some whimsy or another.

She'd even made a coffee mug for him, painted blue with a laughing sun in gold. It was in one of the downstairs cabinets.

Sometimes, when insomnia struck or he simply woke early, he would get dressed and just sit next to her bed in the refinished rose velvet chair, watching her peace. Dawn would bloom through her windows, flushing the sheer curtains, and each moment showed something new in her face, things that kept surprising him. Like the curve of her cheek, or the exact shape of the little space under her lower lip, or the perfection of her eyelashes, or…

Nothing had changed. She still slept just as deeply and trustingly as ever, breathing softly enough he had to get up and check to see if she was still alive. He'd planned on sleeping on the couch in front of the fireplace—after all, it was where he spent most of his nights—but he ended up getting a pillow from the hall closet and settling himself on the floor next to the bed. Still, he woke every half hour or so, sitting up to make sure she was breathing, and when a gray damp dawn came he gave it up completely and watched as the light discovered her face by increments yet again.

Met her at a coffee shop on Fourth and Ringold. The shop itself was closed now, but then it had been a trendy bistro on a rainy day. He came in, intending to get a latte, standing at the counter when he noticed—again, having marked her habitually upon entering—the woman at one of the tables with a sketchpad, chewing on her pencil and pushing back a single strand of glossy brunette hair. She looked half-lost in a large bulky green sweater, and her eyes matched the sweater almost exactly. Those eyes met his, and she stared for a moment, then gave him an impish grin and began scribbling on her sketchpad.

By the time his latte was ready, she had finished scribbling and torn the page off. Then, pretty as you please, she rose to her feet and approached him.

He froze like a deer in the headlights, but she merely presented him with the paper and a smile capable of rocking him back on his heels. "Here you are," she said. "I'm practicing my motion-capture sketches, and you've got a good face. Thanks."

She'd captured his stance in swift strokes, even though she prob-

ably had no idea why he stood the way he did. She'd paid attention to his eyes, and to the dampness in his hair, not to mention the way his coat hung. She was good.

"This is…very nice." *Mentally kicking himself.* Christ, can't you think of something more intelligent to say?

She beamed, and that smile was high voltage through every nerve he owned. "Thank you. Well, back to the salt mines."

She'd just left her purse behind her at the table in blithe disregard of common sense, and the soft, long wave of her hair had swung as she spun on the balls of her feet like a dancer.

He couldn't help himself. "Hey."

She paused, looking back over her shoulder. "What?"

"Can I buy you a cup of coffee?"

Much to his surprise, she'd accepted. Even given him her phone number.

She was a *civilian*, for God's sake. Her reaction to his line of work had been genuine; so had her brother's. She had no contact with the shadow side unless it was through Josiah himself.

That was an unpleasant thought. Was someone trying to draw him out?

Ridiculous. But still, if someone wanted to use her to flush him out, half their work was done.

Whatever had happened, he had her in his house and in his bed; her brother was dead and she had nobody else to depend on. She wasn't going anywhere. Not this time.

Josiah waited until the sun had fully risen before padding noiselessly out of the room and ghosting downstairs. He wanted a cup of coffee, and he had a few arrangements to make before she woke up.

Chapter Eight

God's breath." The voice was male, shaded with dark amusement. It wasn't familiar; the accent sounded British. Or Australian.

"Yeah." Josiah's sounded hard, the words dipped in metal. "She was in bad shape. I brought her in, patched her up."

"What's she holding?"

"Don't know yet."

The first voice sounded a little scandalized now. "You didn't look?"

"No, I didn't."

"Is it her?"

"Is it who?"

"The girl. The one you keep the phone for."

Anna swam up out of deep water. Her head hurt. Her back hurt. Everything hurt. Her back most of all, but her ankle and her foot and her shoulders each had supporting roles, especially the right shoulder. Her face throbbed, hot and aching-cold at the same time. Her eyes were closed, and she didn't especially want to open them. It was such a relief to be stationary and horizontal.

And safe. Don't forget safe.

"I thought so." The first voice sighed. "What do you want me to do?"

"Her brother, Eric Caldwell. Journalist, and she says he's dead. Dig a little—but *quietly*. Don't trip any wires. Set Willie to getting clothes in these sizes. A girl who likes to dress a little professional, grays and light colors for a brunette. Also, some weekend wear. She likes low heels."

"I'll bet she does." The first voice sounded amused. "Does she have a preferred weapon?"

Josiah's tone got sharp. "She's a civilian."

Silence. The first voice was soft when it spoke again. "I'll keep that in mind. Eric Caldwell, journalist. Television?"

"Print and web. With the *Post,* last I heard. A dying breed. Be soft and easy; we don't want anyone to know we're interested."

"You wound me. I'll have Willie send up some toast. And a cuppa. Since we're nursing the poor little bird back to health."

"Did I ask for an editorial, Hassan?"

"*I'm* no journalist, boss. Just an observation. Nice to see you happy."

"Who says I'm happy?" There was a light sound, scuffling feet. Male horseplay, maybe. Anna lay very still.

The first voice laughed. "You think I've lived with you this long and I can't tell? I'm going, I'm going. She's awake, you know."

"I know. Get out." Josiah did sound happier than she'd ever heard him, really. As if he was holding back laughter.

Anna opened her eyes. It was dark through the window, an early winter dusk, and the lamp on the bedstand gave a soft glow. Golden light touched the ceiling, and Jo leaned over her, pulling up the covers as if she were an invalid.

Anna's hand shot out, feeling for the purse. Josiah's fingers closed gently around her wrist; he guided her hand to familiar rough black canvas. "It's there." Softly, soothingly. "I haven't even taken a small peek. Relax."

If I relax any more, I'm going to fall right through the mattress. She opened her mouth to say so, blinked, and shut her lips tightly, watching him. He was wearing a different shirt; his hair was damp and combed back as if he'd just gotten out of the shower. *How long have I been asleep?*

He squeezed her wrist briefly, comfortingly, then nodded, letting go. His eyes looked almost blue in the electric light, the green in the hazel coming out. Change-color irises; how often had she studied them, watching the light refract?

"How do you feel?" As if she'd been sick, and was just now recovering.

Oh, God. What am I supposed to say? "Like hell." She sounded flat, hopeless, and tired. "How long did I—"

"You slept all night and all day. Are you hungry?" He settled down into a chair by the bedside. Anna pushed herself up on her elbows. The sweatshirt—*his* sweatshirt—had rucked up under her breasts, and she had to move carefully to get it pulled down. Her hair fell in her eyes, and her mouth tasted like the bottom of a gutter. She wanted a hot shower, some icy white wine, and—of all things—a Reuben on rye.

Eric's favorite sandwich.

The loss hit her again, right in her stomach, in the place where she had a hole now. The abyss that kept opening to remind her he was gone, where the vision of the terrible bloody grin in his throat lived when it wasn't climbing up to torment her.

"Not hungry," she managed around the lump in her throat. "A shower sounds good, though."

"The bathroom's over there." He indicated another door with his chin. "I'll get you some ibuprofen; you've probably stiffened up." Josiah leaned forward, his elbows braced on his knees and his hands loosely clasped. He looked very alert, and sharply handsome with his hair slicked back, drawing attention to the lines of his face. "Even if you're not hungry, you should eat. You're probably still numb, in a kind of shock."

You've dealt with a lot more dead people than I have, Jo. Is that how you know? She pushed herself up all the way to sit, despite the screaming in her shoulders and lower back. Her hair kept falling in her face, and it felt greasy. *She* felt greasy. Did she still have mud from George's pond between her toes?

Nausea rose in a swift wave. Maybe she didn't want a Reuben after all. Or anything else.

Josiah kept talking. "Once you've cleaned up and had something to eat, I need you to tell me everything." He didn't lean farther forward, but she felt the shift in his attention. His eyes had turned darker now, blue turned to hazel shading into brown. "I've got to know every detail you can dredge up if you want me to help you."

I don't want to remember any of this at all. "All right." She pulled her knees up, slowly, wincing as her left ankle reminded her that it was *not* happy with the abuse it had endured lately. Anna found herself hugging her knees under the comforter, making herself as small as possible. It reminded her of when her parents died, and she'd been afraid Eric would lose custody because he was so young.

Josiah looked down at the floor. She was glad; his gaze was piercing and cold. Instead of remembering Eric's throat and the wet barking sound George had made when they shot him, now she was thinking of Josiah's hand between her legs and the shameful acid bite of heat bolting through her. Revolted desire, frustrated jumbled pain and pleasure all wrapped together.

As many times as I want. And you'll act like you like it.

She'd never heard him speak so coldly. She was lucky he was willing to help her at all.

Considering the alternative.

"Anna?"

She actually flinched. She'd forgotten he was in the room with her; her brain was jagging around. Mental hopscotch. "I'm losing my mind," she muttered. "Okay, I'll tell you everything. I just want to…I really need a shower. Please." The lump in her throat had come back.

"No problem. I'll find you something to wear. Willie—the housekeeper—she's taller than you, but you're both pretty slim; she should have something that will fit you until we can get you some decent clothes. You can't go back to your apartment, not now and maybe not ever. You know that, right?"

Jesus, why do you think I've spent the last three days running around town like a chicken with my head cut off? She just nodded. He was the last person she could afford to get sarcastic with. "I know." To her dismay, her throat had closed up again. *God. I'm so sick of crying.*

"Anna?" His tone had gentled. "Look at me."

She came back to herself, staring at her knees under the white down comforter. Her left knee still throbbed dully, scraped raw. There was a bandage on her heel and she was full of a muzzy-headed thickness that came with sleeping more than twelve hours at a stretch. *I don't want to look at you.* "I'm sorry I bothered you," she whispered to her knees. "I didn't have anyone else who could help me."

"Hey. *Hey.*" The chair squeaked as he rose, then the bed

made a different sound when he dropped one knee onto it. The mattress gave under his weight and she leaned away, panicked by the sudden movement. Her purse slid on the comforter; she grabbed at it and looked up just in time to see his hand come up. He cupped her chin in his palm; his skin was warm and hard. "Look at me. *Look*."

His eyes were dark again, shadowed in the dim golden light. He examined her face, from forehead to chin, met her gaze again, and his mouth turned into a thin, harsh line. "I thought you'd call sooner or later. It's why I stayed here." His thumb feathered over her lips, just the way he used to touch her, a light, intimate caress. Her heart gave a huge half-strangled leap in her chest, and the lump in her throat turned into her pulse. "I didn't think you'd be in trouble, but I thought you'd…I don't know. Just want to talk to me. I was always good to talk to, right?"

Until I figured out I was the one doing all the talking. She didn't want to irritate him, so she agreed. "Yes." *Just let me go take a shower. Please. Just let me go.*

Another thought swam through her mind, dragging panic in its wake. Maybe he wanted her to start paying now?

Oh, Christ. I don't know if I can do it right now. Maybe I could just lie still and let him do what he wants?

Shame followed the panic. What was she *doing*?

Josiah seemed not to notice how fast she was breathing, or her discomfort. He was staring almost *through* her, an odd and uncomfortable scrutiny. "I was hoping you'd call, no matter the circumstances. Let's just be clear about one thing: I'll take care of whatever trouble this is, but I don't want to hear one single peep from you about *how* I do it. Okay? No petty moralizing, no name-calling, and no goddamn temper tantrums. From now until I finish this out for you, you do *what* I say *when* I say it and keep your editorials to yourself. You got it, baby?"

Well, I've agreed to hire a murderer and pay him with sex. I don't think I'm going to cavil at much else. "I got it." Her lips were cracked; she was suddenly very thirsty and acutely aware of how good he smelled. He didn't wear cologne, so the scent was Ivory soap and his shampoo, with the simple base of healthy male underneath. Clean, uncomplicated, and very familiar. She'd slept with one of his shirts left at her apartment for a year and a half until it had faded. "I won't cause any problems. You're the boss."

So what would he tell her to do now? Anna closed her eyes and waited, swallowing hard.

He didn't move. "About yesterday."

Her heart sped up again, slamming against her ribs as if she was running away again, hearing the *pockpockpock* sounds behind her and wondering when a bullet was going to slam into her flesh. She bit her lower lip, keeping her eyes closed.

You have to get back in the game, Tasha was always saying, whenever she brought a fresh round of drinks to their table. *Come on, Annie!*

She'd never see Tasha's cheerful, snub-nosed, and freckled face again.

He sighed. "Go get cleaned up, and I'll find some clothes for you. Just try to relax. You're safe here, and there's nothing we can do right at this moment. Can I look through those papers while you're in the shower?"

I certainly can't stop you. She didn't open her eyes until he'd moved, letting go of her chin and sliding off the bed. "If you want."

He settled back into the chair. "Did Eric ask you to hold them for him?"

Tears rose again. She denied them, with all her strength, and found out she could sound relatively steady, even to herself. "About h-half of them. The other half were in a safety-deposit box; I got the key in a letter from Eric that m-morning, I don't know why he posted it instead of...I...I went to ask him what he wanted me to do with it and I f-found Eric in his apartment. They had c-cut his throat." Her voice broke on a sob.

Had he gone pale? The only other time she had seen him this white was during the fight, when she'd thrown the pictures at him, the typed sheets fluttering like wounded bird wings.

"He'd told me not to call the cops. I...I don't know. I left his apartment. I was c-crying so hard I couldn't see, but I was in the lobby and looked out the door and noticed a black car. It made me think, I'd seen the c-car outside h-his office the d-day he gave me the first batch of papers. I went out the b-back and I spent the n-night in a flophouse off Seventieth; I was stupid and paid with my Visa. The d-day after, I went to his editor George—"

"Jesus Christ." Not only was he pale, but he might have been sweating, too. "You didn't call me?"

"I didn't know *what* to do." Her voice had firmed, become natural. She could tell the story as if it had happened to someone else now. She felt blessedly, wonderfully numb. "I called George. He told me to come to his house, the office might be watched. I went to the bank, took the papers out of the safety-deposit box, and I went to George's."

The numbness spread down the inside of her chest, a sudden relief. She took a deep breath, finding the constriction in her throat had eased.

Oddly enough, Josiah stared at the floor. He *was* sweating; she observed this with her newfound numbness and found it didn't matter.

She pushed the covers back. Her legs were very pale against the sheets, starred with fresh, ugly bruising. She slid her feet out of the bed. It hurt to move, but she suddenly wanted a shower very badly. "George's wife was there. So was his daughter. Emmaline. Thirteen, and home sick with the flu."

"Anna—"

Let me finish. "His wife let me in and I went up to his home office. She made me tea. He got there ten minutes later." Anna touched her bruised cheek; she'd almost forgotten about it. "George told me that the cops couldn't be trusted. He'd already found out a few things. He was standing by the door, getting a cigarette out, it was the only place Kara would let him smoke, and we heard this…noise. Someone had broken the back door in. Then I heard gunshots. And yelling." She stared at her toes, at the bruising and swelling around her left ankle. "George told me to run. He pushed open the door to the garden and I grabbed my purse. I almost froze. They came in and shot George in the stomach. Then I saw his h-head explode."

Her hands were shaking, so she turned them into fists, digging her broken fingernails into her palms. "I kept thinking I couldn't stop. I ran through the garden. They had a pond, and I slipped on the rocks and fell. There were chips of stone flying around. If I hadn't tripped…I got through and I ran down the street. I ran. I hid under a hedge and there was a black car, the *same black car,* driving past very slowly. Looking for me. I was cold. It was so…cold."

"Anna."

She jumped, startled, and leapt to her feet—or tried to, her aching body arresting her halfway. She had to grab the hem of his sweatshirt, pulling it down far enough to be decent, and when he caught her shoulders she flinched and let out a startled, wounded little cry. "Shhh, baby. Shh." He put his arms around her, and Anna went utterly still, breathing in shallow, rapid gasps. "Christ," he muttered into her hair. "Jesus Christ."

Is he shaking, or am I? It's probably me. "I tried to think of who to call, but...I couldn't put anyone in danger. I went to an all-night restaurant, but I didn't dare stay very long and I couldn't eat. I tried to sleep in an alley. I threw my cell away, I thought they could...Morning came and I walked to a phone booth. And I called you." Laughter clawed at her throat. "The phone b-booth stank."

"I'm sure it did." His arms tightened. He smelled so *clean.* "You should have called me when you got the key."

"I didn't know." Guilt crashed into her. If she hadn't tried to meet George, his wife and daughter might still be alive. "I'm sorry. I didn't know what to do."

"Shh. Don't worry." He was quiet for a few moments, holding her so tightly she couldn't get a deep breath in. "You're with me now. I know what to do."

Good. Because I'm clean out of ideas. I don't even know how to begin *handling this.* "So what should *I* do?" The words vanished into his chest. He was solid, warm, and familiar. She could almost close her eyes and pretend none of this had ever happened. His heartbeat thundered reassuringly against her cheek.

"What I tell you, and you'll be all right." Very cautiously, he untangled himself from her. Held her at arm's length for a moment. "Go get cleaned up, use my toothbrush. We'll figure everything else out after you have something to eat."

The change was so sudden she almost stumbled when he let her go. He stood looking down on her for a moment, his face shadowed in the light from the lamp.

Anna took a few unsteady steps. Her ankle hurt viciously every time she put weight on it, and the scabs on her heel and knee cracked as she moved.

At least she was still breathing. Shame bit at her again.

She reached the bathroom door, an expanse of white tile and a clean toilet spreading behind it. That alone was enough to make her feel better. She hadn't seen a clean toilet since leaving her own apartment.

"Anna."

"Yes?" Anna looked back over her shoulder, her neck screaming with pain. He didn't look at her; he stared at the window, where night had fallen.

"About…about yesterday. I told you that you had to pay me—"

"I heard you, Jo." She was too busy hobbling to flinch. "I haven't forgotten," she managed through her cracked lips. "As many times as you want, Josiah. And I'll act like I like it." She limped into the bathroom, the tiles cold and slick against her feet. "Just let me get cleaned up."

Chapter Nine

Wilhelmina, her hair pulled severely back into a bun the size of an extremely ambitious cinnamon roll, clucked her tongue. "You poor thing." She was easily six feet tall, wrapped in a dark fluttering silk kimono that whispered its own commentary.

Anna, her towel-dried hair lying against her shoulders, blinked at the vision of dark-eyed, angular grace. Willie's face was three-quarters beaky nose; her hands were large and capable and her mouth was usually a wide, genuine smile.

She was also deadly with a pistol or a knife, and could move so quietly even Josiah had trouble sensing her. Wilhelmina Safrich was, after all, a butler whose secondary duty was as a bodyguard.

She descended on Anna, who was now in a pair of Willie's silk Chinese-style pajamas in robin's-egg blue, absurdly too large and rolled up at both wrist and ankle.

Clucking her tongue, Willie had Anna bundled into the freshly made bed in a matter of moments, then took the tray from Hassan and settled it at the foot of the bed. "I didn't know what you'd want, so I made scrambled eggs and toast and cut up some strawberries. There's hot chocolate, too. Do you need a pillow? Your poor face, that will need some arnica. We might have to wrap that ankle, too. Now, *Liebchen,* lift your knees a little—there. Better for your back? Now, do you have any food allergies? No? Good. Jo told me you didn't, but it's best to be sure. Settle this across your knees. Now eat the whole thing. There's plenty more. Anything you would especially like, you let me know. You must tell me, what is your favorite?"

Anna blinked owlishly, staring at the loaded tray. She looked stunned.

Josiah could relate.

"Food?" she managed, and Hassan's mouth twitched.

Hassan stood in the shadows by the door, his dark eyes gleaming as he leaned against the wall. Josiah stood next to him, automatically placing himself out of the man's fire line.

"Found out what we're into yet?" Hassan's low tone didn't carry to the bed, where Willie had pulled a chair up and was busy fussing over Anna, who gingerly took a bite of toast as if she suspected poison.

Why did I say that to her? "Not just yet." The files tucked in the crook of his arm, some of them the worse for wear from being jammed in her purse, deserved a close examination. He would get to that soon enough. "We're going to do that now. Anna?"

Her eyes were round. She almost dropped the toast. Willie had produced a set of knitting needles and a large ball of violently orange yarn, casting on with quick, deft fingers.

Josiah had to hold back a smile. Willie's knitting was a sure sign of approval. "This is Hassan, and you've already met Willie. You can say anything in front of them." He crossed the room to stand at the end of the bed. *I should kick my own ass. Why did I say that to her?*

All the patience in the world, and he'd blown his chance almost as soon as it occurred. Three years of waiting, hoping, and enduring...and five seconds and his goddamn libido had probably wrecked it.

Anna studied Hassan for a long moment. "You look familiar," she said slowly.

"Eat." Willie's needles began to click, and her tone brooked no disobedience. *She must be mildly annoyed. With whom, though? That's always the question.*

"I've got one of those faces." Hassan was British-educated, but he could sound American as apple pie if he needed to. He also did a very good Muscovite Russian, and Spanish with a pure Valencia accent. "Don't think I've had the pleasure, Miss Caldwell."

"No. I've seen you before." Very certain, the line between her eyebrows deepening. Still pale and a little glaze-eyed, she sounded disconcertingly certain. "I can't remember where, but I've seen you somewhere."

"Curse of being handsome, everyone thinks they know you." Hassan grinned, revealing white teeth. His dark, liquid eyes were cheerful, but he didn't move from the shadows near the door. "Willie never gives *me* strawberries. She must have made a special trip for them."

Anna still stared at him, ignoring the attempt at levity. Josiah studied the bruise on her cheek. She hadn't mentioned how she got it; he decided now might be a good time to ask. "Anna? Your face. How did you get that?"

She dropped her gaze, stared at her plate. "I think I fell. I don't know. They were shooting at me."

He cast back through memory, found the name. "George's. The editor."

"Eric's editor."

Damn your brother, for getting you involved in this. All the same, if he hadn't, Josiah might not be standing here looking at her right now. Was it wrong to be grateful? "Hassan and I are going to take a look at these files. When you're done eating we'll take you through what you remember. So eat. That's an order."

"Okay." She didn't glance up, just picked up a single slice of strawberry and slid it into her mouth. Her lips closed over the red fruit, the tip of her tongue taking a quick swipe to catch any flavor left over on her lower lip.

Josiah had to look away. Hassan followed him over to the couch.

"What do you do, Anna?" Willie, deliberately cheerful, the ghost of her accent making the words dark and dense.

"I'm a secretary. But really I'm an artist. Mixed media. Right now I'm showing at Fillmore West downtown." Her tone shifted, more hesitant. "Or I was. I guess that's over now."

Willie's needles settled into a calmer rhythm. "That sounds wonderful. I've never been the artistic type, myself. Too practical." And she was off and running, engaging Anna in light conversation, needles flying.

Josiah lowered himself down cross-legged on the floor next to the couch, in a sheltered angle, opening one of the six manila files left over. Stared at it unseeing for a moment, as Hassan settled in an equally sheltered position and held out his hand for papers.

A soft rustling as Hassan opened one of the files. His murmur was barely discernible, pitched low enough not to carry across the room. "If there's trouble, you need to have a clear head."

I know that. Josiah took a deep breath, drawing it all the way down. He had rarely been this badly rattled. As a matter of fact, out of the half a dozen times he could remember feeling like this, Anna was responsible for or had participated in at least four.

He had to blink a few times before he could concentrate on the file. When he did, he felt his eyebrows pull together.

Josiah's eyes met Hassan's. "What do you have?"

"One of these is full of medical charts." The other man flipped the second one open. "This one looks like accounting—debits, credits, that sort of thing. Lot of money changing hands, if that's what it is."

Josiah opened the second file in his stack and stared at a black-and-white picture, taken with a telephoto lens, of a man with a heavy-jowled face leaving a brick-and-glass building. There was something familiar about the face, and Josiah turned the picture over. There was spidery writing, Eric Caldwell's familiar scrawl in blue ink.

Denton, 1456 E Morris. And another notation: *1st treatment.*

There was a date, too. Some eight months ago.

The folder was full of pictures, each dated, each featuring the same brick-and-glass façade. They were of six men, and Josiah recognized four of them. One of them was the mayor, and another was the chief of police.

The dating was odd, and he couldn't quite think of why until he had spread four pictures of Denton—the police chief—out in a row and stared at them for a few minutes. Denton was beginning to look better, his fat face smoothing out, and something in the carriage of his shoulders looked subtly different. As if he'd been working out hard at the gym.

"Huh." Josiah stared at the four pictures, barely listening to Hassan breathing and riffling through his own stack of papers. *What the hell is this?*

Pictures. Pages of scribbled notations in Eric's script, most of which made no sense—they seemed a kind of code. There were two flash drives and four blank CDs, and a large manila file full of random bits of paper—receipts, lists of contacts and appointments, and—bingo—laser-printed transcripts of interviews, each neatly labeled.

Taped to the inside of the largest folder was a small key. Safety-deposit box, maybe? Next to it, printed in block letters: MAIL TO NABOKOV. 473.

Then, there was a letter, laser-printed just like the interviews, and dated for Tuesday.

Dear Annie,

If you're reading this, something's very wrong. I'm onto something big, and it's getting weird. If anything happens, go to George. He knows what I'm working on, and he'll help you get out of town. Listen to him. This is the important: Get out of the city as fast as you can if you get this letter. Drop everything and go. I am not kidding and if you read this, you'll know I'm not. Go visit my ex Susan in Cedar Falls, she always liked you better. And stay there. Do not, under any circumstances, stay in the city. Just get out and go. I love you.

The letter was unsigned, sounded unfinished. Josiah thought about this for a few seconds, turning it over in his mind the way he would turn a knife in his hands, testing the balance.

There was one more thing. A scrap of paper, with more block printing on it. The telephone number Eric had written was as familiar to Josiah as his own breath.

It was the number Anna had called yesterday, the one he'd switched to a new phone and kept active just in case.

Just-in-fucking-case. The worst goddamn words in the English language.

There was a question mark at the end of the number, too.

Christ, Eric. I would have come to see you, at least. For her sake. If you gave your goddamn stamp of approval she would have at least listened to me. You were her big brother. Why did you get her mixed up in something like this, whatever it is?

He looked up to find Hassan engrossed in his own work. Anna had asked Willie about textiles; the older woman was deep in a discussion of the pros and cons of silk yarn.

All in all, this seemed a pretty tame collection of paper to have killed four people for.

He grimaced slightly at the pictures. They bothered him, still. He turned to the interviews, and began to read.

Half an hour later, he heard Willie softly fussing Anna into the bathroom and waited until the butler had brought her back and tucked her into the bed.

"Can you take these downstairs?" He looked up to find Hassan studying him, with a faintly lifted eyebrow that looked as perplexed as Josiah himself felt.

"There, snug as bug," Willie said. "You look tired. It was all the hot chocolate, I think."

"I feel like a lump." Anna's voice slurred under the weight of the sedative added to the hot chocolate. Willie hadn't been happy about using it, but Josiah was the boss, and after an eagle-eyed stare and a few precious minutes lost in discussion, she'd agreed. *Just to settle her nerves. She needs it.*

He felt a brief flash of guilt, discarded it. Hassan righted his papers with quick, efficient motions. "Downstairs it is. This doesn't make any fucking sense, Wolfe."

"Not yet. But maybe it will. Willie? Thank you."

"Poor thing." The wide fall of orange knit cloth would eventually be a sweater, Josiah guessed; Willie bundled it up, settled it on the spent tray, and sighed. "It looks like someone punched her. That ankle—and her knee. Very bad."

Now, that was strange from practical, capable Willie, who had seen no little bloodshed in her day.

Josiah rolled his shoulders back precisely once, dispelling an incipient ache. "She'll be all right."

He meant, *I am going to take care of her,* but Willie pressed her lips together and gave him a look that would have been scorching if his own conscience hadn't been twice as painful. She considered both Hassan and Josiah himself borderline morons when it came to women and sticky things like emotions, as well as the proper way to make hot cocoa. Josiah didn't precisely *disagree,* but it was a little disconcerting to think that Willie in half an hour maybe knew more about Anna's emotional state than *he* did.

Hassan drifted out of the room on cat-soft feet, Willie sailed out with her knitting and the tray, and Josiah found himself standing and looking down at a peacefully sleeping woman.

Eric Caldwell was indeed dead. That much Hassan had quietly found out; he hadn't begun digging into the matter of George Moorhouse's death yet. Nobody was talking about *how* Eric had died, and the files just didn't make a hell of a lot of sense. The interviews were odd, to say the least. None of the interviewees would say what they were scared of, and it was always the same—Eric gaining the trust of his subjects, then an abrupt notation at the end of each: *Gone,* with a date at least a day but never more than three after the interview.

Anna turned onto her side, her long hair spread out on the pillows. She belonged in her own messy, unmade maple four-poster with its mound of pillows and brightly colored sheets. Josiah was suddenly shaken with the urge to close the door, brace a chair against it, and get in next to her. Take her in his arms and pretend that she was sleeping because she trusted him, because she wanted to.

His hands itched to touch her. In the end, Josiah backed away from the bed, one slow step at a time, and closed the door once he was in the hall. He spread the fingers of his hand against cool wood for a moment, imagining he could still hear her breathing.

Josiah was very fond of things that made some sort of sense. Either he didn't know enough, or someone had gone after Anna to draw him out…or something else was happening here, something that probably had a rational explanation but for right now was looking irrational as hell.

It was anyone's guess.

He peeled his fingers away from the door, one by one. *Don't worry, Anna. Sleep tight. I'm on the job.*

Disgust rose acid in his throat again. *As many times as I want, and you'll act like you like it.*

It didn't matter so much *that* he said it. What did matter was that it was at least partially true. He was going to take whatever he could get from her, as often as he could, and he was going to make it good for her. As good as he could.

On the job and already neck-deep. He turned sharply away. He couldn't wait to hear what Hassan thought of the interviews.

"What the hell is this shite?" It was the first time Hassan had ever sounded baffled and angry at once. "Some kind of practical joke?"

Josiah folded his arms. "Someone killed Eric for this. I doubt it's a joke."

"Oh, come *on*. This is pure top-grade shite. A collection of fucking fairy tales. They never say exactly what the treatment is, and everything in the interviews is just scared bibble-babble." Hassan's accent had turned crisp. He picked up the beer bottle, tossed the last swallow back.

Willie leaned on the other side of the breakfast bar. "The charts don't make any sense." Her dark eyes were troubled. "Blood transfusions? Morphine in massive doses? The notations, they look like amputations. Cutting off fingers and toes."

"You haven't read the Grimm's edition yet." Hassan tapped his bottle on the counter, a short sharp noise. "One of the interviewees swears he's seen someone levitate. I hate to ask you, Wolfe, but are you sure she's not snowing you? Or a few cuckoos short of a Black Forest cake?"

If I didn't know you had a legitimate reason to ask, I'd hit you, whether I owe you or not. "Anna isn't in any condition to lie. And her brother's indisputably dead."

"Yes, but this…" Hassan shook his head. Willie silently crossed the kitchen, opened the fridge, and brought him another beer. She glanced at Josiah, who shook his head slightly.

No, thank you, Willie. "It doesn't make sense right *now*. Maybe it will once we've done some other quiet digging. I'll take first watch tonight. Cancel the housekeepers, too."

Willie moved her teacup. It made a precise little click, and he looked up to find both her and Hassan watching him.

I hope I don't look as worried as they do. "I'm thinking this could get messy. So if you want to excuse yourselves…"

"You're determined to take this seriously. Levitation, morphine, and all." Hassan lifted his fresh bottle in the usual salute to Willie, then brought it to his mouth and took a long draft. His throat worked, tanned skin and muscle moving.

Let's count this up, shall we? Josiah held up one finger. "A dead reporter and stacks of confusing documents. Interviewees shutting up, or disappearing—we'll find out which tomorrow." Another. "Pictures of the chief of police, the mayor, other city officials." Another. "A dead *editor.*" The last one. "And a woman so terrified she starts to stutter when she talks about finding her dead brother. You may not know her, but I do." *Whatever's going on, she's innocent. And going to stay that way.* He looked down at the untidy stack of paper. "My instinct tells me this is going to get messy. I *am* determined to take this seriously, and I am further determined to finish this matter to my satisfaction." He took in a deep, soft breath, the last before the plunge. "I'm on the job."

Hassan let out a short sigh. "For Christ's sake. You *retired.*"

"Consider this a last hurrah."

Willie shook her head. "I don't like it."

"Are you out?" He didn't relish the thought of losing her as backup.

She thought about it for a long moment. Then she nodded once, very softly but decisively. "God knows you have no sensitivity in your entire goddamn body, Josiah Wolfe." The tall, spare woman tilted her dark head. "I don't like anything to do with morphine and amputations and dead reporters. But I'm in." A trace of native German worked its way out through her words, precise and throat-deep.

Well. That's a relief.

Hassan drew his finger through a ring of condensation left by the cold beer bottle. "If you're on the job, this is a bloody sloppy way to begin." His tone was excessively mild.

"You're right. Tomorrow morning we're going to rectify that." A cold, calm clarity slid through Josiah's head. It was the only feeling that didn't seem to lead directly to the woman sleeping upstairs. "Starting with finding out what exactly the story is about Eric's death and the editor's, then tracking down some of those interviewees. We're going to poke the anthill, see what comes up."

Chapter Ten

Anna turned, sheets sliding, and felt a jag of pain from her ankle, a deeper bar of pain in her lower back. The bandage on her heel rasped against the material. More darkness wrapped around her, submerged her in deep, heavy water.

Running. Her breath came in short, hard gasps; she couldn't get enough air in, and the little pockpock *sounds of bullets burying themselves in wet turf were a demonic sewing machine as she struggled not to freeze; if she stopped running she would die, they would shoot her and—*

Then, in vivid screaming color—Eric's distorted face, painted with puffy bruises and blood. A horrible wide grin yawned under his chin, and his shirt was clotted with crimson stickiness.

"Anna." Hands on her shoulders, fingers digging in, and she was pulled forward. A familiar smell enveloped her, and for a moment she was confused, her heart pounding and slick dampness on her palms. *A horrible nightmare. I dreamed you were gone and Eric was dead and I was sleeping in an alley. God.*

Disorientation swamped her. He held her shoulders; she thrashed fruitlessly. "Just a dream, Anna. It's all right. I'm here."

Josiah? The room was dark, a faint cold spill of moonlight outlining a rectangle on the floor. "God." The word cracked in the middle, fell useless to the floor. Her face burned, her bruised cheek sounding a deep bass beat of hot pain.

"It's normal to have bad dreams." He waited until she was steady, let go of her shoulders. "It's okay. Just relax."

How would you know? Do you ever have them? The silk pajamas were soft, and she was finally warm again, but her back ached as she tried to sit upright. She felt funny, her head full of soft, blue cotton instead of the gray of shock. Even the hot pain of her cheek and her lower back was muted. "I feel funny."

"It's normal." He sounded so *calm;* he was a familiar shadow against this unfamiliar room with its bare walls and the leather couch, the pristine bathroom seen through a half-open door. So stripped-down, minimalist.

She'd never liked that movement. It was baroque for her, curlicues and velvet and softness. If this was who Josiah really was—this bareness—what had he thought of her messy, plush, comfortable apartment? He'd barely ever taken her to his home; the one time she'd spent the night at his apartment she'd wondered at how nakedly white the walls were.

"Normal?" She had to try twice to get the word out.

"When you see someone you love dead, and when you've been thrown into a high-pressure situation...yeah, it's normal." He sat on the edge of the bed, his hands dropped loosely into his lap and his head half-turned so he could watch her. "You're a civilian, Anna."

Civilian. High-pressure situation. "Did you...do you have bad dreams?"

He shrugged, an easy, familiar motion. "Not when I was with you."

A traitorous spike of warmth went through her chest. She pulled her knees up slowly, her joints creaking like an old woman's. Added to that was the fuzzy realization that she was in his bed, and the spike became a spreading heat. "Was that why you…"

"It wasn't why I got involved with you, and it's not why I'm helping you now. You should lie down. Or do you need something for pain?" He shifted his weight slightly, as if he was going to stand up, but then settled back down.

"Were you watching me sleep again?" *Why did you always do that?*

He didn't respond. Her throat was dry, and her mouth tasted a little funny. Metallic.

She reached out. Her fingers touched his shoulder, the slightly rough texture of his sweater and the hardness of muscle underneath. It was an instinctive movement, and as soon as she did it her heart began to pound again. He was probably still angry, but it was still so familiar. Even the sound of his breathing was the same.

Three goddamn years, and he still felt just as comforting as an old pair of slippers. She'd forgotten how he could make her relax, his almost infectious calm. Like there was nothing he couldn't handle.

At least, she really hoped there was nothing he couldn't handle.

Even his profile was watchful, thoughtful, silent. She had sketched his face so many times, and now, looking at the set of his shoulders, she realized he was edgy.

He used to get like this. Not very often, just once every couple of months. Tense, and startlingly affectionate at the same time; he would come up behind her and hug her, follow her into the kitchen, be waiting for her when she left work. She'd thought it was love, before.

Now she wondered. Her hand moved almost of its own volition, her palm polishing his shoulder under the sweater, and he sighed.

"Josiah?" *I sound like I'm fourteen years old again. Hell of a time for a blast from the past.*

"You should rest." He finally moved, just a little, leaning into her hand.

"What about you?" *How often do you sleep here? Are you visiting some other girl's apartment nowadays? Watching another woman sleep?*

She wondered why the thought made a fresh sharpness jab through her chest.

He didn't move. "I'm on watch. No sleeping allowed. Do you want something for the pain?"

Why do you keep asking me? "No." Her hand dropped away; she pulled her knees up slowly. Hugged them, ignoring the ache in her lower back. "What's going to happen?"

"We're going to do a little digging, find out exactly what we're dealing with. Might leave you in a safe place while we work." He dropped his gaze a little. Her gaze picked out the line of his jaw, the curve of his cheek. The shell of his ear. He was so handsome, in his own quiet, unassuming way. "For right now, you're supposed to rest."

I was out like a light. I barely even remember brushing my teeth. "I've got money," she heard herself say. "And…the other. I'll pay."

"Don't, Anna." Calm, quiet, and inflexible. "I shouldn't have said that to you. Just go back to sleep."

How can I? "I don't think I can."

"You've already done a hell of a lot you didn't think you could. This isn't any different."

"Was it any different for you?"

"I'm not normal." His jaw set, and for the first time his tone was shaded with something other than quiet evenness. "I'm going to go check the house. Stay up here and try to sleep, then."

Don't go. The words stuck in her throat. *Talk to me, like you used to. Tell me something, anything.* "I'm sorry I called you."

"I'm not. Looks like your brother was on to something." He made a swift movement and was on his feet, his eyes glittering in the dimness. "I'm going through the files. There's odd stuff in there. I want you to take a look at it...."

The silence was immediate, and Anna looked up at him. Her dark-adapted eyes caught a swift movement and the gleam of metal, and he ghosted across the room to the door.

"Josiah?" The whisper curdled in her throat.

"Be quiet," he whispered back. "Stay there."

Then he was gone, out through the door.

Anna shivered. She knew what that gleaming was, the knowledge springing into full terrible life inside her head.

A gun. Josiah was carrying a *gun*.

Her heart pounded so hard it filled her head with blackness, and her palms were wet again. She pulled the blankets up, suddenly cold, staring at the window.

Moonlight bloomed thin and hurtful against the cold glass panes. She stared at the square of pale whiteness against the hardwood floor. The deep, warm, soft bed seemed to get a little colder.

The nightmare wasn't going to end.

A faint scratching, like fingernails on smooth, slick glass, startled her. Her head jerked up, her pulse pounding in her ears.

What was that? They've found me? I don't even know who "they" are.

How was that for crazy? She didn't even know who wanted her dead so badly.

Moonlight, pale and innocent, lying on the floor. Only now, there was a block of shadow in the sterile white light. A strangely rounded shape, and the scratching noise intensified.

The window rattled.

Jesus Christ, someone's out there. Her throat was desert dry, her heart thundering in her temples and ears, shivers sliding down her spine in waves. *Someone's trying to get in.*

She remembered stairs coming up to this room. Lots of them, too.

Get out of the bed. Get away. Frozen, she stared at the bobbing shadow in the moonlight. It *did* look like a head, and shoulders, floating up and down like a balloon.

Anna scrambled for the other side of the bed, forgetting her injured ankle and aching back. Her face throbbed with pain. *Get into the bathroom and bar the door with something. No, that's a dead end, God help me.*

Still, she skidded across the floor and onto chill, slick tiles as glass shivered, breaking. Heavy feet smashed onto the floor near the window. She heard popping sounds and slammed the bathroom door, looking wildly for something to brace it with. Nothing showed up, and she fumbled for the lock on the knob with more hope than actual trust in its ability to stop anything coming through.

Darkness smothered her, broken only by the night-light's faint gleam and its reflection in the mirror. Her breath was very loud in her ears, just like the gasping in a horror film.

So that's why. It's what terror sounds like.

There was a massive crunching, and she didn't stop to think, just tumbled into the claw-foot bathtub, smacking her head against the tiled wall and smashing her knee against the lip, too. A hot flare of pain slammed up from her ankle, the shower curtain tangling in plastic ripples. It was an old-fashioned curtain, on a ring bolted to the wall; she screamed and thrashed, thinking for an instant that someone had grabbed her.

More crashing jolts. Anna swallowed the remainder of the scream. *I'm an idiot. I've been attacked by a shower curtain.*

Something smashed against the bathroom door again, and she choked back another cry, casting around for a weapon and closing her fingers around the shampoo. *Great. I'm going to hold them off with a bottle of Prell.*

Another impact against the splintering door. Anna struggled up to her sore knees, searching for another weapon. *You'd think a contract killer would have a gun in his bathtub. I don't even know* how *to shoot one. A fine time to wish I'd learned.*

More crashing sounds, thankfully receding. Anna clutched the shampoo bottle and looked around wildly for something else to use as a weapon. *I don't want to die in a bathroom, I don't want to die in a goddamn bathtub, dear God....*

"Anna!" Josiah, frantic, somewhere else in the house. "*ANNA!*"

I'm okay, I'm just crouching in here like an idiot. "Jo?" Her throat was two sizes too small.

The bathroom door rattled. She gulped back a gasp, eased herself back up onto her knees, the shower curtain rings clattering. *Dammit. Be quiet. Hide.*

And brain them with a shampoo bottle when they come in. Wonderful. As a plan, that really sucks.

"*Anna!*" The bathroom door flew open, banging against the

linen closet. Anna flung the shampoo bottle, he ducked, and the next thing she knew, Josiah was hauling her out of the bathtub, the curtain hoops rattling like a snake's tail. "Jesus Christ. What was that?"

How the hell should I know? You're the professional. "Someone was at the window." *I'm not stuttering. Hallelujah.*

"What did she say?" This was the slim dark familiar man with the faintly British accent. He held a gun with both hands, pointing it down at the floor. "Christ, look at this. Be careful, Willie, there's glass on the floor."

Tiles were still slick and chill against Anna's bare feet. Josiah hugged her so tightly she couldn't breathe, her heart pounded, and she suddenly had to use the toilet very badly.

"Jesus." His breath was warm; he buried his face in her hair. "Are you all right? Tell me you're all right."

I wish I could, I really can't tell. "I'm all right." Her bladder felt about three sizes too small, too. Everything on her was shrinking. "I'm okay. There was someone in the window."

"What does she say?" The woman's voice. Willie. What a name for a woman. "*Mein Gott.* How the *hell* did they get out through there?"

"They didn't; it's broken *in*. Look." Hassan's voice. There were soft footfalls, metallic clicks. "Watch *out* for the glass, Willie."

"I *know*, silly man." Willie didn't sound impressed.

"Tell me you're all right." Josiah's hands closed over her shoulders; he held her at arm's length in the bathroom's dimness, lit only by the single night-light. He shook her a little, and Anna had the sudden overwhelming urge to laugh and scream at the same time. "Are you all right? *Anna!*"

"Stop it," she heard herself say. "Stop it. I promise I'm fine. Calm down."

"I'll calm down when I know what's going on." His tone promised violence, a new, unsettling thing. "Light. Close your eyes."

She did, and his hand briefly left her shoulder. Light exploded; she blinked furiously and peered up at him. He examined her face, used his grip on her shoulders to spin her around and looked at her back. Then he jerked her back around and hugged her again. "Anna."

If he doesn't let go of me I'm going to wet myself. She struggled, pushing him away. "I think I need to use the toilet," she said primly. "Please. I might also throw up. Not to mention cry. And scream. That sounds good. *Really* good."

His jaw went tight. He looked down at her, his eyes darker than usual because he wore a gray sweater, the sleeves pushed up; the gun was tucked into the waistband of his jeans. "No screaming. Stay in here; we'll make sure the house is secure and I'll find you some shoes. There's glass."

"It came in through the window. It was scratching, and then it came in. I ran in here." *I'm babbling.* She pushed her shoulders back and her chin up, suddenly aware that the tile was freezing and her legs were bare. Gooseflesh raced up her arms. Nausea warred with the need to visit the toilet. "I really think I'm going to throw up."

"All right." He let go of her, one finger at a time. "Stay in here. If you hear gunshots, get back in the bathtub. Good choice."

"Thanks." *Forget throwing up. I want to pee. And you'd better get out of here, or there's going to be a puddle on the floor.*

He stepped back, had a little trouble getting the door to shut properly; the doorknob was broken. How many people had tried to break it down, including him?

I didn't lock it. All they had to do was turn the knob. Some pro-

fessionals. I'm glad they didn't think of just opening it. Her teeth wanted to chatter; she set them tightly together and turned around. *Toilet. Let's take care of business first and worry about whoever tried to kill me later.*

It was, she reflected, almost getting fucking mundane.

No. Not really. She extended her arms and looked down at her hands. They shook so hard her fingers almost blurred.

Chapter Eleven

They couldn't have come in through the window," Hassan said flatly. "Look out there, and up to the roof. The angle's all wrong. It's not impossible, but why should they bother when they already had penetration to the second story? Answer me that."

Willie, sweeping up the broken glass, glanced at him. She said nothing, but her agreement was clear. Her dark hair was mussed out of its usual sleek tight bun and she had the sleepy-eyed look of a woman who had been rudely awakened, despite her calm smoothness as she went from one task to the next.

Not like Anna, who sat on the bed, her hands clasped and her eyes huge, looking at the floor whenever she wasn't sneaking little glances at Hassan and Willie.

Josiah folded his arms, leaning against the doorjamb. He needed a moment.

How could anyone have known Anna was here? He'd been circumspect, scooping her up at the hotel and making sure he was free of pursuit before bringing her in. His name wasn't connected to hers in any professional circles. At least, he'd done what he could to make sure.

That wasn't what bothered him the most, though.

"The bodies." His voice cut through Hassan and Willie's muttered exchanges. "Did either of you see what I saw?"

Hassan rounded on him, dark eyes aflame with something Josiah recognized.

Fear.

"Don't start, mate." The slim dark man's accent wore through the words, turning each one into a bullet. "What the *fuck* is going on here? You better start talking, or I swear I'm going to…" Apparently no threat was dire enough, because the slim man trailed off, his jaw working and his dark eyes ablaze.

"What precisely are you going to do? Head for the hills while the getting's good?" Josiah folded his arms, the gun a comforting weight pressing in against his side. "I saw the same fucking thing you did, man. The same thing."

Hassan shook his head, wordless. His pulse beat visibly in his throat. The dark man turned on his heel, his gaze coming to rest on Anna's bowed head. "You." His tone had turned chill. "What the fuck did you do? Nobody had a fucking clue she was here, Wolfe, right? So she must have—"

"She hasn't had a *chance*, Hassan. Think about it."

"That's just it, mate. I don't want to fucking think about it. I say we search her, inside and out."

"Don't be rude," Willie sniffed.

Hassan took a step toward the bed. Josiah sighed inwardly.

"Well?" the other man demanded. "How did you tell them you were here? Huh?"

"I didn't," Anna said, quietly, in a dry cricket whisper. "I *couldn't*. I…Josiah…"

"Leave her alone." He restrained the urge to pinch the bridge of his nose and sigh. "You saw what I did, Hassan. Admit it."

"All I'm admitting is that I want some answers from *her*." Hassan jabbed an accusing finger at Anna, who pushed herself up to her feet—or tried to, only to halt halfway and sit down, hard, as if her legs wouldn't quite hold her up.

Willie's handheld broom paused in its steady whisking.

"Hassan." Josiah's tone was soft and cold. "Stop it."

The air boiled with tension; Hassan threw up his hands, a short, sharp movement that almost, *almost* made Josiah twitch.

"For God's sake." He shook his dark, sleek head, and the strange, nervous tension evaporated. "You're mad. I'm mad, we're all mad here. You saw it too?"

Scalding relief swept through Josiah. *Now* Hassan was thinking clearly—and, bonus point, Josiah was suddenly very sure he hadn't gone crazy himself. "Of course I saw it. I'm just not sure what *it* was."

Willie's steady sweeping resumed. Anna was now staring at Josiah as if he'd grown another head. Her eyes were very wide, and very green.

"I'll fucking tell you what it was." Hassan shoved his hands in his pockets. "They turned to *dust*. I slit that punter's throat; he should have been gushing. But *no*, there was a fucking *poof*! And the next thing I know, I'm staring at a handful of sand."

Willie's sweeping stopped again. She leaned back on her haunches, her dark gaze moving from Hassan to Josiah, then swinging over to Anna. "I shot two of them," she added, matter-of-factly. "Both right in the *kopfe*. Nobody came to haul the bodies away, but they were gone, and I'm going to have to run the hoover down there." She waved the little handheld broom idly, as if for emphasis. "Something very strange is going on. Anna? Can you shed any light on this?"

All eyes on you, Anna. He let himself look at her again, at the gleaming of her hair and the dazed, uncomprehending beauty of her face.

She'd folded her hands in her lap like a little girl. "There was someone outside the window. The shadow was bobbing up and down, and I heard scratching. Then I ran for the bathroom." A flush rose in her cheeks, and she looked down at her clasped fingers. "I didn't know what else to do."

Well, you showed far more presence of mind than most civilians, sweets. Bolting into the bathroom and getting in a cast-iron tub. Josiah's chest hurt. Realizing they had slipped upstairs past him had caused such a sharp upswell of panic inside his ribs he'd almost thought he was having a heart attack. Getting into the room and seeing the empty bed was one of the worst things he'd lived through yet, and *that* was a surprise. He did, after all, have a good long list of bad-to-worse things in his life.

"Scratching at the window?" Hassan was pale under his caramel coloring. He didn't glance nervously at Josiah, and that was faintly unsettling. He wanted Hassan more worried about *him* than about what had just happened, for any number of reasons, one of which was Anna herself.

Thank God he's being reasonable. If he goes off the deep end I'm going to have to do something drastic.

Anna nodded, a tendril of silken hair falling in her face. "Like a cat. And the shadow was bobbing up and down. Like a balloon." She shivered. Her feet rested on hardwood; the slippers were Willie's, embroidered with red dragons, and too big for her. "Are they going to come back?"

She looked at him as if he knew all the answers, instead of only knowing one or two and suspecting a hell of a lot of unpleasant ones. "Not tonight, baby." *Wish I was as sure as I sound.*

"It's near dawn, and they had one hell of a surprise. We'll move out, get to a safer location."

Willie finished sweeping up the glass and stood, smoothly, dangling the paper bag full of broken window. Chill air made the drawn curtains move slightly, and the faint, indirect glow from the open bathroom door wouldn't help out anyone with a scope.

"You mean we can't stay here?" The fresh color drained out of Anna's cheeks.

"They've tried once, they'll try again. They'd be fools to come back without debriefing and reinforcements. This was just a raid, and it tells us that no matter what else, they want to keep this *quiet*. Nice and swept under the rug." He sighed, a familiar pain beginning to knot up the muscles at the base of his neck. "They don't have a secondary wave, or they'd be on us now while we're recouping. That means we have a chance of slipping away."

Her fingers twisted together, her knuckles turning white. She said nothing else, and he wanted to be on the bed beside her, to put an arm over her shoulders and console her, let her lean on him, and reassure himself that she was all right.

That was a party of sweepers; they came to leave nothing in here alive. We have got to get out before they can scramble some surveillance. They underestimated us as much as I underestimated them.

Then there was the little matter of the exploding bodies.

For a moment, the fact that this didn't disturb him as much as it should was…troubling. If he decided he didn't really care about anything but the next logical step, that he would think about it later, everything got a lot more manageable.

Manageable is good. Manageable is very good. "So Hassan and Willie are going to go out of town one way. We're going to go another. And we'll hook up someplace nice and quiet, and go about our business." He met Willie's gaze with a sense of relief; the tall, dark woman was outwardly calm and seemed only mildly puzzled.

"I don't think that's a good—" Willie began.

"Wolfe, without backup, you—" This from Hassan.

"I'm not leaving," Anna said flatly, and glared at him. He was immensely cheered to see that furious, green-eyed stare. It meant she was angry instead of terrified. "I hired you to kill whoever killed Eric."

You and I are about to have a talk, sweetheart, and I don't think you're going to like it. "You two get packed. I want you ready in ten."

Willie subsided, but Hassan evidently thought it was still under discussion. "Come on. We don't even know exactly what we're dealing with here. At least we should—"

"Ten minutes. Now, get out." His tone didn't admit argument. Willie reached forward, wound her fingers in Hassan's left sleeve.

"Come on. Help me pack." She drew him out, closing the bedroom door—miraculously unharmed by the night's fun—with a firm click.

That left Josiah with one pale and shaking Anna, who sat on the bed and stared as if seeing him for the first time.

"Do you think this is a game?" His tone was harsher than it had to be. She was alive. In one piece. Safe. "*Do* you?"

Anna pushed herself up to stand, making it without much trouble this time and wincing as she put weight on her swollen ankle. The bruise on her face mocked him. "I hired you." Her tone was much softer than his, but still sharp enough to cut silk. "You told me I'd hired you. I am not leaving until whatever Eric was working on is done and the people who killed him are—"

Well, would you look at that. She still manages to infuriate me without even trying. He made a concerted effort not to yell, an effort that curled his fists. "You promised no temper tantrums, baby doll. I told you, I am going to handle this in my own way, and you are going to *shut the fuck up* and do what I tell you, when I tell you."

"Yes, *sir*," she shot back. Her eyes glittered, and if his fists were tense hers were outright clenched. "You're the *professional* here, right?"

It was, he told himself, absolutely normal. She was exerting some control in a situation where she didn't have any. It made sense for her emotions to be all over the map, and he was the only person she could feel even halfway safe taking this out on.

Still, it pinched at him, right where he needed calm and control the most.

"Just be glad you're fucking alive." He shook his hands out. *She's not going anywhere. Relax. Just…fucking…relax.* "Damn right I'm the professional. I get more for a single goddamn event than you can make in a decade, and your mother's paltry little nest egg wouldn't even make a dent. It's as close to a charity job as I've ever—"

"*Fuck* you!" she yelled, taking a step forward onto her good leg. "I promised you what you wanted! *I* want whoever killed Eric to *pay,* and if you're such a goddamn hotshot, it should be no *goddamn problem for you!*"

He realized too late what he'd just said to her. At least she wasn't sunk in apathy anymore. If she was angry at him, at least she wasn't crying about her brother, and it showed she still felt *something* for Josiah himself. Just what, he wasn't sure.

81

He'd never been sure what she saw in him.

On the minus side, however, he was handling her badly. As usual. He seemed to do nothing *but* handle her badly.

A completely predictable civilian reaction, whipsawing on the fine edge of panic and rage. He'd seen it often enough in the untrained.

The *normal*. He hadn't really been one of them even before he'd found out what he was made for.

The important thing right now was to stay calm. *The situation is what the situation IS,* one of his trainers had said, a long time ago. For a tautology, it was pretty effective.

Take it from the top. Willie and Hassan could have been collateral damage; *he* might even have been. The sweepers were after Anna. She was too dangerous to someone to be allowed to live, and if Josiah didn't watch it, she *would* end up dead.

How had they found her? That bothered him.

It bothered him a *lot*.

First on the list of necessary items was calming her down. Reassuring her, as far as he could. "I did not take this job to exact revenge on whoever slit your brother's throat, Anna. I took it to keep you alive." *And to keep you with me, no matter what.* "The situation has undergone a rather drastic change that requires reevaluation. I'm not going to evaluate sitting here."

Her eyes flicked toward the window, the thought transparent on her face. Another raw civilian reaction, one with a little more presence of mind than most.

She was so goddamn stubborn. He could admire it, unless it would get her killed.

"Go ahead." It was work to get the words out past the rock

in his throat. "I'm the best chance you have to stay alive. You do something stupid and I'll handcuff you. I advise you not to push me on this."

She dropped back down on the bed, glaring at him as if she could happily boil him and eat him for lunch—which was all right. "You never used to be this much of an asshole." Her voice broke, unsteadily.

Which was bad. He wanted her furious at him, not unsteady and aching.

I was. You just never saw it. "You never had professional erasure teams after you before. I'm going to find you some clothes. You should get ready to go."

"Go where?" Her jaw set, her eyebrows drawing together, and the urge to take the few steps between them, take her face in his hands, and kiss her breathless almost took his legs out from under him.

Business first, hormones later. "Anna. Go and brush your teeth, wash your face, do whatever you have to do to get ready. Stay away from the window; it's a two-story drop straight down anyway. If you hear anything strange, get in the bathtub again. Stay here until I come get you."

She went extraordinarily still. Indirect light from the bathroom's night-light shadowed the bruised half of her face.

He had to persist. "Is that absolutely clear, Anna?"

Her gaze dropped to the floor. "Crystal."

"What are you going to do?" *Make her say it, for God's sake. Make her understand.* His hands ached. He wanted to touch her, wanted to take her shoulders and shake her. Reaction was setting in for him, too, delayed and unwelcome. He wanted a little more time before he had to process this.

"Get ready to go. Stay in this room. Until you come to get

me." Her chin jutted a little, defiant, and her shoulders hunched. It was impossible for her tone to be any blander.

"Good girl." He turned to the door, paused, and found it impossible to leave without saying something else. "I mean it, Anna. Every single word."

"The part about you just letting my brother's killer get off scot-free? Or the part about me whoring myself to pay you for whatever you feel like doing?"

He winced inwardly. *I probably deserve that.* "I'm not going to let your brother's killer 'get off.' I'm going to make damn good and sure you don't end up like Eric did. Get ready."

He left her in the room, closing the door quietly, and took stock, only to find that his hands were absolutely steady. He was in operating mode now.

The next move was his.

"I don't like it," Willie said softly. She looked down at a pile of fine, grainy ashen grit, all that remained of one of the attackers. There was a deformed, flattened lump of metal on the carpet in the short hall leading to her bedroom—the bullet, stopped by something solid that had exploded into ash. "If I wasn't sure none of us were crazy…"

"Let's not make any assumptions just yet." Josiah rubbed at the bridge of his nose, looking down at the pile of ash. He could still feel the drag of flesh against the knife in his hands and the sudden imploding as a body turned to this fine, glittering crystalline dust. "We could all be having some kind of hallucination."

"A mass hallucination? Now *that's* ridiculous." She blew out a long, soft breath. "Hassan's having trouble with this. So am I. I don't think we should separate."

Josiah thought this over, staring down at the distorted bullet. A thin curl of steam lifted from it; the metal was still warm and the house was chilling rapidly due to broken windows. "This will probably get messier than I thought."

"You need someone to herd the *fräulein*. Not only that, but you can't untangle this and keep her out of it at the same time." Willie avoided the pile of grit on the carpet as she stepped away from him. "Just think about it."

"You're right. But I don't want to drag you and Hassan—"

"How safe do you think we're going to be, when they dig into the records on your staff and find his history? Not to mention mine." She waved her hand over her shoulder, disappearing into her room.

Damn her. She's right. As usual. I hire a butler and get a god-damn den mother. He took a deep breath, turned on his heel, and headed for the stairs. He'd given them ten minutes, and they were going to be ready in five. He had an armful of clothes that might fit Anna, and they would have to get to a transfer point and change to clean vehicles.

Then he had to settle down for a little while and think clearly. His head was getting a little odd inside, things shaking loose and nasty assumptions rising to the surface.

They turned to ash, dammit. Like a bad fucking special effect. What the hell is going on?

It didn't matter. The important thing was, if he shot one of these things, they ended up dead. What happened to their bodies afterward, he decided, was academic. And bodies that turned into gritty dust were easier to get rid of than the other sort.

With that thought to keep him company, he trudged up the stairs, bracing himself to face Anna again.

Chapter Twelve

Anna huddled in the backseat of the dirty, primer-spotted Taurus. It looked like a heap from the outside, but it ran very quietly. Willie sat next to her, Hassan was in the front passenger seat, and Josiah—who hadn't said much since bringing her back an armful of clothes and telling her to get dressed—drove.

Silence. Not even the radio broke the sound of tires on pavement. She stared unseeing out her window, orange streetlight paling with the gray advent of false dawn.

A pair of jeans fit if she rolled them up, and a soft cashmere sweater in pale gray was too big for her but still warm and comforting. The shoes were all too big, but there was a pair of boots that weren't bad if she wore bulky wool socks. At least she was warm. She had her purse—her ID, her useless bank card, ten dollars in cash, and all the other detritus that accumulated inside a woman's bag. There was ibuprofen in there, and she wished suddenly it was Valium. Or something stronger.

Tasha always swore by Ativan. *It makes me care fuck-all,* she'd often said, and took one before every opening night. Thinking about leggy, beautiful Tasha, who lived for ballet and moaned if she gained even an ounce, could have been consoling, under other circumstances. As it was, Anna just kept hoping whoever was after her hadn't gone after her friends, as well.

Anna shivered, crossing her arms and wishing she could pull her feet up, curl into a ball, and forget all about this.

I know what I saw. Something was bobbing up and down outside the window. She had peered out the window, pushing the drapes aside and ignoring Josiah's warning. It was a two-story drop, and she couldn't see how anyone could hang off the roof and break into the room. She supposed it was *possible,* sure. It just didn't seem very likely, especially with the bits of whispered argument she'd overheard.

I've gone crazy. I have to be.

Bodies turning into ash? Things floating outside windows? *Crazy* was a polite term for it.

Totally fucking nuts was probably the proper description. She was beginning to wonder if maybe she should have taken her chances going to the police anyway, despite Eric's warnings.

Every time she thought so, though, the vision of Eric's throat, the necklace of a bright red slash across it like a wide clownish smile, rose up in front of her.

If my house is tossed, I'm not calling the police. You get me? Back when he had been alive. Why hadn't she tried to stop him, demanded to know more? Suggested he get a hotel room or something? Would he be alive if she'd asked some questions?

A spiny mouse made of guilt lodged in her chest, nestling in and nibbling at the empty place where her brother used to be. Anna's hands twisted themselves together, tighter.

When Josiah finally pulled over and stopped on a quiet residential street, he and Hassan got out of the car without a word. Hassan carried the files, and Anna's heart leapt into her throat.

Willie laid one long, slim hand on her arm. "There's a twenty-four-hour copy place right around the corner. They'll be back in under ten minutes, and we'll be on our way to a transfer point; there'll be clean cars and a cache of supplies. It's standard procedure, *Liebchen*."

"So this is normal?" *Jeez, what do you do for fun? Rob a few banks, invade a foreign country?*

"Not so much normal as a matter of training, just in case." The woman's eyes glittered as she glanced out her window, then peered at the rearview mirror. "Just watch. Jo wants to get through this without any of us dying."

That would be nice, wouldn't it. Anna pulled her hands back inside her sleeves and studied Willie's long, pale face. In the dim gray almost-dawn, the tall woman looked ghostly, and now Anna could see pitted scars under her makeup. It looked like she'd had *really* bad acne. "I'm sorry." The car ticked as metal cooled, shrinking.

Willie shrugged. "Hassan and I both knew there was a chance. It was almost a given."

"Because of what he does?" *Murderer.* She closed her eyes, wishing her heart would stop pounding. *What does that make me? I'm just as bad as he is. Worse, I'm a hypocrite.*

"It was a good career. Very…lucrative." Willie's tone, at least, was kind. Out of all three of them, she seemed the most approachable. The most…well, normal. "You knew?"

Only what Eric dug up. "My brother was suspicious. He…well, he got pictures. He had a contact somewhere in the government and he…I saw the file. Pictures of things, horrible things." *Almost as horrible as what happened to him, as a matter of fact. God.* "I broke up with Josiah. We were just about to elope."

"Ah." Willie sounded as if a private hypothesis had been confirmed. "I see."

"He didn't tell you?" *I never told anyone. Even Tasha. Only Eric, and he...*

"I didn't ask. Hassan knows a little, I think. All I knew was that Jo carried that phone with him everywhere, and he was always listening for it."

"Which phone?"

"The one you called him on."

The darkness behind Anna's eyelids turned hard, uncomforting. She looked out at the quiet street. There were houses, lawns, mailboxes. People sleeping behind dark windows. Normal people who hadn't run through a manicured garden, listening to bullets thud into the ground and zing off rocks as they fled for their lives.

I wish I was home. Click your heels together three times, Annie, and see what happens.

Willie shifted a little, glancing at the passenger-side mirror. "I used to tease him. Tell him that I would find him wife like good matchmaker should. He would only smile. One day Hassan took me aside and told me that there had been a girl, and something had happened. I didn't tease him again, but I wondered. And now, here you are."

Here I am. Wonderful. The number was the same, from Josiah's cell phone. He'd kept it all this time, for some reason. It was only a few dollars and some hassle to change a number, right? Maybe he just didn't want to go through all that.

Anna closed her lips firmly over the urge to ask more.

The two men returned, Hassan carrying two crisp new manila stretch folders. The burst of night air, as they got into the car, was laden with cold and the iron tang of potential snow.

"How are we doing?" Josiah asked quietly, buckling his seat belt. The light inside the car didn't go on when the doors were opened, which gave Anna a faint funny feeling.

"No sign of anything out of the ordinary." Willie buckled herself in, too. "You?"

"Nothing but a sleeping clerk behind a counter. God bless coin-op machines." The car started with a swift, sweet purr. "Anna? You okay?"

No, I'm not. I don't think I'll ever be okay again, dammit. "Fine." The word tasted bitter, chopped short, hard. *I don't even have any clothes.*

She longed to go back to her apartment, crawl into her familiar bed, and pull the covers over her head. Let the world do whatever it wanted outside her door. If she did, maybe this would all turn out to be a bad dream. She didn't even know what all these people wanted to kill her *for.*

Well, Eric was always a pest. Someone decided to shut him up after he came across something big. I know that much. "Josiah?"

"What?" He pulled away from the curb. Hassan stared at his lap, and Willie let out a soft sigh.

"Can I ask a question?" One of their old games—next he'd say, *you already did,* and they would both laugh.

Except those days were gone.

"You can." He sounded, of all things, amused. His hazel eyes flicked up to the rearview mirror. Was he watching her?

I hope not. He's driving. "What's in the files?"

Hassan's dark, curly head jerked up. He half-turned, looking over the seat at her.

"Information," Josiah said steadily. "I'll go through it with you when we're safe, okay?"

I thought I was safe, but someone broke into your house, too.

Now you're running away. And there were other people, too—his friends, if that's what Willie and Hassan were.

Now they were in danger. All because she hadn't been able to think of anything else, and *still* couldn't.

Except Eric's discolored face, and that horrible slashed necklace. Her brother, who had held her hand on the couch one night while the policeman said *there's been an accident,* and gone white as a sheet, but never broke down. Eric, who had just shook his head when they wanted to send her into foster care.

She was beginning to suspect she'd never feel safe again. Ever.

"Fine." Another short, sharp, bitter word. Her cheeks turned hot, and she was glad it was dim inside the car. She closed her eyes again, leaning back. The car kept moving like an oiled ball bearing, sliding along with a sound that threatened to crawl into her head. "Where are we going?" *Am I allowed to know?*

"To a transfer point. Everything's taken care of. Try to rest." Josiah said nothing more, but Hassan made a small snorting sound, as if choking on laughter.

Anna didn't care. She just kept her eyes firmly shut.

The "transfer point" was a warehouse in the industrial part of town; Hassan pulled the garage door shut behind the car and Josiah cut the engine. A flurry of activity ensued, with the three of them working and Anna feeling foolish and useless—Josiah just handed her the original files and told her to sit in a new car, a sleek, anonymous white sedan. She did, resting her too-big boots on cold concrete, the open door creaking slightly when she pushed at it.

Willie and Hassan, after a long sotto voce conference, took the other car, a dark blue Jeep. They drove away through another door, Josiah silhouetted for a moment against the pale light of a cloudy winter morning as he pulled it closed. He came back to the car she was in, put a few more things in the trunk from boxes on the concrete floor, and finally got in on the driver's side. "You still okay?"

"Fine," she repeated. *Just dandy. Will you quit asking me that?*

He studied her for a long moment as she pulled her legs in and slammed the door. She arranged the messy pile of paper in her lap, settling her feet on either side of her purse; he started the car but kept it in park, still watching her.

"I'm sorry," he said finally. "I shouldn't have said that to you."

You've said a lot of things to me lately. I guess we're about even, when it comes to verbal nastiness. "Said what?" She patted the papers into neatness, suddenly very concerned with their edges and creases. Eric's notes were always coffee-stained and reeking of burning tobacco; for someone with such a logical, organized mind he was chaotic at best and hideously messy at worst.

The image of Eric's office, paper and coffee cups everywhere, his shapeless battered plaid jacket hanging on a peg by the door, rose inside her head. Hot water scorched her eyes. She swallowed twice, quickly.

Josiah was silent for a long moment. The engine thrummed along under that dangerous quiet. "There's a whole list of things I shouldn't have said. I'm sorry about your brother."

Her vision blurred, came back. The entire world wavered, uncertain. An iron fist closed around her throat. "Eric," she managed.

"I'm sorry he's…dead." He did *sound* sorry, too. Not calm or ironic or just slightly amused. Josiah actually sounded like it mattered to him. "My job is to make sure you don't join him. Revenge is pointless, Anna. There's no profit in it."

92

Who cares about fucking profit? He's my brother! "You won't help me?" *This is a fine time to tell me, Jo.*

"I *am* helping you. This is bigger than we thought. We're going to lie low for a little while, and I'm going to call in a few favors." He paused. "You don't have to pay me."

What does that mean? Did I take all the fun out of it by agreeing to let you do whatever you wanted? "I said I would," she insisted, stubbornly. "You were very clear about what you wanted." Not to mention it was looking like the only bargaining chip she had, at this point. He could just tell her to get out of the car and drive away, really.

He started the car with a vicious twist of the key; Anna almost flinched. He chose yet another exit, this one with an automatic opener that made a ratcheting sound as it pulled the thin segmented metal plates up. "I was…upset, Anna."

Oh. And now you're not? "You said you'd help me." Carefully, cautiously, she measured the distance between her hand and the door handle.

"I *am* helping you," he repeated, maddeningly calm, easing the car out between piles of discarded, rotting siding.

"How?" It was out before she could stop herself, and she bit her lip. *Don't piss him off. He's the only chance you have now, unless you* do *want to go to the police. How about it? Both Eric and George warned you not to.*

"By getting you somewhere safe so I can work."

"Oh, yes. Your…work."

"Yes, my work. The only thing I ever lied to you about." He braked smoothly, glancing in the mirror to make sure the door was closing, checked the deserted street, then pulled out and turned left. "I didn't even really lie. I just didn't tell you."

It was probably good sense not to continue down this road.

Unfortunately, something inside her was boiling, and she couldn't help herself. "Oh, so omission makes it all right?" *Calm down. Come on, don't make him angry.*

"Think about it logically for a minute—" His voice was rising.

So was hers. "*Logically?* You should have *told* me!"

"Oh, really? When should I have told you, huh? When I bought you coffee? On our first date? Maybe the first time we slept together, or that time you almost got mugged and I scared the guy off? When *should* I have told you? When would be a good time to say, *Oh, by the way, I do contract work for domestic and international intelligence, I'm referred to as a liquidation consultant?* You answer me that, when would have been a good time to tell you? Huh?"

She pulled into herself, crossing her arms. *Don't make him even angrier. Jesus, Anna, you could make the Dalai Lama lose his temper.* Scolding herself didn't really work, because it sounded just like Eric.

"Answer me." Josiah's tone had gone chill. "When would have been a good time to tell you, Anna?"

Don't respond. Suck it up. She scrubbed at her cheek with the back of one hand. Said nothing.

"That's what I thought." His voice was quiet, and quietly vicious. "Do me a favor and stop arguing with me. I have to think."

It was hard work to keep the words neutral, even, and reasonable. "About what?"

He made a short, almost-annoyed sound, as if she'd changed to the Food Network during a documentary. "About my next move. This is just like chess; each move either narrows or widens prospective alternatives. Mostly narrows. I need to plan out my next few alternatives and contingencies, and you need to rest. We'll get some breakfast on our way out of town."

Wait, what? "I can't leave." Panic welled up inside her chest. "I *can't.*"

"It's only temporary. Right now I can't be worrying about you being recognized somewhere."

She studied the hood of the car, trying to name the exact Pantone color of the paint. There had to be hundreds of white sedans in the city just like this one.

Josiah's knuckles were white on the steering wheel. He stared at the road as if it had offended him; his eyes had lightened and were almost piercing green. Change-color eyes on a chameleon man, he looked different than he had in the warehouse, and more different still from in the lobby of the Blake. His profile was still clean and classic, but his mouth was drawn tight and his eyes blazed.

Her fingers relaxed. She had been clenching them, making a fist. She reached over, touched his shoulder under navy merino. "Don't. Please."

Well, now I sound like an idiot. Don't leave me? Or don't be mad at me? Or don't leave me to the wolves, because I don't know what to do?

He let out a long breath, then reached forward and flipped the heater on. Her hand dropped back down into her lap, limply.

She shouldn't have touched him.

The lump in her throat eased. A thin film of self-control stretched like Saran Wrap over the big squirming ball of panic and grief that was all she was right now.

I'm worse than useless. I've never even taken a Tae Bo class, for God's sake. Even Tasha knows how to take out someone's knee.

"That's what dancers do when you've really *pissed them off, Annie!"*

"Don't worry so much." Josiah was himself again, impossibly calm. "Did you ever wonder why Eric didn't suffer?"

She had to swallow twice. The newfound calm wasn't quite numbness, and it was fragile. If she didn't move too quickly or speak too loudly, she wouldn't shatter. "What?"

"He obtained a top-clearance file on me. If I was the bad guy you think I am, I would have liquidated him. Him having that fucking file was a major breach of security that could have gotten me killed and did end up costing me almost everything. But I kept quiet about it. For *your* sake, I might add. I didn't turn him in." He turned right, toward the interstate. Morning sunlight fell between still more warehouses, made train tracks gleam and showed a thin layer of frost edging weeds and grass. "Besides, if Eric had the connections to get that file on me, he probably stumbled over something bigger than I can handle with just myself and superficial backup this time. I want you out of the way if this all goes south."

Liquidated. Clearance. Breach of security. Superficial backup. I know he's talking English, but I barely understand. She fastened on the first thing that occurred to her. "You would have killed Eric?"

"I seriously considered it." He turned onto the freeway on-ramp, smoothly, under a green light. "But no, I wouldn't have. It wouldn't have changed anything."

Miles began to slip away under the car wheels. "You considered it?" *What else did you "consider"?*

"You want the truth? There it is. I thought about it. It would have been tremendously satisfying, in the short run. He destroyed the only thing I valued." His eyes flickered up to the rearview mirror, back down to the road. Traffic was light this early in the morning, and he kept the car at a respectable two miles under the speed limit.

The heater blasted her with warm air, just like yesterday—or the day before. Time kept slipping away from her. The whole thing was a bad dream, a waking nightmare. If she could just wake up in her own bed…

Anna watched the white line at the edge of the road, unreeling in its smooth ribbon, and flinched when her humming brain served up the most recent horror.

Scratch-scratch. Like a cat scratching at a door.

"How did they get in the window?" She sounded childish even to herself, but there probably wasn't a better time to ask. Her brain just wouldn't let any of this rest, zigzagging from one hideous event to the next. "And the…the bodies. What happened to the bodies?" *I heard what you said, but it doesn't make any sense. None of this does.*

Maybe she was going insane instead of dreaming. Was Josiah a figment of her imagination?

Well, maybe not. For one thing, he was just as irritatingly imperturbable as he'd ever been.

He was silent for a full thirty seconds. "I wish to God I knew."

That seemed to finish everything up, and Anna stared at the files in her lap. What had Eric seen? What had he been pursuing?

He destroyed the only thing I valued. She turned the sentence over in her mind, examined it from every possible angle.

A horrible thought floated up past the thin new layer of calm, drifting into the forefront of her mind.

Was it possible that Josiah was involved somehow?

No, he seemed as baffled as she was. Then again, he'd lied to her before, lied so well she hadn't suspected anything was amiss. Lied every time he touched her, every time he kissed her.

"We'll stop for breakfast soon." He hit the turn signal and changed lanes to avoid a wallowing semi. "Just relax. There's nothing we can do right now."

"Relax. Right. Sure." She didn't mean to sound sarcastic at all, just tired. Her back hurt, her ankle and face throbbed, and her heart hurt worst of all, a deep, drilling emptiness of grief rolling itself tighter and tighter, into a diamond ball. She stared out the window, the feeling of deadly, shock-induced unreality growing with every mile of familiar-strange freeway taking them north.

Chapter Thirteen

The cabin sat on a pristine scallop of lakefront property, its windows golden stars in the gathering dawn. Firs, pines, and the occasional bare-armed maple or aspen crowded close. Josiah braked to a stop on the rise, spotting the dark blue Jeep right where it should be, and waited until one of the lights in the upper window flickered. A slow count of five, then it flickered again.

He waited for a slow count of ten, shut his headlights off. Five more seconds, and he turned them back on and descended the ribbon of indifferent paving jolting down the hill, finally pulling the sedan in a tight circle and backing into the space left for him.

Anna, asleep almost since they'd hit the freeway, breathed softly next to him. He'd wanted to stop for something to eat, but she looked so peaceful he ended up simply driving, ignoring the gnawing in his stomach. Even now, with her head tilted back against the seat and her long dark hair mussed against gray cashmere, she looked so tranquil and exhausted he almost didn't want to turn the car off.

But he did, and sat watching the flush of sleep in her un-wounded cheek as her eyelashes fluttered. She woke with a small start, looking wildly around, and his hand shot out, fin-gers closing around her wrist. "Easy, relax. We just stopped." *I'm here.* Comforting words stuck in his throat; he swallowed them.

She blinked owlishly, green eyes suddenly vivid and the bruise on her face a bit better. Rest did wonders for anyone. "Oh." She glanced down at her lap, checking to make sure the files were still there. Her lashes momentarily veiled her eyes, and her hair fell forward over her shoulder, and he remembered what it was like to walk down a snowy downtown street with her on Christmas Eve, looking in deserted shop windows as they headed toward her brother's apartment for dinner.

Anna next to him, and everything right with the world; he remembered her having a little too much wine, and he'd promised Eric he would get her home safely.

Counting on it, Wolfe, her brother had retorted, with an odd gleam in his green eyes that matched his sister's. *Just see that you do.*

All the things he wanted to say to her climbed back up into his throat, fighting for free air. Trapped, they congealed, and he had to swallow twice before he could talk again. He let go of her wrist, one finger at a time. "How do you feel?"

"Shaky. Tired." She gave him a shy, tentative smile. "I thought you said we were stopping for breakfast."

An uncertain détente filled the space inside the car. "You needed sleep more. Stay here for a second, I want to check the house."

She examined the surroundings, gray-rising dawn light turn-ing her into an ivory statuette. "Isn't that the Jeep that they took? Your friends?"

Clever girl. "I don't want any surprises. Watch in the mirror. If anyone other than me comes out that door, you turn the key and burn rubber out of here. Got it?"

She nodded, brushing her hair out of her eyes with a slight irritated movement that made his pulse speed up a notch. "Where am I supposed to go?"

It was a good question. "Over the state line to the next major city, and talk to the FBI. It's worth a try." *It probably won't do any good, but let's not mention that. I have no intention of it ever becoming necessary.*

Still, what he intended and what actually happened were sometimes wildly divergent, especially where Anna was concerned.

"Oh." She rubbed delicately at her eyes as he glanced in the rearview mirror again, checking. "Okay."

Fortunately, five minutes later he ushered her into the snug, cozy little cabin. Willie had started a fire, and it smelled of pine sap and frying bacon. "Breakfast," Willie said smartly, subtracting Anna from him with barely a nod. "Come along, *Liebchen,* you made good time. There's coffee; it's not very good, but it'll do. The garden is lovely, and the window looks right out onto the lake—" Her words faded to indistinct muttering as they went into the kitchen, the door closing quietly.

Hassan appeared at the foot of the stairs, shaking his head. "I did some phoning and Willie worked her magic on the laptop. I talked to Abramoff." Hassan wasn't pale, but he sounded like he should, by all rights, *be* pale. "Something weird is going on."

Josiah stretched. First one side, then the other. His gaze slid over the interior of the cabin, checking for weak points, looking at cover. They would have to move the old comfortable hole-eaten gray couch and brace the rocking chair against the window. "Now you realize this?"

Hassan's mobile mouth made a small moue of distaste, and he folded his arms—Willie must have packed that red flannel shirt for him. His shoulder holster held a very nice little Sig Sauer. "Don't give me any shite, Yank. Abramoff says there's not a whisper. Nobody looking for you, or for anyone connected to you. But get this, he did drop me a word about a little visit someone paid to Machen on the Lower East Side."

"Machen." He cast back through memory, found the face. "Thickset fellow. Knives. Hangs out with Holly's crew." Now *there* was someone he wouldn't care to tangle with—Hollister the Fence might be getting older, but certainly not mellower.

"Yep. Some guy from the cop shop—they have a working relationship—comes to visit him, asking if anyone had been hiring mercenaries lately. Machen thinks about it, says no, nothing out of the ordinary. The cop tells him something big and quiet is going on, and to keep his head down. Just before he leaves, the cop says something weird."

Interesting. Do they think maybe I hired a few professionals, or that Anna did? "What?"

"He asks Machen if he's got any silver bullets and tells him to buy a crucifix. Then he laughs, and leaves. Machen thought it was weird enough to mention."

Silver bullets. Crucifixes. Okay. "And Abramoff thought it was weird enough to tell you." He met the younger man's worried gaze, finally. "Anything else?"

"That isn't enough? Well, here's another one. I had Willie look up that building. The one in the pictures." Hassan's mouth turned down at the corners, a sure sign of trouble. "Guess who holds the deed."

"Who?" *This is beginning to get strange.*

"The chief of police, our dear Lock-'em-Up Denton himself. Guess what *else* I found out?"

This isn't the time for games, Hassan. But he took the bait. "You've been a busy boy. What?"

"Those interviewees? All of them? Missing. A few had reports on them, but not many. A couple just up and vanished. Here's the kicker: Nobody knows Eric Caldwell's dead yet. His editor's not even listed as missing. The cops aren't pursuing, either."

That stopped Josiah for a full fifteen seconds, time he spent looking across the room at the merry, flickering orange dance of flame in the stone fireplace. Red checkered curtains, shabby furniture; all this place needed was dead animal heads on the walls. He hadn't gone quite that far yet with the interior decorating. Hunting lost a lot of its savor once a man knew what it was like to be shot at. "Nothing about *any* of them?"

"And no missing-person's report on your little lady, either, even though she's been gone from work for a few days. This is all bollixed up, and badly."

It does alter some things. "Look on the bright side. It gives us a certain latitude of action we wouldn't otherwise have."

Hassan snorted. "Well, that's comforting. When you say *latitude of action* all I hear is *shite's going to get messed up.* This isn't going to be another Cairo, is it?"

Josiah's skin chilled all over, a brief cold caress. "Of course not. I'm not suicidal." *Not this time.* "Besides, we've got a civilian to keep out of this, and Willie to think of. Anything else?"

That earned him a lopsided smile. Hassan was back where he was comfortable, gathering information and being cheeky. "Christ, you haven't given me any time yet. We've been busy fighting off bodies that turn into a fucking Hoover commercial. You should be on your bloody knees thanking me for all I've done already."

"I'll send you a Christmas card."

Hassan replied with a scathing and unrepeatable term in Russian, and Josiah laughed. The banter was so familiar, he almost wondered why he'd retired.

Then he heard a muffled burst of female laughter from the kitchen—Willie's high and carefree, Anna's half-guilty and surprised. It was good to hear her, but it reminded him of plenty of things he didn't want to think about.

Number one on that list was bodies that turned into dust. Crucifixes. Silver bullets.

Enough. Just got to get through the day, then I want a drink. I need to think about this.

Willie kept Anna busy all day, cleaning the already-spotless cabin, making lunch, preparing dinner. The little domestic chores would calm both of them. Normalcy—or at least some approximation of it—was the best thing for Anna at the moment.

Hassan settled in a chair by the front window, watching the road, alternately humming a tuneless melody and leafing absently through his old, battered copy of the Koran. That was a little disturbing, but at least he wasn't oiling his knives yet.

Josiah knew better than to think he'd forgotten about dust-exploding bodies, either.

He spent the day shoring up the outer defenses and alarms, trudging through muck and coming back in time for lunch and again for dinner. By the final time he scraped thick cold mud off his feet the light had failed completely. The wild darkness of countryside pressed thick against the windows of the little cabin, an almost-full moon mounting higher in the sky, its reflection rippling on the surface of the inky lake.

Dinner was almost a disaster. Josiah said little, Willie tried to keep the conversation going, and Hassan took his bowl to the window and settled down to watch, a high-powered rifle braced against his chair.

Anna tried to play the politeness game with Willie, but ended up eating only a few bites and staring into her soup, occasionally darting uncertain looks at Josiah.

Finally, however, it got the better of her.

"What are we going to do?" This she directed at Willie, who was pragmatically enjoying herself.

Willie had taken the opportunity to make her justifiably famous potato-and-leek soup, and was dipping her bread—store-bought, but she'd cheerfully remarked that sacrifices had to be made—with great relish. She glanced up, her hair back in its large, sleek chignon. The light was kind to her, smoothing out the pockmarks on her cheeks and forehead just like her makeup did. "Now we wait."

Anna's eyes glittered. She laid her spoon down, and her expression called Josiah out of a worried rethinking of the short list of people he wanted to contact in the next few days.

"Wait for what?" Anna sounded deceptively calm, but he'd heard that tone before and sighed internally.

"Wait for Josiah to decide it's safe to move again. Wait for the next disaster. Wait for it to be safe enough for us to go back home." Willie shrugged. "It's the worst part about something like this."

"I thought..." Anna bit her lip, continued. "I thought we

would *do* something. Take the files somewhere. What's *in* the files, anyway? What's going on?"

"It's probably safer if we don't know." Willie set her own spoon down, precisely. The tiny click was very loud in the stillness. "Really. The best thing to do is just…wait."

"They didn't wait to kill my brother." Anna laid her hands flat on the table. "I can't go home, I saw George get shot right in front of me, they broke all the windows in Josiah's house, and we're just supposed to *wait*?"

"Wait, and eat your dinner." Willie nodded. "That's it, exactly."

Anna cast him an imploring look. Josiah shrugged. She wasn't going to listen, but he told her anyway. "She's right. Ninety-nine percent of any operation is the waiting. We need to be careful."

It wasn't anywhere close to what he wanted to tell her. *I would do just about anything to fix this for you right this fucking instant, Anna girl. But I can't, and I have to make sure we don't have another nasty surprise.* He found himself examining the shape of her mouth and dragged his gaze hastily up as her eyes slid away.

Her head dropped. She looked down at her bowl, and her shoulders trembled once. Her hair, freed from a messy ponytail, swept down to curtain her expression.

Christ, say something useful to her. Something comforting. "We're going to give the situation some time to calm down. Then I'll go in and call in a few favors. If all goes well we won't even have to lift a finger; everything will be taken care of in the—"

"Excuse me." She stood up, suddenly, the chair scraping against wood flooring. It was such a quick movement he almost twitched. "I don't think I'm hungry. I'm sorry."

"Anna—" He'd handled it badly, again.

She fled, stopping only to scoop up the original file and blindly stumbling up the stairs. He listened, marking each familiar squeak and groan, heard her slam the door to the upstairs bedroom.

"Civilian." Hassan snorted, only mildly disparaging. He slurped a very large spoonful of soup for emphasis.

"Be kind." Willie sighed, dunking a slice of wheat bread into her bowl. "It's not every day a girl finds her brother dead and her life depending on punks."

"Punks?" Hassan inquired mildly, arching an eyebrow. The combination living and dining room was so small he could deploy sarcasm or inquiry for maximum effect at short distance.

Josiah suppressed a small smile, despite his stomach turning in on itself.

Willie's short chuffing sound of unwilling amusement was a balm. "Like you, Hassan. You're a punk. Come on over and sit down."

"Watching the road, woman."

"Who's going to come down the road? Nobody knows we're here." Willie was trying, bless her. Almost too hard.

Josiah pushed his chair back, slowly, and stood up. Willie glanced at him, and for a moment he saw a flash of fear in her dark eyes. "Don't worry." He sounded odd even to himself. "I'm not going to do anything stupid."

"Again," Hassan mumbled, and immediately took another huge mouthful of soup.

Josiah let it go. He left the table and trudged up the stairs, his footfalls silent. Stood outside the firmly shut bedroom door. Spread his fingers against the rough wood and imagined her behind it, maybe lying flat on the creaking single bed and silently weeping. God knew she wouldn't let him see her in tears if she could help it.

What am I going to do? His fingers rested on the doorknob.

It was enough to make a man helpless, pulled forward like iron to the magnet. No use in struggling. He twisted the knob and walked in like a man heading for his own execution.

Chapter Fourteen

The door creaked a little, theatrically. "Anna?" Softly. As if he wasn't quite sure what he'd find in the room.

That made two of them, she guessed.

Oh, God, can't you leave me alone? She hunched her shoulders, her fingers running over the edges of manila folders. "Go away." She couldn't say it very loudly, and he came in, shut the door, and ghosted across the floorboards. He seemed to avoid each squeak and groan a normal person would wring out of lumber.

The bed creaked a little as he sat down next to her, though. She had pulled herself up, tucking her injured ankle and approximating a cross-legged position, a weight of paper in her lap. Thin moonlight fell through the windows under their cheerful clichéd red gingham, and she was suddenly shaken by the urge to scream. *Did you have to make this place so fucking ugly? I could rip all the curtains down and make better ones from diseased flea market quilts. I know I could.*

Homesickness tasted like bitter metal in her mouth. Anna pulled her lips tight, pushing the words down, away. The thin film of self-control was getting a workout, but at least she didn't feel like she'd start screaming anytime soon.

Well, not very loudly, anyway.

Josiah pushed a strand of her hair back, tucking it behind her ear. He touched her swollen cheek, smoothing his finger down. "Ouch." His tone took her by surprise—thoughtful, and gentle. "You bruise so easily. I used to think I should pad all the sharp corners for you."

Her stomach turned over, hard. He sounded just like he always had. Calm. Quiet. Controlled.

God, how she'd loved that about him, the way he took everything in stride, from a flat tire to a bad cup of coffee. He'd always made her feel steadier and more reliable, too, instead of just the fruitcake little sister, the scattered artist.

She'd liked it, after being irresponsible all her life. *You have two left feet and a brain stuck on glitter,* Eric had yelled at her, once, when he tried to teach her the cha-cha.

He'd only been twelve, but still.

"I hate this." She stared down at the file. "All this time, I haven't even had a chance to look at it. Now I'm afraid to."

His fingers curled around the messy stack of paper. There was a short struggle, not even deserving the name since she didn't fight very hard, and he subtracted the whole bundle from her limp fingers. "Not right now." He set it aside on the nightstand—an indifferently painted, chunky stripped-pine piece that had been further insulted by a shapeless seventies amber-glass lamp—and turned back to her. "I know you're…really upset. The rug's been pulled out from under you, and I'm sorry. But you've got to eat, Anna. And you've got to stop yanking my chain. I can't do my job if you—"

Upset? I'm upset? A laugh, bitter and sharp, spilled out of her mouth as her temper snapped. "I thought that's what you wanted. A good chain-yanking. A little roll in the hay, yanking the old ball and chain. Right? I'm useless for anything else."

"Jesus." He slipped his arm around her shoulder and pulled her close.

She wanted to hit him. She wanted to break the horrible amber lamp, wanted to smash the entire room, wanted to scream and scream and scream. Instead, she found herself breathing into the comforting space between his neck and his shoulder, shuddering. He had somehow pulled her into his lap, and was stroking her hair while she struggled to stop hyperventilating, to calm herself down. The entire cabin smelled like sap and unused air, the dusty, disused tang of a house closed up and left uninhabited for a while. Her ankle hurt, but she didn't fight him, didn't shift to a more comfortable position.

For the first time since seeing her brother's body, Anna felt...well, completely safe.

He smelled like outside, like cold air and more pine sap and just plain Josiah. "I hate this," she whispered into his sweater. "I *hate* it." *And I hate you,* she was tempted to add, but that would have been childish.

"Shhh." His breath was a warm spot on her scalp; he ran his fingers through her hair and rubbed her back in small circles, his expert fingers finding little spots of soreness and working at them gently. He murmured soothing little nonsensical words just as he had when her cat Caravaggio died. "I know. It's all right. Shh."

The shudders peaked, her teeth chattering, and eased slightly. Eased again. She was left with her face buried in his neck, damp tendrils of hair clinging to her forehead, listening to the sound of his breathing. Even, regular, as if she hadn't upset him in the slightest.

Silence crouched over both of them. His fingers kept going, a gentle massage. Her head felt heavy, as if she'd cried herself out, but her eyes still burned with unspent tears. *Stop it, Anna. Stop your whining.* "Sorry." It was a pale little word to contain what she felt.

"It's all right." He inhaled, a long, smooth movement. "It's normal. I'd be worried if you didn't hate this." A short pause. "I'd be worried if you didn't hate me a bit, too, right now."

I wish I did. It was warm and dark, and she kept her eyes tightly closed. There seemed nothing else to say.

He seemed perfectly content to hold her, though she was probably giving him a cramp or two. Her neck started to hurt, and her lower back was unhappy. Her ankle twinged.

But he smelled so good she stayed where she was, and finally found something else to say. "I missed you."

He made a small movement. "You have no idea how much I missed *you*."

That made her smile, a sad, forlorn trickle of relief pulling the corner of her lips up. "How much?"

"I nearly got myself killed in Cairo, missing you. Wasn't thinking clearly. Hassan had to bail me out. He saved my life."

Well. I'm sorry I asked now. "Oh."

His fingers curled into her hair. He kissed the top of her head. "You missed me?"

If you only knew. "I did."

"Regret breaking up with me?"

Not really. I had to. "I wish you'd told me."

"I couldn't."

This is so fucked up. The awareness of just how completely insane and absurd her life had become hit her, down low in the pit of her belly. "I know."

"Anna?" He kissed the top of her head again. For a moment the intervening years fell away, and the only thing larger than the relief was the sickening thump in her chest when they came back.

"What?" She moved, restlessly, and he let her go. A moment's worth of rearranging ended with her looking up at him as he knelt on the bed, the light from the lamp describing the stubbled line of his jaw, the curve of his cheek.

Her fingers itched for charcoal and paper. She did her best thinking while she sketched.

"You don't have to pay me." He levered himself off the bed in one swift graceful motion and pulled his sweater down a bit, a completely unconscious rearrangement. "I shouldn't have said that. I shouldn't have done that, either."

Embarrassment scorched her cheeks—and other parts of her, as well. "I didn't think you worked for free."

"I don't." He turned on his heel and stalked for the door, his shoulders hunching slightly, as if he expected her to throw something at him. "But I'll take what you give me, Anna. I always have. Try to rest."

"Josiah—"

The door closed.

Well, that went as well as I'd expect after the last few days. Anna sighed. She stared at the unforgiving blank wood, wondering if she would hear him going down the hall unless he wanted her to.

It was eerie, how quietly he could move. She'd dropped a bowl, once, when he just seemed to appear out of thin air in her kitchen, and her short yelp of surprise had given them both the giggles.

What was she supposed to do now? Forgive him? Act like nothing that happened three years ago mattered? As if Eric wasn't dead? Or as if Josiah hadn't held her against the wall and whispered *as many times as I want, and you'll act like you like it*?

Maybe as if she didn't care? Was there a Miss Manners guide for this sort of situation? There should be.

She reached for the bedside table, touched the stack of paper.

There was nothing else to do. She scooped up the file and dumped it into her lap. Someone had killed Eric because of this, and Josiah suddenly didn't seem really committed to hunting down her brother's killer or exposing whatever story he'd been pursuing.

"Not that keeping me alive is a bad thing," she muttered, and flipped the first folder open. "I'm not saying that at all."

But something had to be done. If Josiah wouldn't do it…it was up to her. For once in her life, her big brother needed something from her. The big brother who had always protected her as best he could.

Ever since grade school, Eric had been the one to look to for a solution. He'd always seemed to know what to do, never at a loss in the wide, drifting world like his almost-useless, dreamy, artsy younger sister. He knew how to fix a car or a broken lamp, and as scattered as his office was he was never late for an appointment. When their parents died two days after his nineteenth birthday, he'd moved from one task to the next, organizing the funeral, getting cards sent out, booking a chapel for the memorial service, signing the papers—and refusing to even listen when they wanted to send Anna into foster care.

I'm her brother, he said steadily. *I'm over eighteen, and she stays with me. Do we need to get a lawyer to explain that to someone?*

The thought of Eric not having a funeral of his own was a sharp spear through the middle of her chest. The monstrous, ugly idea of him stopped like a watch, unable to smile or laugh or play Scrabble anymore, was so hideously unfair it threatened to choke her.

It's up to you now, Annie.

Anna reached over, turned the lamp up a notch, and began to read with burning eyes.

Chapter Fifteen

The room was dark, all the lights turned off and only the pale coldness of moonlight falling through a few windows, marred by the shadows of naked tree branches. Josiah settled into the couch, lifted the glass to his lips, and downed the fiery liquid.

It burned less than his conscience.

"You're drunk." Willie's dark eyes glittered. With her hair loosened and a cashmere navy sweater blurring her outline, she was an angular, narrow-hipped shadow. Thick felted boots—she hated going barefoot, and would sleep in them—made soft familiar whispers.

Josiah poured himself another shot of whiskey, offered her the bottle. "I'd put the bar at *mildly intoxicated*." He had a little trouble with the last word, it came out *intoxshicated*. "Want some?"

She took the bottle, set it on the table. "*Mein Gott.* She really gets to you, doesn't she." It wasn't a question.

He saluted her with the shot, downed it. "Only one who ever has. Only one who ever will."

"I believe that." Willie perched on the arm of the couch

with a sigh, sweeping her ponytail back with long fingers. "This means you're not expecting an attack."

"Not for another twelve hours at least." *Plenty of time to drink a little.* He stared at the bottle, at the shot glass. He had to stop soon or he would be of no use to anyone.

But oh, the oblivion promised by the bottle looked *really* good.

"I suppose it wouldn't do any good to tell you I approve." Willie folded her broad, capable hands. "Even *you* need someone."

Need. Bad word for it. Just like a goddamn junkie. "Don't need anything." His chin set stubbornly. He had no right to even touch Anna in the first place. Should he feel guilty he was all she had to depend on now?

"Even a hermit needs a world to isolate from." She said it solemnly, her voice dipping from alto into light tenor for a moment, but her eyes were twinkling. "In any case, I think you've had quite enough." Willie scooped the bottle up neatly, avoiding his halfhearted grab for it. "Drink some water. Your head will be unhappy tomorrow."

For Christ's sake. If I wanted a mother I would have hired one. "Unhappy's the human condition. Give that back." He'd already made up his mind not to press too hard for the bottle's return.

"No. You've had enough." She stood up and skipped back, avoiding his other feeble grab with regrettable ease. Liquid sloshed, and her teeth—all new, the crowns had cost quite a bit—showed in a rare, complete, very wide smile. "Go to sleep, *mein Herr.* You'll need it."

"Isn't that the truth," he mumbled, listening to her footsteps retreat toward the kitchen. Then toward the room she and Hassan had bunked down in. He should have a quiet talk with

Hassan soon, so that the man understood Willie might *say* she didn't want a ring, but…

On the other hand, that was probably an awful idea. When it came to women, Josiah was striking out with depressing regularity. He was used to two or three months, presents, easy uncomplicated sex, and a gradual letting go as the girl found someone else. Right from the beginning he'd known Anna was different, in some significant, ineffable way. Instead of calling the shots, he was pretty much at the mercy of whatever small crumb she let him have.

That was distinctly uncomfortable. Control meant survival. Lack of it might cost him his life, cost his backup theirs.

Or, God forbid, cost Anna hers.

The world reeled out from under him. He found himself on his feet, the stairs not creaking as he ghosted habitually up, avoiding all the iffy spots. He was in stocking feet anyway, useless if there *was* another attack. Maybe he should take Willie up on her offer of felt boots; she had learned about them in the Baltic.

But he'd have warning, and plenty of it, from the rings of defenses and alarms he'd set up. There would be enough time to get shoes, and get her to safety if anything happened.

Or at least, he told himself so. He shouldn't be drinking.

Goddammit, sometimes a man needed to. The situation was approaching the ridiculous, and he *still* didn't want to think about fine crystalline ash glittering on a carpet. He needed all his wits to deal with this.

The trouble was, a man with a perpetual hard-on wasn't the best candidate for rational, logical thought. Especially when that man was Josiah and she was right upstairs. Sleeping the sleep of the innocent.

The sleep of a woman from the normal world, his only remaining link to the man he could have been, if he hadn't been so goddamn good at killing people. Moral adaptability, they'd called it. Along with physical durability and lack of emotional turbulence.

Like any man who was very, very good at what he did, he supposed he preferred to do what he was best at—and avoid the rest. It was too late for him to go back, and he wasn't even sure he wanted to.

Even for her. *Especially* since going back would rob him of any chance to keep her, now.

You shouldn't think about it that way, Josiah.

Too late.

The room at the end of the hall was a dark cave, a faint knife-thin bar of moonlight falling between the curtains. He could hear her breathing, if he stilled his own and listened until red spots danced through his vision. The door didn't creak if you opened it the right way, slowly, with the pressure in the proper spot.

A metaphor for life, Josiah reflected. If you went slow, with the pressure in the right place, all sorts of things would fall nicely into your lap.

Where was the right pressure to apply to Anna? Did he even know? If he knew, would he do it?

If he did, would she remind him so much of the man he could have been?

Josiah told himself sternly to quit second-guessing, just as the sound intruded through the peaceful quiet.

Skritch. Skritch-scratch.

His hand blurred, came up with the gun. His mouth tasted sour, and he blinked several times, everything inside him freezing into crystalline disbelief for a few endless moments.

A shadow bobbed up and down in the rectangle of moon-light lying on the floor, slightly distorted by the edge of a striped, frayed thrift-store throw rug. It took a moment for the shape to make sense to his baffled brain—the silhouette of a head, of shoulders.

The window's latch clicked, a soft deadly sound.

Anna sighed in her sleep; she turned over and buried her face in her pillow. Josiah saw the curve of her hip under the blankets, a long strand of dark hair visible against the white pillowcase.

He should have been in the bed next to her, keeping her warm. The thought circled his mind once, submerged into the clear, dark water of waiting for an enemy to show himself.

How did he get through the defenses, dammit? There shouldn't be anything for acres I don't know about. Am I slipping? What the fuck is this?

The window, incredibly, drifted up without a sound. Curtains fluttered on a soft, chilly breeze. The shadow in the moonlight swelled.

The bigger question, of course, was how in the fuck was this man climbing up into a second-floor window, one that had no direct line from the roof? The ground underneath was soft and there were no ladders; it was vanishingly likely that whoever this was could have brought his own. He should have tripped a wire and set something off.

I'm not that drunk, Josiah decided. The hair on the back of his neck stood straight up, an instinctive bristling he'd only felt once or twice before, when a job had gone sideways and precious little would halt the sliding.

Anna made another soft sound, burrowing deeper into the covers. The gangly shadow-intruder swung a leg over the win-

dowsill and ducked gracefully in. The scratching noise continued, then stopped dead

You son of a bitch. Josiah's finger tightened on the trigger.
Coming in for a midnight rendezvous, are we?

The only thing preventing Anna's being at this man's mercy
was a half-drunk liquidation specialist, who had let his better
judgment get besotted one time too many. Great.

The new player was slim but tall, moving fluidly and noiselessly along the periphery of the room, avoiding the squeaks
and bumps in the floor as if he had spent years living here.
Josiah, in his pool of deep shadow, kept the gun down only
because if he squeezed a shot off now he couldn't be completely sure.

Also, something bothered him. The shadow was a glitter of
eyes and a shock of hair; the man didn't seem to be in camo or
have any nighttime gear.

Nor did he have any shoes. His bare feet glimmered pale as
he drifted. Pale, and oddly thin, malformed in some way.

Josiah's brain struggled with this. *What the fuck?*

The man reached the nightstand. He was less than three
feet from Anna, who murmured again. A pale misshapen hand
reached down, touched the stack of paper.

Eric's files.

Josiah lifted the gun.

"I can hear your pulse." The voice was male, flatly accented,
and stilted. There was a terribly *wrong* quality, a dead bell struck
at midnight. It was barely a whisper, insinuating itself into cold
night air. "And smell the liquor on you."

The words dried the inside of Josiah's mouth and made his
stomach clench around alcoholic warmth. "Get away from her."

A glitter of sharp white. The man pulled his lips back in a

snarl, visible in the reflected moonlight. A slow, deadly, liquid hiss filled the room.

Josiah barely thought about it. His own lips peeled back, an animal's instinctive baring of teeth, but he didn't echo the sound. The man studied him, thin shoulders hunching as if he expected a blow.

Just wait a second. The same instinct, born of years of working the edges of violence and death, made Josiah wait. The attackers at his house had been geared to the nines, in tac and black webbing. This guy was *barefoot*.

"Where is the ring?" The man's voice didn't improve the second time. It was even worse. A hiss like that belonged in dank underground cells, water dripping down crumbling stone walls and rusted chains still warm from the last prisoner to die in them.

What? "What ring?"

"Eric was to bring me my ring." The creature held up one thin, pale-glowing hand. Three of the fingers were missing, only thin, spidery stubs remaining. The shape of the man's bare feet was odd, too, because he was missing toes, and livid dark weals stood out on the fish-belly-white flesh, visible in the moonlight. Either Josiah's night vision had gotten better, or the moon had come out from partial obscurity. "He promised. He did not return."

"Eric..." *Get the fuck out. No way.* "Eric Caldwell?"

Anna's breathing changed. She moaned, softly. The man looked down at her, an oddly reptilian movement of scrawny neck and dark-haired head. "Eric," he breathed, and bent down.

"Get *away* from her!" Josiah's voice rose sharply, and he took a single step forward. Nine and a half pounds of pull would squeeze off a shot, and he was at eight and three quarters. Body shots, because he wanted to ask this motherfucker some questions—but he could change that, if he needed to.

If the situation required.

The man hissed again, taking a single step back. He didn't totter on his mutilated feet, and that was wrong, too. Nobody should be able to balance so lightly on such damaged appendages.

"Eric Caldwell's dead, my friend." Josiah's voice was absurdly steady. "Someone slit his throat and is trying to kill his sister, too. Who the fuck are *you*?"

The scarecrow cocked his head. He glanced down at Anna again, who stirred and turned over onto her back, pushing the covers down. Innocent as a fucking little lamb. A bomb could go off outside and she'd probably sleep right through it. Once she passed out, she was gone until morning.

He adored her for it, even while he cursed inwardly.

Josiah took another step, the gun trained on the man's head. He felt a lot better about his shot chance now. "I said, who the *fuck* are *you*, and what are you doing in my fucking house?"

"Sister." The hissing freak shook his head, greasy matted hair falling forward to curtain his expression. "Sister..." The word trailed away, turned into a long, sibilant exhale.

"Jo?" Anna, pushing herself up on her elbows. Just like Sleeping Beauty, blinking prettily at a prince.

Only this woman didn't have the prince she deserved. All she had was him.

The intruder twitched. Josiah squeezed the trigger and kept shooting, moving forward, *knowing* he hit the man who scrambled for the window. The gun muzzle flashed with each burst of noise, and he cursed being in stocking feet as he slid on hardwood. Glass shattered as the pale, misshapen streak launched himself out into the night, and Anna let out a short cry as Josiah got to the bed, grabbing a fistful of her shirt and dragging her out. She hit the floor and he pushed her head down, sure that would provide her with a little cover, and he went *over* the bed and ended up next to the window, waiting for return fire.

None came. He risked a glance.

A stick figure lay spread-eagle below on the leaf-strewn ground, dappled with moonlight through the bare grasping branches. Broken glass glittered, and splotches of weird fish-belly skin gleamed. As Josiah watched, the man rolled onto his side and up to all fours, shook himself like a dog, and darted away into the underbrush on pale, mutilated hands and knees, so fast he almost blurred. His bare white feet flickered.

All the breath left Josiah's lungs in a walloping rush. He leaned against the wall, the cold breeze touching his face, and felt utterly chill-cold sober.

Footsteps behind him. He heard Anna's harsh breathing, and his own. He'd shot the man four times, and the bastard had just gotten up and run off. Barefoot. Missing toes and fingers.

Jesus. Jesus Christ.

Hassan burst into the room.

"Check her," Josiah snapped, pointing at Anna, who was peering up over the side of the bed. He sounded like he'd been punched.

I suppose I have. He would have checked Anna himself, but his legs didn't seem to want to behave. *Silver bullets and crucifixes. Jesus.*

It was time for a radical rethinking of just what Josiah was willing to believe.

"What's going on?" Anna sounded terrified. He didn't blame her.

"Wolfe, get out of the goddamn window!" Hassan barked. "*Josiah!*"

"In a minute." Josiah looked out over the moon-dappled ground. *A two-floor fall and four bullet holes. I know I hit him. Kevlar? But he was barefoot, goddammit, and missing fucking toes as well.* "Is she all right?"

"Right as rain." Hassan's accent wore through. "A little shaken up, but all right."

"Jo? Josiah?" She gasped, and he wanted to look across the room. He didn't; he kept staring out the window at the silver-dappled shadows. *The other ones exploded into dust. This one didn't. Because they weren't head shots?*

You know, another drink would go down real well right now. His mouth was still dry. *Think, goddammit. If you act like you're scared she'll go right over the moon.* "It's all right, Anna. You okay?"

"Let *go* of me! Let *go*!" There was the sound of tearing cloth, and Hassan cursed.

"Just be bloody calm, you heard the man! Someone could be out there with a rifle. Get out of the bloody *window*, Josiah!"

He did. He leaned back against the wall and closed his eyes. *Be calm. Anna's here, she needs you, be calm.*

It did manage to keep him from the edge, but only just. He opened his eyes to find Hassan with his arm over Anna's throat, holding her back; she struggled uselessly and tried biting him again.

The sight of someone holding her while she struggled, even Hassan, threatened to tip Josiah over the edge.

Be chilly. Nice and cold. Josiah kept the gun pointed down and away, but he pointed his chin slightly at Hassan. "Let her go. Anna, there's glass. Be careful."

She flew across the room and almost collided with him, flung her arms around Josiah, and squeezed. Rewarded with a faint huff of breath, she squeezed harder; he kept the gun free and found his other arm around her shoulders. "Jesus," he whispered into her hair.

On the one hand, her closeness reassured him she was safe. On the other, it made his hands shake just a little, the trembling working through his bones, as he thought about how fucking *close* it could have been.

"What the fuck is going on?" Hassan sounded just two short steps away from opening fire.

Josiah hugged her, unsure of why she was clinging to him but happy for it all the same. "I think one of Eric's contacts just visited us. And shook off four direct hits, right before he flew out the window." He met Hassan's worried dark gaze as his skin prickled with gooseflesh.

This is like that woman with the rats. Remember that? Her eyes, and the way they all looked at her, right before she gave that little whistle? And the bones in her hair, click-clack.

You saw a lot of weird shit when your job was liquidating troublesome people. The world was much, much stranger than nine-to-fivers assumed. All sorts of rumbling strangeness snuggled down in the cracks between the daylight surface and the gray world of infiltrate, double cross, liquidate, intel, vanish.

He took a deep gasping breath, and her softness pressed against his body. There was a good way to make everything inside a man settle down and behave reasonably. Unfortunately, now wasn't the time. *Down, boy. You've been a bad agent, no cookie for you.*

"This is getting Hollywood weird," Willie remarked from the shadows just on the other side of the bedroom door. Dark hair shawled her shoulders, and the rifle in her capable hands was a blessing to see. "Is everyone all right?"

"I'm not," Hassan said glumly, letting out a gusty, deflating sigh. "I'm miserable. Can't we have one bloody night without gunfire and broken fucking windows?"

"You are in the wrong line of work for that," Willie observed, reasonably enough, and the twinkle of merriment in her gaze was even more welcome.

"I was dreaming," Anna said into his chest. He closed his eyes again, resting his head against the wall and feeling her in his arms. "What happened? Josiah? Are you all right?"

I don't know. "Just a little snag in our plans, baby. Nothing we can't handle."

Lying to her. Again. For the moment, he simply held her, and was glad to do so. She was warm and safe and alive, *willingly* touching him. He was just enough of a bastard to be happy about it, even though his legs wouldn't quite hold him up.

The files sat on the table, and Anna held up the flat key with its trace of blue paint. "Why didn't you tell me there was a key in there?" She'd pulled her legs up and hugged her knees, bracing her heels on the lip of the chair. It was a familiar pose, one Josiah recognized. "And the note."

"We had other things to think about." Hassan, his hair a wild mess, flipped a knife over his hand, caught the handle, repeated the motion. The glitter of the blade threw a random reflection of candlelight onto the ceiling. The candle wasn't for romance. It was easily snuffed, and wouldn't destroy Josiah's night vision or give someone with a rifle and scope a clearly lit shot.

Willie rubbed at her upper arms, her palms rasping on heavy

navy wool. She'd pulled her hair back, and her felted boots held traces of floor dust. "*Gott in Himmel.* This is ridiculous."

"I'm not that drunk." Josiah finished pulling his boots up. He'd been lucky to avoid a foot full of glass. "I know what I saw. He took four bullets and scurried off into the underbrush like a cockroach."

"Kevlar?" Hassan hazarded.

"After falling out the window, two stories down?" He set his boots on the floor. "What's the key to, Anna?"

"A post office box." She stared at the table, closing the key in her fist. "Eric had it under another name—Sebastian Knight. He was so amused by it. It was for his contacts. If anything...I didn't know he had an extra. Or maybe this is his first one. I don't know." She hugged her knees harder, not looking at him. "He called it *mailing to Nabokov.* After the novelist, you know? Because...because he's dead."

"Very touching." Hassan spun the knife again. "What the fuck is going on, Wolfe?"

Josiah sighed. "Isn't it obvious?" He pulled his chair up to the table. "That was one of Eric's contacts. And I don't think he's strictly human."

This extraordinary statement was greeted by silence. Hassan stopped tossing the knife, which was good. Willie sighed, leaning back in her chair a little. Anna made a little movement, as if shaking away water. Her eyes widened.

"I don't know about the rest of you," Josiah continued, "but I'm fairly willing to start believing in a little weirdness here. Like the rats in Tunisia, Hassan." *Or that snake dancer in Moscow, the one with the strange eyes.* Another weirdness tucked in a corner, the crackling sound behind a frosted glass pane as the man's jaw distended, and Josiah's target—the petty criminal lord he was to deliver alive to Evgeny—began to whimper like a child instead of a grown man who had ordered beatings and killings for a good fifteen-plus years in the subarctic cold.

"Don't remind me." Hassan outright shuddered. He hadn't been in Moscow, but could probably hear that low, whistling exhalation from Tunisia in his dreams just like Josiah could, and the scratching of tiny feet, the dragging of naked tails...and bones clacking, click-snack, in a woman's tangled hair.

"Rats?" Willie raised an eyebrow.

"Don't ask." Hassan scrubbed at the back of his left arm, where the faint scratching scars were often hidden under his sleeve. "God's breath, Wolfe. You expect me to believe..." He didn't finish the question. It would have been idiotic, because Hassan sounded like a man convinced.

Still, someone had to say it out loud, and it looked like Josiah was nominated. "You cut a throat and got a shower of grit, so did I. Willie shot them and got ash, or dirt, or whatever. We just had a barefoot man, shot four times, launch himself out the window and run away. I might be a little buzzed, but I'm not *nearly* fucking drunk enough to be hallucinating. We have witnesses missing, a dead reporter *and* editor whose murders are not being investigated, we have assassins who turn into ash, and we have this new wrinkle, this asshole who claims Eric was going to retrieve something for him." He set the gun on the table, with a slight click. "I say we retrieve whatever is in Eric's PO box and take a look around this brick place on Morris. And I've got a friend or two I need to meet up with." *Although "friends" might be stretching it a little. More like "non-enemies so far." That might be more precise.*

The shaking in his hands had gone down, so he popped the

clip out of the gun and racked a new one in. Always better to have a fresh clip; sometimes you couldn't stop to reload.

Better not to take the chance. Much of his life had been lived according to that maxim.

Most of the parts that hadn't were enough to give anyone normal nightmares. Then there was Anna—the flip side, maybe. A good dream, one he didn't deserve but was selfish enough to want to keep anyway.

"Wait a minute." Anna, not staring at her knees anymore, the bruise glaring on her cheek and her sandalwood hair mussed. She only looked puzzled, not frightened out of her wits. "Witnesses? Not human? What *exactly* are we talking about?"

"Well, we've had two suggestions: silver bullets and crucifixes. This guy didn't explode in a shower of dirt like the other ones—"

"Dirt?" Her eyes were very wide, and very green. "I thought you were joking. They really turned to…" She let out a short, sharp breath. "Jesus."

He looked at the bruise, at the heavy circles under her eyes, and the vulnerable, breakable curve of her wrist. *I thought she'd be safe here. Safer than this. Still, he didn't hurt her.*

The reptilian little movement the pale barefoot man had made was enough to make Josiah's stomach twist against itself, and he pushed the sensation away. *I'm really doing very well with this. I should be going crazy by now. Hands aren't even shaking. Much.*

"What we have here are some odd occurrences," he continued, pedantically. "The last of which is the barefoot man who in all likelihood floated up to your window tonight and broke in like a bad Romeo. There's no ladder there, no marks from a grapple, and the angle's wrong from the roof, *again*. If he used some trick to get up there I can't figure out what it is." He slipped the gun back in its holster. "Plus, our little friend didn't trip *any* of the alarms or anything else I had set out there on the approaches to the house. Not a single one, coming or going. Either I'm getting sloppy or we're looking at something weirder than snake shoes. If there's a rational explanation, it's escaping me right now; I'll be damn happy when it finally presents itself. Until then, I'm going to take a few irrational precautions. Hassan, you're going back into town tonight to set up a meet with Chilwell and another with Vanczny."

"You want to meet with Van?" Hassan's jaw all but dropped.

"That's right. And I'll be taking her with me. Willie, I want you to run backup on Hassan. Get a room in town. We'll rendezvous at fourteen hundred tomorrow, past that restaurant on Clark Street going east. I'll make contact. If not, we'll try in twenty-four, on Lasko, then it's the regular protocol. You know where I mean?"

"I know." Hassan gained his feet in one smooth motion. The knife disappeared. "Dammit, I wanted some sleep tonight."

"You'll need clothes for her." Willie sighed. "And what will you do, cook for yourself?"

As if that was the worst thing she could think of. An unwilling smile twitched at one corner of Josiah's mouth. "Don't you worry about her, she's in good hands. I'll just have to rough it without your soup for a while. You're already packed, that's the beauty of it."

They were both professionals, and ready to go in a short while. He gave Hassan all the spare ammunition for the Sig, but kept the shotgun and rifle rounds as well as the clips for his own gun. "Be careful," he cautioned one final time. "Be *very* careful, all right?"

Hassan snorted. "Bloody fairy tales, and he wants us to be careful. Come on, Willie, let's go somewhere quiet. You can rub my feet."

Willie muttered something that didn't sound like a compliment, and Josiah waited, peering out through the curtain on the front window, until their taillights vanished up the hill, into the darkness that suddenly seemed very close. He pushed his hands in his pockets and braced his shoulder against the wall, looking back at the inside of the cabin.

Anna hadn't moved, still huddled like a kid on the hard wooden chair. Her eyes were very dark, and she stared at him through flickering mellow candlelight. She looked lost, and a little forlorn. He wanted to pull her up and hold her, stroke her hair and reassure both of them.

He didn't quite trust himself yet.

"How much of the file did you read?" His tone surprised him, brusque and businesslike.

Her shoulders hunched, candlelight picking up gold highlights in her beautiful hair. "The first two. The…interviews. I went through the photos. There were some charts, but I didn't—"

"What did Eric tell you? Anything? Anything at all?"

She shook her head, tangled hair sliding over her shoulders. "Just to hold the files. That he was onto something big, a corruption case. He had informants, he said. He wanted me to hold the files because he thought his house might be burgled. *Tossed,* he called it. I went to ask him about the safety-deposit box key and…" The words husked to a stop, and she dropped her chin, her hair falling forward.

And you found him dead.

"I found him," she finished, haltingly. "He…"

"A corruption case." *Fingers and toes, and blood transfusions. I'm missing a piece or six or seven; none of it makes any goddamn sense.* "Did he say anything to you about a ring, or about any of his contacts? Anything at all?"

Her mouth was so soft; she bit at her lower lip before replying. "No. Nothing. He didn't tell me a lot about his stories, they were confidential."

Yeah. Right. What you didn't know wouldn't hurt you, right? Except in my case. He swallowed bitterness, forced himself to think. "How was Eric acting, lately? Preoccupied? Did he seem afraid?"

"No more than usual." Her gaze met his, those wide expressive eyes windows all the way through her, and he knew she was lying. Her face couldn't hide it, not from him.

Josiah stared at her, his hands physically itching with the urge to touch her, yank her up out of the chair, and sink his fingers into her hair, bring her mouth up to his. "Tell me." Delivered softly, but it was still a command.

Was she pale, or was it the uncertain light? "He had his will drawn up. I know because I went with him to the lawyer's office to sign some papers. He had me as his beneficiary." Her eyes shone wetly, and her arms tightened, pulling her knees in harder. As if she could curl up tightly enough to close all this madness out. "He just seemed a little distracted, that's all. But you know Eric."

Seemingly distracted but shrewd, that was Eric Caldwell. Josiah nodded. "A lot of his papers seem to be in a kind of code. You know anything about that?"

"Oh, yeah. We made it up when we were kids. He liked ciphers."

"Can you decode it?"

She nodded, loosening up a bit on her knees. The bruise on her cheek mocked him, just like the sudden hopefulness in those wide, pretty eyes. She was looking to him to make it better, to do what Eric had always done and step in, take care of everything. For a moment, a great weariness settled over him, one he accepted even as it dragged down his shoulders and aching legs.

He'd been smoothing things over and taking care of things and fixing problems for a long time now. Too late to stop.

Besides, he *wanted* to fix her problems. He wanted her shoulders to come down and the shadows under her eyes to go away. Once she relaxed, she could show him how to do it.

How to feel human again. He wanted more of whatever effortless magic she'd worked before to soften the wasteland inside him.

First things first, though. "All right. Tomorrow you're going to start decoding it for me, after we do a couple things."

"We're not leaving right now?" Her eyebrows came up, the very picture of surprise, just as she always used to look when a design program behaved in an unexpected way or a driver cut her off in traffic.

"Not yet. If Eric's contact comes back, I want a word or two with him. Nobody else knows we're here." He rolled his shoulders back, dispelling tension and settling himself into work mode again. "I suspect moving and tiring ourselves out won't do any good. Not if what I saw tonight was any indication."

Chapter Sixteen

A thin gray morning crept in with cotton-wool fog, the entire world hushed and eerie. Josiah drove, and when they broke out of the fog on the interstate and thin winter sunlight blazed over the road, Anna actually gasped, the relief was that intense.

Her back ached. So did her ribs, and her ankle, and her knee. Sleeping fully clothed on a couch might be okay for a teenager but wasn't so hot for a battered thirty-year-old. She'd managed broken, fitful rest, and her feet were swollen since they'd been in the boots all night.

Waking up from an almost-nightmare to the rattling buzz of Josiah's cell phone sitting on the table hadn't done much for her blood pressure. As a matter of strict fact, it had scared the living blue bejesus out of her.

The few cryptic exchanges he'd muttered into the phone hadn't helped, either.

"You okay?" Josiah didn't look away from the road. It was the first real conversational gambit since this morning's short, brisk commands—*get your shoes, here's some coffee, let's go, hurry up.*

That was just fine with her. Sticking her head in the sand and being extremely quiet sounded like a *great* option. She'd already had the stupid too-big boots on, too, which felt like a faint victory.

"Fine." Her own voice sounded brittle, barely audible over the humming of tires on pavement. When she moved her purse shifted, and a copy of the files made a slight rustling sound.

He gave her a single glance, probably gauging her truthfulness. "We're going on a meet." He returned his gaze to the road. "A clandestine meeting. There are rules to this sort of thing, and you will obey them. Got it?"

My, haven't you become a little Napoleon all of a sudden. Yesterday she might have said it. Today she only nodded, looking at the dashboard and how it fit over the glove box. The curve, she decided, was wrong. She could draw a better one.

She flat-out ached to draw again. Even just to doodle on the copies of Eric's notes would feel heavenly, but Josiah had the only pen.

Apparently just nodding was the right thing to do, because he continued, as calmly as if he was discussing the day's weather. "I wanted to keep you out of this part of it. After today, the information that I'm involved with you is going to be out there, and what's out there can be sold. Always." He took a deep breath, maybe for effect. Today his eyes were dark green, helped by a black sweater and a dark coat; he wore jeans and boots like she did.

I bet his boots fit, though. She suppressed an irritated sigh. Nodded again, a movement he was sure to catch out of the corner of his eye.

"After today, you could be considered an agent by anyone working in the gray." He hit his turn signal, changed lanes smoothly. "Someone looking to get a certain type of information from me might try to use you."

Her heart was taking this surprisingly well. Not pounding. Her hands were steady. *I'm actually doing all right. I think.* She looked out the window, at the paintbrush green of fir trees marching along the side of the road. They were just about to come over the hill and into the suburbs from the north. Her head ached, and she wanted more coffee. And her drawing pad, and a whole handful of pencils as if she was in grade school again.

That would be nice. Along with a bubble bath and some very cold Chablis. The ribbon of gunmetal-gray road unreeled under the car, filling up the interior with the sound of travel and two people not speaking.

Finally, Jo cleared his throat. "You just stick with me and you'll be fine. All right?"

She managed a shrug, which sent an interesting cascade of pain down her side and into her back. "You've done all right this far."

He seemed to find this funny. At least, Josiah smiled, and it was a new expression, one she'd never seen on him before. Bitter, resigned, and full of cynical black humor, he grinned at the road the way an old wolf would at a wounded deer flopping in the snow. "Well, you're still alive. That's something."

My ears are still ringing from last night. I'm getting uncomfortably used to the sound of gunshots. She folded her hands primly in her lap. There was still a smudge of fading cadmium blue across one knuckle; now she would in all likelihood never finish that painting. She would never be able to give Tasha her birthday present—the sketchbook of her friend in thirty-six *attitudes*. Or give Robbie and Tor their wedding present, the two *raku* bowls, one glazed silver and the other black, both fitting together to make a whole. She'd fired piece after piece, trying to get that right, and been down to oranges and coffee before payday last month. "I can't complain."

Really, what good would complaining do? She'd veered out of real life and into some sort of black nightmare comedy. Maybe, if she just went along with it, someone upstairs would look down and notice a huge mistake had been made, and she would wake up in her own bed again. The first thing she'd do would be to call Eric, just to hear his voice mail message.

You've reached Eric Caldwell. Leave a message, willya?

The thought sent an unbearable, lancing pain through her chest and she breathed in sharply, wondering how a heart could go on beating when something like this happened. The feeling was strangely familiar—after the accident, both Mom and Dad gone, the same hurt.

Except now, there was no chance to lean into Eric's shoulder again, holding his hand as the caskets lowered, their parents sliding side by side into eternity. Nobody to fight with, or mourn with, nobody who remembered the pickle sandwiches or the Great Baseball Incident of Eric's eighth-grade year, nobody who remembered Mom's singing voice or Eric's perfect SAT scores.

Nobody except Anna, and she was a very thin straw to hang so much on.

It's up to me now. Everything is.

Josiah reached over, tucked a strand of her hair behind her ear. She didn't have anything to tie it back with, and there was, he said, no time to dye it today. Besides, in the picture on her driver's license it was much shorter, and pulled back as well. "I'm sorry it has to be like this."

Does it? Does it have to be like this?

She swallowed. "Me, too." Silence stretched out, thin and tensile; his hand returned to the steering wheel. "Josiah?"

"What?"

"I want whoever killed Eric dead." *I am actually having a little trouble with how much I want that.* The burning inside her chest didn't alter at all. Emotional heartburn. Too much grief salad.

His knuckles whitened on the steering wheel. "There's no profit in revenge, Anna."

For a smart man, you are surprisingly dense. "It's not *profit,* for God's sake. They killed..." It stuck in her dry throat. "They killed my *brother.* I want them—"

"Can't promise anything." His jaw had gone tight, too.

Her jaw clenched, threatening to crack. "Then teach me how to do what you do."

He didn't say anything. The miles slipped away beneath the car's underbelly, and whatever breakfast she'd managed to eat—funny, she couldn't even remember it now—turned into a hard, cold lump inside her stomach.

"I will," she repeated, "learn how to do what you do. I'll do it *myself.* That way you won't be burdened with me, either. You just teach me, and I won't be your problem anymore."

"You're not my problem." Calm and reasonable as ever. "I can't teach you how to kill. You either can, or you can't. *You* can't."

Oh, really? For whoever cut Eric's throat, I'll sure as hell learn. "You don't know that."

"I'd say I'm the resident expert in this car. You have no fucking idea what you're talking about, so please just stop."

Fine. "He was my brother. He's all I have." She shut her mouth, tightly, sealing her lips together.

He was all she'd *ever* had. Friends, even parents, were temporary. She'd learned that when she was twelve. A brother was safety, was certainty. That night at the dinner table, both of them staring at their plates, and Eric raising his head finally. *I won't let them take you away, Annie. I promise.*

She should have promised *him*, too.

Josiah loosened one hand on the steering wheel and apparently changed his mind, clenching it tighter than before. His eyes had lightened two deadly shades, but that could have been the sunshine. That betraying little movement of his jaw was like a flag, the only sign of frustration he would show. Otherwise, he seemed only absorbed in driving.

She returned to staring out the window. They crested the hill, and the pine trees began to give way to strip malls and small housing developments. "It doesn't make any difference." She didn't recognize her own voice. "I'll learn, whether you want me to or not."

It was the first time she ever felt like she'd actually won an argument with him. The feeling of triumph was amazingly short-lived. Anna settled herself down to watch, to pay attention, and to figure out everything she could about this horrific new world she found herself in.

"Keep your hands loose. Don't make any sudden moves. And for God's sake, keep your mouth *shut*." Josiah unbuckled his seat belt. "You hear me? You don't say a single word, you don't nod, you don't shake your head, you don't make a sound. Got it?"

They had cut through the suburbs and ended up on the edge of the west side of the city, across from the parking lot of a shabby, tired-looking apartment building. A few children far too young to be outside alone played in the parking lot, bright, tinny voices and inadequate coats. Thin winter sunshine picked out broken glass on cracked pavement. Half the cars in the lot were up on blocks, and other frowning apartment buildings closed off the street on either side.

"Not a word," she promised. *God, those kids don't have coats. What are they doing out here? It's too cold.* Who on earth could Josiah be meeting *here*? It looked the least likely place in the world for an assassin to hang out.

Of course, that was probably for the best, she decided.

"Give me the copy." He was all business now.

She dug the manila folder out of her purse. "Who are we going to meet?"

"Better if you don't know. But his name's Vanczny. He's Polish but he works for the local Mob. Which is why it's so goddamn important that you keep your mouth sewn up." His tone was level, chill. "I'm not joking."

I heard you the first time. "And so far you've been such a barrel of laughs. I *get* it, Josiah. I'm not stupid."

"Stupid and quiet might help you live a little longer. Smart people who get mouthy get weeded out quick." He reached for the door latch, his watch's face turned to the inside of his wrist for some reason. "Stay there. I'll come around and get you out."

What a time for you to get all chivalrous. He'd always insisted on holding the door for her. Before.

I liked him, Tasha had said, once. *Easy on the eyes and quick to pay for drinks. What happened?*

Creative differences, Anna had replied, lightly, through the rock in her throat. Tasha had merely given her a funny look, sweeping her dreads back with one lean ebony hand, and that was that.

Anna nodded. He got out of the car, studied the apartment

building for a moment, then came around the front and opened her door, reaching down to take her hand. His fingers were warm. He didn't look at her, just kept looking at the apartment building's leaning frame. "I don't like this," he muttered. "Van usually likes to meet in restaurants."

She hoped the no-talking rule didn't apply yet. "Why?"

"More exits. Plus, he's a fat fuck, and he loves to eat." He glanced down at her, his eyes gone opaque. Unreadable. "No more talking."

Anna opened her mouth, thought about it, closed it. Nodded.

"Good girl." He looked different, and she took advantage of the walk across the parking lot to study his face in small, furtive sips. He was no longer the quiet, calm Josiah she knew, the man with a slow smile and utter confidence over a sweetness she never would have suspected if she hadn't seen it.

This Josiah was a blank wall, nothing betraying any emotion. Even his walk was different, more of a prowling stride, matching his pace to hers but also somehow always managing to stay a step ahead. She knew he was wearing a gun under his coat; she'd seen him strap it on this morning. The firearm and the expression on his face combined to make him a stranger.

Was this face a façade, or was the one he'd always shown her before the false one? Were both of them true?

How much did she really know about him, anyway? He'd never given much in the way of personal information, always more interested in what *she* had to say, and she'd fallen for it. What woman wouldn't like a man who listened to everything, who asked questions that *showed* he was listening, and occasionally turned up with little gifts—nothing too expensive, but nothing too cheap—that seemed designed to show how much attention he paid to her offhanded comments? A bracelet she'd admired. A bottle of wine she liked. A clutch of white roses and a bird of paradise—her favorite flowers.

She'd fallen for it, never dreaming anything was wrong until she found the file in Eric's home office—the second bedroom in his apartment, the very room he'd died in—while digging for her birth certificate so she could get her passport renewed.

That innocent-looking manila folder with *Wolfe* written on the tab. She could still remember being on her knees in front of the file cabinet, opening it out of curiosity…and then, the pictures. The *proof.* The newspaper clippings as well as dates she recognized, because Josiah traveled a lot.

For business, he always said.

The entryway was cracked linoleum, a bank of mailboxes, a short hall, and stairs covered with indifferent carpeting. She wrinkled her nose at the smell, a combination of poverty, cigarette smoke, and fried food, sticky and oily. It was horribly familiar; she and Eric had lived in places like this after their parents died. His second semester of college and her sixth-grade year had passed in a haze of numb grief, both of them barely able to make it through classes, Eric coming home to fix two doses of ramen or something similar, eating silently together on the ratty orange couch they got from the curb, its cushions still reeking of weed smoke, and retreating to sleeping bags in the one bedroom.

Once, and only once, she'd asked him if it would be easier if she weren't there. *Don't be stupid,* he'd snapped, and gone back to work on a paper, writing in his cramped sideways cryptic scribbles.

The memory hurt more than usual. *Oh, Eric.*

Josiah led her up two flights of stairs and through a propped-open fire door giving onto a narrow, dimly lit hall. He knocked once on the third door on the left, after pushing her aside and telling her to stand still against the wall with a single significant glare.

A stranger's look. *He's telling me to stay here because…hm. Maybe they could shoot through the door? But then, he's right there.*

The door opened, and there was a metallic click. A low, muffled thread of sound, someone talking fast and soft.

Josiah, of all things, replied in the same language, heavy on the *k*'s and *z*'s. His voice had changed again, becoming harder, disdainful.

The door opened a little more and he glanced at her, a single look that told her to follow. She did, meekly enough, stepping into a dim front hall of an apartment that smelled foreign. The air was blue with cigarette smoke and the drapes were drawn; this was a studio apartment and the only furniture was two couches set facing each other. Cheap beige carpet was worn down the middle; a door off to the left showed a slice of brightly lit bathroom, in no way clean but not overly filthy, either. The kitchenette to the right, bare and empty except for a hulking man in black with an honest-to-God submachine gun in his beefy paws, could have used some bleach and hot water, too, especially in the corners.

Anna's heart jumped into her throat. *Jesus.*

Their host was a quick, rotund little ferret with a lit cigarette, black hair oiled slick to his skull over a round pockmarked face. He wore a cheap gray suit and twitched a little nervously when he turned back and caught Anna looking at the fabric. He spat something that sounded uncomplimentary; Josiah made a short, sharp reply.

The hulk of Submachine-Gun Man moved forward inside the empty kitchen and gestured at the door. He crowded close behind them to sweep it shut, the dead bolt clicking home as Josiah and the obese ferret moved forward.

There was another man in the dimness, sitting on the couch with its back to the right-hand wall. Josiah had suddenly gone tense. Just how she could tell she couldn't quite explain, but he seemed suddenly, hurtfully aware of everything in the room.

Just like he used to every few months, following her around, sticking close to her, waiting for her outside her building. She'd thought it was love, that he was paying attention.

All those "business trips," too. How many of them had ended up with someone dead? With more than one someone dead? He was always a little more affectionate when he came back.

Josiah half-turned, reached back with his left hand, and grabbed her wrist. Pulled her forward, into the studio space, then slid his left arm over her shoulder and brought her close to his side. He made another short remark, and the burst of nasty male laughter made her exposed skin feel grimy.

The third man laughed loudest of all, his wide, dark eyes never leaving Anna. He gestured, blue smoke trailing from the end of his cigarette, and when he spoke in English it was almost a shock.

"Pretty little piece, *lupo*. You always did have taste." A slow Mediterranean accent wound through his words. He had a long nose, dark skin, and soft, curly, oily hair; he was wearing a very *good* suit, silk if Anna didn't miss her guess, and exquisitely tailored. Good shoes, too; calfskin, tailored as well. A briefcase sat next to him on the sagging couch, like an obedient angular dog.

"A man has to have a weakness, *signor*. How's your health?" Josiah pulled her forward, managing to make it look like they were walking together. He pushed her toward the couch opposite the long-nosed man.

"Ah. Getting older, getting older. Having daughters gives a man many worries, many indeed. Sit, sit, *bambina*. Does she want a drink?"

There was a low, cheap coffee table between the couches. Anna sank down, her knee and ankle protesting. Not even the ibuprofen was helping.

"She doesn't." The new Josiah grinned, laying the file down on the table with an easy movement. "But I'll take one, *signor*. With thanks." He settled down next to her, pushing her aside slightly. Anna tried to make her face as impassive as his, with a sinking feeling of failing miserably.

The man on the couch studied her avidly. "Rough trade?" he asked, and laughed again. It wasn't a nice laugh, she decided. It bore a stunning resemblance to a hyena's cackle. His cigar fumed and smoked.

"Someone didn't play nice with her, so she came over to my part of the schoolyard." Josiah leaned forward, his elbows on his knees and his hands dangling loose. "How's the *signora*? I hope her health is good?"

For a few moments the banter went back and forth, Josiah asking about the man's family and listening patiently, the man inquiring after Josiah's own health and prospects. It sounded like the numbing kaffeeklatsches her mother had loved, hens clucking at each other over weak coffee and small stale cakes hour after hour.

Only these hens were watched by a man with an AK-47.

Was it an AK-47? That was the only gun name she knew. Eric would have known; he'd done a piece on endemic violence in Guatemala.

Funny, that he would have survived that and come home, promising never to do any combat reporting again. He didn't talk much about what had actually happened, and she got the idea the worst of it hadn't made it into the articles he wrote. He drank a little more afterward, that was all.

The whole thing was mind-numbingly boring, and she had almost relaxed by the time Oily Round Ferret brought two glasses with a few finger-widths of amber liquid in each, no ice.

The glasses were sparkling clean. *That* was odd. Anna tried to rearrange the scene inside her head, design a better one, and failed. Maybe if she worked in gouache she could capture the dinginess, and there would have to be a lot of straight lines, the perspective just subtly altered to induce the dreamy feeling of unreality.

As if that was a signal, Josiah pointedly glanced around the apartment.

The other man breathed out through his nose, a loud huff of air. "You think I want to be seen talking to you? Even if you are retired." His eyes slid slowly over Anna again. "Pretty piece." The remark was delivered in a thoughtful tone.

"Thank you." Then, amazingly, Josiah began to speak in another language. It sounded like Italian.

That led to a conversation that would have sounded beautiful and rolling except for the slow narrowing of the other man's dark eyes. Josiah leaned forward, slowly, and tapped the file. Then he—still slowly—pulled the gun from his shoulder holster and laid it on the file.

There was a soft, metallic click behind them. It took all Anna's self-control not to twist around and look. That click sounded like it came from another gun.

Like maybe the one the gorilla was carrying.

Oh, my stars and garters. Maddeningly, she heard her brother's voice in her head, his tone of mock surprise, used plenty of times when she was a little girl and he had a surprise for her—pleasant or unpleasant, a gift or an Indian rope burn. *Look at what we have here.*

She was suddenly very aware that she was on a dingy couch in a room with three men she didn't know and one she might not know as well as she thought, all four of whom probably had more than one weapon and the willingness to use them. Even Josiah probably had another gun on him. A thin thread of sweat trickled down the channel of her spine, and she suddenly wished they had been able to find some clothes that really, truly fit her. The sweater was too baggy and the jeans had to be rolled up, and the boots were loose even though her feet had swollen and the socks were the heaviest she'd ever worn.

Christ. I'm sitting in this room and worrying about my clothes. I must be insane. But isn't this why I came to Josiah? Although I have no goddamn idea what he's doing.

Whatever it was, she hoped it was worth it. She was suddenly hoping, too, that he could indeed handle this.

"*Lupo, lupo.*" The dark-eyed man shook his head, waving one caramel-skinned hand. "No need to get suspicious. We are old friends, and you have always been reliable."

"Then tell your man behind me to get his finger off the trigger and go take a walk somewhere useful, like out in the parking lot." Josiah didn't bat an eyelash. His expression stayed interested, bland, open. "And tell the Polish to stop sniffing. His snort's about due and you're purposely keeping him here. He sounds like a goddamn adenoidal bulldog."

The man laughed. Another stream of liquid Italian, and the

door opened and closed, clicking securely shut. The third man was gone. "I forget how cautious you are, sometimes."

"As I forget how wily you are." Josiah didn't relax. "And the second half of it is this, *signor*. I am calling in the favor."

The air in the room went very still. The man's eyes slitted, and he studied Josiah with interest. "The favor."

"If I should meet with an accident, this one—" He tipped his head slightly, indicating Anna. "She goes to a safe *pensione* and these papers get distributed widely to the press. *Every* press. My staff is given twenty-four hours to clear out."

"Even that fucking raghead?" The profanity was suddenly shocking, since the tone had been courteous so far. This, Anna suspected, was real business.

A thin curl of irritation lit behind her breastbone. It wasn't that Anna particularly *liked* Hassan, but that...term...was gratuitous, and nasty.

Josiah's calm remained unruffled. "Even him."

"You ask much." The man's eyes began to take on a satisfied gleam Anna didn't like at all. "This is not the old days, friend, when a man's word is his bond."

Josiah sighed. Anna's stomach contracted even further, bile threatening to crawl from the back of her throat out and into the world.

The dark-eyed man on the couch had produced his suspected gun, and had it pointed at her. The mouth of the barrel looked wide, deep, and very black. She let out a small, shocked sound, unable to help herself, and the man laughed.

It was not a nice laugh, even though his belly shook with Santa Claus jollity.

"Giuseppe." Josiah shook his head, like a disappointed uncle. "Not you too."

The man shrugged, his suit wrinkling in interesting ways. "As I said, I have daughters. Who would not want to live forever?"

Josiah said nothing. Anna couldn't look away from the gun, fascinated by its yawning black eye. Her first thought was completely ridiculous. *Eric, I am just going to kill you for this.*

Then she remembered her brother was dead, and she began to feel light-headed.

Josiah made a brief movement, and the gun clicked. The Italian man still held his smoking cigar in his left hand. "Please. I have nothing against you, *lupo,* and I do owe you. But the *bambina,* she is to be brought to some mutual friends, and made to tell all she knows. It is business, my friend. Nothing more."

There was another click, and the ferret-oily man had another gun, to Josiah's head. The dark-eyed man on the couch opened his mouth to yell, and things got very confused.

There was a stunning impact against the side of her head—Josiah had pulled Ferret-Face down and across his lap, somehow, and Ferret's skull cracked against the side of hers. She forgot the prohibition on talking again and yelled, more with surprise than actual pain, slithering off the couch as something zinged over her head and there was a high scream of pain across the room. Her knee hit the coffee table, and an amazing jolt of pain speared her thigh. She ended up on the floor with deadweight on top of her, and for a moment she thought he was trying to pin her to the carpet. Anna thrashed, kicking, another scream caught in her throat, her heart slamming in her chest so hard little black sparkles danced in front of her eyes.

"Stay where you are, Anna." And damn the man, Josiah sounded *calm.* "Now, Giuseppe. Let's have a little chat."

Anna found her eyes squeezed tightly shut, and the childish

thought that she could just keep them that way and avoid the whole situation occurred to her in slow, syrupy motion.

Oh, God. She opened them, and sucked in a sharp breath.

Fat Ferret-Face hung over her, one of his eyes glazed. From the other eye protruded something she had to stare at before she realized it was the leather-wrapped handle of a knife. His mouth was slightly open, and his good eye stared at her as if he had just had a whopper of a great idea and was working it around inside his head before he let it out his gate of a mouth.

Hot, acid, gooey bile whipped the back of her throat again.

Don't you dare *throw up, Anna Maria Caldwell.* It was Eric's voice again. *Just lie there for a moment. Yes, I know it's a dead body. Just stay there. It's what he told you to do.*

The absurdity of her dead brother telling her to do what Josiah wanted and stay still under a dead body made a dark, screaming noise fill the inside of her skull. It was like the rushing that had filled her head when the cop showed up at the door that rainy evening her parents died. *Caldwell? Eric Caldwell? There's been an accident. You'd better sit down.*

Babbling in Italian. High-pitched, squeaky. Then Josiah's voice, terribly even and calm.

I can't. I can't do it. She struggled free of the heavy body on the floor, rolling it aside. Her throat scorched; she was losing the battle with whatever breakfast she'd managed to choke down.

Now, of course, it was even worse. She ended up squeezed between the body, the hilt of the knife hitting the floor with a hideous *thock*, and the couch—which smelled none too clean.

Nobody had made any attempt to freshen up *this* piece of furniture. Why bother, when someone was just going to get stabbed on it?

Do not throw up. For Christ's sake don't throw up now.

She suspected she wouldn't even be able to draw this.

Da Vinci did corpse studies. You're just following in the master's footsteps, right?

There was a wet, gurgling sound. The world faded out to a gray haze for a moment, came screaming back as copper filled her mouth. She found herself grabbing the lip of the coffee table to haul her clumsy, unwieldy body half-upright. Her back gave an amazing flare of fresh pain, her knee screamed, but she didn't care.

Josiah pushed the man on the couch over. Another knife hilt of leather-wrapped wood stuck out of the man's neck, and Josiah knocked his wavering gun away. There was a horrible stink that couldn't be what she thought it was, a real bathroom stench.

Then Josiah calmly leaned over, wrenching the knife back and forth inside the flesh, making little squicking sounds. He had braced his knee in the man's midriff to do so, and the man gurgled again.

"Have the grace to die quietly," Josiah said, softly, as if thinking aloud. He glanced over, his gaze lighting on Anna. His eyes were dark, not piercing green anymore. "I thought I told you to stay down. He managed to squeeze off a shot."

She stared at him, swallowed hard.

This isn't what it's like in the movies. She'd always enjoyed mindless action flicks with popcorn and explosions, but she suspected she wouldn't anymore.

Not after this.

Josiah made a swift movement and the body slid off the couch, landing bonelessly on the other side of the coffee table. He checked his watch against the inside of his wrist, then put one hand on the back of the couch and hopped over, gracefully, and strode to the window. He proceeded to peer cautiously between the edges of the cheap curtains, not moving them. "Christ," he muttered. "Of course they would be in on it. Anna, you okay?"

I really don't know. The sensation of the world skewing sideways and normal angles and ratios failing to apply made everything tilt around her, a hideous carnival spinning. "F-fine." She hauled herself up, her shoulders protesting and the jolt of her wounded knee making her wince. "I think I hit the table on the way down."

"Sorry about that. I wanted to give you some cover. Bring me my gun and the file, there's a good girl." He sounded just the same as ever. Completely, madly calm. "Fucking two-faced bastard. I suspected this."

Her fingers were cold and numb, and she swayed, her knee a bright spike of pain. "You *suspected*? Then why did you—"

He gave her an amused look she couldn't quite classify as contemptuous, but it wasn't extremely encouraging, either. "This was the only way to find out. Now we'll see."

He had just killed two people. As calmly as if he was taking out the trash. "Jesus," she breathed. The world kept doing its funny sliding, first one way, then the other. "Who *are* you?"

That earned her a shrug, which was even worse than that look. "Are you deaf? Bring me my *gun*. And don't leave that file lying there, either. Move, woman!"

Nothing made any sense. Mechanically, she scooped up the heavy gun, holding it awkwardly. The man on the couch gurgled again and flopped. The stink was tremendous.

"Ignore him." Josiah was still peering out the window, moving from one side to the other, looking down. "It's just nerve death. He'd be suffocating on his own blood if I hadn't broken his neck as well. Son of a *bitch*." He turned on his heel, sharply, away from the window, and strode across the room.

Anna flinched as he bore down on her. He merely yanked the gun out of her hand and checked its clip, sliding it back in with a click. "Are you going to throw up? Or scream?" Businesslike, as if he were inquiring whether she wanted fries and a Coke with that.

Both. Neither. Jesus Christ. She steadied herself on her throbbing knee and glared at him. "Neither." It took everything she had to lift her chin and push her aching shoulders back. "What's next?"

It was almost worth it, to see him nod. "Good girl." Nothing in the words but that awful, inhuman calm. "Now we move. Can you run?"

Oh, let's see. I think I've pulled most of the muscles I own and you hit me in the head with a dead body and I am going to have more nightmares than I ever thought possible, if I ever sleep again. "If they're shooting at me, I'll find out, won't I?" She didn't mean to sound so flippant, but there was only so much a woman could take.

The world still didn't look quite right, every surface oddly luminous. Even the couch looked more graceful and serene. The only things that didn't match were the two…bodies. Even drawing in charcoal wouldn't capture their slack wrongness.

Two breathing human beings, vanished, now. Gone.

Just like her brother.

She couldn't tell if that made it better…or worse.

Chapter Seventeen

She was too pale, feverish spots of crimson bloomed high on her cheeks, and her eyes looked a little glassy. Worst of all, she flinched when he got too close, a betraying little movement that might have made his heart crack clean through if he hadn't been too busy to worry about little things like how he *felt*.

There wasn't any time; he hurried her down the stairs in front of him and cursed inwardly, a steady, comforting, monotonous cavalcade of obscenities in every language he knew and a few that he only knew the purple words in. He knew bodyguard protocol, but it wasn't his favorite, too many variables.

Ironic, that now when it counted he was using the one skillset he felt least confident about.

Anna's hair glowed under the fluorescents as she reached the bottom of the staircase and bolted through the entryway. She was rabbiting blindly, only moving because he was behind her. He reached up, couldn't catch her shoulder; his fingers sank into her hair and he yanked, sharply.

Her head snapped back. "*Ow!*"

That stopped her, but it wasn't the way he'd wanted to. He

pushed her aside, into the scant cover of a laundry room doorway; a dryer was running and the smell of fabric softener filled the air. His hand closed over her mouth; she swallowed a second cry and a shiver went through her, one he would have loved to soothe her out of.

No time.

"Stop." He wasn't gasping from adrenaline and motion, but his lungs burned. Back in the zone again, every nerve raw and his brain clicking through trained-in codes and percentages. It was familiar, and how he hated it. "Wait a second."

He eased forward, cautiously, checked this side of the building. Thin golden light blanketed the alley that cut through to Eighteenth Street on one side and the parking lot on the other. Good cover, but if he was them he'd have snipers on the roof.

Of course, he wasn't them, and they were worried about exposure, or needed Anna at least conscious for questioning. He didn't have to be worried about anything other than saving his miserable hide—and her infinitely more fragile one.

There was a strange sliding sensation inside him when he realized this was Anna's first brush with serious violence.

Josiah didn't feel like telling her they might be surrounded. He especially didn't feel like telling her the parking lot was crawling with plainclothes cops, most likely alerted by the gorilla with the machine gun. Or even by Giuseppe himself when Hassan phoned Vanczny to set up the meet.

Well, now at least he knew the Mob was involved. He'd dangled both himself and her as bait, and some very interesting fish were rising.

Now he just had to get them both out of here.

He shut his eyes for a moment, filled his lungs. Anna's breathing came harsh and hard; he suspected she was crying but when he glanced back over his shoulder she slumped against the side of the door, rubbing at her neck as if it pained her, fiercely dry-eyed. The bruise on her cheek glared in the harsh light, and her throat worked as she swallowed, still staring wide-eyed at him as if he was the enemy.

He'd half-expected her to be a sobbing heap by now. His mind kept ticking through percentages, standard operating procedures, and the layout of the terrain. "All right. They won't put snipers on the roof and they can't afford choppers at this point; both would alert the press. You go out this door and to your left. When you get to the street, make a right, walk until I pull up behind you, and you get in the car. Simple."

"What are you going to do?"

Maybe she was in shock. Paper-pale, shaking visibly, and bruised, she stared at him with a wide, haunted look that would get her marked as prey in any neighborhood, even a nice one.

"I'm going to go get the car." He stroked a strand of her beautiful gold-threaded hair back, tucked it behind her ear, and flattened his palm against the curve of her bruised cheek. Her skin was hot, feverish, and his instincts screamed at him to *get going come on for Christ's sake get out of here time is running out!* "All you've got to do is trust me, Anna. Okay?" *If you can. You have to. Please let her trust me.*

"What if you don't make it?"

Shit. Had she guessed there was someone out in the parking lot? Of course, the way he was acting it was a fair assumption. If he showed any sign of uncertainty now, she would be in an even worse position. "That's not an option, Anna." He let his tone carry confidence he didn't particularly feel at this point. Everything depended on his enemies being unwilling to make much of a fuss. Between the police and the Mob, you could never tell when they would decide it was acceptable to have some sort of public spectacle that could be misinterpreted rather than let a loose end dangle any longer.

It reminded him of Eastern Europe, of Krakow in spring and the rifle in his hands, knowing they were on his tail, cat-and-mousing with remnants of Soviet secret police. Instability made for a lot of work in the private sector, and he'd been contemplating retirement even then.

He'd been young, but not stupid, and knew he wasn't invulnerable. But the money was so good, and—useless to deny it—he knew what he was good at.

The same bitter taste of copper, and the same frantic, trained calm behind his thoughts. He *had* to get her out of the critical zone. "Not an option," he repeated. "You just go. Walk like you're heading somewhere, and I'll bring the car around."

"Okay," she whispered, and it hurt to see her straighten just a little bit more. He was trained for this; she wasn't.

It wasn't hard to figure out who was the braver one here.

His heart gave an amazing, painful leap. "Get going." He took his hand away, gently, and led her to the door. Opened it, checked the alley, checked the slice of roofline he could see. "All right. Go. Walk like you're headed somewhere, and don't look back."

She did. He wanted to go with her, but he had a little business first. To see her stepping slowly away down that alley in Willie's sweater, her hair a little mussed and an obvious limp dragging down her right leg, made his heart hurt even more.

He was about to duck back into the building and cut through to the other fire exit, where he could slide across the street and retrieve the car, when he heard what he'd been hoping for all along.

The *rat-a-tat-tat* of submachine fire. He could guess what had happened, see it in his mind's eye—Guiseppe's meathead flunky slinking out to place a call to Guiseppe's higher-up, then stationing himself in some unobtrusive corner and waiting for the single shot that should have meant Josiah's death.

That shot was instead thrown wide because of the knife in Giuseppe's shoulder. One shot was the signal, and the gorilla had probably been coming up the stairs on one end of the hallway to check back in with his *patrone* just as Josiah and Anna vanished down the other end. Seeing both his *patrone* and the slimy little Pole dead, the assumption of a deal gone horribly wrong would wend its way through even a mind unaccustomed to working for itself.

Cops in plainclothes would only add to the confusion. In the best of all worlds, Giuseppe Torrafazione's idiot flunky would mistake the men in plainclothes for another Family or faction, and Josiah a double-crosser luring a Family man to his death.

Let me be lucky, huh? In situations like this, though, a man often made his own luck.

Josiah bolted. Everything now depended on speed, and how stupid the made man with the submachine gun was.

Giuseppe Torrafazione was not known to pick his muscle with an eye to their brains. It was why he was a bottom-feeder, and one of the lightning calculations flashing through Josiah's brain when he stepped into the apartment and smelled hair oil and cigarette smoke had taken that into account.

Josiah ran smoothly, orienting himself from the steps he'd counted since they walked into this place. The fire door finally loomed in front of him, submachine gun chatter interspersed with the reports of police-issue Glocks sounding thin and tinny.

The cops thought they'd been double-crossed, the Mob gorilla probably thought *he* had been, and in the confusion Josiah could slip away nicely.

He was four steps away and slowing down a little when the fire door opened and two men charged in, guns drawn.

No time, too close. He took the first one with a fast strike to the throat, cartilage making a strange wet popping noise as knuckles met larynx. The man folded, and the second one—blond crew cut, hazel eyes, a scar on his chin—almost had time to get the gun up before Josiah half-spun on the ball of his left foot, his other boot striking with unerring precision at the knee. That put him in a perfect position to knock the gun away, metal skittering along the cheap, harsh carpet of the hall, and then he had the man's head in his hands.

Can't leave any witnesses. For a moment he was glad she wasn't here to see this, then training took over and he made the short sharp movement. The crack sounded like a good hard axe strike against seasoned wood in just the right place. The choking of the first man had turned frantic; Josiah scooped the Glock from nerveless fingers. This man was dark haired and handsome, a wedding ring glinting on his left hand as he clawed at his throat. *For what it's worth, I'm sorry. They'll pension your wife, at least.*

The sound of the shot was lost in the chaos happening two floors up. Or at least, so Josiah hoped. Quick, clean—or mostly clean; blood spattered against the wall and more matter and blood fouled the carpet. He gave the gun a quick, efficient wipe with a handkerchief rescued from his coat pocket, folded the blond man's fingers around it again, and stepped out into winter sunshine on the quiet side of the building, far away from the pitched battle.

Three and a half precious minutes later he was in the car, driving sedately away as sirens brayed nearer and nearer. Sixty seconds afterward he spotted Anna, who glanced nervously over her shoulder when he pulled up alongside, pushing the button that lowered the passenger-side window. Eighteenth was a street of small shops and gas stations, and if the approaching sirens were any indication, it would soon be crawling with attention from both the cops and the media. He checked the rearview mirror. Clear for now.

He leaned over. "Get in."

She did, dropping down with a small wounded sound and yanking the door shut. Paper crackled in her black canvas purse. She locked the door and stared straight ahead as the window slid back up, closing out the world.

"Put your seat belt on." His heart was suddenly pounding. Or maybe it had been pounding all this time, and he'd just noticed it. There was blood on the back of his hand, a small splatter, and he still felt short blond stubble under his fingers for a dizzying moment before the wall fell inside his head, cutting him off from the chill efficiency of combat brain with a sound he was often surprised nobody else heard. He was himself again, his hands cold and his mouth full of sour copper, death cheated once more. "Are you hurt?"

She said nothing, looking out through the windshield as he pulled away from the curb, checking the street over his shoulder.

"Anna. Are you hurt?"

She stirred finally, folding her hands in her lap. "Not much." It was a pale, soft voice, one he'd never heard from her before. "I just had a dead body tossed on top of me and half my hair pulled out. Other than that, I'm kosher."

"I wanted you to have some cover if the bastard started firing." It was useless to explain more.

"That was nice of you." She sounded almost prim.

"You're in shock." *You still think you want to kill someone, Anna? Do me a favor, leave it to the professionals.* She should never have had to see something like this. He'd wanted to insulate her from it. Just this one little piece of the world untouched by bloodshed and darkness, that was all he'd ever asked for. One single, simple little space inside the circle of her arms, where he could feel warm.

Where he could feel *human.* He still didn't know how she did it. He hadn't even known he was capable of it until she came along.

If he was normal, maybe he could have had the last three years with her, instead of—but that was an idiotic thing to think, because if he'd been a nine-to-five Wal-Mart shopper, she would be helpless right now. Already captured, or dead, or God alone knew.

"You think?" She reached slowly for her seat belt, buckled herself in. "Josiah?"

"What?" The next stage of the game unfolded in front of him. Still too many variables—Eric's fucking fingerless contact, the post office box, the attackers turning into dust, not like the four respectable corpses he'd just left behind.

He still didn't like those goddamn variables.

"The knives."

When you want it quiet, it's a knife or a garrote, and I didn't have time to strangle Giuseppe. Much as I would have liked to. "Necessary, Anna. Or you'd be at their tender mercies right this moment."

"Jesus." She shook her head, slightly, her hair falling forward over her shoulder. He had to do something about that soon; she was just too distinctive with a long mane. But God, he loved her hair. He even loved the way her lower lip trembled and she bit it a little, her eyelashes sweeping down as she looked at her hands in her lap.

It wasn't just the adrenaline rush of escaping the trap making his heart pound. It was the light falling over her profile and the vulnerability of her slender shoulders. It was the fact that she was sitting next to him, safely buckled in and still breathing.

Not thinking straight, Josiah.

"Not Jesus," he said before he could stop himself. "He's got other things to worry about. All you've got is me, baby doll. And you should be goddamn glad, too."

She stared at her hands in her lap, her hair falling forward, shielding her expression. "I guess so." Three tiny words, very soft.

Christ, you're not convinced yet? "We've got to get you some clothes that fit. And something to eat."

"Why are you always bugging me to eat?" The faint note of annoyance was very welcome. Even more welcome was the slight movement, as if she wanted to look at him.

"I can't have you fainting on me. Or getting weak." He checked the rearview again. They were clear. Slipped through the net. Vanished, like two good little fishies.

"I won't get weak. Can I ask you something?"

As long as you're talking, I'm sure you're all right. Or reasonably all right. I thought you'd be screaming by now. Or unconscious. "Shoot." As soon as it left his mouth, he regretted the word choice.

She shifted in the seat, as if she regretted it, too. "How many times did you kill someone while you were with me?"

Oh, Christ. "Now is *not* the time, Anna."

"How many times, Josiah?"

He gave up. "You mean, how many jobs? Six. And two more after you. Then I retired. What else? Do you want to know how, with what, the body count? You're taking this really well, I might add."

Anna said nothing. When he glanced over, wishing they didn't have to move so he could stop, pull over, and try to explain, he saw she had leaned her head back against the seat and closed her eyes.

Whatever reaction he'd expected, it wasn't this. He settled for forging ahead. "There's been a slight change of plans. We're not going to see Willie and Hassan today. We've got a meet at sixteen hundred."

"Another one?" That got her attention. She wasn't as blasé as she wanted him to think, thank God. He'd underestimated her, and even though that was a cheerful surprise, it also gave him a nagging sense of…well, his life depended on making precise estimations of everyone.

Anna, however, defied them every single time.

"Relax." He took a left on Henry Street, falling in behind a plumber's truck, its bumper sticker asking HOW AM I DRIVING? and giving an 800 number, as if anyone would bother. Sirens began to recede, and *now* he could admit it had been a close call. Far, far closer than he'd liked. "This one's not a trap. Let's go get you some clothes."

Her sizes hadn't changed much, and she just nodded when he suggested various articles of clothing in a big-box store off Hanon Way. Jeans, a nice dark blue merino sweater over a black T-shirt, a pair of boots that wouldn't give her another blister—she was stepping with the exaggerated care of a footsore soldier by now. He also bought more bandaging as well as more ibuprofen and a few toiletries. He was a little more sanguine about their chances now; she had clothes that fit, a few pairs of shoes, and two dark coats. They had a clean car, and he had managed to tangle up both the cops and the Mob.

It was a good day's work, all told. Winter dusk swirled into corners and alleys, rain clouds moving in from the north as Josiah settled himself across the table from Martin Chilwell.

The dapper man's gaze flicked over Anna once as he laid his tan driving gloves down on the red checkered tablecloth with prissy care. Here in the back of the restaurant, the booth was relatively safe, chosen for its position near the fire and kitchen doors as well as the shelter afforded from peering eyes on the street.

Chilwell was all narrowness, from his slit eyes to his compressed balding head, his slender shoulders, and his skinny, polished wingtips. He wore a natty double-breasted suit tailored to fit over the bulge of his sidearm, and his long dark coat shouted *spook*.

Unfortunately, Chilwell wasn't CIA. If the intelligence community was a family, Chilwell would be the cousin nobody ever wanted to talk about or see, working for an agency nobody would admit to even suspecting the existence of. He'd been Josiah's contact for a good decade, from back in the heyday, and was now—if you could believe the hints he gave—mostly retired, or doing administrative work.

The busboy came, silently setting out goblets of ice water with lemon. "Thank you," Anna murmured habitually. She always thanked servers, bank tellers, even florists and dry cleaners. It was one more thing he'd missed about her, the tiny graceful manners she took as a matter of course.

Chilwell's eyebrows went up a little. This was his preferred type of meeting place: good food and several potential escape routes, not to mention a slightly shabby type of elegance. Chilwell's meets tended to be in cafés that had either outlived their best days or were trying to muscle their way up, right on the fringes of the popular districts. For a man so thin and wasted, he certainly spent significant time stuffing his face.

Josiah laid the file on the table, close enough that Chil could take it if he wanted to. The threadbare red velvet on the wall muffled all sounds. Schumann played softly through hidden speakers and the tables were lit by tiny oil lamps. "Evening, Chilwell. How's the wife?"

He had no idea if the man was married, though he wore a wedding ring. Often, Chil's answers were maddeningly imprecise and perverse, and could be taken to refer either to a flesh-and-blood Mrs. *or* the agency he had given his life to.

"Demanding as ever." Chilwell's voice was colorless, a simple murmur. "What is this, Wolfe?"

Josiah laid it out in a few clipped sentences: a journalist, dead; interviewees, missing; the editor, dead; his own tangle with the Mob and the police. The file, in which some very odd accusations were made—but what would doubtless interest Chilwell more, the debits and credits portion. Someone was making a hell of a lot of money with this, and it could, Josiah hinted, have a bioterrorism aspect.

The agency was extremely sensitive to those kinds of things.

Plus, Chilwell had been Josiah's handler in Tunisia long ago, and had believed Josiah and Hassan about the woman with the rats. He'd had to; she'd sicced the animals on all three of them. After that, the man had started hinting at retirement.

Who could blame him?

So Josiah told him just enough about the attackers turning into dust to whet his appetite, and closed with the tidbit that neither Eric's death nor Anna's disappearance was being officially investigated.

This was long work, especially with the waiter gliding up at intervals. Chilwell ordered tomato bisque to start with. By the time Josiah finished, plates of roast lamb à la Grecque with new potatoes and winter greens had appeared for both Chil and Anna, who waited for Josiah's nod before she ate.

She had such exquisite manners. The bruise on her face was going down, thank God. He hadn't even suggested hiding it with makeup; that would only accentuate the discoloration. He wished he was here alone with her, refilling her glass, listening to her low clear laughter.

Being as normal as someone like him could ever be.

Chilwell thought about it, picking up his wineglass and swirling the rosé inside. "How is it?" he asked Anna, solicitously.

She glanced at Josiah again. He gave a fractional shrug. "Very good, thank you." Her tone was just as soft and polite as his. "The vinaigrette is particularly nice."

"The chef here is a traditionalist." The narrow man sighed. "Wolfe, you've gotten yourself into trouble this time."

You don't think I know that? "So I've noticed."

"I can't offer you backup."

"Don't want it anyway." *I never have, you had to twist my arm to get me to work with Hassan.*

"Nice not to ask for what you can't have. What *do* you want?"

"New identities for me and her, a guarantee for my staff, and latitude to finish this off. Plus any help you can provide making sure this"—he tapped the file with two fingers—"gets to the right people."

"Who do you think the right people are, Josiah?" Chil took another bite of lamb, closed his eyes briefly.

"The agency. If there is something with…potential…in here, they might be well disposed toward me for bringing it to their attention. In any case, if this gets out, or into the wrong hands…" He left it at that.

"Indeed. We can always count on your self-interest, can't we." The man's gaze rested on Anna, who studied her plate, a faint flush rising in her unwounded cheek. Her eyelashes veiled her own gaze, and that natural elegance of hers made everything around her seem a little brighter. "Which is why this is…surprising, to say the least."

"Call me sentimental. She's a witness, she needs protection." *If you didn't know I was involved with her, you're radically redefining my status as trustworthy. I kept this secret successfully, I'm sure I did—if only because I infiltrated and found my files held no mention of her, even after I retired.*

Still, nothing was certain. His file could have been doctored. Eric got hold of part of it, too. Friends in high places? Or had a reporter's snooping alerted the agency that Josiah had entanglements?

Lots of unpleasant alternatives to be had, in this situation.

"I'm interested in exactly how she came to your attention." Chilwell signaled the waiter for a fresh basket of bread. "More wine, Miss Caldwell?"

"No, thank you." She set her fork down. Conversation ceased until the waiter was out of earshot again.

"Her brother left my contact number in the file. I was bored." Josiah shrugged.

"Is that so."

It's the only explanation I'm going to give. "She's a noncom, Chil. Come on."

"Sometimes there must be sacrifice, Wolfe. You know that."

"Not this time." *I gave you everything else. Her, I'm keeping. And if you try to hurt her, you're going to be one more obstacle in my way. You taught me to be very, very good at getting rid of obstacles.*

"Don't tell me you're involved." Chil's tone was more eloquent than a whole book. Disbelief and artful half suspicion.

"Does it matter?" Josiah's heartbeat hitched up a notch. In a few moments he would turn cold, getting ready for God only knew what and estimating just how much blowback killing Chilwell would generate.

This was not a good turn for the conversation to take.

"Are you going to do something stupid?" Chil permitted himself another sip of wine.

Why are you even asking me? "Not yet."

That evidently wasn't the right answer. "You've gotten yourself into some deep waters here. I'd feel a lot better if I knew you weren't going to be led around by your dick."

"My dick's the least of your worries, Chil." He leaned forward, hands flat on the table. "I did my time, goddammit. I'm bringing this to you rather than hopping the border and taking what I know to a foreign fucking power. I need identities when this is over, and I need contacts who can break this thing. I don't trust anyone local further than I can throw them."

"Don't get dramatic." Chilwell sighed. A faint blush had kindled in his sallow, freshly shaven cheeks. "I must admit, I was a little surprised to hear from you. Especially since…well. This is a delicate situation."

Josiah's skin shrank two sizes and grew a coat of ice in the same second. *There's another operation going on out here. Fuck. Isn't that just my luck.* The smell of the wine drifted through his nostrils, the alcoholic tang suddenly very attractive. Getting really drunk seemed like an excellent avoidance mechanism, except he'd already tried it and *that* hadn't worked out well at all. "Delicate." He managed to make the word as flat and unhelpful as possible.

Chilwell actually *laughed,* a dry cricket-rustle of honest amusement Josiah had heard only once or twice before. "Don't worry. I'm not going to cut you loose; you're too potentially useful. We want to know what's going on inside that brownstone on Morris, and we want to know what Denton and Marshall are selling that had so many investors flocking to the table."

Marshall? The mayor. Great. "How many other agents have you sent in?" It was only a guess, but a good one. The man's face puckered as if he was sucking on a lemon.

"Four. None came back." Chilwell's gaze skittered over Anna, whose eyes had grown very large. "None of them were liquidators. Just coverts." His fingers stole out, whisked the file off the table. Josiah let him. "Which is why it's so surprising to hear from you. Your name was...shall we say, bandied about?"

Think. Think very quickly, Josiah. And for God's sake be careful. If the agency had considered a liquidation agent with Josiah's record for a domestic operation, something else had to have happened. Not only that, but Anna was squarely in the middle of the tangle, the one place he didn't want her to be. Chilwell had a visual on her and there was enough in the file for them to dig—and if they did, they could put two and two together about Josiah's sudden change from a cold, levelheaded liquidator to a half-suicidal monkey who'd needed help to handle a simple erasure in Cairo.

That would make things decidedly sticky.

"Always nice to be popular," he said easily. "I assume I'm given the usual prerogative?"

"License?" Chilwell tapped his fingers precisely once on the tabletop. He wasn't batting an eyelash at Anna's continued presence during this conversation. Again, very bad. The game had suddenly mutated into a new shape, one Josiah didn't like the look of at all. "We've never had a complaint about your methods. Bring us usable information, that's all we ask. Will a safe house be necessary for your... witness?"

Fuck it all, they know. "She's staying right where I can keep an eye on her. Standard fee?"

"You mean, standard fee plus the new identities and guarantees for your two misfits? I suppose you can't simply do this as a favor. For old times' sake."

You cheap son of a bitch. "No."

"I didn't think so." Chilwell reached for his pocket, nice and easy. His hard, narrow hand came up with a brown paper envelope, which he placed on the table and pushed toward Josiah. "The rest will be deposited in the usual account. I assume the number's still good?"

It certainly is, but after the money gets there it will be bounced a few times to one I know is clean. "Pleasure doing business."

"Josiah." The man's gaze was level and cold as a dead fish's. "It has been remarked that you thought to bring this to us. We appreciate your discretion and loyalty. But this is very, *very* delicate. We will disavow, and we will cut loose, if necessary. *Be careful.*"

Josiah's throat was parched and sandy. He rose smoothly. "Thanks for the warning." He managed to sound normal.

At least, he tried to sound normal, and Chilwell didn't push. There wasn't a need.

Anna gained her feet with a lurch. It was painful to watch her move; she was obviously hurting. "Thank you for dinner," she said, awkwardly, as if she had been slightly embarrassed at a party. Her hair fell forward over her shoulder, glowing under the mellow golden light. It was hard to look at her and keep the wall in his head up, keep his mind ticking through the maze of percentages and alternatives.

"It was my pleasure." Chil sounded genuinely pleased. "We do these things so we can have people like you on nice sunny streets, Miss Caldwell. I hope Josiah doesn't forget it."

That's enough. "Leave her out of this, Chilwell."

"Take your own advice, Wolfe." He fluttered his long, skinny fingers. "You're ruining a good meal. Go away."

"See you."

Anna didn't protest. She limped alongside him; Josiah's arm slid over her shoulders, both to hide her distinctive gait and to offer a little comfort. He scanned the front of the restaurant, the windows not blind with approaching night because the street outside was lit by lamps and the pale glow from shop windows. Not a hair out of place, not a single wrong note.

So why did he feel so unsettled? Chil would cut him loose in a heartbeat to serve the agency's needs, but the agency needed Josiah alive, especially if they'd lost four ops in the brownstone.

Anna pulled her coat closed. "What do we do now?" she whispered as he palmed the door open, nodding to the maître d'.

He waited until the door was closed, taking a deep breath of night air tainted with exhaust and full of shifting shadows from the trees lining the street, their bare limbs turning the street glow into lace. It smelled like damp, rain on the way. "Now we find a room, and you get some sleep. Tomorrow's going to be a busy day."

"We're not going to the post—"

"Not enough cover in the middle of the night. Come on." His arm tightened, pulling her closer as wind ruffled the ends of her hair.

"Josiah?" Dammit, she was going to start asking questions again.

After the conversation he'd just had, he wasn't sure he wanted to answer any more goddamn questions today.

"Be quiet, baby doll. In a minute." *Let me get my head together. You're bad for my detachment.*

And I've never needed it more.

"Never mind," she said quietly, and the note of finality in those two words managed to do what Chilwell had not.

It hurt.

Chapter Eighteen

He took her to a hotel off Maple, ironically not so far from the Blake but not nearly as nice. The check-in clerk barely glanced at them *or* at Josiah's ID, and Anna managed a glimpse at the names Jo signed them in under. Apparently they were now Bob and Kelly Duncan, and the ID was from Idaho.

She felt only a faint weary surprise and a low hum of physical pain, her back and shoulder and head and feet all contributing their voices to the chorus. Jo kept glancing at her, as if he expected her to start talking again, but she kept her mouth firmly shut.

There really wasn't any point, and she just wanted to sleep. Even the meeting in the restaurant with the man who looked like her ninth-grade English teacher had taken on a dreamlike quality. It felt like she'd pulled two or three all-nighters in a row, either in college or for work, with the world comfortably behind a distant haze broken only by whatever task she had to finish next.

He gave up trying to talk to her. Anna took the small blue pill he offered and fell asleep in one tightly made twin bed without even brushing her teeth or taking her shoes off. Her last conscious thought was *that feels good,* when Josiah worked her left boot free of her aching foot.

Whatever was in the pill made her sleep dreamless-deep. She woke in the blackest part of night, the hushed time a few hours past midnight when sunlight is only a distant memory and even nurses and cops get lethargic.

She surfaced, in fact, with an immediate jolt and the sense that something was terribly, hideously wrong.

Cool air drifted across her face as she struggled to sit up, her body singing its concert of aches and pains. Her head was stuffed with fuzz.

I hope I don't catch a goddamn cold to top everything off.

Two realizations hit her at once. One, the window leading out to the breezeway running past all the second-floor rooms was wide open, cheap motel curtains blowing in the freshening rain-heavy wind.

Two, there was a slight shuffling and an exhalation of effort. The picture she saw didn't make any sense at first, but as she reached stupidly and habitually for a lamp—reached out to the wrong side, too, as if she was trying to turn on her bedside tensor at home—she realized that someone was holding someone else up against the wall across from her bed. The sharp little sounds were punches striking home.

Josiah! She thrashed uselessly out of the bed, stocking feet hitting the floor, and scrabbled for the gleam of cold metal on the nightstand. It was there, heavy and solid; she remembered Josiah laying the gun down and giving her an odd look, his eyes suddenly dark and distant. Shuttered.

For the first time in her life, Anna Caldwell held a gun, and she lifted it with trembling hands. "Josiah?" The word dropped down into the dark well of the room, vanishing without a ripple.

Both figures jerked. One—the one with its back to her—had long, deformed hands and hunched shoulders. He had Josiah against the wall, and a random reflection of light showed a bone-white curve of cheek, long strands of greasy hair. Her brain, used to putting together shapes before drawing them on paper, struggled briefly with the utter impossibility of what her eyes were relaying.

Then the man dropped Josiah and rounded on her, and impossibility became terror.

I'd shade in those cheekbones, if I were you, a weary, practical voice spoke up in the middle of her head. *But I wouldn't worry about it too damn much, because you've gone crazy. There's no other explanation.*

The face floated in midair, mostly because he wore dark clothing. He wasn't just pale. Luminescent skin stretched tight over wide, low cheekbones and a thin mouth, heavy eyebrows painted with a thick brush over coal-black pits that had to be eyes, except for the glittering vertical slots of red revolving in their depths.

His lips hung slightly open, the creature making a small asthmatic sound because he couldn't quite close his mouth properly.

Because of the *teeth*.

Long, sharp canines, glowing and nacreous, protruding from the top lip and dimpling the thin lower lip, only they didn't look like a dentist's job or a fake Halloween decoration.

No. Their wicked little points looked real. The wheezing breaths were all *too* real.

Copper filled Anna's mouth. Her stomach gave a violent lurch and her fingers spasmed tight around the gun. She was barely aware of backing up until she ran into the second twin bed in the room, her abused ankle sending a red jolt all the way up to her hip.

It paused, cocking its head, and took a deep, whistling breath. Sniffing the air, its head making a small lizardlike movement. Her art school roommate had once had an iguana as a pet, and the little flick of this human-shaped thing's head reminded her so much of Mr. Handbag that her stomach gave another huge, cramping twist.

"Oh my God," Anna whispered.

There was a small click. "Take another step toward her, and I will kill you." Josiah sounded terribly hoarse, and exhausted. "I don't care *what* you are."

Silence filled the room, dark water in a cup. Anna's knees gave out; she dropped down onto the bed, barely remembering the gun in her hands. The springs squeaked.

Oh, my word. She sounded prim even to herself. *This just keeps getting better.*

The creature straightened, slowly. Then it spoke. "I could kill you both, with little trouble. Your bullets are quite the wrong sort."

Anna's left hand freed itself from the gun and flew to her mouth, clamping over her lips with hysterical strength. With those teeth, the man sounded like he had a minor speech impediment. *Your bulle-th are quite the wrong thort.* Rancid giggles rose in her throat, but she swallowed them with an effort that left her shaking. Her stomach lurched again, settled, and promised more trouble in the future.

"Wrong or not, a hollow-point in the brain might not be a bad idea. Back away from her, goddammit. Now." There was another little metallic click. Josiah had never spoken to her like this, and she was suddenly grateful.

There was no warning. One moment the man was there, the next he was halfway across the room, at the foot of the bed Anna still stupidly sat on. She blinked, letting out a blurt of surprise that might have been funny if she'd been watching someone else enduring this, and things got very confused for a few seconds.

Her wrist gave an agonized shriek of pain as it was twisted. There was something hard and thin across her chest; she was hauled up and across the bed in one movement.

The thin man with the funny teeth and the bone-white cheeks held her a good foot off the floor, with no apparent effort. Anna's feet dangled, making small, fruitless motions, and her shoulders both hurt because he *squeezed,* hard enough to keep her hanging but not choking her. Josiah took a few steps forward, to the end of the second bed, and his eyes glittered dangerously.

The man had grabbed her, and had his back to the wall, Anna held in front of him like a ludicrous shield. She kicked, thrashing, until his arm slipped a little and the pressure mounted. "I can snap your neck in a trice, fair Anne," he whispered, his voice as flat and wrong as a badly tuned piano. "Be still. And you, with your *gun.*" Terrible contempt shaded the creature's tone. "Close the window, so we are not heard at our parley. I give my word I will not harm her unnecessarily."

"Very comforting." If Josiah could have sneered, he probably would have. "I'm not about to turn my back on you."

The arm tightened. Anna bit back a gasp, creaking pain mounting in her chest, and saw Josiah's shoulders tense in the dim light.

The creature made a small amused sound. "Turning your back is not necessary. Closing the window *is.*"

Josiah did back up, carefully, and managed to shut the window without lowering the gun. He even locked it.

Then he reached over and flicked the light switch.

The creature hissed and Anna blinked, her eyes stinging. The rattling sibilance in her ear made her think of dark riverbanks, of fanged things lying in wait in thick silt. Things with long claws, bad tempers, and reptilian plating.

Hungry things.

"Oh God," she whispered. She blinked away the stinging, Josiah a blurred shape across the room, comforting and solid.

"God has not forsaken you. You are, after all, still alive." The arm, hard as a bony iron bar, loosened slightly. He set her on her feet again, but didn't let up on the pressure across her shoulders and chest. "Your brother, fair Anne. I can smell him in your veins. Where is he?"

The mention of Eric was like a pinch in a sore spot. "He's dead." Her voice wouldn't work above a cracked whisper. "I found him d-dead, in his apartment." Eric's puffed, discolored face rose in her memory like a silent scream; she closed her eyes and tried to push the sight away. Her stomach was exceedingly unhappy with this turn of events.

"Ah. That explains…" But apparently the creature still wasn't satisfied. "How did he die?"

Josiah sounded coldly furious. "For God's sake, leave her alone. Whoever killed Eric slit his throat and left him in his apartment with the heat on high to speed decomposition. The police are sitting on the news of his death. There's no investigation. Nor is there any goddamn investigation of his editor's death. If you want anything out of either of us, stranger, I'd counsel you to let go of her and start giving some goddamn answers."

Tension crackled in the air. It felt like a lifetime before the slender bony arm slithered away from her collarbones. He even pushed her away, gently. "Eric is truly dead." It didn't sound like a question.

"He is." Josiah moved forward, smoothly.

Anna spotted the gun on the floor. She'd dropped it, like an idiot. She was about to bend to pick it up, her feet unsteady, when it was scooped up by a luminous white hand missing three fingers. Only the thumb and the index finger remained, and the stubs of the other three moved in concert, as if trying to grasp the heavy metal.

Bile scorched her throat. She looked up into the face of the creature who had just let go of her.

The teeth were gone. Now he looked like a thin, weary, but still-attractive man, deep lines scored into his face by pain and experience, his dark eyes no longer tainted with red, their depths fully human. His hair fell over his eyes, greasy dark tendrils moving like dreadlocks. A scar ran across his forehead, and another livid one up his cheek, plus a band of thick scarring across his throat. His long-sleeved T-shirt was torn, and the jeans he wore were crusted with dark stuff she didn't want to think about. His feet were as mauled as his hands, and she saw more ropes of shiny pink scar tissue on his ankles and wrists.

Her mouth was dry and smooth as glass. *He looks like he's been through a blender. It's cold out there, why is he running around barefoot?*

The man cradled the gun in his wounded hand, examining her. She got the idea he was waiting for something.

"I think we have a spare shirt," she said finally, straightening to brush her own hair back. She heard a slight sound behind her, as if Josiah had sucked in a harsh breath. "But I don't think any of Josiah's pants will fit you. Or his sh-shoes."

The man regarded her steadily. Then, of all things, a twinkle of actual amusement came into his eyes. He presented her with the gun, neatly. "You are much like your brother, child. I thank you for your bravery."

It's not bravery. I'm too tired to be scared. "You knew Eric?" *I sound like I'm eleven years old. And frightened. It's not my fault. I can't breathe. How can he move so quickly?*

"Not very well. Your brother came into that hellish place and loosed my bonds. He promised to meet me in the church of St. Simeon and bring me my ring, since I could not approach its hiding place without betraying it. I waited among the candles, but no sign of him appeared unto me. Given my status, I cannot say I was surprised." The eerie sibilance had gone out of the man's voice. He now looked normal, as normal as any beggar with mutilated hands and ragged clothes.

"Your...status." Her hand was numb, but she closed her cold fingers over the gun. Josiah made another slight sound, and she felt his hand wrap around her shoulder, warm and comforting.

The other man's flesh was cold as marble, or at least, the finger she could feel pressing against her own was. He grinned, a wide terrible grin, and she saw his canines again. Abnormally long, and looking very sharp; his front teeth were a little too small, so the canines were set forward, curving viciously.

"My jaw distends," he said, calmly. "So the teeth can drive in. Do you require a demonstration?"

"No. No thank you." She backed up a hurried two steps, bumping into Josiah, who pushed her aside. He had another gun, and kept it trained on the man. *I am going crazy. I've finally snapped. I am believing something I shouldn't.* "Who *are* you?"

It wasn't what she wanted to ask. She wanted to ask *what are you?* and stopped herself at the last second.

"My name is Christopher. You may call me Kit, fair Anne. I come with explanations, and if your protector will lay aside his weapon and speak with me, I think we may find more profit in league than in adversity."

"Anna?" Josiah, pushing her aside even further. She would fall on the bed if he kept this up.

"Stop shoving me," she found herself saying. "All right, you—Christopher. If you knew Eric, then tell me something about him."

The man's smile didn't falter. He dropped his mangled hand back down to his side. When he stood still, the reptilian quality of movement wasn't so pronounced. He looked almost human. "He smoked Lucky Strikes, and often took a shot of Jack Daniel's before going on a 'mission.' To find the truth. Not because people deserved to know, but because he *wanted* to know. To lift the veil."

Her shoulders dropped. She reached, meaning to push Josiah's hand with the gun down. Josiah took a half step away, subtly moving forward. He was, she realized, trying to get between her and the other man.

Her heart hurt, a swift flash of pain. "Josiah—"

"I'm a little harder to convince." Josiah's eyes were locked with the other man's. "You *bit* me, you son of a bitch."

"It was necessary. Put the gun down. It will wake someone, if you fire."

The tension in the air ratcheted up another notch. Then it snapped, and Josiah lowered the gun. He cast a swift look at Anna, as if gauging her reliability. Now she saw a thin trickle of blood threading down his collarbone, vanishing into his dark sweater. Her head started to feel very light, and a rushing sound filled her ears.

"Her pulse has increased." Dry, academic, the pale man made no movement. "She may swoon."

I have never fainted in my life. I'm not about to start now, dammit. She struggled for self-control, won by a bare thread. "I will not. Come on, Josiah. Please."

Josiah didn't look convinced. He was wearing his stubborn expression, the one he used to use often during fights, his voice growing calmer and softer as Anna's rose higher and sharper. "He *bit* me."

"He's on Eric's side. I wonder if the ring's in the post office box?" As soon as she said it, Josiah cast her a withering look, and she realized she probably shouldn't have mentioned that little tidbit.

The second man said nothing, but Josiah slid his gun back into his shoulder holster and reached over to take the one from Anna's nerveless fingers. "Give me that." His eyes never left the other man. "All right. Anna, dig in that bag over there, the black one, and bring me the first-aid kit. You, Christopher, whoever you are, sit down there, at the table. And you better start talking. None of this is making any goddamn sense."

"Here is something that does make sense, then. There is a brownstone building, at 1487 East Morris Street. The rich and powerful of this city go there for injections that make them younger." Christopher padded soundlessly across the carpet with his mutilated feet, brushing past Josiah, who stepped gracefully aside and turned on his heel—at least *he* had his shoes on—to keep him in sight. The thin man folded himself down in one of the two cheap chairs. "The fools are after immortality."

Anna paused. Their luggage was between the two beds, and

she saw the little black bag. "Immortality?" She sounded like she'd been kicked in the stomach; she was having a little trouble breathing. Her head suddenly hurt, a sharp pain to match the one in her chest. "But that's...it's impossible."

"It isn't as difficult as you might think. But they have gone about it the wrong way." Christopher pushed up his tattered sleeve, his mangled hand having a little trouble with the fabric.

Scored into his arm were track marks, hideous ropes and tunnels of scarring. "These will fade," he said quietly. "They had trouble finding a vein, near the end; I was running dry. Like a well. Despite bleeding me from arteries in my fingers, and hobbling my feet with less care than a horse's. Your brother, fair Anne, may never have believed I could escape, even with the service he did me of loosening my bonds."

"Jesus God." Anna's left hand clamped over her mouth again. Her stomach rose in revolt; she pushed it down with an effort of will.

"Immortality?" Josiah sank down on the bed Anna had slept in. She couldn't see the bleeding side of his throat, and she knew she should bring him the first-aid kit. But she stayed where she was, staring at the ruin of Christopher's arm. How many needles had poked and probed there? To take blood?

A shiver ran from her heels to her scalp, an electric zing. *Jesus. This is insane. Completely, totally insane.*

"Yes." Christopher's face was suddenly entirely human, under the ropes of greasy hair. "They are convinced they've found a way to have it without the Thirst. Now they have only what they have managed to hoard, and are desperately seeking to repossess the fount of their newfound good health." He smiled, a grin that carefully didn't show the tips of his canines but was nonetheless wide and feral.

Josiah gained his feet in a single galvanic movement. "The file is right there on the table next to you," he said, just as quietly. "All the information Eric managed to gather, unless there's more hidden in the post office box. I assume moving around after dawn is going to be a problem for you."

"In my current state, yes." The dark eyes flicked past Josiah, rested on her. "She looks ill, and her pulse is still high. Dangerously high."

"I'm all right." To prove it, Anna opened the black bag and started rooting around in it for a first-aid kit. There were clips of ammunition, heavy and clicking against each other as she pushed them aside, and that made her feel even woozier. *Don't you dare throw up, or faint, or do anything stupid.* "I'm fine."

"Don't lie." Josiah was suddenly looming over her. He held out a hand, she took it, and he pulled her to her feet only to push her down to sit on the tangled bed. Now she could see the wounded side of his throat. The trickle of blood came from two punctures, neat and aesthetic, over the jugular.

She stared at them and swallowed dryly.

Josiah untangled his fingers from hers, but not without a reassuring squeeze. He gave her a tight smile, too, one that didn't light his eyes. "What about the other assholes, the ones who turned to dust?"

"Dust?" Christopher cocked his head. "Ah. So they *were* trying the gene therapy. I wondered why they wanted bone marrow."

"Gene therapy." Josiah dug in the little black bag, coming up with the first-aid kit in a matter of seconds. "Holy Christ. This hurts."

"My apologies. You are a canny adversary, for a mortal."

"Do me a favor and *don't* say things like that." Josiah set the small blue plastic box on the bed next to her, then did a strange thing. He half-bent over, cupping Anna's face in his hands. His palms were hard and warm. "Anna? Baby, you okay?"

His eyes were green again, deep enough to drown in, and very close to hers. He searched her face, almost nose-to-nose; she saw the faint scar at the end of his right eyebrow and the flecks of gold in his irises. This close, she could see other long-healed scars and the beginnings of crows' feet at the corners of his eyes. He wasn't a young man, really.

Not anymore.

"I think I'm all right." To her immense relief, her voice didn't tremble. "Just a little…shaken. That's all."

"That's my girl." His smile was genuine, even if tight. He leaned forward, kissed her forehead. It was odd, he had gone so long without touching her, and it still felt as natural and welcome as it ever had. "You just keep breathing, and we'll get through this. Okay?"

She stopped herself from nodding just in time. If she moved, she would dislodge his hands, and she didn't want that. The warm touch made the spinning nausea lessen a bit. "You're taking this really well," she muttered, and watched his eyes light up for a moment with genuine amusement.

"When you've ruled out the impossible, whatever remains, however improbable…" His thumb stroked her cheekbone, a light feathering touch. "Don't worry. Everything's under control."

Her chest still hurt, but it was a sweet pain. She bit her lip and wished she hadn't, because his gaze dropped to her mouth and his smile widened just a little, before vanishing entirely. Josiah gave her another soft, almost platonic kiss on her forehead and straightened, the wound on his neck still trickling a thin thread of blood. *He's bleeding, and he's still taking time to make sure I'm all right.* She had to swallow twice, looking down at her hands clasped in her lap. The next thought was completely unexpected, and it hurt even more.

I should never have left him. No matter what he is.

Was she a complete and utter hypocrite now, or had she been one then? Or both?

Josiah flipped open the first-aid kit and found a package of sticking plasters. "All right, Christopher. Start talking."

"You may call me Kit. And you are?"

Josiah's eyebrows drew together. It was his *I-am-dealing-with-an-idiot* look, the one he used to use with dimwit waiters or shop clerks who tried to overcharge her. It usually appeared right before he intervened with a quiet word and a significant glare, and oddly enough, it made everything about this madness seem…well, manageable.

At least he didn't let out one of his maddeningly dry, ironic observations. "It's Wolfe. Now let's get down to business. Take it from the beginning, and don't leave anything out."

Chapter Nineteen

Josiah's stomach felt like someone had tipped a bucket of worms in. The bite on his throat burned fiercely, as if already infected. Just what he needed. "So the gene-therapy ones are the ones that turned into dust?"

"They are trying to re-create me, without much success." The mangled man leaned back in the chair, his chalk-white face drawn thin and tight. His lips were so pale they were almost blue, just like a drowned, frozen corpse. "Your bullets affected them because they are young, and only pale copies of a true...well, still mostly human, after all. The gene therapy stresses their physical structure. Makes it unstable. So, a sudden shock—a bullet, a knife wound, a broken bone—introduced a fatal chain reaction."

Anna still sat cross-legged on the bed, half-turned to face Kit. She was heartbreakingly pale, and he began to wish he hadn't given her the sedative to help her sleep. But she'd needed dreamless rest.

Probably still did.

She stared at the man, who sat with his mutilated fingers

quietly in his narrow lap, his broken feet lying obediently together on the floor. He perched, motionless as a cat, having glanced through the files with apparent interest and absorption. Josiah got the idea his ears might twitch at any untoward sound. Anna's gaze was intent and troubled, a slight vertical line between her eyebrows as if the man were a painting she wanted to pay special attention to. She had sometimes studied Josiah like that, usually with her mouth slightly full from a kiss and a wondering intensity filling her beautiful eyes.

He didn't like her looking at someone else like that, giving her whole attention, her hair slightly mussed and begging for a man's fingers to straighten it. When Josiah spoke, his tone alarmed even himself—combative, and just slightly disdainful. "So poof. They turn into dust. What about the mayor, the chief of police? When the injections stop, what happens?"

Kit shrugged. "They will age rapidly. Their own cellular structure has been stressed, and without the stabilization of more infusions they will deteriorate." He paused, thoughtfully. "It is not a pleasant death."

"How do you know?" Josiah found his fingertips resting on the bandage on his throat. Made his hand fall back to his side. Kit's face didn't change, but Josiah had the sudden sense that he smirked.

Anna still stared at the man, biting her lower lip slightly. Her pale silence filled the spaces between their words, as if she was trying to speak.

"It has been tried before. There are those who crave to be as I am."

I'll just bet. "How many of you are there?"

This made Kit cock his head slightly. "It is," he said very softly, "safer for you not to know." For a moment his eyes glittered, a flash of red like a badly taken photo, and Josiah could have sworn his canine teeth lengthened just a little. The two puncture marks on his throat throbbed.

Forget it. I have a better question. "How did they find me?"

"If they have a sample of Eric's blood, tracking fair Anne would not be difficult. Kinship has its own scent, and the living leave it everywhere."

Great. Which means no place is safe for more than a day or so. "How long does it take them to track—"

Kit shook his head. The greasy ropes of his hair moved like fat snakes. "I have confused her trail, for the time being. Consider it a gift."

Right. Great. A gift. Josiah had to restrain the sarcasm, and that wasn't a good sign.

The freak was strong. Inhumanly quick, as well. By all rights, Kit should have been a corpse on the floor. There weren't many people who could tangle with Josiah and walk away breathing. But this…thing…had not only overpowered Josiah, he'd done it easily and *bitten* him as well, right on the goddamn neck. Bitten him and held him pinned against the wall as effortlessly as Josiah might hold Anna, as easily as he might hold a child.

And the sonofabitching bite *hurt*. Red-hot needles drilling into the skin, and a tender soreness swelling around the spot.

He didn't want to think much about that. His head was only provisionally clear at the moment. Josiah suspected that in a couple of hours he was going to have some very unpleasant mental messiness. His wrist ached, too, and his knuckles. Not to mention his legs. And his shoulders. A dull heavy pain, as if he'd had a hard workout. The stress was catching up with him. "So we fetch your ring, and you what? Go on your merry blood-sucking way?" Something inside his head that strangely enough had Anna's voice was trying to tell him to calm down. He wasn't handling this right.

Kit's eyes didn't flame with red again. They merely narrowed. "Then I return to the place of my captivity and raze it to the ground."

The way he said it, it sounded almost doable.

"Wait a minute." Anna held up her hand like a fifth grader uncertain of the answer but willing to give it a try. "*If* Eric even managed to get his hands on the ring. If it's in the post office box. What is this ring, anyway?"

"It is mine." Kit's eyes didn't flash red, but his voice dropped a few chill degrees. "And it is to your profit to aid me. If those who sought to use me are dead, fair Anne, you are safe. And your brother may rest avenged."

Josiah swallowed a derisive laugh. *That's one way of looking at it.* "Still not a good deal for us. You could take your ring and disappear, leaving me with the whole mess." *I'll bet Chilwell would love to get his hands on you. The agency would, too. You would be solid gold for them, an unstoppable agent only vulnerable to…what? Sunlight? Silver? Garlic? Crosses? I don't know nearly enough about you, friend.* He couldn't stop staring at the missing fingers and the blue corpse lips, the eerie immobility and the skeletal thinness. Kit's knees were knobs and his elbows bigger than his biceps, but he'd held Josiah up off the ground with one hand. With no discernible effort at all.

Kit didn't answer. He sat still in the chair, his head tilted just so, and his eyelids dropped halfway. Underneath the heavy hooding his dark eyes turned flat and sleepy, his attention turning inward. A slow rattling hiss sounded in his narrow chest.

The world slowed down, every motion wrapped in syrup.

Great. Now I'm going to have a dead body in this room to handle. If I can kill him. His hand jerked toward his shoulder holster. Anna gasped.

In the next eye blink Kit was suddenly *there,* his cold, marred hand clamped tight around Josiah's. "Stop," he hissed, chill breath tickling Josiah's nose. It reeked of dirt and chill open air, instead of the normal sourness of a human mouth. "Listen. My hunger for vengeance has kept you alive. You are useful to me as you are, do not force me to kill you." A slow, meditative pause. "Or worse."

"*Stop* it." Anna didn't shout, but it was damn close. "Just *stop,* both of you!" The springs creaked as she bounced up off the bed.

NO! Goddammit, Anna, stay still!

The creature's gaze bored into Josiah's, crimson streaks revolving in their depths. Anna padded closer, and Josiah's world narrowed with each step. "Stop," she repeated, quietly but firmly. "Snarling at each other isn't going to help anything." Her hand touched Josiah's shoulder, and he could feel the trembling going through her, a high fine voltage of fear. Was she also touching the other man?

Anna, for Christ's sake, get away from him. He couldn't make the words come out; his mouth was dry and his throat closed up. Looking down would mean submitting, and Josiah was pretty sure it wouldn't be a very good idea to show this son of a bitch any weakness.

"Please." Anna's voice started to tremble. "Please, both of you. Stop it."

Kit looked away first. He made a swift movement, pushing Anna so she stumbled. Josiah half-turned to catch her, his left hand blurring out instinctively. Between one blink and the next, the slim, pale man was at the door. His distorted hands had curled into fists, and as Josiah pushed Anna behind him, hearing her trip over a suitcase full of clothes, Kit's canine teeth stretched with a slight crackling sound, curving viciously down into the bloodless lower lip.

Oh, Jesus Christ. He leveled the gun and tried to tell his hands to stop shaking. Anna let out a short cry of surprise, choked off halfway as she fell, banging into something on the way down.

Kit was trembling, too. His face had become feral, contorted with rage; he bared the rest of his teeth and hissed with a reptilian twitch. A thin trickle of sweat slid down Josiah's back, tickling.

If he comes for us he'll kill us both, but he's going to have to take me first. That might give her a chance to get away, to run.

The door opened. Josiah caught a slice of fog pressing between the lights out in the parking lot, having crept in on little cat feet during all the fun and games. The door swept closed, and he let out a long shaking breath before bolting across the room to lock it, almost skidding to a stop in his boots. It wouldn't do much goddamn good, but it made him feel a hell of a lot better.

His eyes glued themselves shut. "Fuck," he whispered, and began to curse methodically, in a monotone-whispered rosary. In every language he knew.

Little soft sounds told him Anna was struggling to her feet. Josiah braced himself against the door, his arm bent and the cool metal of the gun pressing his fevered forehead. *Think, goddamn you, Anna's in here and she needs you to think. There is no alternative.*

The first answer was the easiest, an immediate change of

scenery. *Rule one—when a hole is blown, the agent moves, especially a liquidator.*

She was exhausted, he wasn't much better, and they'd been clean coming here. A corpse with superhuman strength finding them wasn't like being found by any enemy he'd ever dealt with. And *how* on God's green earth had it found them? By *smelling* her relationship to Eric? Blood thicker than water, and all that.

He said he's confused the trail. God. Dear God.

The bite on his neck twinged unpleasantly. He held the cool metal against his forehead until it warmed up, gathering himself.

Logic. Think about this logically.

Only there was no logic to the game. It just kept getting more and more fucked-up-weird at every turn.

"Josiah?" She sounded uncertain. "What do we do now?"

She doesn't know what the hell, and she thinks you have a plan up your sleeve. Great. "Did he hurt you?" His voice didn't shake. That was good. He opened his eyes, lowered the gun, and looked back at the hotel room.

She stood at the end of the bed, her hair even more mussed, her eyes wide. She wasn't panicked yet, thank God. "Hurt me? He *bit* you, for God's sake!"

"That he did." *I sound calm.* "Did he hurt *you*?"

"I guess not. I fell, though. My back is never going to forgive me, and my ankle seems to be swelling again." She took a step forward, winced as her ankle buckled.

He reholstered the gun. "Do you want another pill?"

She shuddered, visibly. "The last thing I want is to be drugged and helpless if *he* comes back. Or more of *them*." Her arms came up; she hugged herself, blinking. Her eyes shone.

A single, glittering tear slid down her unbruised cheek, slowly, while he watched.

Oh, Christ. It took him six steps, but he reached her and took her in his arms, helpless not to. He buried his face in her hair and inhaled, suddenly aware of the thing that bothered him the most about the corpse-man.

Kit didn't *smell* human. *She* did, gloriously so, and it called up memories of lazy mornings spent in bed, of lifting up her long mane and kissing her nape, surrounded by *her,* without any perfume.

She was *home.* Warm skin and softness, a safe haven.

Like heaven, as a matter of fact.

Josiah threaded his fingers through her hair, pulled her closer. And closer still. The marks on his neck settled into an even, persistent throbbing, easy enough to ignore. The other throbbing, down low, wasn't easy to ignore at all. "I'm pretty sure I'm still sane." He kissed her hair. "I feel sane. This feels sane."

"You saw what I saw, right?" Her voice was muffled in his chest. "Long teeth. Glowing eyes. And he moved—"

"Don't think about it. Just don't think about that right now." The feeling of the world tilting sideways slid through him in waves. If he didn't let go of her immediately he was going to do something he'd regret.

He held on. Kissed the top of her head again. Then, wonder of wonders, she tilted her head back, as if trying to get free. Her arms came up, and the next thing he knew she had tangled her fingers in his hair and pulled his head down.

Their mouths met. It had been too long, but he hadn't forgotten. How could he, when she was pure sugared heat, when his skin suddenly felt too tight and all he could think of was getting every thin layer of fabric out of the way and getting closer to her? Close as he could.

She was ripe, and she was willing, and he was the lowest bastard on the face of the earth to even *think* about taking advantage of the situation.

As many times as I want. And you'll act like you like it.

Was that what she was doing? She pressed against him, and the slight movement drove every sensible consideration out of his head. Anna had always done that, gone through his nerves just like a drug and robbed him of careful control. It had all been over from the moment she looked up from her sketchpad and grinned at him.

He kissed her greedily, even as his fingers curled around her shoulders and he slowly, gently, pushed her away. It took some doing, especially since his entire body protested.

Protested? No. Screamed in agony, demanding her. She was battered and bruised, and if there was any justice in the world she should never have had to suffer this. She should be with a normal man, with a house in the suburbs or a penthouse suite with enough art materials to keep her happy and busy for a very long time. In a safe, *sane* world where there was no place for a man like Josiah Wolfe *or* this fucked-up situation.

Anna made a small surprised sound as their mouths broke contact. Her breathing came light and quick; his was harsh but just as fast. He sounded like he had just finished a four-minute mile. He made one last grab for the good angel sitting on his shoulder, the anemic barely used one.

"No." He barely managed to get the word out through the gravel in his throat. The bite on his throat pulsed hotly, echoing that other pulse. It was normal, actually. Getting close to death, being terrified, always made the human animal want a little heat.

A little? Hell no. He wanted all the heat she had to share.

Her lips were slightly swollen, and he cursed himself again for not being gentler with her. Anna blinked, with the heavy-lidded look she wore after a particularly intense make-out session. He felt like a teenager again, sneaking a few sweating minutes behind the gym with a cheerleader too desirable to be a mortal creature.

Mortal. The sensation of ice cubes trickling down his back managed to bring him back to himself. "No." He repeated it, but he didn't sound any surer the second time. "You'd better… rest. You'd better get some rest."

The flash of hurt in her eyes was a knife to his heart. "I thought you wanted…" She trailed off, her shoulders slumping.

You have no idea how much I want. "I do. But you need rest." *There. I'm being decent, see? I'm being a good boy.*

"I don't want it." Stubborn, her chin lifted just a little. She reached up to touch him, and he had to straighten his arms to keep her away. He'd had daydreams about her touching him again. None of them had ever felt this good. "Josiah. I don't *want* to rest."

Be a good boy, Jo. Then go take an ice bath. "You have to. You'll be no good tomorrow if you don't."

"I don't care." Another tear spilled out, glittering in the warm electric light. This one tracked down her bruised cheek. He had to turn the light off soon, and take another look at that parking lot. Keep watch.

But she leaned forward in his hands, as if she wanted to touch him as badly as he wanted to touch her. "Please. Josiah."

Oh, Jesus. God help me. Please, God, help me. His fingers loosened. She pushed forward, into his arms again as if she were coming home. She ran her fingers over his cheekbone, down the stubbled rasp of his jaw, almost touched the plaster over the aching wound. He caught her hand, and the movement broke all stasis. His mouth met hers again, and he was lost; his only thought was to get his sweater off, and hers. The backs of her knees hit the tangled bed, and they went down, her fingers working at the button to his jeans. He had enough presence of mind to lay the gun on the nightstand before he descended into red haze, and it was every bit as good as he remembered.

Chapter Twenty

The next day dawned foggy and turned into rain splatting dully against the windshield as Josiah drove. The windshield wipers beat irregular time, and Anna kept sneaking glances at his profile. He hadn't said much, but he certainly looked a little happier. Which was nice, but Anna's entire body ached, and she had to be careful even with limping. Her ankle hurt like hell, and her back was a solid bar of pain. Plus, she was hungry, and she needed coffee.

Still, she couldn't help smiling a little. It had been a long time, and he was just as careful and sweet as ever.

Even the thought that he might just consider it payment couldn't dampen the first halfway decent mood she'd had since finding her brother dead in his office.

The thought of Eric dispelled all trace of even that faint pleasure. She slumped in the seat, watching newly strange buildings pass by outside the windows. The city she'd lived in since beginning college now looked like a leering mask over a twisted, unfamiliar face.

Even fresh clothes and an oblong white painkiller—*be careful with these, I've only got a few,* Josiah had said with a smile, before he ruffled her hair the way he used to and went off whistling to the bathroom—didn't stop the way her heart hurt whenever Eric's battered face rose in front of her.

Why hadn't he told her? If he had, would she have believed him, or signed him up for the rubber room?

She could just imagine the conversation. *Sis, I've got a contact. He's nocturnal, has blue lips, let's not even talk about the teeth! Oh, and he lives on blood. Got any silver bullets? Maybe a crucifix?*

She liked to think that she would have believed him. She'd believed him about everything else since their parents had died. Eric had worked two jobs, attending night school and getting the job at the *Post* even though he was talented enough to get a spot on a New York paper, or something way more secure. New York wasn't safe for kids, as he often pointed out. *And you're a kid, dearest sis.*

Why hadn't he *told* her? Trying to protect her, again?

She carried the unfinished letter from the file, tucked into her purse. Eric's last words to her.

Just get out and go. I love you.

Not even a memorial service, because she had to hide. The police, if what she was hearing was any indication, didn't want to look too closely into this. Whoever wanted to…use…that creature Kit had stolen her brother, and the life her brother could have lived—who knew, maybe even a Pulitzer; that had been his cherished dream. He had a lot of dreams, like settling down with someone special and maybe breaking a huge story or two.

All of them were gone now. Finally, irrevocably gone.

"You're quiet." Josiah hit his turn signal and turned left on Greenboro. They were very close to the post office, and he was going to circle the block once or twice to make sure they were, in his terms, "clean."

I don't know if I'll ever feel clean again. "Thinking." She stared at the sidewalks, full of umbrellas and hooded jackets, the occasional bareheaded person, hats bobbing up and down. The hard, cold feeling in her chest was new. She had never felt dangerous before.

"About?" He sounded only mildly curious. This politeness between them was new, brittle and fragile and full of things left unsaid. Had last night been payment? After seeing something no rational person would admit existed, they had clutched at each other like shipwreck survivors. He had two round little sticking plasters over the wounds on his neck; she'd watched him apply them this morning.

The two little rounds did more than anything else to unsettle her. She could have comfortably consigned last night to a particularly bad and vivid dream if they weren't there glaring at her, clearly visible proof. She couldn't even pretend Josiah had nicked himself shaving.

"About Eric." She swallowed the lump in her throat. *What the hell, what can it matter now? I might as well say it.* "He didn't tell me, you know."

"What?" Josiah checked traffic, took a right on Fortieth.

"Eric didn't tell me about you."

"Huh."

Damn the man, did he have to pick *now* to get all male and grunt? "I found the file. I was looking through his safe for my birth certificate, I wanted to get my passport renewed before we...before we eloped, so maybe I could go with you on some of your trips. I found the file. I don't know how long it had been in there. He didn't tell me."

"Is that so." Even, unsurprised. His profile didn't change, clean and nondescript, handsome in his own unremarkable way. His irises didn't lighten, either. He looked completely unmoved.

So she kept going. Might as well tell him the whole thing. "I went to see him after I left your place."

"After you dumped me." A small, precise correction. He touched the brakes. They passed the post office, a large granite block built in the fifties. People marched up the steps, marched down; the bus stop in front was packed with people huddled in the flimsy shelter. She craned her neck to stare as they rolled past, looking for anything out of the ordinary.

If she kept looking out the window, she might be able to keep discussing it as if it didn't matter. "Yes. After. He told me I was an idiot. He was furious with me for taking the file. He also told me that when I was with you he didn't worry so much, but now he was going to have to start worrying all over again."

"An implicit vote of confidence." Josiah didn't take his eyes from the road, and she had a sudden intense longing to *shake* him, to make him react. This calmness was infuriating.

She took a deep breath, stared at the rivulets of water sliding down the windshield as they reached the end of the block and Josiah hit the turn signal again. Her mouth burned with the memory of his lips on hers, and a few other places on her body twinged. Last night she hadn't cared about her back or her ankle. This morning, however, she wished she hadn't been quite so athletic. "I want whoever killed him to die, Josiah."

Did she imagine it, or did he take in a short, soft breath? "If I get you out of this without any more bruises it'll be a miracle. It will be an even bigger miracle if neither of us comes down with a serious case of lead poisoning. I am *not* in this for revenge, goddammit."

"Then what are you in for? You told me that if I paid you, you'd kill whoever killed Eric." Her jaw set stubbornly, aching. *Why am I doing this? I know better than to push him when he's like this.* Miserably compelled, she forged ahead. "*You* made the deal, not me."

"That's not quite what I said. Seriously, Anna." He turned again, circling the block, his eyes light blue now, piercing as he looked through the windshield, scanning. His knuckles were white. "Now is *not* the time."

"Then when? We haven't exactly had a lot of time for discussion lately, in case you haven't noticed." She shifted in the seat, easing her back slightly. The painkiller he'd given her was beginning to work, blunting the pain. The welcome relief didn't bring relaxation in its wake, though.

"If it would bring Eric back for you I'd get my hands on some Semtex and a freelance backup crew and blow up half this fucking city. But it *won't*. This is bigger than either of us thought. That nice polite man we met yesterday, in the restaurant? If he thinks he can get his hands on that thing we saw last night, we'll never see the light of day again. If that thing comes back and we don't have whatever he thinks Eric was holding for him, it could get even uglier." He took a deep breath. The windshield wipers went back and forth. "The cops are looking for us, and yesterday I pulled the resident organized-crime syndicate's tail so hard they're probably cursing my name in between trips to Wal-Mart to buy more ammunition. I have *no* backup, little gear, and you to look out for. Liquidation isn't my primary objective on this run, Anna. Keeping your ass in one piece *is*."

Well, isn't that a compliment. "So you enjoyed yourself?"

"I forgot how temperamental you can be." He took one hand from the wheel, ran it back through his dark hair, and sighed. "Of course I fucking enjoyed myself. That's never been the problem. The problem is, you clutter up my goddamn head and twist me around so hard I don't know whether I'm coming or going. And if I don't think clearly, we are *both* going to end up dead."

"You promised." She couldn't help herself. *Life's not fair, Anna,* Eric had repeated over and over again. Still, the injustice of it filled her eyes and her throat at the same time.

"Even if I *had* promised, I wouldn't do it. Not as things stand now." By this time they had completed another circuit of the block, and he whipped neatly into a parking garage across the street from the post office. He rolled his window down and took the ticket from the machine, glancing up as if to reassure himself. Anna looked up, too, and saw a security camera aimed right at the car. "Don't worry, it's not loaded." Josiah's tone held a great deal of dry humor. "That's why I chose this place; the cameras here are fakes." He crept through the garage until he found a spot that seemed to satisfy him, and cut the wheel hard, pulling into it.

"I want whoever killed Eric to answer for it," she repeated, searching for the words to make him see, make him understand. "He was my brother. He was all I had."

"He was not all you had. Give me the key." He reached over and actually took her purse. She grabbed for it, but he was too quick. "Relax, I'm not going to die of embarrassment if I find tampons in here, for God's sake." Paper rustled, and he had the key that had been tucked into the second copy of the file. "Now, one last time. You're going to stay here. You're going to wait for me. You will not get out of this car for any reason. Is that perfectly, completely clear?"

She stared at his profile. His gaze kept flicking over the dripping cars waiting silently for their masters to return. An elevator sign glowed next to a fire exit stairwell; a small sign proclaiming 2 and STAIRS was painted next to an unprepossessing door laden with layers and layers of chipped yellow paint.

I am not going to just sit here. To hell with that. "What if you don't come back?"

"Then I'm dead and they'll scoop you up in a matter of minutes too. Don't worry so much; we're clean and nobody knows about the post office box, or they would have already dangled the ring in front of Dead Boy like a worm on a hook. I want to hear you say it. Tell me you're going to stay here and not get out of this car for any reason."

Fine. "I'll stay here." She tried not to sound sulky.

"Good girl." He did look at her then, his hair falling across his forehead and faint dark circles smudged under his eyes. They had darkened a bit, the hazel turning deeper. He wore a little armor-clad half smile. "Work on decoding that file. I'll be back in two shakes."

"Exactly how long is two shakes?"

"Temper, temper." He reached for the door handle, paused. Turned back to her. "Anna."

Oh, for Christ's sake. Her eyes were full, and she was sure there was a box of Kleenex in the back. She wanted him to get out and get away so she could blow her nose, at least. Why was she such a weeping idiot?

"Eric wanted me to take care of you. That's what I'm going to do. I don't know why he didn't call me, but it doesn't matter. He wasn't all you had." The door creaked as he yanked savagely on the handle and pushed it open, almost smashing a dent into the red SUV parked next door. "You have me."

With that he was gone, the door slamming, and she watched him walk quickly to the entrance to the stairs. Fluorescent light glinted in his dark hair, and he moved gracefully, with a smooth economy of motion—and a little bounce in his step that hadn't been there yesterday.

"For fuck's sake," Anna whispered, as the yellow fire escape door closed behind him. She swallowed the tears, and looked at the ignition. Today he'd taken the keys with him. Her hands ached for paper and pencil, just long enough to draw something to steady her mind a little.

She stared at the steering column for a long minute. It felt like an hour. When she lifted her head, silent rows of parked cars mocked her. Eric's apartment was less than eight blocks from here.

The church of St. Simeon was twelve.

What are you thinking, Anna?

Her hand stole toward the door handle, dropped to her side. Staying with Josiah was her safest bet, true. He'd just admitted he wasn't likely to do anything more than just get her out of town safely. There was no "profit" in revenge.

Really, that was the best course of action, wasn't it? Getting out with her life was seeming more and more like the most she could hope for.

Two left feet and a brain full of glitter. Run away and hide, little Annie.

She'd always counted on Eric to make things better. Now she was counting on Josiah. She might get out of this alive, sure.

Would she be able to look herself in the mirror if she did, though?

What's really bothering me? Other than her brother dead and her own frantic running away and whining? Well, a lot of uncomfortable things she hadn't had any chance to voice or even think about too deeply.

The deepest of them, a half-formed, nagging little suspicion, suddenly became a full-fledged certainty. Whatever "agency" the narrow little man in the restaurant worked for probably wouldn't care much about the truth surfacing. If they were a government agency, the potential use for someone with Kit's abilities would be staggering. What if the government itself locked Kit away underground and bled him dry? Instead of a mayor and a chief of police getting younger—and the pictures Eric had snapped were thought-provoking, to say the least—there could be a President getting younger, or Chiefs of Staff. The effect of Kit's blood could be bargained to the military or even foreign countries, the "gene therapy" used to create supersoldiers, and Eric, wherever he was now, would throw up his hands in disgust.

To find the truth. Not because people deserved to know, but because he wanted *to know. To lift the veil.*

That had been most of it. Eric had also wanted to make things *right*. It was why he'd gone to Guatemala, why he'd broken the big corruption story eighteen months ago that ushered Denton into office.

Now it was up to her.

Not so incidentally, what would stop Josiah from giving this "agency" the truth, as unbelievable as it was? He had the marks on his throat and the file as proof. More proof was probably in this brownstone everyone was talking about.

Take the chain of logic one step further, Anna. That thing bit him. What if he's somehow infected? They could take him, too, just to find out. That's probably already occurred to Josiah. He's smart enough. This isn't a good position for him to be in.

He could get hurt. We already know these people shoot to kill.

Her hand crept out again. Rested on the door handle. How many exits did this place have? Also, could she walk for a while without getting noticed? The painkiller was a good one, and her head was starting to get a little blurry. Her ankle hurt, and she was limping badly, but if she walked slowly...

He told you to stay here. He's done everything he can for you so far, up to and including falling back into bed with you. Which was your own idea, Anna, even if he did make it an explicit condition of his helping you.

Would Eric still be alive now if she hadn't found the file and hurried off to punish Josiah? Would Eric have come to Josiah and maybe gotten some protection or at least some good advice if they'd still been involved?

Would Josiah have eventually told her everything?

Quit dithering. It's time for you to take some action. Eric is depending on you to see this thing gets out, not just swept under the carpet. Josiah also might get himself hurt or worse if this went any further. She *had* to do something.

Eric had done what was right all his life, no matter the consequences or the cost. Now it was Anna's turn.

She pushed the door lock open. Josiah would be back soon, depending on how quickly he could cross the street and get into the post office.

"Come on," she whispered. "It's not so hard. You just get out of the car and start walking."

Here was safe, though. Doing what he told her was *safe*. Or at least, safer than anything she had in mind.

Safer for *her*, but what about for Josiah?

The vision of Eric's battered, swollen face rose up in front of her again, so vividly she let out a small hurt sound. Her fingers curled around the door handle.

What makes you think this idiotic, stupid, crazy plan will work?

It had to. As much as Anna needed revenge, the creature called Kit seemed to need it even more. She didn't think for a moment that *he* was hampered by any of Josiah's sudden caution, either. Not to mention, he was probably a lot less likely to end up...dead.

Maybe he's already dead, in which case it's all academic, right? He won't even be there, Anna. Come on. You're being stupid. If this was a horror movie you'd be shouting, "Don't do it!" at the screen right now. It's idiotic.

Her fingers curled around the door handle. She pulled. With a loud, decisive click, the latch released. She only had to push the door open and wriggle out, since Josiah had parked next to an old black Jeep that had apparently been piloted into its space by a drunkard.

Don't do it, Anna. Don't.

Anna told the little voice of cowardice inside her head to shut the fuck up, and pushed the car door open.

Rain drummed against the windows, a steady, monotonous sound underscoring soft chanting. Some form of service was in session. Mom had been a lapsed Catholic, Dad a Presbyterian, and Eric an atheist almost to a fault, so Anna had rarely ever been in a church except for a few weddings and funerals. The ranks of candles, the wooden pews, and the soft hushed singing from the choir loft as a robed priest lifted something above his head all made her dizzy. Not to mention the heavy, cloying incense and the echoing space inside the cathedral. Her hair dripped and the new boots squeaked a little as she edged along the wall, hoping nobody would notice a half-drowned artist. The coat Josiah had bought for her had shed most of the water, but her jeans were wet almost to the knee.

St. Simeon was a towering pile of faux-crenellated stone, and even though there was no sunlight to make them burn, the stained-glass windows were comforting. She moved aside, into a windowless narrow room holding small statues in niches behind racks of candles, some lit, some not; she came to a halt in front of a small wooden Madonna and Child varnished with dark age.

The Madonna's face was kind, and under the layers of darkness her blue robe could still be seen. She was perfectly proportioned, too. Chipped, beaten, repainted, and obviously antique, the Mother of God looked right through anyone standing before her, jotting down and forgiving each human frailty.

A small box of white matches crouched in a little wrought-iron holder, hanging below the rack of candles. Anna took one with trembling fingers.

It's daylight. Even if he's here, which I seriously doubt, what am I going to do? Besides, shouldn't he not be able to come into a church? Not to mention that he was supposed to meet Eric here how long ago? This isn't going to work. He won't be here, and I'll…Jesus, I'll do what? What can I do?

I'll figure out something.

The match lit with a sizzle when she held it in a candle flame. She lit a short white candle, for Eric. Thought about it, lit one for Josiah. Then, before the match burned her fingers, she lit a third.

It certainly couldn't hurt.

She shook the match out, grimacing, and dropped it in the little jug set aside for the purpose. The singing wound to a soft close, and a quiet, flat voice in her ear startled her.

"Did you come here to pray?"

She jumped, and might have fallen into the candle rack if his mutilated hand hadn't closed around her arm. The grip was like a vise, and she looked up into weary, dark eyes with no trace of red.

He examined her, then cast a glance around the small room. "Where is your protector, fair Anne?"

Relief boiled up inside her. Relief, and fresh terror. *I didn't think this out very well, did I.* "I...he has the key. He's getting the ring. I came here." Her throat was parched dry, despite rainwater dripping from her hair and clothes. "Aren't you supposed to be—"

"Lying in a grave, appearing dead instead of passing my time in a papist church? Sanctified ground is not my enemy, and I had too much of sleep in my captivity." He let go of her arm. His cheeks were flushed with unhealthy fever, and his hair was no longer as stringy and greasy. The livid scars on his neck and face were also rubescent, as was his mangled hand. All in all he looked much less like a corpse and much more like...a fresh corpse. Not much of an improvement. "I must apologize. I did not...last night, I almost did what I should not."

I really wish I had some sort of idea what to say. "Oh, that's all right." Rain dripped from her hair. She studied him, he examined her, and the silence was full of small, sharp things. The singing intensified, and there was the sound of shuffling as people got to their feet. "I wanted to talk to you. Is it...can we go somewhere?"

"Not until dark. Not while I am as you see me." Kit shifted

his weight slightly, leaning back. He was still barefoot, and she wondered why nobody noticed a barefoot dreadlocked man with missing fingers and toes in here.

"Don't you need shoes or something?" *Why am I whispering?* Her voice shook, but no more than it had lately. "You look cold."

He shrugged. The torn sleeve of his black T-shirt flapped, and she caught a glimpse of the horrible track marks underneath. "Why are you here?"

Here goes nothing. Her ankle almost rolled as she straightened, her lower back creaking. "I want whoever killed Eric to…to face the consequences."

That was good for a long fifteen seconds or so of silence, during which Kit stared at her. His gaze ran down her body and back up, and Anna shivered. It was like being eyed by a shark. "And your canny young man?"

Canny's a good word for him. Exactly the right one, in fact. "He says there's no profit in revenge." *It's a little too late to worry about what he's going to think now. He's going to be furious. I don't blame him.*

Kit nodded, slowly. Thoughtfully. When he moved that slowly, the reptilian quality of his movement was a little less marked. "He is right."

Anna drew herself up to her full height. "Eric's—was—my *brother*." Her conscience gave a sharp twinge; she told it to shut up. "I want whoever killed him to pay and I want his story on the front page. I don't care if there isn't any *profit,* or if nobody will believe in you or what those people did to you."

The candle flames reflected in his eyes, little points of brightness in the endless depths of his pupils, before he looked down at the floor. Fat snakes of matted hair fell across his forehead.

"Women," he muttered. "The Queen her Grace had a mother like you, except her gaze was darker. I heard she witched the king, God save his soul." He winced, his lip lifting in a swift snarl that thankfully didn't show much of his canines. "Imagine that. Here in a popish church, after so long, I still beg God's forgiveness for that whoring peacock. You should beware of men, fair Anne, they are creatures of habit."

She swallowed dryly, tasting metal and dusty stone in her mouth. *Tell me something I don't know.* "I thought you could help me."

"How could I? Does the lamb ask the wolf for help? No. The lamb cowers in fear, and well she should." He cocked his head. "Mass is heavily attended today; they must suddenly fear for their souls in this city. Come with me."

He brushed past her, the candles bowing away from a sudden cold breeze. The flames danced as her skin rose in goose bumps. He seemed to take it for granted she'd follow, so she did.

The end of the hall was a blank stone wall, but he turned aside just before that. An ancient dusty velvet curtain hung, pulled back from a niche where a painting of a thin bearded man sitting cross-legged on a pillar peered at her from under his halo. He wore a beatific smile, and two fingers pointed to heaven. The perspective was wrong; she automatically corrected a few lines inside her head, her busy brain suddenly worrying about how to fix the mistake.

Kit pulled the curtain aside, and she saw a small wooden door. He pushed it open, with not even a theatrical creak. "You have no idea what I almost did last night, do you?"

Behind the door, stone steps went down, lit by a bare bulb overhead. "No." *But I think you might have wanted to bite me, too.*

213

I don't think I'd like that very much, thank you.

A ghost of a smile touched his garish flushed lips. "That is very good. And you also have no idea, fair Anne, of who is also lurking in this church, waiting for me to show my face." He stood aside so she could go through the door and followed her down, his step silent behind her as the door swung shut.

Chapter Twenty-One

Josiah leaned against cold concrete, hot blood slipping through his fingers clamped around his shoulder, and marveled again at how a simple job could go completely fucking sideways without even a shred of warning.

Hassan racked a fresh clip into his 9mm, chambered a round. "How you doing, mate?"

They've taken her by now. Or killed her. Dear God. "Fine. How did you find me?" The machine inside his head was stalling, a product of cotton-gray shock. He squeezed his shoulder; the resultant flare of spiked, scalding flame pushed the gray cotton back. *Have to be careful; keep using the wound like that and it'll lose its punch.*

"Police scanner. They were watching the PO, started chattering about ten minutes ago, Willie tagged it and told me to go. I got down here in time to see you coming out the front door."

What Hassan didn't add was, *right into a trap.* The only thing saving Josiah had been the animal consciousness of *something not right,* the little intuitive tickle on his nape sending him back into the post office, glass shattering as he dove for cover. The back door had been watched, too, but Hassan had dropped in, neat as you please, and rid the alley of two plainclothes John Q. Laws with some very illegal and powerful rifles.

They weren't taking any chances.

So someone had known about the post office box. Of course, there were ways of finding those things out. A simple pawing through Eric's desk would have probably yielded the information on a receipt or a reminder note.

Eric, for all his shrewdness, had been a fucking amateur.

Josiah swallowed, his throat slick and dry. "Anna." A hundred wet stinging needles from the slice of iron-gray sky visible overhead kissed his face, a fine penetrating rain. The bite on his throat throbbed, a star of fetid heat. "Jesus. I left her in a car. Second level, garage across the street." *They have her, or they've killed her. Anna.*

"Let's hope she's still there. Come on, soldier, move. Willie's coming for us."

Josiah squeezed again, the pain a bright red smashing kaleidoscope inside skull. *Make your brain work, you idiot.* "How did they ID me?"

"You haven't exactly been inconspicuous lately." Hassan eased back, taking a look at him. Water ran down his face. "Vanczy, probably. Let's go, old man."

Hassan took point, leading Josiah farther down the alley. The gun was a warm, comforting bulge under his left arm, his right hand clamped over the bleeding hole in his left shoulder. A high-powered rifle, capable of taking a good chunk of him wherever it hit; he was lucky.

Too much goddamn luck going around lately, good and bad. This isn't normal. He gulped down cold, wet, exhaust-laden air, intense prickling flushing along his skin. The most unpleasant part of being shot—aside from the pain and the blood—was the feeling that he might simply vomit from the agony.

It never got any easier.

"If I know Willie, she'll nip over to the parking garage and collect your girl; their units on the roof must've moved by now. Hurry up." Hassan kicked at a door, taking it down in two hits, then fished in his pocket and extracted a cell phone. He thumbed a call and Josiah wanted to laugh, the past curving over onto the present. Anna's voice through the phone, soft and husky.

I need your help. I need your help.

Too bad this was all going south. He didn't have enough backup to run this type of operation successfully. He wondered what type of backup would be better—a priest, maybe? Or just anyone with garlic and stakes.

And guns. Lots of guns.

His head was getting fuzzy. His throat hurt, the bite molten-hot. Was it infected? Christ.

"I need eyes, woman," Hassan snarled into the phone. "Where are they?"

Whatever he heard must have been good news, because he barely slowed, bursting through another door that gave onto the sweat-hell chaos of an industrial kitchen. Someone gasped at the sight of two men, one with a gun and the other bleed-ing, both running hell-for-leather, the tiles underfoot slippery with steam. The smell of food made his stomach turn hard, and suddenly he was sure that this time he really was going to puke.

Anna. I'm coming. If they get to you just hold on, hold on—

"Good." Hassan slapped the phone back into his pocket and snarled a curse in Spanish at a wide-eyed busboy, who scurried out of the way. "Come on, Wolfe. I get a little tired of dragging your ass out of these things."

Josiah knew Spanish, but what came out of his mouth was strangely slurred and in Muscovite Russian as well. "But without me you'd never have any fun."

"You have the strangest idea of fun, mate." Another door swinging open, and they were in a long concrete hall lit by fluorescents. Hassan whipped out a red bandanna and paused long enough to prop Josiah against the wall, fishing another square of cloth out of his pocket. The rough compression bandage helped, though Josiah couldn't lift his left arm now. "There we are. Good thing your coat's dark." A few sani-wipes to get the worst of the blood off his jacket and hand, then Hassan checked his pupils and nodded. "Here. Take one." He popped a bitter-tasting pill in Josiah's mouth and snorted at the resultant involuntary grimace. "Good enough. Willie's got the first-aid kit; she'll pick us up on the other side of this block."

Josiah let out a sigh, the world snapping back into its accustomed dimensions, shock receding. His eyes burned, and before long the pill would start to work. "Let's do it, then." *God help anyone who gets in the way. I'm not feeling cautious right now.*

The wall inside his head lifted and the machine took over, turning over percentages, working angles, alternatives, possible moves. *First objective, getting the hell out of here. Second objective, get to Anna. Make sure she's okay.*

If she's not—no, don't think about that. You can't *think about that.*

Outside, the rain made a dull leaden curtain. The alley was long and crooked, the type of terrain perfect for escape or ambush. They went quickly, not running but loping, a ground-eating pace any mercenary or agent could keep up, even wounded, for a long time. Everything depended on getting enough of a lead to disappear into thin air. Neatest trick of the week, put a rabbit into a hat and watch a Wolfe disappear.

Just be safe, Anna. Hold on.

Hassan slowed, reaching into his pocket again and producing the cell phone. "Make it quick," he said, short of breath. His hair was soaked by now, droplets shaken free as he moved. The end of the alley was drawing close, and Josiah could see cars gliding past at the end, people walking. They would come out on Madison and hopefully be lost in the lunchtime rush; Willie would swoop by with Anna in the car and pick them up. Neat as you please. His side ached, a stitch tearing into his ribs and the bandage mercilessly tight on his shoulder. Lucky. He was lucky.

Get to her in time, Willie.

Hassan flipped the phone shut. He didn't say anything, just slowed to a safe crowd-insertion pace. Josiah didn't ask. If it was trouble, Hassan would tell him soon enough. If it wasn't, he didn't need to know.

Thank God he had left her in the car. If she'd been hit in that crossfire—

No, I went around the block, there was no way for them to see where I came from. Willie only knows about that garage because of that time we went to the Bach concert.

His brain jagged sideways again. *They were shooting to kill. Oh, God. Anna. Be safe, baby.*

He should have dropped the whole thing and gotten her out of town after meeting Chilwell. They could have been on a beach by now, Anna with a sketchpad balanced on her pretty knees, listening to the rhythms of heavily accented foreign words or sucking on lemon ice. He could be watching the sun pick out gold highlights in her hair instead of stumbling behind

Hassan, hoping like hell his backup was good enough because the shock from the bullet had come back, closing around him in a heavy gray blanket. The pill made everything very calm, a placid blue lake with veins of orange pain spearing down his arm.

Be safe. Just be safe.

The crowd closed around them without a ripple, and Hassan's shoulders were tense. The guns were gone, holstered automatically. Now was not the time for firepower; now was the time for blending in. Rain blurred down, telescoping the sound of sirens in the distance. Drips of water falling from Josiah's numb fingers were pink. Nobody noticed, too occupied with seeking shelter from the intensifying downpour. The world rippled underfoot, then Hassan ducked aside, opening a car door. Josiah followed.

"How badly is he hit?" Willie, her accent turning the words guttural. Dark hair scraped back into a huge bun, a welcome sight in the driver's seat. Rain bulleted against the windshield, the wipers going full speed.

"He'll live. Get us the *fuck* out of here." Hassan pulled the coat down Josiah's arm; there was a sharp barking inhale of pain that didn't sound like it was coming from Josiah at all. "Sorry, mate."

"Anna..." His voice, slurred and slow, as he fought to hold on through the gray carpet of shock. His neck burned, *burned,* jolting him. "*Anna...*"

"You didn't tell him?" Now Willie sounded shocked, and Josiah registered something.

Anna wasn't in the passenger's seat next to Willie. She wasn't in the backseat, now full of Hassan and a bleeding, suddenly very tired Josiah. Nada. Zip. Zilch.

That managed to rouse him. "Where is she?" *I'm yelling. Can't yell, attracts attention, dammit—*

"She wasn't in the car!" Hassan yelled in reply as Willie took a left turn and accelerated. The sirens were very close, and Josiah found himself in a wrist lock, his wounded shoulder screaming, too. "She wasn't in the bloody *car,* now calm the *fuck* down!"

I left her there, I left her safe, think I have got to think my God where is she?

Hassan had his wounded arm as Josiah feebly thrashed, shock and blood loss finally taking its toll. A sharp prick, needle sliding home, and numbness rolled up to his shoulder. The bite was a necklace of fire. "She wasn't in the car," his backup—and best friend—repeated. "Willie would have brought her, if she was. The bloody bint's got snatched; she's bait. Or she's dead. Just calm the fuck down, Wolfe, and let us work. You're no good to us half-dead." It was *'alf-dead*, his accent wearing through, too.

They were frightened, and well they should be.

Hassan sighed. "That's right. Relax." He probably had no idea how unsoothing he sounded. "Just bloody relax, mate. We'll sort this all out. We've got you, mate. You're in good hands."

Josiah passed out.

The bullet had gone right through the meat of his upper arm, a wing shot. He was damn lucky it hadn't hit bone, and even luckier shock hadn't disabled him further. To top it all off, he was fucking lucky that both Hassan and Willie hadn't even considered leaving him to the tender mercy of his pursuers. Loyalty, that one variable hardly ever accounted for in operations going sideways, had saved Josiah's ass.

He should have been grateful.

Another fog-wrapped night pressed hard against the windows of yet another dim motel room as Willie stitched and bandaged his arm properly. Hassan poked around in the kitchenette, making sandwiches and heating up soup. This place was an extended-stay motel; they had paid for two weeks in a two-bedroom suite. Hopefully it wasn't a waste of money. There was ready access to cash just about anywhere in the world they landed; it was simply an agent's habitual running over alternatives that had him worried about liquid resources.

The lights in the kitchenette and bathroom were on to give Willie enough to see by, but not enough to silhouette any of them in the draped window. The television was on, the sound muted. He stared at its flickers as Willie, her touch butterfly-light, finished the bandaging. "You're going to have good scar there." Her tone was deliberately soft, soothing.

She was trying to be kind. He searched for something to say. "I shouldn't have left her." Flat, hopeless, the words came out of the hole in his chest, the whistling emptiness widening another few centimeters. "Shouldn't have left her there. But if I'd taken her in…Rifle fire. They meant business."

"Of course they meant business. They had two SWAT teams coming in. Whoever opened fire on you made a mistake. Probably being disciplined right this moment." She laid the bandaging aside on the table, pushing aside the pile of bloody cotton balls. There was a hole in the sleeve of his jacket now. Someone's aim had been off, or Josiah's reflexive dive had saved his life.

Anna had no reflexes. She would have been standing up as the bullets plowed past, making their deadly little whistles, cleaving air and smashing glass.

Gone. Vanished into thin air.

"We have laptops?" He thought he'd done a pretty good job of keeping his voice steady and level. But Willie glanced at him, and he saw a flash of fear in her dark eyes. The rain had dotted her makeup, and normally she'd have fixed it in the car while waiting for him and Hassan.

Little things like that were the first to fray during a mission.

Willie nodded, carefully. "We have a full kit. I went shopping yesterday. Hassan didn't think I should, but I had one of those feelings. Besides, I didn't know if you were going to have to ditch your car after meeting Chilwell." Her thin mouth pulled down at the corners. She rose, and her large, gentle hands moved efficiently, sweeping the gauze package and the cotton together into a small wad that went into a plastic bag, and inside another one as well. The antiseptic wipes and the leftover suture material vanished as well. She would get rid of it quietly in a dumpster as soon as possible.

"Good. Are you able to work for a few hours?" He tested the arm. Range of motion was impeded, but it was his left. He could still use a gun, and probably a knife if he had to; if he wasn't worried about tearing sutures he could do more.

The bite on his throat was less swollen now. God knew what that thing—Kit—had in his saliva. A reflexive shudder worked its way down through Josiah's spine.

Anna.

He closed the thought away, shutting the doors on it with a mental click.

"I can work." Willie finished clearing the mess on the table. "You should rest."

Not yet, my dear. Not even close. "Was there any chatter on the bands about Anna? Anything about a female apprehended or shot?"

"Nothing. Plenty about you, but nothing about her. I don't think they have her, Josiah."

"If they do, they'll offer a trade. It's the logical thing to do." *They wanted to kill her before. If they have her she's dead; I'm deluding myself. But my God, the car...* "The car?"

"Locked and empty. There was nobody there." Her long, capable hands loosened; she leaned back, pressing her fists into her lower back as if it hurt. "You should rest."

"Not going to. Get me everything you can on the mayor. And Denton, and whoever else was in the files. I want a full workup on their homes. Understood? A *full* workup. Get me everything you can and don't leave any traces."

Hassan came around the corner. "Food. And just be glad I didn't spit in it. What are we into now?"

"Josiah wants target files." Willie scooped the plastic bag up, stalking to the bathroom. "Talk to him."

The slim dark man set a platter of sandwiches down on the table, bumping aside the medical kit. "What now?"

"Denton. The mayor. Everyone who paid to have this treatment." Josiah tested the arm again. She did good work. *Wish I'd had her in Veracruz that one time.* "Kit said their cellular structure was becoming unstable. Shouldn't take much to—"

"Hang on. Who?" He dropped down in the other chair. "Cellular structure?"

"Eric's contact. There's some kind of...Jesus." The unreality of it hit him between the eyes again. His head was getting funny, between the shock and recent events. "You're not going to believe me. I don't even know if *I'd* believe me."

Hassan lifted an eyebrow. "Does it have something to do with that thing on your neck? You're bleeding there, by the way."

Josiah reached up. His fingertips came away wet and red. No wonder his throat felt hot. "Fuck." He pulled the first-aid kit across the table, digging in it for another sani-wipe. "Listen, Eric's contact is…weird. He said they were bleeding him and injecting his blood to make themselves younger. But it stressed their cellular structure—"

"Younger?" But Hassan didn't sound disbelieving. He dug in the bag in the chair next to him, coming up with a fistful of the original file. "I took a closer look at the digital files on here; some stuff was scanned in that isn't on the hard copies. If there is some sort of medical breakthrough, some kind of therapy, it's worth *millions*. Can you fucking imagine what people would pay for it?"

"I dunno." Josiah eyed the sandwiches. He had to eat, to fuel his body through the rest of the night. There were things to be done, serious work. "If it makes you fall apart in dust like those assholes the other night, it might not be worth it."

"There is that. Goddamn you, Wolfe, you'd better eat. You left a few pints back there." Hassan scooped up half a ham sandwich on wheat, held it out. Maybe a peace offering. "Come on."

Josiah's chest hurt. It wasn't a physical pain, God knew there was enough of that. It was just…Anna, maybe in a cell somewhere, suffering God knew what. If the hostiles had her and wanted information, she wouldn't have any to give beyond his name, and that phone number. Torture would be useless; she didn't have it in her to resist.

Anna wasn't outright weak, but she hadn't been trained. There were also…things that could be done to a female subject. Distasteful methods a liquidation agent didn't use, but still, part of the kit bag. Part of the work.

She would be broken, and it would be his fault for not anticipating his enemies correctly.

Maybe they lured her out? How? His mind wouldn't stop pawing at the problem, turning it over inside his head, probing at it. *How,* for God's sake? She had been safe enough, as safe as he could make her.

It just hadn't been enough.

"Josiah." Hassan's tone was kind but firm. "You have to eat. Take it, goddammit. Willie's going to get the laptops and start working, and I'm going to go through and get all our gear inventoried. You need to rest that brain of yours and come up with approaches if you're really looking at doing multiple liquidations in a city crawling with cops who know what you look like now. They're probably bringing in mercenaries, too. You've all but declared war on the Torrafaziones, too, because you never do anything halfway, right? The entire city wants your head, Wolfe. You should get the hell out of here."

"Not without making them pay." It came out flat and hard. He took the proffered sandwich, bit into it with little relish.

"Are you even hearing yourself? This is not a good situation to be in. We don't even have agency backup."

Hassan was right. The agency wanted whatever information it could gain, but they would cut Josiah loose and disavow if anything truly tangled went down. Losing four agents inside a domestic hole would make the big brains nervous. They might decide to torch and send in the hot squad, and if Anna was taken…

He had to swallow before he could speak. His throat burned. "How do you know?"

"Don't insult my intelligence. You're getting punchy. Eat, and then you'd better lie down. Don't worry about that girl of yours; she's a little brainier than she lets on. She recognized me, after all."

His skin felt too loose, a by-product of escaping death and adrenaline overload. He was just beginning to suspect he'd actually survived. "Where from?" *Hassan, you sneaky bastard.*

"Was just curious. Two years ago, talked to her during a gallery showing. Didn't think she'd marked me."

Curious? Anna never forgets a face; she's as good as an agent that way. "How'd you find her?"

"It was in your bloody file, Josiah. Eat."

His heart turned into a stone fist. The personnel file he'd acquired with so much trouble had been edited for his benefit. They had known about her. It brought up the starkly terrifying idea that perhaps the agency had taken her for leverage.

Which meant she was better off tortured and dead.

He ate. Hope was like revenge; there was no profit in it.

Still, if I have to, I'll take revenge.

Eating came first. Then resting his tired body, so he could be clear and calm and ruthless when the time came.

I'm going to need guns. The right guns. And I suppose it won't hurt to get a few grenades.

"Wait a second." Willie stood in the bathroom doorway, a faint blush beginning on her high cheekbones. "You're not going to encourage him, are you?"

"Encourage him? Have you ever tried to get between Wolfe and an objective? Not the best place to be, ducky." Hassan shrugged and took a huge bite of a chicken salad sandwich. He'd probably added sweet pickles to it, the philistine.

She looked about to protest, but three soft knocks sounded at the door.

Hassan was out of his chair, in cover position as Josiah

scooped up a 9mm on his way to his feet. Willie half-turned, pulled up the rifle leaning against the wall, and settled it against her shoulder.

The knocks came again. "Housekeeping," Hassan whispered. "In the middle of the night. What fun."

Josiah motioned for him to be quiet. He settled himself between the two beds, covering the door. Then his heart leapt into his throat and settled there, because the deadbolt on the door was moving.

Silently, smoothly, the deadbolt jittered open, moving in increments. Hassan sank down, ready to push the table over and provide the first wave of firepower. A little red dot showed on the door—Willie's laser sight; she must have some pressure on the trigger.

The deadbolt eased fully open.

Next, the door handle—a spring-loaded lock, and supposed to remain shut unless the person outside had a key—began to turn down. Smoothly, very smoothly. And so very silently.

His heart thudded dimly, thickly in his ears.

The door eased open, drifting and letting in a flood of rain-washed night air. "Put your weapons away," a familiar voice said, calmly enough. "You cannot harm me, but she is fragile."

The bite on Josiah's throat crunched with wet, hot pain.

Yellow light from the hallway lay on the short carpet, and a scarecrow shadow lay inside it. Kit's pallid face and hands floated, his fish-belly feet dragging as he ghosted forward. The red dot of laser sighting from Willie's rifle settled on his thin chest, still clad in a ragged black T-shirt.

"Holy *fuck*," Hassan whispered.

At the edge of the door, a pair of familiar green eyes appeared. Anna peered around the corner, her tangled hair falling down as her fingers curled over the jamb. "It's okay." She sounded hysterically calm. "He's a friend."

"I would not go so far, fair Anne." The creature paused, his terrible black gaze coming to rest on Josiah. "Put your weapons away, children. We have much to speak of."

Chapter Twenty-Two

The entire room held its breath, Anna did too. The air turned uneasy, staticky, before Josiah laid his gun down.

Josiah crouched between two beds, his shoulders slumped wearily but his face set. He looked like hell—bare-chested, his shoulder had a glaring-white bandage, and his hazel eyes had gone bleaker and colder than ever. "Stand down."

Willie lowered her rifle, but Hassan stared wide-eyed at Kit. She didn't blame him. Her own heart beat thin and fast in her wrists and temples; she was sweating. Josiah's eyes were locked to her face. The bruise on her cheek hurt, but less than it had, and she moved gingerly into the room behind Kit.

"Hassan." Josiah's tone brooked no disobedience. "Put your fucking gun *down,* soldier. You two, get the hell in here and close the fucking door."

Kit took another step forward. His gaze flowed over to Hassan, who turned pale under his copper coloring. His pupils dilated, then shrank as the gun dropped to his side, held loosely with fingers locked outside the trigger guard. "Holy fuck," Hassan repeated.

That's what I thought, too. Anna swung the door shut, flipping the deadbolt. Her hair was still damp, and she suspected her socks would never dry out. She leaned against the door, all the strength leaving her arms and legs in a trembling rush.

Safe. Or as safe as I'm likely to be, around him. It was odd to think of Kit as "him." As *human.*

Especially after what she'd seen him do.

Josiah rose, fluidly. He strode across the room, brushed past Kit, grabbed her shoulders, and proceeded to shake her so hard her head bobbled. Once. Twice. Three times. "Where. The. *Hell.* Were. You?"

It was the most emotion she'd ever seen from him. His eyes had turned dark, almost black, and his mouth drew against itself in a grimace of pain or rage. He had trouble getting the words out, his teeth were locked together so hard.

"She was safe enough." Kit sounded dismissive. He moved forward, touching the mirror hanging over a low bench meant for shoes or luggage; the two fingers remaining on his left hand left no streak on the glassy surface.

It was a relief to see he had a reflection, at least.

Anna shuddered, hearing the wet crunching sounds and the screams again. "There were cops in the church," she whispered as Josiah pulled her forward, hugging her so tightly her ribs creaked. The smell of safety closed around her again. "Regular ones, and ones that turned to dust. If I'd gone all the way in they would have seen me, but they were waiting for *him.*"

"Jesus." He breathed into her hair, his arms tightening even further. She couldn't breathe, but she didn't care. He was solid and warm and *real,* not cold or horribly fever-damp like Kit, who had clapped his hand over her mouth and hissed for her to be quiet while he "cleaned" the rest of the church. Not to mention the moldering smell of his small room, a cellar or closet with rotting books and clothes piled on shelves and racks, a narrow pallet of a bed, the entire small space full of a cloying iron-hard scent she now knew was blood.

Spending the hours until dusk in that little room, trying to be interested in the bare, weeping walls while the pale, mangled creature stared at her, was one of the worst things she had ever experienced.

Almost worse, even, than finding Eric dead.

Afterward, the fight in the darkened church, seeing how silently and ruthlessly Kit had killed first the men who exploded into dust and then the regular ones...but before he killed all the normal ones, he *drank*.

Josiah's grasp loosened, only so he could grab her shoulders and shake her again. "I told you to stay in the *car*. Do you have any *idea* what it's like, thinking someone's taken you? Jesus *fucking* Christ, you *goddamn* idiot, you could have gotten *killed*!"

Kit piped up again. His voice, soft and wrong, cut like a cold knife through hot butter. "Save your sweet murmurings for later. Where is my ring?"

Josiah appeared not to hear him. "*Killed*, Anna! Do you understand me? Or what they'd do to you would make you wish you were dead. I told you to stay in the *car*. What happened?"

Anna tried to find the words. None came.

Kit made a small hissing sound. "I weary of this. Where is my ring?"

Josiah spared him a single glance. "Shut the fuck up, freak. I'll get to you in a goddamn minute." His hands were shaking, and that was vaguely frightening. She'd never seen him like this, not even during the last big fight. "What happened, Anna? You tell me what happened."

She found her voice, surprisingly steady. "Calm down."

"Calm…" Words seemed to fail him. He tipped his head back, his jaw working, and the shaking in his hands invaded her body. Shaking like an earthquake, like everything coming apart.

Oh, God, Josiah, you have no idea what I saw. "You have *got* to calm down. You're scaring me." Her hands crept up, grabbed at his wrists. His skin was warm, human. Not waxy and resilient. "Please, Josiah. *Please.*"

A galvanic shudder ratcheted through him. He let out a long sigh. "Josiah," she persisted. "Jo. Look at me."

Another sigh, or a breath so deep there was no difference. He finally tilted his head back down, slowly, his throat working as he swallowed. The thin trickle of blood oozing from beneath the plasters on his throat was black in the dim light.

His hands left her shoulders. He cupped her face, leaning forward so his forehead touched hers, and closed his eyes. "You're all right?" As if he wasn't sure. "You're okay? Hurt anywhere?"

It felt like a bar of hot lead was buried in her lumbar region, her shoulders ached, and her face throbbed. Not to mention her ankle, freshly angered by trotting; if she took her boot off it would probably swell like a basketball. Her face hurt, too, a small pain in the middle of the orchestra of aches. "I'm fine," she whispered back. "Just a little bruised, the usual. I need a vacation."

He made a sound that was probably intended to be a laugh. "Anywhere in the world you want, baby. You just say the word."

It was her turn to make a pale, forlorn attempt at laughter. "Even the North Pole sounds good right about now."

"Too cold." Steady, now. Which meant he was marginally calmer, probably. "I swear, Anna, if you ever do that to me

233

again…" His thumbs moved, brushing her cheeks, an exquisitely gentle caress. Then he kissed her forehead, pushing her gently away and examining her face. "If you ever do that again you won't be able to sit down for a week when I finish with you. Understood?"

So he remembered that particular joking exchange with Eric, and their lighthearted arguing. It was an unexpected balm, and tears pricked at her eyes before she blinked several times, denying them. *Better. He's calmer.* So she gave the next line. "Chauvinist. You won't hit me."

"Who said anything about hitting?" He sounded like himself again, and wrung a small surprised laugh out of her. His eyes were no longer so frightfully dark, and she was suddenly aware that he wasn't wearing a shirt, his chest hair hadn't changed one bit in the intervening three years, and that everyone else in the room, including Kit, was staring at them. "That's my girl. Sit down, there's food. We have pain meds for you, and Hassan can make some tea. He does good tea. Hassan?"

Hassan's jaw closed with a snap. "Tea? You want me to make bloody *tea*? What is…*that*?" He pointed at Kit, who wore a faint smile as he stared disconcertingly at a point too high to be Hassan's chest and too low to be his chin. "What the fuck is going on here?"

Josiah let go of her, suddenly calm and in control again. "Hassan, Willie. Meet Christopher, 'Kit' for short, freak by occupation, and the reason why this is all so fucking weird. I'd offer him something to drink but I don't think we'd like it if he accepted. Sit down, Kit. Let's get to business." He pointed at the table, where a pile of sandwiches looked absurdly good.

Kit's faint smile turned sardonic.

Hassan shook his head. "Jesus Christ, Wolfe. Jesus fucking Christ."

"Tell me about it. Get moving." Josiah pushed Anna's shoulders, gently, as Hassan reluctantly stepped back into the kitchen, the gun dangling in his hand. "Sit down, Anna. You look ready to fall over."

"This is all very well." Kit's tone didn't change, but the air cooled a few degrees when he spoke. "I will ask one more time, young man. Where is my ring?"

"In a safe place." Josiah pushed her past the pale scarecrow, her feet moving automatically, a spike of pain jolting up from her abused ankle with every step. "Willie is about to get us the information we need to strike. When we finish eradicating everyone who's been in that brownstone, I'll give you the location of your precious ring."

Anna sank down gratefully in a chair, but her mouth had gone dry. Josiah leaned over her, flipping a first-aid kit closed. She saw another dark room through an open door, luggage stacked against the half-wall between the main room and the kitchenette, bags and cases, and Willie lowering a long nasty-looking rifle from her shoulder.

Josiah passed behind her, scooping a navy sweater from a pile sitting on the closest bed, and she painfully craned her neck to see a swift snarl pass over Kit's face.

"I do not bargain," he said softly. "I have returned your wayward woman. You will give me my ring, and *then* you shall aid me in slaying my enemies." There were little red slits revolving in the depths of his irises, and his tongue had difficulty with the sibilants—*probably because his teeth are growing.* Anna shivered. *Oh, God, Josiah, don't piss him off!*

Josiah finished pulling the sweater on. The bandage vanished. He moved impossibly gracefully, despite a slight hitch in his left shoulder. "I give you this 'ring' and before I know it I have no leverage and no way of ensuring you stay on my side. No dice. I'm holding on to your ring until this is finished, and then you can have it, and welcome to it. Otherwise, just fuck off and watch a real professional work."

Kit was silent. He studied Josiah as if a new and interesting bug had just crawled out from under a rock. Her throat turned dry as the Sahara, and she glanced nervously at Josiah, who scooped up his gun from the bed and checked it, maybe a trifle unnecessarily.

"The way I see it," he continued, calmly, as if he wasn't being stared at by a creature out of nightmares and books, "you would have already taken these guys apart if you could. You need me. After all, they trapped you in the first place and bled you white. They haven't caught me yet. So just sit your freaky self down and listen. You might learn something."

Anna opened her mouth, meaning to protest, to forestall the inevitable explosion. A new sound intruded, a kind of whistling wheeze. Kit's face contorted, the flush high along his cheekbones intensifying, becoming almost purple.

Anna's mouth hung open. *My God. He's laughing.*

Josiah dropped down in a chair to Anna's left, his back to the kitchenette. That meant he was facing Kit, and he still had the gun in his hand, resting casually on the table. Willie had barely moved, and Anna suddenly realized they were preparing to shoot the scarecrow if he moved the wrong way.

The wheezing finally tapered off, and Kit moved slowly forward, his feet barely seeming to move as they brushed the carpet. The ugly red-purple flush faded bit by bit as he did. "You remind me of Walsie. He was inflexible when he believed he had the winning draught." He sounded thoughtful, and lowered himself slowly into a third chair. Caught between him and Josiah, Anna braced herself.

Josiah's left hand came down on her wrist. He squeezed once, reassuringly. "Whoever he was. Did you like him?"

Kit shrugged. "He is the one responsible for my present…condition. It was a choice between certain death or becoming a creature glutted with other death. I count myself lucky I was given that much."

"That's okay. You don't have to like me. You just have to do what I say for a little while, and then we can go our merry ways and never see each other again. Willie, check on Hassan and that tea, then start working on target files." Josiah stared at Kit, unblinking. They held each other's gazes for a long, breathing eternity as Willie moved, edging back toward the kitchenette, where running water and clinking ceramic almost covered up the sound of Hassan swearing under his breath.

"Have you wondered how I found *you*, canny one?" The pale man sat utterly still, his eyes hooding. His lips were red, and a shudder went through her because she knew where that crimson came from.

"You fucking bit me; that's probably how you found me. Or you can smell me. Either way I don't care, as long as *those* bastards don't find me. Anna?"

She blinked at him. A switch had flipped, and he wore his old calm mask as he glanced down, his fingers going through the first-aid kit. She wasn't sure she could ever believe that placid smooth surface or small half smile ever again.

"Take this." He produced a small bottle of Tylenol PM. "You

need some rest, and it'll help with the pain." He pushed a half-full bottle of mineral water toward her, too.

She took a couple of the Tylenols. He nodded approvingly, and Kit didn't look at her throat as she swallowed.

Small things to be grateful for. "I'm sorry." The words caught her by surprise. "I should have—"

"Don't worry about that right now." He touched her wrist again, with just his fingertips. "Eat something. You need a shower before that hits, or anything?"

She eyed the sandwiches, but her stomach revolted at the thought. She kept hearing the wet meaty crunching of a broken neck, the gasping as the thing buried its teeth in another throat—or the pair of bright blue eyes as the last man Kit had drained dry stared at her while she huddled terrified behind a pillar.

The fact that the blue-eyed policeman had been pointing a gun at her when Kit appeared only made it worse.

"A shower first. P-please." She had to speak slowly. Pure relief was almost as terrifying as fear itself.

He eyed her for a long moment. "All right. Bathroom's in there. I'll send Willie in with fresh clothes. Don't take too long, you'll fall asleep and drown."

"Okay." But she didn't move. Kit was so still she could almost forget he was there, but his black eyes glittered avidly, watching. "Josiah?"

"Just go, Anna. Get some warm water." He was back to staring at Kit, their gazes still locked, as if they were going to play a telepathic game of chess. "I'll wait right here."

It was hard to push herself up from the table. It was even harder to skirt Kit, trying not to cringe, and turn her back on both of them.

Just before she closed the bathroom door, she heard another slight chuckling wheeze. "If she were a boy, I would change her. Those eyes."

"You'll keep your teeth off her." Josiah sounded serious, and dead level. "Thanks for bringing her, by the way."

"She came to me, thinking I would provide vengeance." The creature had no right to sound so amused.

"Well, she doesn't have to worry about that now. I'm on the goddamn job. Tell me something *useful.*"

Anna closed the door with a quiet click. She fumbled across the bright white, antiseptically clean bathroom like a blind woman even though the lights were on, finally figured out how to turn the shower on. Rushing water covered any sound of conversation from the room outside—and it also covered any sounds she might make as she sobbed under the hot torrent, her ankle swelling and her back afire with pain. As much as she tried, the images of bloodshed just wouldn't go away.

And she thought, over and over again: *Oh, God, Josiah was right.*

She had been so wrong.

The sleepy stuff in the Tylenol filled her head with fuzz and made the pain retreat. She lay in one of the double beds in the second room, the covers pulled up, sinking into warmth and softness, hearing the soft murmurs of conversation. When sleep closed over her head it was a blessing, welcome oblivion.

A church rose out of a pool of red shimmering. Crimson fluid lapped at the front steps, Venetian gondolas sliding past with foaming wakes. Impelled, she opened the heavy doors and walked into incense-scented gloom.

Josiah stood at the altar, straight and quiet in a tuxedo, his hair combed just so. Sinking horror began as Anna realized the church was full of people staring at her expectantly, and that it was a wedding. Sprays of white flowers decked the end of each pew and the altar, exhaling a cloying reek. Her feet were bare, and as she looked down at them she saw she was missing toes, and her skin was corpse white.

She lifted her hands, slowly, and saw her fingers were mere stubs. It was too late, she was at the altar, and as she turned with syrupy slowness she saw the muttering congregation was full of bright eyes and long, sharp canine teeth dimpling their scarlet-smeared lower lips. Her arms and legs weighted with dreamy terror, she saw the priest in his cassock, lifting something above his head.

The priest was suddenly Eric, the necklace of sliced flesh gaping terribly as he gasped, inhaling, his face a grotesque ruin as he toppled forward.

And Anna began to scream....

She jerked into full wakefulness, someone's hand over her mouth and warm skin against her back. "Shhh," Josiah whispered in her ear. "Shhh, just a dream, I'm here. Just a dream. Wake up."

He stroked her shoulder, and she finally relaxed, muscle by muscle. The tank top pulled up under her breasts; she felt the peculiar constriction of sleeping in her clothes. There was a dull silence from the other room; Anna froze.

Had she disturbed anyone else?

"You all right?" he whispered, warm breath tickling her ear. His hand cupped her shoulder; he was warm as he had always been. Sleeping next to him had always been pleasant; he was a stove on cool nights and even in the middle of sticky summers it was nice to feel him next to her.

She managed a nod, holding herself very still. He had curled against her back, her second-favorite sleeping position; his hand slid down her arm and pulled the covers up, tucking her in securely and diving below the blankets to touch her ribs, his arm circling her waist and pulling her back against him.

There was a very definite pressure against her left buttock.

He's got a hard-on. And we're in a room with a flimsy door and other people out there. The thought that Kit might be in here, in the dark, sent a fresh jolt of panic through her.

Josiah kissed the top of her head, pulling her back even farther. "Relax." A mere murmur, unlikely to disturb any sleepers. "Go to sleep."

She squeezed her eyelids shut so hard tracers of green and blue exploded in the darkness. "Kit?" She couldn't help herself.

His hand flattened against her bare midriff above the waist of the pajama pants Willie had brought her. Calluses scraped against her softer skin; she wondered if his shoulder was hurting him. "He left. Had to find a safe hole since his other one was blown."

Thank God. She sagged in relief. He stroked her belly, gently, soothingly, just like petting a cat.

Then, his fingers slid below the elastic waistband. "You need to relax." Murmuring in her ear again, his breath tickling unbearably.

There's two other people sleeping practically right next door, Josiah. Not now. She tried squirming away, stopped when that only made things worse. Now, as well as being acutely aware of his arousal, she was uncomfortably aware of her own, and excruciatingly aware of the presence of others just beyond the closed door. His fingers slipped down, curving, and she froze again.

"Not now," she whispered.

"Lighten up. They're sacked out." God *damn* the man, but he seemed to have grown another few fingers, teasing and probing. "I feel like a teenager."

She struggled with laughter, biting the inside of her cheek, and tried again to slide away from him. He was having none of it. "Stop it," she finally whispered, fiercely. "I want to talk to you."

"I'm listening." His breath blew a strand of hair across her nose, adding tickling to her list of worries.

"I can't think when you…" She hissed in a soft breath as he stroked, with just the right amount of delicate pressure.

"That's the idea."

It *was* like being a teenager, she decided, her heart hammering behind her ribs. *I am going to die of embarrassment.* "Stop it, Josiah. Please."

He did stop, but he didn't move his hand. "You're no fun."

It was exactly like the time they had been in the back of his car at Huntington Leap, the lights of the city glimmering in the distance and the fear of another car—or a police cruiser pulling up—adding to the close confines and the sticky leather against her bare, sweating thighs. She'd never been incredibly adventurous, but the wine and the heat and his hands on her had done the trick that particular night.

He was waiting, she finally realized, holding himself still and breathing into her hair. She wondered if he was angry. Probably.

"I want to talk to you." She tried not to wriggle. "Please?"

He let her move, managing to silently express reluctance at the same time. They ended up with her head propped on his right shoulder; she could see the glimmer of the bandage on his left. Her ankle twinged every time she moved, and it took a little bit of wriggling and settling before she was comfortable. He kissed her forehead, and she heard his heartbeat again.

If she shut her eyes it was almost as if the intervening years had disappeared. She traced the arch of his ribs, feeling him breathe, and the last cold, clammy fingers of the dream faded. "He bit you." She tried to whisper softly, not to disturb the air.

"Yeah." He reached up, touched her cheek with his left hand. If his shoulder hurt, he made no sign. His tone was soft, considering. "So?"

"So? If they find out, they might decide to do the same thing to you they did to him." It was hard to keep her voice down. "And what if the government—the real government, not just the mayor—finds out about Kit and locks him up? What if—"

His finger came down across her lips, silencing her. "For Christ's sake. Don't borrow trouble. By the time I finish, nobody alive will know and we'll be long gone. We're going to have to leave the country, go somewhere they can't find us. I'm trained for this, goddammit."

"I think that man knows."

"What man?"

"Chilton."

"Chilwell," he corrected. Now she felt stupid as well. "I'll take care of him. The thing now is to get you out of town with Willie and Hassan. You'll wait for me in a safe place. I'll tie this off, get rid of Corpse Boy, and all will be gravy."

Was that tight feeling under her ribs panic? "I don't want to leave."

"You couldn't wait to get away yesterday morning." Mild and whispered, the words still stung. "What the fuck were you thinking, Anna?"

I had an attack of bravery. I might have another one, you can't ever tell. "Will you listen to me?" When he subsided, she went on. "What happens if these people—this *agency*—believes you about Kit? There's nothing stopping them from making you disappear. The implications—"

He made a small, annoyed movement. "They already know, or they wouldn't be sending me somewhere four agents bit it. Chilwell wouldn't have paid me, either. Don't you think I'm accounting for that? How stupid do you think I am?" He took a deep breath, his ribs rising under her fingers, and she had the sudden urge to tickle him. She knew just where the sensitive spots were.

After a moment, he continued. "I know what I'm doing, Anna. You just have to trust me. Is it so fucking hard?"

"Josiah—"

He overrode her whisper. "I am already doing what you wanted me to do. I'm getting you your goddamn revenge. There. Are you happy? I'm going to kill them because I thought for a few hours that they'd killed *you*, goddammit. Don't you get it?"

It was her turn to reach up, lay a finger against his lips. Her thumb stroked his stubbled jaw, rasping. *I don't understand you at all, Josiah. I thought I did, but then I saw my brother murdered and twelve men killed in a church by a dead man who locked his fangs in their throats—the ones he didn't outright murder, that is. I thought I understood; I was wrong.* "I thought if I could make them pay…" There was something in her throat, a huge smooth egg of despair.

"You thought it would bring him back." His lips moved against her skin. He caught her hand, squeezed just a little, kissed her fingertips.

And here I thought I was just being brave. Maybe he was right, though. Sharp pain speared her chest. "Let's just both go, just get out of here. Give Kit his ring and get the hell out. We can take the file with us—"

"Something else you don't understand." He had shifted from a whisper to a murmur, a thin thread of sound. "The ring wasn't in Eric's PO box. I don't know *where* it is. If I blow town now he might come after us."

The stone in her throat swelled. She shivered. He hugged her, pressed her fingers against his lips for another brief, silent kiss.

"Listen to me," he whispered, soft and distinct. "If I don't finish this off, you won't be safe. I thought something had happened to you. I thought you were dead or worse, Anna. I never want to feel that way again. One way or another, I am taking those motherfuckers down. And if I can manage to eliminate Corpse Boy as well, I will. He's a threat to you, and I will not *allow* threats to you. Is that clear?"

"Shh." She pressed her fingers against his mouth, hoping it would calm him down. "Be quiet."

"You'd better understand." He stroked her hair, his lips moving against her skin. "You had just better."

"Be quiet. You'll wake them up."

He did calm down, at least audibly. Kept stroking her hair. A slight movement ran through him once, scalp to toes, a subtle frisson she wouldn't have felt if she hadn't been so close.

Let's try it again. "Why don't we just leave?"

"We're past that now." He touched her cheek, skated his fingers delicately over the curve. "Go to sleep."

How can I sleep? "Got any more of those pills?"

"Just close your eyes." He was back to a whisper, his touch warm and forgiving. "You're safe."

She squeezed her eyes shut. Took a deep breath. Another.

Her head did feel heavy, and her arms. Her legs were made of lead.

"That's it," he whispered. "Trust me, Anna."

"I do."

She wasn't sure if he'd heard, but he held her until she fell asleep again, comforted by the steady beat of his heart and the rhythm of his breathing.

This time there were no bad dreams.

Chapter Twenty-Three

I don't like this." Willie stuffed another handful of clips in the bag, her hair slicked back. "At least let Hassan go with you."

Josiah stared at the computer screen, hearing the shower running. Hassan was drowning himself in hot water, and Anna made little shuffling and clinking sounds in the kitchen, washing dishes and making a fresh pot of coffee. The rich illusory smell filled the suite, and if he concentrated he could hear her humming, a familiar wandering melody.

"I don't recall asking for your input on this issue." He tapped the return key twice, pushed the laptop back, and opened the first target file. Scanned it, his attention submerging, making connections. "Hassan is going to be busy taking you and Anna out of town."

"I can take the *Liebchen, mein Herr.* I'd feel better about this if you had some backup." It was the fourth time she'd said it, in a slightly different way with each repetition. "So would Hassan. We've talked it over."

When did this become a democracy? "You are not the prime point on this run, Willie. You and Hassan are taking Anna. End of discussion." Rainy morning light flooded the windows, and his tone held mild warning, nothing more. He found the third file, cross-referenced a location, stored it in the little drawer in his head.

He'd awakened this morning with Anna sleeping in his arms, her cheeks flushed and her hair tangled, the faint light creeping through the curtains sliding over every curve of her face. For a half hour of complete silence, he'd held her, each second spilling like a grain of sand through an hourglass, infinitely precious and now irretrievably gone.

Then Hassan had coughed, and he'd heard Willie's sleepy murmur, and the machine he was trained to be rose inside his head. Cold calculation made the plan, and now he had to stick to it.

It was the only way.

"What about the *Liebchen,* Josiah?" Willie's tone was soft, worried. "This is not the best course of action. You should—"

"More coffee, anyone?" Anna sang out in the kitchen.

It sounded so familiar, so normal. Josiah forced away the urge to close his eyes. "Black for me, please."

"Willie?" More soft shuffles, and she peered around the corner. "Coffee for you?"

"Yes, please." Willie subsided, shoving more ammo clips into the bag. "Cream. Sugar. And big stick to pound in idiot head here."

Anna blinked. The bruised swelling on her face was turning yellow and purple, even more glaring and conspicuous. "Is he being stubborn again?"

"Ach, yes." Willie closed the bag with a swift yank, grabbed the first-aid kit, and started to reorganize it for the second time. "*Still.* I have not managed to talk sense into stupid head."

You have no idea how close to the edge I am, Willie. Don't push me. "I thought I told you this discussion was over." He heard the chill in his tone, pulled the fourth file toward him and opened it, checked the address against the list. There was an error.

Damn it all to hell and back. His temper thinned, and he took a deep, calming breath. He was starting to deconstruct under the stress, and that was the last thing anyone here needed.

Anna sighed. She shuffled back into the kitchen.

"*Mein Herr,*" Willie started, and he looked up at her, his face hardening. She swallowed the rest of the sentence, her cheeks paling.

He switched to his Berlin-accented German, so he could be absolutely sure she understood. "No, Willie. That is final. I'm counting on you and Hassan to get Anna out of here safely. I am *trusting* you two to get the *only* thing that matters to me in this fucking world out of here and to a good hidey-hole, so I can concentrate when I need to. Do me a favor and don't fuck with me right now, my dear. I'm not in the mood."

She stared at him, her large, dark eyes suddenly very full and shining. In her mouth, the precision of the German was softly blurred. "You will get yourself killed."

Not if I'm careful. Which I can't be, with Anna around. "Only if you keep distracting me. Now be a good girl and make this laptop behave."

"Coffee." Anna came around the corner, bearing two steaming mugs. "Sounds intense. What's up?"

It was a relief to think in English again. It was also a sucker punch to see her, her hair falling in a glowing wave under the electric light and her stocking feet shuffling. She dragged her right foot and winced just a little.

Just making sure everyone understands what's going on here.

"Just getting some things clear." *Definitely starting to deconstruct. Wish I had a heavy bag to get all this out.*

Willie leaned over, pulled the laptop toward her. She muttered a particularly foul curse in French, and wiped at her cheek with one hand while the other tapped at the keyboard.

"Are you okay?" Anna's tone was soft, and genuinely concerned. "Willie?"

"*Ja,*" the taller woman replied, accepting her coffee. "There. It should work now." It was a submission, and he recognized it. Anna was as safe as he could make her. Willie would see to it. And if the unthinkable happened, Willie and Hassan would teach her how to take care of herself. More than that he couldn't ask for.

That's my problem. I want more than I should. But thank you, Willie. "*Bitte.* These addresses don't match up. Can you find the right one?"

The tall, spare woman settled into a chair. Anna hovered uncertainly, first glancing at her, then at Josiah. The line between her eyebrows deepened.

"I'll work on it." Willie kept her head bowed. Her bun was back in place, and her thin fingers tapped at the keyboard.

Anna waited. He took the coffee, their fingers touching for a brief second, and gave her a tight smile. *Be calm, Josiah.* "Thanks. Feeling any better?"

She shrugged, a graceful movement. "I've been thinking."

Oh, God. Not you, too. His temper was frayed down to the bone, and if she started in on him he just might slip. "About?" He looked down at the fourth file, taking a scalding sip of coffee. *Dammit.*

"If Eric mailed the ring to his PO box, he might have picked it up. It might have even been a red herring, especially if he suspected someone might steal his files." Anna folded her arms as the shower shut off, and Hassan began to hum a saucy RAF drinking song having to do with a lassie from Leeds with definite needs. It was a good sign. "Was there anything in the box at all?"

"Not a thing. Bare as a bone." Josiah set the coffee cup down, carefully, amid the drift of paper. "Where are you heading with this, Anna?"

"So he'd picked everything up, maybe the day he...died. Or he put it in there in case the files were stolen." Her mouth trembled, firmed. She went on. "Either way, he probably hid the ring."

Assuming he found it, of course. "Where?"

"He had a couple hiding places. I want to go back to his apartment and—"

Jesus Christ. "No."

"Josiah—" She actually flinched. The little betraying movement tore at his heart.

"*No.*" His voice rose, and Willie's shoulders hunched. She tapped at the keyboard industriously. Anna stared at him, her green eyes dark and terribly sad. "Absolutely *not*. Tell me, and I'll see if I can fit in a trip to an almost-certainly compromised location into my day. It might even add a little excitement to my otherwise *boring* life."

"Don't yell at me." Her chin set stubbornly, she scowled at him. "I'm only trying to help."

"Save me from amateurs." For a moment he couldn't believe he'd said it out loud. *Christ, keep your temper down. If you push her over the edge now she won't stop until she's made you react, and that won't be good.* For a moment he remembered every other fight he'd had with her, trying desperately to keep his calm while she grew more and more frustrated. She had never understood what it cost him to keep his composure, especially since she knew every button to press. "The only thing you're doing today is heading out of town with Willie and Hassan. That's *final*. Tell me where Eric likely hid the ring, and I'll get it."

Her almost thirty seconds of silence was all the warning in the world. He braced himself, but she surprised him with brittle calm. "I don't know *exactly*. But if I get in his apartment I can check the most likely—"

"Didn't I tell you *no*?" He took a deep breath. "Make a list of the likeliest places."

"But you said you'd give him his ring!"

How did she do it? No other person on earth could throw him off balance like this. He struggled for an even tone. "By the time I finish this, Corpse Boy isn't going to care whether I have his goddamn trinket or not. He's going to be too busy being truly dead or eluding the agency. You wanted me to handle this; I'm handling it. I'm the resident expert; stop trying to fuck up how I do my *job*. Will you, please? I'm begging you."

Willie pushed her chair back from the table and padded across the room. She tapped smartly on the bathroom door and walked in, through a puff of steam. Hassan's humming stopped.

Anna's chin kept its defiant tilt. "Why are you so upset with me? Because I called you? I'm sorry I interrupted all your goddamn important *plans*. Maybe I should have just let them catch me, so as not to interfere with your busy life."

The words hung in the air for a moment. Her unwounded cheek bloomed with high, hectic color, and under the mottling of the bruise she was blushing as well.

Oh, Jesus. His jaw had seized up. If he ground his teeth together any harder he was afraid one or two of them would break. He shoved his chair back and rocked up to his feet. Anna swayed but didn't move as he grabbed her shoulders, his fingers sinking in.

"I am not very stable right now," he informed her, softly. "I'm having trouble keeping my head clear. You don't make it any easier. I am *not* angry at you, but I am about to go out and get myself in a hell of a lot of trouble, and I can't be the normal guy you need right now. Like it or not, if I was *normal* you'd be dead. I never should have tried to make it work with you, but I *wanted* to, Christ how I wanted." A deep breath; he had to struggle to keep his tone even and calm. "Just for the next few hours, do what I say. After that you'll be out of town and I'll stop worrying about you while I go out and try to get myself killed getting your goddamn revenge. Remember? The one you hired me for?"

Tears trembled on her wet, matted eyelashes. She stared up at him through a blurring welling of salt water, and he wished she didn't have her hand over her mouth, so he could kiss her.

Calm her down. You're making a mess. Is this what you want her to remember about you?

He tried to make his tone a little softer. "I'm not angry at you, I swear. I just have to work now, and you're getting in the way of my work. Help me out here, Annie. All right?" *Quit looking at me like you think I'm going to hit you. I never have, and I won't start now.*

She nodded, and one of the tears brimmed over, touching her hand. Her hair fell forward, brushing his hands and falling in her eyes. She said nothing, blinking furiously. He uncurled his hands from her shoulders slowly, wishing he could keep the feel of her skin against his bottled up somewhere it wouldn't hurt.

Anna took in a deep, jagged breath. "I don't mind. About you not being a normal guy, that is. I never did."

Jesus. His heart compressed itself to a lump of coal inside his ribs. If it was a lie, it was a kind one, and she might even believe it. *Why did you run away from me, then? You took everything with you when you slammed my front door.* "Good enough." He was trying to be kind in return, but the flash of hurt in her eyes told him he'd failed. She probably meant he'd been weird even while dating her. No matter how well you faked it, anyone close enough could begin to tell if you weren't…

Well, if you weren't *human.*

He hadn't minded, before he met her.

Goddamn woman, twisting him into knots. Everything he had ever wanted to say to her swelled behind his throat, but there was no room for it now. He had work to do.

Still, he leaned forward, pressing his lips to her forehead. Gently, very gently, though he wanted to do a hell of a lot more. It would be more enjoyable than a session with a heavy bag, that was for *damn* sure. He could be clear enough and cold enough to think afterward.

No, you won't. You'll find fifty reasons to rabbit, just take her and go and leave this whole operation unfinished. What's not tied off is dangerous, you know that. You leave with her now, you'll be running for the rest of your life and most definitely the rest of hers. Stick with the plan you made while you were cold and reasonable, Josiah. It's your only hope.

Not only that, it's hers, too.

So he gently, very gently, pushed her away. Held her at arm's length, and told the persistent pressure below the belt to settle down. Work to do, the constant refrain of his life.

"I don't mind," she repeated, and her eyes were just as big

and dark as ever. Anna looked up at him as if saying it again would make everything all right, turn back time, and untangle the whole mess. "I'm sorry, Jo. I shouldn't have—"

If she went any further he was going to do something stupid. "Don't." *Don't apologize.* "We'll talk about it later. I promise. Now go back into the kitchen. I need to think."

He thought she might give him more trouble, but she stepped back out of his hands, and it took everything he had not to take the single step forward and grab her again. *Don't listen to me. Ask me to leave again. With you. Tell me you didn't care about what I am, tell me you don't care now.*

She simply shuffled back into the kitchen, and a sharp, precise agony uncoiled inside Josiah's chest. He shelved it, promising himself he'd think about it later, and looked back down at the papers on the table. For one terrifying vertiginous second he couldn't remember who he needed to kill.

Reality returned with a snap and a rush. He settled down in his chair again, took a deep breath, and waited for Willie to come out of the bathroom so he could get the address he needed. While he waited, he collated a few more files.

And wished his recalcitrant hands didn't ache so badly for the feel of her skin again.

Chapter Twenty-Four

Don't stop," Josiah said, in that odd flat tone he'd suddenly developed.

Anna's fingers were folded in so hard her entire hand hurt. Her purse lay obediently in her lap, and she stared down at its black canvas.

Josiah leaned over, bracing his arm against the driver's-side door. "I mean it. Don't stop until you get them both out of here."

"You're being an idiot." Hassan turned the key in the ignition. "I'll take good care of them both, Wolfe. Safe as little baby chicks under mother hen."

"Just be careful." Josiah didn't look at her, his profile clear and sharp, his eyes light and piercing. "Godspeed." He stepped back, light misting rain weighing down his short dark hair.

"Don't do anything stupid." Hassan put the car in gear, and it smoothly slipped forward. Willie's head bowed, her bun visible as her shoulders came up.

Anna twisted in the backseat, ignoring the creaking pain in her neck as she struggled to catch a glimpse of Josiah. When the car turned, nosing out into traffic, she could view the entire parking lot. He was nowhere to be seen.

Vanished, into thin air.

Why am I not surprised?

Silence crackled thick and uncomfortable inside the car. Hassan turned the windshield wipers on.

Willie finally spoke as the car slid into the left-hand-turn lane on 188th. "He is crazy. Will get himself killed."

"Knows what he's doing." Hassan glowered out the windshield. His shoulders were stiff, and his fingers gripped the wheel. "Don't, Willie. You're a professional."

"And I tell you, professionally, he will get himself *killed.*" Willie's head came up with a quick jerk. "He is not in his right mind. I am surprised at you, Hassan. You know better than—"

"He has his reasons. For Christ's sake, I already have a headache."

The words tumbled out before Anna could stop them. "What do you mean, he's going to get himself killed?"

"Don't you start in on me, too." Hassan's dark eyes flicked up to the rearview mirror, pinned hers, and just as quickly cut away. "He's doing this for you."

"Leave the *Liebchen* alone. Look, you take us out of town, then, *ein-zwei-drei,* you come back, help him. I look after *Liebchen,* and we all become happy big family." Willie turned to stare at Hassan's cheek. "You know I'm right."

"Don't make me the bad guy. I'm doing what he wants and getting what matters to him out of the fire zone." The light turned green and he pulled away, turning left and joining the lane for the freeway on-ramp. "He's been walking around half-dead for years. Now he's alive again, and thinking. He's got a better chance now than he did before."

"Half-dead?" Anna's fingers locked so hard her bones were about to begin groaning.

The car piloted itself toward the freeway, smoothly accelerating. "You left him," Hassan said quietly. "Tore him up so bad he couldn't think straight. He was never the same. *This* is the old Josiah. Suppose I should thank you—to tell the truth I'd rather wring your neck for taking a good man down. But Wolfe wants you nice and safe, and I owe him. Nice and safe is what you're going to be, ducky, until he comes to collect you."

So it's my fault? Anna's lips clamped together. *I didn't leave because I wanted to hurt him. I left because he lied to me about killing people for a living.*

Back when I had no idea what that meant.

"You are being a bastard." Willie folded her arms, her chin lifting. "You apologize."

"Like you never wanted to get your hands on whoever broke him." Hassan made a short, rude noise. "Like you never—"

"*I* never did." Willie shook her head and her large, finely modeled hand came down hard on Hassan's thigh. "I said apologize. Horrible man."

"Fine, I'm sorry. Doesn't make it any less true." His jaw jutted out stubbornly.

"Don't listen to him, *Liebchen*. All this time, he is the best friend Josiah has. Now, jealous like a woman."

"You're a spiteful lass, Willie." The broad British accent turned the words into sharp edges.

Anna turned her head, stared out the window at the freeway slipping away beside the car. Just like a magic carpet. She ignored the further sound of bickering, staring at the white stripe at the side of the road, swelling and retreating according to a random fluctuation of speed.

It's true. It is my fault. Whether she meant Josiah, or Eric, or anything else, she couldn't tell.

They drove all day, stopping only for a hurried lunch at a roadside diner. By the time Hassan checked them into an anonymous hotel, they were over the state line in the middle of a dark rainstorm. Anna's back ached, but Willie gave her ibuprofen as Hassan laid an armful of gear on the bed, shaking water out of his hair. "Good Christ. I wasn't born to be a mule. What did you *put* in these?"

"Lead pipe." Willie set up her laptop on the table, unplugging the television cable and deftly plugging in a long cord from the computer's side. "Useful for all occasions."

His laughter was a bitter snort of nonamusement. "How is she doing?" He spared one look at Anna, who pulled further into herself.

Why do you even care, if you dislike me so much? Still, she couldn't blame him. She would feel the same way if someone hurt one of *her* friends.

Friends she'd never see again, but still.

"How do you think, you horrible man? As well as can be expected. Lie down, *Liebchen*. You are safe with us."

Safe. What did that even mean, anymore? Did it just mean *alive*?

I wish Josiah was here. A swell of self-disgust rose in her throat. *I wish I knew what to do. What* can *I do?*

"Bloody hell. I'm going to get that last load from the car. I'll do the usual." Hassan stretched, various creaks and pops sounding as he moved. "I *hate* these kinds of operations." He paused, his eyes coming to rest on Anna again. "Listen...Miss Caldwell. Anna. I didn't mean it, love."

Anna stared at her knees. Her entire body hurt, but her heart worst of all. *Leave me alone. I hate you. If I had a gun…*

But she didn't, and it wasn't right to be angry at him anyway. Hassan sighed. "Willie?"

"Leave her be. You are terrible cruel." She waved a hand at him. "Get everything from the car, Hassan."

"Women." He went out the door, muttering.

"Don't take it personally, *Liebchen,*" Willie said in the sudden silence. "He says things he doesn't mean. Like Josiah."

Josiah doesn't say something he doesn't mean. Anna sighed, folded her hands in her lap like a schoolgirl. *Would you teach me what I needed to know, if I asked you?* "We're just supposed to sit here? For how long?"

"Until Josiah makes contact." Willie turned the laptop on. "Or until it's too dangerous to stay. Then we'll get out, by train or plane. Probably by train, then plane. Or we might drive up over border. It all depends." She shrugged, her huge bun bobbing as she settled into the chair, producing a gun that clicked as she settled it on the table within easy reach. "Important thing is to keep you out of it."

God. "I shouldn't have called him." Anna shut her eyes, hugging herself. *I'm responsible for this. I didn't know, but that doesn't absolve me.* "I should have just let them kill me. Or I should have tried to find out what Eric knew and—"

"Does no good to blame yourself." Willie's fingers tapped the keyboard. "Bloody hotels. No security at all."

"You say he's really going to get himself killed." It was one thing for her to think it, quite another to hear these "professionals" saying it out loud. "It's my fault. I wish I could do *something.*"

"The best thing to do is *wait.* Silly little girl. We are specialists, let us…" Willie stopped. The sound of her fingers tapping the keyboard stopped as well.

Anna's eyes flew open. *What's wrong?*

Willie eased out of the chair. "Get down," she whispered. "Beside the bed, *Liebchen*."

Anna didn't hesitate. She almost fell off the bed in her hurry, her back spasming and her ankle sending a bolt of pain up her leg. She peered over the top of the rumpled coverlet and saw the door handle moving. "What if it's—" she whispered.

"He would knock. Get down." Willie moved aside, crouching behind the long, low dresser holding the TV. Seeking cover.

Anna found herself nose-to-carpet, listening with every fiber of her body. The carpet was short, stubby, and peach colored, probably a bitch to clean without steam and heavy-duty solvents. If they ever *did* clean. Her hair was a hot weight against the back of her neck.

I'm spending a depressing amount of time in hotel rooms lately. A sardonic laugh rose in her throat, was strangled, and died away, clawing at her chest as it went so her eyes turned dry and her entire body into a hypersensitive canvas, nerve endings straining. *It must be my personality.*

The door rattled. Willie let out a soft breath.

Four knocks. A pause. Two knocks. Another rattle against the door.

"Stay still," Willie whispered.

The door clicked and opened. "Stand down." Hassan was hoarse. "Check the window, Willie. They're here."

"Who?" Willie gained her feet in a lunge, and the light died. Anna blinked.

"*Them* again. The fucking exploding men." A skittering

sound, like sand poured from a pail at the beach. "I knifed one at the door. *Move*, woman!"

"How many?" Willie eased to the window.

"Four of 'em I saw. The other three hung back—be *careful*." Hassan was hoarse. "Christ. I hate this."

"Get the rifle. I see one. Standing right down there in the light." Willie tweezed the curtain aside delicately. "Stay down, *Liebchen*."

"She behind the bed? Good." Little clicks. "You sure you want to open fire?"

"Not sure, no. A silenced shot from here..." She accepted the rifle. "What are our options?"

Anna's back spasmed again, and she wished the ibuprofen would start working. *Oh, God. This just keeps getting worse.*

Hassan brushed ash from his shoulders. "I even have this shit in my hair. Our options are to fight, fight silent, or run."

"I like the second."

"I like the last." He stepped back. "Willie. They came in the window at the house."

"I know. I've got a visual on two and three. You sure you only saw four?"

"I saw—"

Whatever Hassan had seen remained unsaid as the window shattered and Anna screamed, frantically scrabbling to get *away* and failing miserably as the man landed on the floor and launched himself at her. Two guns spoke at the same instant, one silenced and the other not, and the man's head exploded.

Literally, truly *evaporated*. Flesh runneled, veins of darkness crackling through the flying figure with lightning speed, and an eruption of fine crystalline grit painted the air, breaking into smaller and smaller pieces.

Anna stared. It wasn't the first time she'd seen it, but it never got any easier to believe what her eyes were telling her.

Get up. The voice in her head was new, and cold, married to the same chill certainty that had forced her to keep running in George's garden as bullets pocked into wet earth. *If you freeze they'll get you.*

Funny, how George's head hadn't acted like that. The explosion there had been much more—

For God's sake, stop it. Her legs wouldn't quite work, but she grabbed the bed and hauled herself up with more determination than success. *Get up, Anna.*

Cold air swelled through the broken window. The curtains fluttered, making little noises as they touched the wall.

"*Fuck.*" Hassan moved to the window. "It's fight *and* run. Get the girl and the laptop, lovey."

"And after you brought everything upstairs." Willie eased to the side. "I can take another one from here. He's just *standing* there."

"Don't take the easy shot." Hassan stepped forward and leaned down, grabbing Anna's arm. He hauled her up as if she weighed nothing. "How did they fucking find us? *How?* We're *over the goddamn state line!*"

More certainty clicked into place inside Anna's head. *Me. They're tracking me. Because my...blood...smells like Eric's.* Bile rose in her throat. *I think I'm going to throw up. I really do.*

Puke later, the cold voice replied. *Move now.*

Willie slammed the laptop shut, shoving it into a padded case while Hassan grabbed the backpack and the duffel bag. "Hold these," he said, and Anna found herself with the backpack on, her arms through the straps, her left hand taken up with the heavy duffel. "If I shout *down,* you drop. Let's move."

"They could be out in the—" Willie slung her laptop case across her body and picked up the rifle again, its case discarded on the bed.

"*Move,* woman!"

The curtains billowed, and Hassan shoved Anna so hard she stumbled and fell, her head giving a starry burst of pain as it rebounded from something hard in the duffel bag. He fired twice, three times, bursts of incredible sound followed by a soft explosion as dust flowered through the air.

Forget puking. What about passing out? She made it up to her knees, casting around for something, anything, to use as a weapon.

Hassan hauled her the rest of the way back up, his fingers unforgiving steel spikes. "Off we go, then." Grim good humor filled his voice. "Willie?"

"Right behind you. Stay with me, *Liebchen.*" She, at least, sounded calm. The rifle did something in her hands, clicking and coming alive, and Willie's dark eyes took on a predatory gleam.

Anna had nothing in her hands but the duffel. The entire world was going a bit fuzzy—was it because of the Advil?

Find something to fight with, Annie. "Can I have a gun?" *I sound almost normal.*

Hassan snorted rudely. "Not bloody likely. Worse than having none at all. Come on."

Outside in the hall, dead silence ruled over the harsh broken sound of their breathing. The duffel bag was heavy, the backpack straps cutting into Anna's shoulders. Still, she felt more useful than usual—she was carrying something, at least.

"This way." Hassan shoved her to get her going. "Not the elevator, ducky. Someone's coming up."

"Americans," Willie muttered, like a curse. She walked sideways, the rifle held ready; Hassan had his gun pointed at the floor. "Do you hear that? Sirens."

"I hear it." His voice was pitched low, and Anna stumbled. Her heart beat high and wild-frantic in her throat, and she suddenly longed for a bathroom. Her bladder was two sizes too small now.

Dammit. Now is a really fine time to wish I'd bought a gun years ago. Or learned how to use one, at least.

Then the stairwell door was flung open, and chaos swallowed her whole.

Chapter Twenty-Five

He took the first one—a prominent businessman on the City Council who looked twenty years younger than his real age now—from a rooftop, the recoil of a silenced rifle jarring his hands, the shock against his unwounded shoulder. The second, a district attorney, was a bit trickier, but the rifle still worked wonders. Ballistics would link the two, but that was fine.

It was, after all, what Josiah wanted. He *wanted* them to know someone was picking them off. He also stopped at two, having other work to accomplish that day.

He hardly ever thought about Anna. At least, not for long, not that night. Hassan and Willie would take care of her. They didn't make contact, but Hassan could have decided to take the women even further afield to protect them.

Josiah couldn't worry about that now.

He was grimly satisfied to see the headlines the following morning. There was no more covering it up or keeping it quiet. No, they were called murders and splashed across the front page, the first attributed to a jealous ex-wife—Josiah could have laughed until he choked if the situation hadn't been so gruesome—and the second to a disgruntled felon the DA had prosecuted.

That afternoon found him settled in a cheap hotel room across from the back of the brownstone on East Morris, as planned. From here he could see the rear entrance, not the façade and the front door—and not so incidentally, since he was well camouflaged and in place by 6 a.m., he was pretty much already inside whatever security perimeter they would set up. The fire escape outside his window was well oiled, going down to an alley that would be impenetrably black once night fell.

Josiah settled in and watched the comings and goings—people carrying out boxes of files, cars pulling up, cars pulling away.

The afternoon lengthened, and they started arriving.

Idiots.

The chief of police showed up, looking fit as a fiddle and much younger than his fifty-three years. Two more city council men, both with a bounce in their strides but with worried shoulders. The heads of two hospitals. A man who owned half of downtown. A virtual who's-who of the city and county influential.

Christ, there's so many. All coming to do damage control.

Dusk settled in increments, and they kept arriving, a good double-dozen men who had sold their souls and bled Corpse Boy dry, then used his bone marrow to create their own private army of dust-exploding men. Not to mention killed a pesky reporter and, the only thing Josiah really cared about, threatened Anna Caldwell.

If they would have left her alone I'd have turned this over to the agency and been long gone by now. I'd have taken her to Europe, maybe. Easier to stay out of sight there.

He shifted his weight slightly to keep his circulation going as he crouched in the window, the binoculars in his hand. Hanging out in a sniper's hole all day was almost guaranteed to give one the mental jitters, but he felt better than he had in a while. Once he put her out of his head, he could function more effectively.

Except the thought of her kept coming back. Tiptoeing into his head on little cat feet, touching off the unsteady explosive feeling that had almost gotten him killed in Cairo.

The way her skin smelled, for example. Her steady gaze at a painting she was interested in. The way she would look up at a waiter in a restaurant, thanking him with a quick smile. She never glanced in store windows to check sight lines or woke up damp with sweat, a scream caught in her throat because the dreams were so bad.

She lived in the real world, and she'd made it possible for him to live there, too. Instead of the gray pit of murk where Josiah had sunk for so long he couldn't remember the real, except when he saw it through her eyes.

Don't think about that. She's in the gray now, and you have to get her out. Yourself, too.

He took a deep breath, another, and settled himself more comfortably as full dark began to spread her wings over the city. The streetlamps came on, and he clicked the binocs to night vision. The bite on his neck throbbed with the same hot, infected pulse.

She's seen what I am up close now. How am I going to keep her with me after this? Lie to her about whatever kind of danger she's in? Yeah, that'll go over real well if she ever finds out. Let's face it, Josiah. You're not the man for her.

Soon this would all be a bad dream for Anna Caldwell. She'd visit her brother's grave, lay down some flowers, cry, and get on with her life.

The agency knew about her. She wouldn't be safe without him. Could he possibly make her understand that?

Doesn't matter. She's not going anywhere without me once I finish this. I don't care what I have to do to make her understand.

He patted his hip pocket for the fifth time, the heavy little lump of cold metal in it sharp even through heavy denim. Another car pulled up and he lifted the binocs just as the cell in his breast pocket vibrated.

He held the binocs with one hand and fished the phone out with the other. The car was a limo, and it held the prime mover of the whole thing, if Eric's files were to be believed.

Denton. The man himself. He looked even trimmer and thinner than in Eric's pictures—pictures, incidentally, probably taken from the alley below.

Josiah flipped the cell phone open. "Talk to me."

"Wolfe." Hassan sounded pale. Josiah's heart gave a thump. He controlled it, ignoring the sudden taste of copper in his mouth. "We have a problem."

The wall inside Josiah's head lifted, flooding him with sterile white light. The world stood out in cold, sharp relief, every muscle in his body locking briefly as he stared through the binoculars. The world was green and distorted through them, but once his eyes compensated he had no trouble picking out Denton, the bullyboys around him—probably off-duty cops, maybe with the gene therapy making their cellular structures *unstable*—and another figure, slim and limping, that he would know anywhere, in any crowd.

Her hair was tangled. She moved painfully, and one of them shoved her.

You promised me you would keep her safe. You promised, Hassan.

"They have her," he said flatly. "Where are you?"

"They followed us out of town and overwhelmed us, got us locked up in a warehouse on Starke." There was a sound of shifting, Willie's hoarse voice counting something off behind him. "We were to be liquidated as soon as they took Anna, but Willie managed to get her hands free. And the freak showed up. He said to tell you he's on his way. Josiah—"

"*Where are you right now?*" *That doesn't sound like me. That sounds like a man with something dry and hard stuck in his voice. A man who's just had the wind taken out of him.* It took every iota of control he still possessed to keep the phone to his ear. *This must be what it feels like to have a heart attack.*

"We're on Middleston Boulevard. Willie's got a net up—"

"I'm going in," Josiah heard himself say.

"Wait for us." Hassan's tone was soft and hoarse. "Come on, Wolfe. Just ten minutes."

Oh, no. I am not going to be that reasonable. They have Anna. "No. She's in there now, I'm going in. When you get here, just follow the screaming." He hit the end-call button and Hassan's protest was cut off.

Josiah hurled the phone across the room. It hit the wall with a sound too small to be satisfying. The binocs dropped from his hand, and he scooped up the messenger bag, settling it so the strap lay diagonally across his body. The plastic explosive wasn't very heavy, but he had plenty of ammo. There were more clips on the belt he buckled on, shrugging his jacket over both bag and belt. He tested the clips of the first two guns, and opened the window. Cold air smashed his face. The back of his neck crawled, and he found he was sweating.

Anna.

God alone knew what they were going to do to her. To his connection to the real world. The only thing that had ever made Josiah feel alive, as if he *mattered.*

As if he was real, himself.

Go do it, Josiah. Do what you were made for. Do what you have to.

Whatever happened, he was going to make them pay. Afterward…

Worry about afterward when you're clear of this mess. Now get in there and kill someone, Josiah. Put them down quick and hard.

It was time to do some damage.

The guard perimeter was laughably amateur. Josiah simply came out of the shadows and took both of them, one with a quick twist to break the neck and the other with a knife to the kidneys, pulling back on the man's hair to expose a pale slice of throat. The blade went in with little resistance and came out just as easily. He stepped free of arterial spray and glided up the steps, the terrain map standing out clear and sharp inside his head.

It was like every other liquidation. Except this one had an extraction at its center, a beating heart.

Anna.

His brain jagged to the side, came back. *Can't afford to lose focus.* The back door didn't have just outside guards. If he was running security, he'd have plenty of them inside, covering the hall and fire angles.

Just how amateurish are they? He glanced up, and decided there might be a better way to get in.

"Wait," someone breathed in his ear, and Josiah spun aside, the knife coming up in a sweet solid arc, sinking in with a sound like an axe splitting soft wood.

Kit eyed him for a moment, his eyes half-lidded and carrion breath exhaling in Josiah's face. The bite on Josiah's throat gave a hot agonized pulse.

The knife had passed right through Kit's mutilated left hand, stopped only by the crossguard. Josiah braced himself.

Kit smiled broadly, exposing all his teeth. His canines were long and deadly sharp, touching his bruise-colored lower lip, dyed dark purple by the dim gleam of the lone streetlight standing sentry on Bremont, the street running parallel to Morris. The band of scarring on his throat and the track marks on his bare fish-belly arms—the sleeves had been torn off his T-shirt—writhed madly, flush and fat.

Those dark eyes lit with hellfire, a sickly greenish glow building in the pupils. Every hair on Josiah's body stood straight up. He *recognized* the creature.

This thing…It's a predator.

Not only did Josiah recognize it, but he also found out something that made his entire body into a block of ice.

He *understood* the creature, too. They were, in some mad way, completely identical.

Kit's right hand reached down, the index finger and thumb squirming in ways no human finger was designed for, curving into Josiah's hip pocket. He fished out the ring, its heavy black cabochon glittering with the same greenish fox fire as the thing's eyes. The high curved claws holding the gem—an onyx, or some other black glassy stone—were of no creature that existed on earth.

The ring *had* been in Eric's apartment, the best find of the day. In the very first place Anna had listed in her careful school-girl handwriting—all Josiah'd had to do was drag a chair under the tinkling antique chandelier in the living room and reach up, sensitive fingertips finding a circle of bitter metal ice.

"This," Kit said softly, his mouth having small trouble with the sibilants, "is mine, canny one."

The ring clicked against the knife's hilt as he wrapped the ruined stubs of his right hand around Josiah's. One sharp move-ment and the knife slid free, black blood painting its blade. More blood welled before the hole in his hand closed itself, the hurt healing over.

A painless, hot pang of nausea bolted through Josiah, passed away. He stared. *I am just standing here on the steps. The door's right there. If there's more of a security net I'm in deep fucking trouble.*

Kit's grin widened. The bite had turned hard, a knob of in-fection under the skin. "There were six others. You would have killed them soon enough. Inside, there are more." He let go of Josiah and lifted his left hand. Slid the ring onto his sec-ond finger and let out a sigh of consummation, a very human sound made terrifying by the utter inhumanity of his ruined face topped with long greasy-black dreadlocks.

"Anna's in there." Josiah's voice didn't come out quite right. It was a harsh croak. The only thing more frightening than *un-derstanding* the predator was the fact that he didn't see much wrong with standing here and talking to it. "They have her."

"Then we shall retrieve her. She does seem to wander, this

fair Anne of yours." Kit's face flushed, a sparkle creeping into his gaze. He was looking better every second. "Perhaps you should keep a closer watch."

Shut the fuck up. She's been in there too long. "I have enough plastique to blow this place sky-high. Let's go."

"I shall go first. Their bullets cannot harm me." Kit blinked, a quick reptilian movement, and the cold grin spreading over his flushing face felt familiar as Josiah's own. "Come, then."

Chapter Twenty-Six

She actually saw *stars,* bright speckles in the flood of sterile whiteness. The slap rocked her head back, her wounded cheek burning with fresh scalding pain. Handcuffs jingled against the back of the chair, and the harsh light from the lamp glared in her eyes.

"You'll talk." The stocky, dark-haired one they called Denton sounded like oil poured onto freezing concrete. The name sounded familiar, from Eric's files, but he didn't seem like anyone Anna wanted to know. "Stubborn little bitch, you will."

Her mouth held a thin scrim of blood, the blood that had led them to her. If she tried, could she taste Eric in the coppery salt? The gaunt, feverish man Willie had seen outside in the parking lot had somehow tracked Anna, somehow *smelled* her, and she shuddered whenever she'd brushed against him on the bumpy van ride back to the city. They thought it was funny, especially Denton, laughing at her flinching whenever he twitched—and whenever he made that mewling little noise in the back of his throat, like a kitten crying to be fed.

His eyes, dusty darkness twitching in their sockets, reminded her of Kit's. And all the laughter didn't help.

A long van ride back to the city, her arms aching because her wrists were tied behind her back; Willie's eyes closed as her lips moved silently, Hassan working his hands against each other to try to get free. Each time one of their captors found him doing so, they hit him, and each time they hit him Anna shut her eyes. They kept saying nasty things about Willie, too, just like douchebags catcalling on a city street.

They had no doubt killed Hassan and Willie by now. It was her fault, for calling Josiah and getting them involved.

These men had brought her here, to East Morris Street, and that meant she was going to die as well. She wasn't naïve enough to think they'd dragged her here just to beat her up a little bit.

Not anymore.

Josiah. He's out there somewhere. Going to get himself killed, too. I shouldn't have called him.

Another slap smashed against her face, and someone made a small avid sound. Pounding her wasn't working, despite the fact that her face was on fire and her stomach hurt, runnels of nausea working up her esophagus, burning. How soon would it be before they came up with something worse?

She could think of much worse.

Your imagination just works too goddamn well, Annie. Her brother's voice, tight with pain inside her head, like the time he'd broken his arm and she'd read *Winnie the Pooh* to him all through long rainy afternoons while he was in bed because Mom was afraid if he moved he'd break something else....

Eric wouldn't talk, so these men—or their flunkies—had killed him. They kept asking her questions, and hitting her.

She kept her mouth tightly shut.

"Is this necessary?" Another anonymous male voice. With the light shining in her eyes, she couldn't tell where it came from. The light bored into her, smashed past her eyelids, laid her bare. Her wrists ached, and her swollen ankle pressed heavily against the inside of her boot; both boots were handcuffed to the chair legs. Her back cramped so hard she gasped.

"She knows where it is. This is necessary. Unless you want to end up like Johnson." Fingers slid into her hair, pulled painfully, her head tipping back. A trickle of liquid slid down her upper lip, matching the hot blood painting one side of her face. Her stomach gurgled with molten lead. The oily-sounding man had punched her more than twice, right in the gut. Hard.

Knows where what is? The files, or Kit?

Don't tell them a damn thing, Anna. Eric wouldn't, so you won't either.

The thought was like flotsam to a shipwreck victim. She clung to it. Her teeth had cut the inside of her mouth. Blood slid hot and slick down the back of her throat, full of copper.

The atmosphere inside the small room tensed, cold and strained. Anna knew there was a bed in here, with a high iron headboard; she'd glimpsed it when they dragged her in. With the hot light in her eyes, she couldn't tell how many men there were.

Oh, God.

The bed's head and footboard both had straps dangling from them. Some of the restraints looked ragged, as if the tough leather had been *chewed*.

Had Eric somehow snuck into this cellar, and freed Kit? Her wrists rubbed together, yet more blood painting the handcuffs as they jangled.

"Did you hear that?" Yet another man. He sounded worried. "Gunfire. This isn't what I signed up for."

"Fucking pussy." The oily man's hot fingers cupped her face, one hand still tangled in her hair. "You wanted to live forever, you stinking son of a bitch, it takes a little work. Make yourself useful, and come take a turn. The troops will handle it."

"So far the troops have done jack shit, Denton." *This* voice Anna knew. It was Mayor Marshall, his rich baritone strained and worn raw, not smooth as a campaign ad. "You didn't tell us they turned to dust when you hit 'em. They couldn't even bring this bitch in without getting the whole goddamn city in an uproar. What else haven't you told us?"

"You should have come to us when it escaped." A whining, sawtooth voice. "You should have come right out and told us."

"What would have happened if I did? You'd have all turned into goddamn candy-ass pansies sooner, and we never would have gotten any work done. We can handle this. We're in control here, goddammit."

You don't sound like you're too in control to me. Gunfire? She strained her ears. *I don't hear anything.*

Her heart leapt inside her chest. *Josiah. Oh, God.*

The oily man yanked up on her hair, and a small betraying sound wrung its way out of her. "Just like your fucking brother," Denton whispered in her ear. "He begged, bitch. He broke down and begged once the boys started working on him."

Fury filled her, a hot flood of stinging anguish mixing with the rage.

Anna's teeth ground together. Her wrists worked fruitlessly at the slicing-tight handcuffs. She pitched to one side, hoping to throw him off balance, *do* something, but he yanked her hair again and cupped her throat, his fingers sinking in. The chair didn't move.

Pressure mounted behind her eyeballs, her throat almost blocked, breath whistling past the obstruction. Not enough air.

"I think she needs softening up." The only thing worse than the menace in his tone was the cheerfulness. "Do you like the sound of that, little bitch? The bed's right there."

More silence, and Anna heard a faint chattering sound. It wasn't her teeth. It was bullets in the distance. Everything inside her contracted, leaving her body behind.

Please. Oh, God, please. Not that.

"You are fucking crazy," another man said, in a wondering, thoughtful tone. "You are absolutely fucking *insane*."

"I'm not insane. I'm a visionary." Denton laughed. The sound was a madman's cackle. "And I think she just needs a little time to get to know us. Then she'll tell us where the goddamn thing is."

"Uh, Denton? The noise is getting closer." This voice was from farther away, and Anna could sense them drawing back.

All except for the man with his hand digging into her neck. It was hard to breathe, and it only got harder when his *other* hand slid out of her hair and clasped around her throat as well, tensing. "It doesn't matter. The door's locked both inside and out. I've got the only key. The troops will *handle* it."

The pressure behind her eyeballs got worse. So did the burning need to *breathe. Oh, Jesus.* The thought wasn't even a prayer, more an inarticulate moan. The chair was bolted to the floor; there was no way she could move it. Still, she had to do something. Anything.

Bite him? Maybe I could. Can't kick, my feet are strapped down. Think. Do something.

"I'll tell you," she whispered, her cracked lips framing the words with difficulty. "He's hiding. I'll tell you where."

Silence reigned for a full twenty seconds, ticking through the room as gunfire echoed in sharp spatters. She clung to consciousness by a thread.

The hands around her throat eased. "You'd better make it quick." Denton's tone was almost intimate.

Blessed, scorching-cold air hit her raw throat. "I'm not stupid." She licked her lips, wished she couldn't taste fresh blood every time she swallowed. "If I tell you now you'll kill me. I'll take you there. In a car." *Keep him talking, Anna. It's your only chance.*

"You think *I'm* stupid, you nosy little cunt?" He pulled her hair again, sharply. "Where is it? The thing. The creature."

I wouldn't go so far as to call him a person. But if he's a murdering psycho right now I wonder how much you have to do with it. "So neither of us is stupid." *Mexican standoff? No, they have me tied to a chair and any moment they're going to hit me again.* The light glared in her eyes, even when she shut them. If she lived, would she be blind?

The sound of gunfire abruptly ceased. Somebody gasped, another let out a whispered curse.

"That's enough, Denton." Mayor Marshall spoke up. "This has gone too far."

There was a click behind her—a metallic sound, one she'd heard too many times recently.

Someone was messing with a gun.

"I say when it's gone too far, Ed." Denton's tone was utterly calm, ruthless, and so flat it could give Kit's sibilant whisper a run for its money in scariness.

Sweat trickled down Anna's back, soaking into her shirt. *He's going to shoot me. He's behind me with a gun.* Fruitless thrashing was getting her nowhere; there was *nothing* she could do. The handcuffs jingled as she hunched her shoulders instinctively, the body's dumb need to get away, understanding it was in danger.

A massive impact thudded against the door, as if a bulldozer had rammed it at full speed. Anna screamed, and someone else did, too, their voices harmonizing with freakish beauty for a brief moment. Another huge sound, metal tearing and screeching, and impossibly quickly, a third. Clatters. Falling scraps of metal. Anna blinked against the light in her face, hunching as far as she could, straining her ears, the back of her head alive with a crawling sensation. Where was the gun?

The voice that spoke out of the sterile white light was slightly *off,* as if he spoke with something in his mouth. Something long, and sharp, and deadly. "Did you hear me knocking? Knocking at your chamber door?" An edge of mad glee rode the words. "*Did* you?"

Denton yelled. The lamp hit the floor, glass tinkling into shivering bits, and died. Anna's breath came hard and harsh as her wrists rubbed, slick with blood, trying to slip her hands out of the cuffs. Metal bit mercilessly, fresh hot liquid welling from her wrists as a chorus of screaming bounced off the concrete walls. The ghost of the lamp spread false blue and gold fireworks in the pitch darkness, and she heard wet ripping sounds interspersed with the screams. Other sounds crashed into the darkness. Gulps, like someone taking long drafts of soda on a long hot summer day. A sizzling sound, like bacon frying. The sharp bangs of a gun, its muzzle flashing in the absolute dark. The stink of bullets. A chip of something flicked past her face, stinging her unwounded cheek.

She struggled and kicked, the rattling of handcuffs against the metal chair adding to the cacophony. Someone was screaming, hoarse and broken, and she hoped it wasn't her.

Then the screaming stopped. More silence, the blackness absolute as the bottom of a well. Except for Anna's breathing, deep sobbing breaths as she thrashed against the bonds. *Please, no. Please no, turn the lights on please, please God no—*

Something touched her arms. Anna screamed again, hoarsely. A quick movement and her hands were suddenly free, the bracelets of the cuffs sliding down her forearms. Almost immediately after, her ankles were torn free, metal squealing as it snapped. Vise-grips at her shoulders, hauling her up.

The darkness was complete. Her breath came in short stuttering gasps. The hands stroked her hair, and her ankle gave way as she tried to walk. Her teeth clicked together, chattering, even though she was feverish.

"One good deed," he lisp-whispered as he dragged her, Anna's boots scraping the floor and bumping soft things he stepped over. "To repay another."

Her mouth was dry, her throat coated with metal. Still, she had to ask. She had to know. She peered up at where the face should be, blinking furiously against the complete absence of light.

"Josiah?"

The blackness engulfed as he carried her away.

Chapter Twenty-Seven

The stitches had torn, and his arms ached savagely. He'd taken a hit on the head that trickled warm blood down his neck, and his knee might not ever be the same again. His hair was full of drying blood, dust, broken glass, and other things.

Killing was a dirty business.

Josiah braced himself against the wall. Time was running out. The lab was a chaos of broken glass and smeared substances he didn't want to think about, the entire second floor of the brownstone given over to rooms full of medical and laboratory equipment, dentists' chairs with well-used leather straps, and enough half-trained cops to make the entire fucking thing a tactical nightmare. Kit had disappeared, leaving Josiah to fight his way up; the result was a sweep-and-clear to find the only thing that mattered to him at this point.

She wasn't up here. He cased the entire second level, his hands moving without conscious direction to keep the gun pointed where it needed to be, sweeping the rooms full of broken bodies and shattered glass. He wasn't sure if he'd taken a bad hit or not; he was past caring.

Nothing. She simply wasn't here. His hands, busy little movers that they were, were itching to take out the plastic explosive and burn this whole nightmarish place to the ground. He had a vague idea what the racks of syringes and other equipment were for—and the straps on the chairs looked far too well-used for comfort.

Did they take her out through the front? Got to go, time's clicking, someone's going to come along or report the noise, I haven't exactly been quiet.

Broken glass ground underfoot. He whirled, gun coming up, and the shot went wide as he realized who it was at the last second.

Hassan held both hands up, both with a shiny 9mm loose and easy in slim brown fingers. "Friendly!" he yelled as he threw himself down and aside, rolling behind cover just in case.

Josiah's hands itched furiously for a moment. He almost hadn't pulled back in time.

"There's nobody alive in here!" Hassan yelled. "There's chatter on the bands about tac-teams moving this way and if the agency's going to move in and mop up, now is the time! Can we *go?*"

Not without Anna. He turned back to the room he'd just searched, the bodies no more than insensate lumps of clay. The exploding ones were easiest to deal with; grit showered the floor, crunching like the broken glass. The live ones were tricky, half-ass-trained off-duty cops, amateurish mistakes giving them openings a professional wouldn't take.

"She's *not here!*" Hassan sounded half-frantic. "Come on, Josiah! Blow this hole and get out! I've checked from the basement up to here—if she's not here she's *gone!* Come on!"

Basement? There was no basement. I didn't see… He replayed

284

mental footage as his body moved, heading for Hassan. *It looked like a freight elevator. What if it was to the basement? Or—*

"Come *on*!" Hassan grabbed his arm, and Josiah suppressed a flinch. He was bleeding pretty badly, and his head wasn't right. The objective wasn't here, and if the objective wasn't here *he* had no business being here.

The situation had gone critical.

Where is she, then? They brought her in here. Where's Kit? He's got his goddamn ring; did he leave me in the lurch? Figures.

His feet took care of the stairs for him, a line of blood smeared at shoulder height where some idiot had tried to escape him. The idiot was sprawled at the bottom of the flight—this place had once been a house, long ago when the city was young. It might have been a pretty place, too, except for the use it had been put to.

How many had he killed? He'd lost track.

Anna.

Where was she?

He stopped four times as they made a circuit of the lower level, long enough each time to tamp down the plastic explosive and push the detonator sticks in. Blood and other fluids dripped with monotonous regularity. There were no sirens in the distance. Whoever was approaching, they were coming in low and silent.

The chief of police wasn't among the dead. Nor were the two dozen men who had taken treatments here. The likeliest explanation was they had gone right out the front. But why? This was their bolt-hole; it would have made more sense for them to come in the front and slip out the back, scattering and regrouping at another location. It fit with the whole amateurishness of the operation.

Hassan had a fresh disposable cell out. He was talking into it, quietly, fiercely; he snapped it shut. His hair was wildly mussed and his face looked worse for wear, and he moved like a man who has endured a beating in the past twenty-four hours and was ignoring it. "We've got no time. Willie's got a visual on a black van heading this way along the main approach; if she's seen one there's others. She's packing up and getting loose now."

"Where's our rendezvous?" his voice asked, independent of his brain. Training had him in its iron grip, because he had *failed* and there was nothing else to do. He hadn't retrieved her. Kit had vanished, the men responsible were gone, and all he'd done was clean up their operation.

The agency's going to turn this place inside out. And there's no scientists here, no medical personnel. The agency will round them up, extract everything they know.

It was all bollixed up. Gone sideways. They had Anna.

Then you'll just have to get her.

It was too late. He'd failed in every major objective. Time to tie it off, cut the losses, and run.

The slap of rainy night outside met the pulsing of the bite at his throat, a half-note in the thunder of pain his body had become. What had he done to his knee?

He didn't know. He'd covered the whole house—

There was a dark green SUV with tinted windows parked on a side street. Hassan bundled him into the passenger seat, slammed the door, and went around the front of the car, checking his surroundings unobtrusively.

Josiah let out a soft breath. The mission had gone sideways. He held up the pulser, looking at the sleek chrome and the single button. It would send out the signal, detonating the explosive and cleaning up the operation.

The gun caressed his cheek. "Be very still," a flat, low voice he knew said softly, in the car's deep dark interior.

Hassan opened the driver's side door, climbed up into the seat—and jerked as Kit took his gun away. "And you. Drive." The ring glinted on Kit's corpse-pale left hand, and Josiah got a funny unsteady feeling in the pit of his abused stomach. Had he taken a fist there, too, or was it the one with the nightstick? He couldn't remember.

Kit's left hand was whole and well now. Four long flexible fingers and a thumb, prominent tendons and the knuckles broad and scarred with faintly flushed white lines.

Knife-fighter's scars.

Some lizards grow their tails back. Did he need the ring, or did he need blood? Or something else? Something they stole from him with their syringes and straps?

A ghastly flush crept under pale waxy skin, and the ring gave a flash of green as Josiah twisted slowly in the seat, dust and little bits of broken glass scratching between his coat and the upholstery.

There, on the bench seat, behind Hassan, slumped a very bruised and very tired-looking Anna, huddled against the door and staring out. She looked like she'd been through the grinder, her eyes glazed in the dimness as she breathed, touching the window with a faint cloud.

There's no fog on the windows. How did we not see them? How did I not mark them in here?

"Wolfe?" Hassan was tense and ready.

Josiah blinked. His heart slammed inside his chest, and the gun Kit held seemed laughably small, a toy instead of a real weapon. "Drive." The word scraped his throat.

The pulser was still in his hand, a small, cold chrome weight.

He pressed the button as Hassan started the SUV. The engine roused, swiftly.

The sound of the explosion was distant, muffled. Josiah watched Anna's profile. She was milk pale, and she didn't even look at him. The stare of a catatonic deadened her marred face.

His heart hurt, just like the rest of him. *What did they do to you, baby?*

Kit's gun vanished. Hassan's was proffered, Kit's right hand miraculously with its full complement of fingers too. Josiah couldn't see the creature's face, but that voice was unmistakable. "She is better thus, for a little while."

"Jesus Christ." Hassan wiped at his forehead with the back of his hand. Great beads of sweat stood out on his skin, damping his hair down. "You sure know how to throw a party."

"Where was she?" That was all Josiah wanted to know. "Is she hurt?"

"They kept her where they kept me, in the cellar. Which is only reached from the alley to the side. Once they used it for coal delivery." Kit paused. "They are no longer among the breathing, canny one, those who stole from me. We are at quits."

"Not nearly." Josiah's tongue felt too big for his mouth.

Hassan made a right turn. *Now* the sirens became audible, and he pulled over to the curb to let a cavalcade of spinning lights and noise go past in the opposite direction, mostly cop units and a SWAT team. A black van trailed silent and deadly in the wake of flashing red and blues, the agency coming in to clean up the mess, recover what they could, and probably search for Josiah himself. There would be other units converging from other directions.

A brief flash of Chilwell's bloodless face floated through

Josiah's head, was shoved aside. *One problem at a time.* "I owe you."

Kit paused. He made a brief movement, and all four of his new fingers brushed Anna's bruised cheek, the ring's claws touching her tangled hair. Someone had given her a few good shots. "She will wake in time, and her memory will be blunted. It was the least I could do. Tell her…"

Hassan hunched in the driver's seat. He was still sweating. The stink of fear was a cloud in the car, the defroster suddenly working overtime against traceries of steam starting on the windows.

"Tell her Eric is avenged," Kit finished, as if he wanted to say more. The door opened, let in a breath of frigid rainy air, closed, and Josiah thought he heard rapid padding footsteps vanishing into the night.

"Fucking hell." Hassan's voice shook. "I can't take much more of this."

You can, and you will. "Get us to the rendezvous." Josiah scrabbled for the seat controls and pushed back the top half of the passenger seat. His entire body cried out in pain as he monkeyed backward, Hassan keeping up a steady cavalcade of obscenities in four languages.

Josiah didn't care. He made it into the back bench seat, popped the front seat back up, and grabbed her. She was heavy and unresponsive, but he slid his arms around her. He breathed into her snarled and matted hair, and for the first time in his memory, Josiah Wolfe wept with sheer unalloyed relief.

Chapter Twenty-Eight

There was motion inside her head, black wheels turning at midnight and the sound of his voice. Soothing, calm, and even, just the way he always spoke. The weight of dark water added to the sound of wheels turning, and she no longer remembered why exactly she was staring into the distance, only that she was safe.

Kit had *told* her she was safe, his eyes swelling with green foxfire and red pinpricks, and she had seen—

No. Don't think about that. You don't want to think about the darkness, and the sounds. You'll be a lot happier if you don't.

For a moment she remembered what else Kit had done, and a scream welled up in her throat. She swallowed, hard, and shoved the memory away. It went willingly, an unwanted guest. Her head hurt, a swift flash of pain lost in the general discomfort. Even her *hair* hurt.

She was alive. And Eric's killers were...what? Dead?

God, I hope so.

Sunlight striped through a window, lay across the end of a bed. The mattress was soft and deep, the sheets were clean, and

Anna's back still ached. She was stiff, and her face felt like a bruised pumpkin.

The bed was clean. *She* was clean. The golden sunshine scoured away at the inside of her head, dust dancing in its slanted fall, and Anna realized she never wanted to sleep in a dark room again.

This room was plain—white walls, the window, a skylight, and a television on a low white table. The floor was carpeted in short industrial blue.

It was beautiful.

Her wrists were still bruised and puffy, sliced and scabbed over. Her ankles throbbed with dull pain.

To top it all off, she was completely naked.

The distant sound of traffic intruded. She pulled the sheets and blankets to her chest and craned her neck, painfully, finding a half-open door into a white-tiled bathroom.

The bathroom looked *really* good.

Another door opened just as her gaze touched it. Anna huddled on the bed, her mouth suddenly dry and her heart thumping in her throat. She cast around wildly for anything that looked like a weapon, however improbable.

If they've come back for me I'm going to die fighting. Surprisingly, the voice in her head still wasn't Eric's. It was her own—but harsher, colder than she could ever be. More determined.

A stranger's voice.

Josiah stepped through, softly, as if tiptoeing into a hospital room. He closed the door with a precise little click. He moved a bit stiffly, and he was unshaven but otherwise clean. A dark navy-blue sweater, a pair of jeans, and a pair of dark sneakers completed the picture. His eyes were more green today, a few shades lighter than usual—maybe because of the dark sweater, or because of his stubble. His hair was tousled, shoved back from his face.

Her heart threatened to knock her ribs outward. "Jo," she breathed.

He crossed the carpeting in long angry strides, reached the bed, and stared down at her. His eyes were flat, their depths curtained; his mouth a straight line. He looked terribly, coldly, thoughtlessly furious.

Anna froze. For a moment the absolutely absurd idea that he was going to slap her drifted through her head.

Then he dropped down on the bed, the mattress giving a squeak of protest. His face still held that awful blank expression for half a breath before he blinked and took a deep breath. "Are you all right?"

Anna opened her mouth to reply. Shut it. There was nothing to say.

"The operation's tied off." His mouth belonged to a hoarse stranger; it shaped the words like they didn't belong to him. "The agency's too busy chasing down the medical personnel attached to the brownstone. They might chase Corpse Boy for a while, too. Which will give us enough time to bury ourselves nicely."

The air was chill against her naked back.

He took a deep breath, and his gaze met hers, the hazel tinted with green and wounded under their screen of indifference. She almost flinched. The pain in his eyes was well hidden, but she saw it, and her heart twisted back on itself with another thump.

"I have to tell you, Annie." His voice didn't get any louder. "You're coming with me. I don't want to hear any argument. I let you walk away once, and it almost killed me. Do you understand?" He was breathing like a man walking uphill, despite the set pallor of his unshaven cheeks. There was a slash along his hairline and a bruise on his jaw, under the stubble.

He looked, quite frankly, like hell.

There was still nothing to say. She wondered if his shoulder still hurt him. He'd been shot at and had his home taken away, just like her. If she hadn't walked out on him, would Eric still be alive?

I didn't know. I couldn't have known.

Her heart hurt. Everything else on her hurt, but her heart most of all. Not knowing couldn't salve her conscience.

Nothing would.

"Anna." He reached up with his left hand, wincing a little as his shoulder dipped. His fingers cupped her chin. "What does it take? Does it have to be a bargain? You got your goddamn revenge—"

"Shut up." *So my voice still works.* "The others?"

"Willie and Hassan are fine. They'll meet us in Montreal. We'll go on from there." His fingers tightened a little, her bruised face throbbing. "What's it going to take, Annie? What do I have to do for you? Tell me."

I don't know that you could do any more. I was so wrong about you, Josiah. I was wrong about everything. "We'd better get going." Her face hurt even more when she tried to speak. She'd stiffened up all over.

Still, that look in his eyes threatened to make her heart stop its busy knocking around. It hurt too much. *Everything* hurt too much. "If you have any more of those magic pills, I'd like one. I don't think a Tylenol will do much."

He stared at her, the sound of traffic going about its business in the real, peaceful world outside like the sea lapping the shore.

Normal lives were going on outside the walls of this room. Normal people were going to work, going home to their families, getting into traffic accidents, and buying underwear.

I don't think I'll ever feel normal again.

It was her turn for a deep breath, all the way to the bottom of her lungs. "I'll go with you," she whispered. "You came down there for me."

Josiah's fingers turned to stone. His mouth opened slightly before he shut it, his lips thinning. The indifference in his eyes vanished, pain mute and dark and terribly present in its place. How long had he been hurting like that? Since she'd left him? Since *before* she'd left him?

She'd never known. Never even guessed.

"I remember that much, even though it was dark. I remember…" For a moment Anna was confused. What exactly did she remember? Something dark, and confusion, and somehow, she had been taken up out of it. There had been a green glow, and the sense that she was safe, held in a pair of thin, very strong arms—

A wrenching mental effort closed it all away. *No. Josiah came and took me out of there. That's what I remember, and that's what I'll remember until the day I die. I don't care about anything else.*

"I remember you came for me," she finished. "I don't care about anything else. When are we leaving?"

It took him a few moments. The pain in his eyes spread over his entire face, an awful crumpling like a child in agony, though he spoke with the deep gravel tone of an adult male with a sore throat. "I'm a filthy fucking murderer, Anna. You don't want to know what I'm capable of."

Oh, Christ. "I told you, I don't *care.*" Hot tears welled in her eyes. "Do you want me to go with you or not?"

"I'm telling you that you're coming with me, whether you like it or not. Is that clear?" He set his jaw and glared at her.

Her arms hurt, but she lifted them. Her hands cupped the rough stubble of his face, and she pulled him forward. Their foreheads touched, and she closed her eyes. Breathed in. Breathed out.

"I'm going with you," she said, as firmly as she could. "Just tell me what to do first."

"It's not ever going to be like it was. Anna. You know. You *know* what I'm—"

If he keeps this up I'm going to cry. If I start to cry I'm going to scream. I don't want to do that. Anna gathered herself. "Josiah. Shut up."

He did.

"They had me down there." It was difficult to say it. It was difficult to even *think* of the cellar and the harsh bright light shining through her skull. "They were going to...one of them, he told me Eric..." Her throat filled. She had to swallow the sudden smooth hard stone in her throat several times before she could speak again. "If I could have killed him right there I would have. I would have even been happy about it. I'm not a hypocrite—at least, I don't want to be one." *I'm just as bad as you are, and I can't say I'm unhappy about it.* The words trembled on the edge of her tongue. She swallowed their bitterness.

It was one more thing she was never going to be able to tell him.

"It's different for you." He must have had the same stone in his throat. "You're different."

No. Anna breathed him in, Ivory soap and clean male. *I'm not different, Josiah. Underneath everything, I'm not different at all.*

But she let it lie. "I love you," she told him. "I'm sorry."

"Jesus. *You* shouldn't be sorry. I nearly fucked the whole thing up. If it hadn't…Well, it almost went bad. I'll get you something to wear. We should get out of here soon."

I don't even know where we are. "All right. Josiah?"

"What?" The tension left him, draining away bit by bit.

I can handle this, Anna realized. *As long as he's here I can handle it.* "Do you love me?" It wasn't what she meant to say. What she wanted to know was more like, *Do you still want me?* Or even, *Will you forgive me?*

"Why do you think I kept that phone number?" The sentence broke in the middle; he finished it with a sigh. "You are so goddamn stubborn, baby doll."

She sagged with relief. Josiah pulled her gently, carefully, into his arms. The sheet twisted around her legs and her back shrieked with pain, but Anna didn't care. A cloud went over the sun, and daylight dimmed.

That didn't matter either. She rested in his arms, and if the dark suspicion of a memory remained, even weak sunshine was enough to keep it away.

Chapter Twenty-Nine

If you wanted to bury yourself somewhere, India was a good choice.

Night descended upon Bombay suburbs with shrieks, clatters, and a whole host of other noises that began to seem like home once you'd spent long enough there. It was a world away from the States, full of the smells of curry and hot stone, a crowd of humanity and incense. There were other, less pleasant scents—but there were plenty of places in this city's skirts where expatriates could hide.

So this quiet stone house with its courtyard garden and reliable plumbing, its satellite dish and easily covered fire angles, was one of the best places he'd ever gone to ground.

Of course, any location with Willie's cooking and Anna next to him every morning was a good one. Josiah propped his feet on the balcony railing and closed his eyes.

Listen.

Anna hummed inside, her familiar wandering melody as she opened the cabinet in the dining room. Her footsteps dragged a little as she headed back into the kitchen—she still limped when tired. Just a little.

Willie said something, as a pan lid clattered and something sizzled.

"Watch the curry, love," Hassan piped up.

Night just as blood-warm as the day, dusk gathering between juicy green leaves in the garden. The sky had turned that fantastic shade of blue only possible in smog-choked sinks, an indigo like the robe of angels. Anna liked the colors here, even if the rainy season gave her nightmares.

At least she didn't remember them when she woke up.

Josiah settled into the chair a little farther. The heat was oppressive, the worst thing about India. Unless it was the bugs.

The back of his neck prickled, an animal's consciousness of danger.

"I know you're there," he said to the damp-breathing evening.

The sense of presence sharpened, resolved next to him. "Still canny, I see." Kit lowered himself down to perch on Anna's deck chair, shadowed lamplight from inside falling over his dark hair.

He was no longer the ruined scarecrow. Instead, he was an attractive English businessman in Bombay, his haircut sleekly fashionable and his linen suit of the latest cut. The ring glittered on his left hand as he settled into motionlessness, his eyes hooding. He looked *more* human, true…but not human enough.

Not to Josiah. The gun was heavy in his hand, but he didn't raise it. "I suppose if you meant me any harm I wouldn't have time to use this."

"You would not. Though you are dangerous, for a mortal." Kit cocked his head as Anna's laughter drifted from inside, Hassan swearing good-naturedly. "She sounds happy."

"Whatever you did to her head, it worked. She's bounced back. Mostly." *Though she can't sleep without a night-light. Sometimes, I think she dreams about that cellar. Even if she doesn't remember it.* "They're after you."

"Your 'agency' has suspected the existence of my kind for a very long time. I erased most of the evidence before we made our attack." The creature shifted slightly. "What did you think I was doing, while you distracted them so handily?"

That answered a couple of questions. Josiah sighed. A cold beer would go down really well right about now. He shelved the desire. "Nice to know." *Now, why are you here, you freak?*

Kit got to the point. "They are no longer pursuing you. You are presumed dead in their files, and fair Anne as well."

If I can believe you, that's good news. "They do like to cut down on variables. I suppose you had something to do with that?"

"I am not without methods for such occasions." Kit paused. When he spoke again, he sounded almost uncertain. "The bite has faded."

Josiah nodded. His neck suddenly felt very naked, though he'd grown his hair out a bit for camouflage. Anna liked him with the sun-scorch of highlights. She said it brought out his eyes. "It quit bleeding after a while."

"Were I to mark you again…" The sentence trailed off into the spice of a Bombay night, jasmine in the courtyard exhaling perfume, mixing with the drift of curry from inside. "*Her* I cannot change. You, however…you are like me."

A stone-cold killer, you mean? Willing to do anything and use anyone to get the job done? Or do you mean I'm a fellow predator? He almost winced, controlled the motion. His boots rested against the railing. Josiah leaned back in his chair.

Anna carried a gun now. After some initial flinching, she'd learned how to use it well enough that Willie was satisfied, even if Hassan rolled his eyes. Anna had even learned about cover angles, and how to check a street, and was doing well with some other hard lessons. But she was still…

She flinches. No matter how hard she tries, she's not ruthless enough. I'm glad about that. If I have any soul left it's her. I don't even want to think about losing her, ever again. "Is that an offer?"

"Would forever be too long to spend with her? I owe you a service, canny one. I change you, you change her, and the world is your garden." The ring glittered, a stray random flash of green. Heat lay on Josiah's skin, Bombay heat, wet and close.

At least I get to see Anna in those dresses. She wears a sari like she was born for it.

Josiah sighed and stretched, rolling his shoulders back in their sockets. "My name's Josiah." His voice was clear, pitched low, and steady enough to satisfy him. "You can keep that service you owe me. I don't want it."

"You may change your mind. If you do, call for me. I will answer." Kit sat very still, as still as one of the lizards in the garden. Anna drew the flowers, sketched people on the street, and paled sometimes when a reptile blinked at her.

Josiah thought he knew why. "Thanks." *I won't ever get that desperate. I hope.*

"I have one question." Kit tapped the chair's arm with his fingers, once, a sharp blurring-quick movement.

"Shoot." Josiah grinned, a wolfish leer. *I might, after all. I don't know if the new rounds will kill you, but I might give it a try. They kept going on about silver, you know.*

"Was she worth it?"

Josiah didn't even have to think about it. "What do you think?"

He waited for the answer.

Kit was gone. The wet, jasmine-laden air was full of the skittering of nasty laughter for a moment. Sweat trickled down Josiah's back. He let out a long, uneven breath.

I never want to see you again, mister. But for what it's worth, thank you. I owe you one for getting her out of that cellar, and if the agency thinks I'm dead, I owe you even more.

God help me if you ever come to collect, because even if I owe, I'm not paying.

"Josiah?" Anna, calling from inside. She was coming through the dining room, heading for the balcony where he and Hassan sometimes sat and knocked back a few beers before dinner. "It's almost ready."

Was she worth it?

"Always," he said to the empty, listening night. The garden's sweetness drifted up, the clatter and hum of the city in the distance growing fainter for a moment.

"Jo." She was at the window now. "Come on in, it's time for dinner."

"On my way." He slid the gun back into its holster and stood, shrugging so his T-shirt didn't cling to his sweating back. "Pour me some iced tea, will you?"

"Oh, sure." Her eyes glittered for a moment as she held the sheer drapes aside. She'd cut her hair, and its sandalwood was now thickly streaked with blonde. "Should I put on my French maid outfit while I do it?"

"I won't stop you." He stepped into the dining room, slid his arm over her shoulders. "Sounds like fun."

"Is everything all right?" There it was: the worry. She stopped

301

short, examining him and chewing on her lower lip. Of course, she sensed tension. She was getting damn good at reading him, now.

Not good enough. You're still lying to her, Josiah.

Ask me if I care. "Everything's fine, baby. You said something about dinner?"

She leaned into his side, the gun secure under his other arm. "Lazy bum. Come on, it'll get cold."

"Not Willie's cooking. Hassan won't let it."

Her low laugh was enough to tempt him to say *the hell with dinner* and pull her down the hall into the bedroom, to the wide bed with its mosquito netting and cool sheets. Instead, he pressed a kiss to her damp temple, jasmine and her skin under a thin screen of cooking sweat and the spice of curry. Goddamn edible.

Outside, a yellow moon rose over teeming streets and a thin man in a white linen suit was probably sauntering through the nighttime crowds, on his way to whatever waited next in his immortality.

Josiah let her lead him into the brightness of the kitchen, where Hassan had piled his plate already without waiting, while Willie scolded him.

extras

orbit

meet the author

Photo credit: Daron Gildow

Lilith Saintcrow was born in New Mexico, bounced around the world as an Air Force brat, and fell in love with writing when she was ten years old. She currently lives in Vancouver, Washington.

introducing

IF YOU ENJOYED

BLOOD CALL,

LOOK OUT FOR

TRAILER PARK FAE

Gallow & Ragged: Book 1

by Lilith Saintcrow

Jeremiah Gallow is just another construction worker, and that's the way he likes it. He's left his past behind, but some things cannot be erased. Like the tattoos on his arms that transform into a weapon, or that he was once closer to the Queen of Summer than any half-human should be. Now the Half-sidhe all in Summer once feared is dragged back into the world of enchantment, danger, and fickle fae—by a woman who looks uncannily like his dead wife. Her name is Robin Ragged, and her secrets are more than enough to get them both killed. A plague has come, the fullborn fae are dying, and the dark answer to Summer's Court is breaking loose.

Be afraid, for Unwinter is riding....

A DIFFERENT BEAST

1

Summer, soft green hills and shaded dells, lay breathless under a pall of smoky apple-blossom dusk. The other Summer, her white hands rising from indigo velvet to gleam in the gloaming, waved the rest of her handmaidens away. They fled, giggling in bell-clear voices and trailing their sigh draperies, a slim golden-haired mortal boy among them fleet as a deer—Actaeon among the leaping hounds, perhaps.

Though that young man, so long ago, hadn't been torn apart by gray-sided, long-eared hounds. A different beast had run him to ground. The mortals, always confused, whispered among themselves, and their invented gods grew in the telling.

Goodfellow, brown of hair and sharp of ear, often wondered if the sidhe did as well.

The Fatherless smiled as he watched Summer wander toward him through the dusk. She was at pains to appear unconcerned. His own wide, sunny grin, showing teeth sharper than a mortal's, might have caused even the strongest of either Court unease.

Of course, the free sidhe—those who did not bend knee

to Summer or her once-lord Unwinter—would make themselves scarce when the Goodfellow grinned. They had their own names for him, all respectful and none quite pleasing to him when he chose to take offense.

Summer halted. Her hair, ripples of gold, stirred slightly in the perfumed breeze. Above and between her gleaming eyes, the Jewel flashed, a single dart of emerald light piercing the gloom as the day took its last breath and sank fully under night's mantle.

Someday, he might see this sidhe queen sink as well. How she had glimmered and glistened, in her youth. He had once trifled with the idea of courting her himself, before her eye had settled on one altogether more grim.

The quarrel, Goodfellow might say, were he disposed to lecture, *always matches the affection both parties bore before, does it not?* The Sundering had taken much from both Courts, and that bothered him not a bit. When they elbowed each other, the space between them was wide enough to grant him further sway. Carefully, of course. So carefully, patiently—the Folk were often fickle, true, but they did not have to be.

He let her draw much closer before he lay aside his cloaking shadows, stepping fully into her realm between two straight, slender birches, and she barely started. Her mantle slipped a fraction from one white shoulder, but that could have been to expose just a sliver of pale skin, fresh-velvet as a new magnolia petal. Artfully innocent, that single peeping glow could infect a mortal's dreams, fill them with longing, drive all other thought from their busy little brains.

If she, the richest gem of Summer's long, dreamy months, so willed it.

"Ah, there she is, our fairest jewel." He swept her a bow, an imaginary cap doffed low enough to sweep the sweet grass exhaling its green scent of a day spent basking under a perfect sun. "Where is your Oberon, queenly one? Where is your lord?"

"Ill met by moonlight, indeed." She smiled, just a curve of those red, red lips poets dreamed of. There had been mortal maids, occasionally, whose salt-sweet fragility put even Summer to shame, and woe betide them if any of the Folk should carry tales of their radiance to this corner of the sideways realms. "And as you are an honest Puck, I have come alone."

"Fairly." His smile broadened. "What would you have of me, Summer? And what will you give in return?"

"I have paid thee well for every service, sprite, and have yet to see results for one or two dearly bought." Summer drew her mantle closer. She did not deign to frown, but he thought it likely one or two of her ladies would take her expression as a caution, and make themselves scarce. They would be the wisest ones. The favorites, of course, could not afford to risk her noting such a scarcity, and so would stay.

"Oh, patience becomes thee indeed, Summer." He capered, enjoying the feel of crushed sweet grass under his leather-shod feet. A finger snap, a turn, as if it were midsummer and the revels afoot. "As it happens, I bring word from a certain mortal."

"Mortal? What is a mortal to me?" Her hand dropped, and she did not turn away. Instead, her gaze sharpened, though she looked aside at the first swirling sparks of fireflies drawn by her presence. There was nothing the lamp-ended creatures loved more than her own faint glow by night. Except perhaps the Moon itself, Danu's silver eye.

"Then you do not wish to hear of success? O changeable one!"

"Puck." The fireflies scattered, for Summer's tone had

308

changed. In her sable mantle, the golden hair paler now as her mood drained its tint, her ageless-dark eyes narrowing so very slightly, the loveliness of Summer took on a sharper edge. "I grow weary of this."

"Then I shall be brief. He has worked another miracle, this mortal of science. There is a cure."

She examined him for a long moment, and the Goodfellow suffered it. There was a certain joy to be had in allowing her to think he quaked at the thought of her displeasure. Far greater was the amusement to be had in knowing that the Queen of the Seelie Court, Summer herself, the fount of Faerie—for so the bards called her, though Goodfellow could have told them where a truer fountain welled—had very little choice but to dance to his tune.

She turned, a quarter profile of hurtful beauty, her black eyes flashing dangerous. The stars in their depths spun lazily, cold fires of the night before any tree was named. If an ensnared mortal could see her now, Goodfellow thought, he might well drop of the heartshock and leave the trap entire.

"And what is the price for this miracle, sprite?"

He affected astonishment, capering afresh, hopping to and fro. Under the grass was sere dry bramble, and it crunched as he landed. "What? I am no mortal tailor, to double-charge. All you must do is send your own sprite to collect it. The mortal longs for any breath of you, he entreats a word, a look, a sigh."

"Does he?" Summer tapped one perfect nail against her lips. There was a rosy tint a mortal might mistake for polish on its sweet curve, and it darkened to the crimson of her smile as her mood shifted again. *Changeable as Summer,* the free sidhe said. Unwinter was far less capricious, of course…but just as dangerous.

"Welladay." Summer's smile dawned again, and she turned away still further. "Does his miracle perform, he may receive a boon. I shall send him a sprite, dear Goodfellow, and our agreement stands."

"My lady." He cut another bow, but she did not see the sarcastic turn his leer had taken. "You do me much honor."

"Oh, aye." A girl's carefree giggle, and she moved away, the grass leaning toward her glow and the fireflies trailing. "I do, when the service is well wrought. Farewell, hob. I'll send him a familiar face, since mortals are timid." Her laugh, deeper and richer now, caroled between the shivering birches, a pocket of cold swallowing a struggling swimmer.

"Mind that you do," Goodfellow said, but softly, softly. He capered once more, to hear the dried brambles crunch underfoot, like mortal bones. He spun, quick brown fingers finding the pipes at his belt. He lifted them to his mouth, and his own eyes fired green in the darkness. Full night had fallen, and silver threads of music lifted in the distance—the Queen was well pleased, it seemed, and had called upon the minstrels to play.

He stepped *sideways,* pirouetting neatly on the ball of one foot, and emerged in a mortal alley. It was night here, too, and as he danced along, the breathy, wooden notes from his pipes arrowed free in a rill. Concrete whirled underfoot, the mortal world flashing and trembling as he skipped across its pleats and hollows. They did not see, the dull cold sacks of frail flesh, and only some few of them heard.

Those who did shuddered, though they could not have said why. A cold finger laid itself on their napes, or in another sensitive spot, and the gooseflesh walked over them. None of them suited Goodfellow, so he ambled on.

A little while later, a mortal chanced across his path—a

sturdy youth, strong and healthy, who thought the Fatherless a common, staggering drunkard. With the pipes whispering in his ear, luring him down another path, the mortal boy did not realize he was prey instead of hunter until his unvictim rounded on him with wide, lambent eyes and a sharp, sickeningly cheery smile.

Yes, Goodfellow decided as he crouched to crunch, hot salt against his tongue, bramble *did* sound like mortal bones, if it was dry enough.

Pleased by his own thoroughness, he ate his fill.

SIMULACRUM

2

Jeremiah Gallow, once known as the Queensglass, stood twenty stories above the pavement, just like he did almost every day at lunchtime since they'd started building a brand-new headquarters for some megabank or another.

He was reasonably sure the drop wouldn't kill him. Cars creeping below were shiny beetles, the walking mortals dots of muted color, hurrying or ambling as the mood took them. From this height, they were ants. Scurrying, just like the ones he worked beside, sweating out their brief gray lives.

A chill breeze resonated through superstructure, iron girders harpstrings plucked by invisible fingers. He was wet with sweat, exhaust-laden breeze mouthing his ruthlessly cropped black hair. Poison in the air just like poison in the singing rods and rivets, but neither troubled a Half. He had nothing to fear from cold iron.

No mortal-Tainted did. A fullblood sidhe would be uncomfortable, nervous around the most inimical of mortal metals. *The more fae, the more to fear.*

Like every proverb, true in different interlocking ways.

Jeremiah leaned forward still further, looking past the scarred toes of his dun workboots. The jobsite was another scar on the seamed face of the city, a skeleton rising from a shell of orange and yellow caution tape and signage to keep mortals from bruising themselves. Couldn't have civilians wandering in and getting hit on the head, suing the management or anything like that.

A lone worker bee, though, could take three steps back, gather himself, and sail right past the flimsy lath barrier. The fall would be studded and scarred by clutching fingers of steel and cement, and the landing would be sharp.

If he was singularly unlucky he'd end up a Twisted, crippled monstrosity, or even just a half-Twisted unable to use glamour—or any other bit of sidhe chantment—without it warping him further. Shuffling out an existence cringing from both mortal and sidhe, and you couldn't keep a mortal job if you had feathers instead of hair, or half your face made of wood, or no glamour to hide the oddities sidhe blood could bring to the surface.

Daisy would have been clutching at his arm, her fear lending a smoky tang to her salt-sweet mortal scent. She hated heights.

The thought of his dead wife sent a sharp, familiar bolt of pain through his chest. Her hair would have caught fire today; it was cold but bright, thin almost-spring sunshine making every shadow a knife edge. He leaned forward a little more, his arms spreading slightly, the wind a hungry lover's hand. A cold edge of caress. *Just a little closer. Just a little further.*

It might hurt enough to make you forget.

"Gallow, what the hell?" Clyde bellowed.

Jeremiah stepped back, half-turned on one rubber-padded heel. The boots were thick soled, caked with the detritus of a hundred build sites. Probably dust on there from places both mortal and not-so-mortal; he'd worn them since before his marriage. Short black hair and pale green eyes, a face that could be any anonymous construction worker's. Not young, not old, not distinctive at all, what little skill he had with glamour pressed into service to make him look just like every other mortal guy with a physical job and a liking for beer every now and again.

His arms tingled; he knew the markings were moving on his skin, under the long sleeves. "Thought I saw something." *A way out.* But only if he was sure it would be an escape, not a fresh snare.

Being Half just made you too damn durable.

"Like what, a pigeon? Millions of those around." The bullet-headed foreman folded his beefy arms. He was already red and perspiring, though the temperature hadn't settled above forty degrees all week.

Last summer had been mild-chill, fall icy, winter hard, and spring was late this year. Maybe the Queen hadn't opened the Gates yet.

Summer. The shiver—half loathing, half something else—that went through Jeremiah must have shown. Clyde took a half step sideways, reaching up to push his hard hat further back on his sweat-shaven pate. He had a magnificent broad white mustache, and the mouth under it turned into a thin line as he dropped his hands loosely to his sides.

Easy, there. Jeremiah might have laughed. Still, you could never tell who on a jobsite might have a temper. Best to be safe around heavy machinery, crowbars, nail guns, and the like.

"A seagull." Gallow deliberately hunched his shoulders, pulled the rage and pain back inside his skin. "Maybe a hawk. Or something. You want my apple pie?" If Clyde had a weakness, it was sugar-drenched, overprocessed pastry. Just like a brughnie, actually.

Another shiver roiled through him, but he kept it inside. *Don't think on the sidhe. You know it puts you in a mood.*

Clyde perked up a little. "If you don't want it. How come you bring 'em if you don't want 'em?"

Insurance. Always bring something to barter with. Jeremiah dug in his lunchbag. He'd almost forgotten he'd crumpled most of the brown paper in his fist. Daisy always sent him to work with a carefully packed lunch, but the collection of retro metal boxes she'd found at Goodwill and Salvation Army were all gone now. If he hadn't thrown them away he had stamped on them, crushing each piece with the same boots he was wearing now. "Habit. Put 'em in the bag each time."

She'd done sandwiches, too, varying to keep them interesting. Turkey. Chicken. Good old PB&J, two of them to keep him fueled. Hard-boiled eggs with a twist of salt in waxed paper, carefully quartered apples bathed in lemon juice to keep them from browning, home-baked goodies. Banana bread, muffins, she'd even gone through a sushi phase once until he'd let it slip that he didn't prefer raw fish.

I just thought, you're so smart and all. Ain't sushi what smart people eat? And her laugh at his baffled look. She often made little comments like that, as if… Well, she never knew of the sidhe, but she considered him a creature from a different planet just the same.

"Oh." Clyde took the Hostess apple pie, his entire face brightening. "Just don't stand too near that edge, Gallow. You fall off and I'll have L&I all over me."

"Not gonna." It was hard taking the next few steps away from the edge. His heels landed solidly, and the wind stopped keening across rebar and concrete. Or at least, the sound retreated. "Haven't yet."

"Always a first time. Hey, me and Panko are going out for beers after. You wanna?" The waxed wrapper tore open, and Clyde took a huge mouthful of sugar that only faintly resembled the original apple.

"Sure." It was Friday, the start of a long weekend. If he went home he was only going to eat another TV dinner, or nothing at all, and sit staring at the fist-sized hole in the television screen, in his messy living room.

Ridiculous. Why did they call it that? Nobody did any *living* in there.

"Okay." Clyde gave him another odd look, and Jeremiah had a sudden vision of smashing his fist into the old man's face. The crunch of bone, the gush of blood, the satisfaction of a short sharp action. The foreman wasn't even a sidhe, to require an exchange of names beforehand.

I'm mortal now. Best to remember it. Besides, the foreman wasn't to blame for anything. Guiltless as only a mortal could be.

"Better get back to work," Jeremiah said instead, and tossed his crumpled lunchbag into the cut-down trash barrel hulking near the lift. "Gotta earn those beers."

Clyde had his mouth full, and Jeremiah was glad. If the man said another word, he wasn't sure he could restrain himself. There was no good reason for the rage, except the fact that he'd been brought back from the brink, and reminded he was only a simulacrum of a mortal man.

Again.

A MORTAL FAILING

3

It looks clear. The Gates shimmered slightly, cold metal under Robin Ragged's fingertips. Triple her own height, cruel spikes along their tops frozen with hungry, thorn-carved flowers, they hummed a low warning scrape-noise at her.

She drew back into shadow, afternoon sun rippling as the border between *here* and *there* slid. As long as she stayed just within touch of the Gates, one foot carefully on either side of the dividing line, she wasn't trackable even though she was technically outside Summer's realm. Had Robin a choice, she wouldn't have picked *this* point of egress—but the Queen had ordered her to make haste.

The shadows *there,* in the gray mere-mortal world, all had teeth. Low doglike shapes with moonlit eyes twisted, their slim muzzles lifted between wavering seaweed fringes. If there was any doubt of the watch kept on the Seelie Gates, it was now assuaged most heartily.

Robin whistled tunelessly, concentrating, a silver quirpiece—an hour's worth of work, a paltry insurance against pursuit—clutched in her free hand. Her palm was sweating.

Mortal sweat, perfuming the air around her in long shimmering strands. Her skirt fluttered a little, eternal Summer breathing against her left ankle, a chill almost-spring wind touching her right. Dusk was the best time to slip through unremarked, but too far into nightfall was dangerous.

She could not wait for dawn, the rising sun that would keep most Unseelie at bay. One of the Queen's mortal pets had sent word, so Robin was sent to fetch and carry.

Again.

The Gates were not open, but the postern just to the north of them admitted or released any Seelie who required it—at least, any Summer sidhe not sickened by the damn plague. The Queen wouldn't tread the path leading to the other side of the Gates for another short while. Sooner or later she must, and who could tell if the infection running rampant outside Summer would enter once the actual Gates were flung wide?

Nobody knew, and even the mortal-Tainted of a scientific bent—now petted and cosseted in the hopes of finding a cure, instead of ridiculed and relentlessly pranked by their more sidhe-blooded betters—couldn't tell for certain. There was only one assurance so far, and it was that those Tainted by mortal blood weren't prey to the sickness. A quartering of mortal or more seemed to keep the infection at bay.

Here on the borders, safe in the interference, it was perhaps the only place Robin could allow herself to think that the black-boil plague could be a blessing in disguise if it cleared away the proud and malignant. Still, if the fullborn sidhe were all gone, what did that leave for the mortal-Tainted, even the most blessed of mixtures, the full Half?

Once the wellspring was gone, would the smaller freshets dry up? It was an article of unquestioned faith, how the fullborn kept both Courts sideways to the mortal world.

Which still left those with only a measure of sidhe blood in an uncertainty. Maybe a new plague would spring from the old. Or would they simply escape into the mortal world and leave Summer and Unwinter both, not to mention the Low Counties, as fading, dry-leaf memories?

She could have refused to tread outside Summer's borders. But there was Sean, now at the Queen's dubious, thorny mercy. The Queen would not let her Robin loose without a silken thread tied to the leg. What else did Robin have left? Her sister was dead, and well so, for it meant she could not be used against the Ragged; grief was a luxury to be shelved so she could *do,* and just perhaps find a way to slip the leash.

She buried that thought as soon as it rose. Even if it was fairly safe here, the reflex was too strong. *Think on something safer. Something that will help you survive.*

Her fingers relaxed, undyed nails tapping the silvery metal of the Gates. *Clear enough, at least, and it's likely to become no clearer for the waiting.* It would be chill in the mortal realm, but she wouldn't feel it, not with the warming breath and her own half of sidhe blood. Besides, it was easy enough to steal clothing.

For a moment she toyed with the dangerous idea of losing herself in the mortal world, abandoning the sidhe to their own problems. There *was* a valley or a city that would hide her somewhere in the wide, wide world. The Queen would no doubt forget her after a while.

Unless she did not.

Sean. The child's face turned up to hers, his golden hair smoothed by Robin's own fingers every day. Her shoulders hunched, and she suppressed a shiver. All the stars of Summer's dusk, and his soft voice following hers as she taught him the constellations. Would it be easier to be fullblood, and able to set down a pretty mortal child and forget it? Regret was, as far as she could tell, only a mortal failing.

Half were oft presented with the choice of being like the sidhe, or like the mortals. As far as Robin could tell, neither side of the coin lacked tarnish.

I'm stalling. She cast a look over her shoulder, an impatient toss of her curls. Fields sloped away behind the Gates' bars, a sweet green valley opening up and each copse of trees drowsing under golden afternoon sun too richly liquid to be mortal. The Queen would be in the orchard today, because the pennants were up, snapping and fluttering on a brisk hay-and-apple wind. Thomas Rinevale would be harping; he was high in favor at the moment. The ladies-in-waiting would be draped across silk and satin pillows, and the Queen would be resting in the tent, her white cheek against her pale hand, smiling just slightly and very aware of her own beauty as Sean brought her another cup of *lithori* or a bunch of damson grapes.

If the blackboil plague breached the Court, that white skin might be raddled in days, and that golden hair a snarl of dishwater. Her graceful slenderness would become a jenny-hag's bony withering. Eventually, Summer might choke out a gout of black brackish fluid, and expire, her eaten body collapsing into foul wet dust.

A comforting thought, and one Robin kept despite the danger. She turned away from Summer and faced the mortal world again. Everything now depended on luck, speed, and her native wit. Her whistle became a high drilling buzz, lips pursing and her hair lifting on a breeze from neither realm. Robin Ragged's blue silken skirt snapped once, her heels clicking as she stepped with a jolt fully into the mortal world, slipping through a rent in the Veil just her size and shape. Her fingers left cold metal, the Gates' thrum disappearing like a train rolling into the distance, and the alley closed around her. Bricks, garbage, the effluvia of combustion engines and decay.

For all that, it was an honest reek, and she welcomed it as she took a few experimental steps. The world rippled around her, cautious as it always was to accept a child of the sideways realms, then firmed like gelatin.

She made it to the alley mouth, peered out into the city. Night gathered in corners. It was the perfect moment of dusk, when the tides between all the realms, sideways and mortal, turned and the interference made it difficult to track *anything*, much less one ragged little bird with a whistle that trilled into silence.

She cocked her head. She'd gone unremarked.

At least, she *thought* she had, until the ultrasonic cry of a silver huntwhistle lifted in the distance, and she thought perhaps *they* had been watching far more closely than even the Queen had guessed.

It was whispered that Unwinter himself had loosed the plague, and even now reveled in its destructive force. Certainly Summer had openly hinted as much, when the black boils began to cut a swath through the unaligned. The free sidhe often named themselves the lucky ones who bowed to no master—at least, not fully, though there was always the Fatherless.

Don't think about him. If all goes well, you won't see him tonight. He won't even know you've been out and about.

Robin slid out of the alley and set off down the deserted street, cars humming in the distance and every nerve in her body quivering-alert.

Now let's see how well I run the course. Her heels tapped the sidewalk as she lengthened her stride, her much-mended skirt whispering and her curls bouncing. She was not so foolish as to think fear of any reprisal from Summer would keep her whole should Unwinter's hounds have orders to bring the Ragged to their liege.

She was, however, just arrogant enough to think perhaps she could outrun them, and if all else failed, there was always the song, its thunder under her thoughts a comforting roil.

Dusk closed around her, and Robin hurried.

introducing

IF YOU ENJOYED

BLOOD CALL,

LOOK OUT FOR

THE GIRL IN 6E

A Deanna Madden Novel
Book One

by A. R. Torre

My life is simple, as long as I follow the rules.
1. Don't leave the apartment.
2. Never let anyone in.
3. Don't kill anyone.
I've obeyed these rules for three years. But rules were made to be broken.

Chapter 1

I HAVEN'T TOUCHED another person in three years. That
seems like a difficult task, but it's not. Not anymore, thanks to
the Internet. The Internet, which makes my income possible
and provides anything I could possibly want in exchange for my
credit card number. I've had to go into the underground world
for a few things, and once in that world, I decided to stock up
on a few fun items, like a new identity. I am now, when necessary, Jessica Beth Reilly. I use my alias to prevent others from
finding out my past. Pity is a bitch I'd like to avoid. The underground provides a plethora of temptations, but so far, with one
notable exception, I've stayed away from illegal arms and unreg-
istered guns. I know my limits.

The UPS man knows me by now—knows to leave my boxes
in the hall and to scrawl my name on his signature pad. His
name is Jeremy. About a year ago he was sick, and a stranger
came to my door. He refused to leave the package without seeing me. I almost opened the door and went for his box cutters.
They almost always carry box cutters. That's one of the things I
love about deliverymen. I stayed fast, refusing to open the door,

and he stayed stubborn, arguing with me until he grew tired and left, taking the damn package with him. Jeremy hasn't been sick since then. I don't know what I'll ever do if he quits. I like Jeremy, and from my warped peephole view, there is a lot about him to like. Muscular build, short dark hair, and a smile that stretches quickly and easily over his face, even when there isn't a damn thing to smile about.

The first shrink I had said I have anthropophobia, which is fear of human interaction. Anthropophobia, mixed with an unhealthy dose of dacnomania, which is obsession with murder. He told me that via Skype. In exchange for his psychological opinions, I watched him jack off. He had a little cock. I think he was right on the second half of that diagnosis. But I don't fear human interaction. I fear what will happen when I get close enough to a human to interact. Let's just say I don't play well with others.

While I may go out of my way to avoid physical human interaction, virtual human interaction is what I spend all day doing. To the people I cam with, I am JessReilly19, a bubbly nineteen-year-old college student—a hospitality major—who enjoys pop music, underage drinking, and shopping. None of them really know the true me. I am who they want me to be, and they like it like that. So do I.

Knowing the real me would be a bit of a buzzkill. The real me is Deanna Madden, whose mother killed her entire family, then committed suicide. At the time it was big news, the "tragedy strikes perfect family" story of the summer. My name was attached to sympathy, notoriety. But then other tragedies occurred and my family dropped off the grid. I inherited a lot from my mother, including delicate features, long legs, and dark hair, but the biggest genetic inheritance has been her homicidal tendencies. That's the reason I stay away from people. Because I want to kill. Constantly. It's almost all I think about.

My inner demons have driven me here, to apartment 6E, my world for the last three years, all I need contained in nine hundred square feet. I've learned, from inside these walls, how to generate and optimize my income. From eight a.m. to three p.m. I work on a website called Sexnow.com, which has a clientele of mostly Asians, Europeans, and Australians. From six p.m. to eleven p.m. I'm on American turf, Cams.com. In between shifts, I eat, work out, shower, and return e-mails—always in that order. I spend my days on a strict schedule. It helps to tell my brain when to behave a certain way and helps to keep my impulses and fantasies under control.

Whenever possible, I try to get clients to bypass the camsites and use my personal website to book an appointment and pay. If they go through my website, I make 96.5 percent of their payout, plus I can hide the income from Uncle Sam. The camsites pay me only 28 percent, which officially constitutes highway robbery. I charge $6.99 a minute. On a good month, I make around $55,000 from camming—on a bad one, about $30,000.That income makes up about 70 percent of my total dough; the rest comes from my website's subscription memberships, which allow men to watch a live video feed of my different cam sessions. I broadcast at least four hours a day and charge subscribers twenty bucks a month. I wouldn't pay ten cents to watch me masturbate online, but apparently 350 subscribers feel differently.

The $6.99 a minute grants clients the ability to bare their sexual secrets and fantasize to their heart's content, without fear of exposure or criticism. I don't judge the men and women who chat with me and reveal their secrets and perversions. How can

I? My secret, my obsession, is worse than any of theirs. To contain it, I do the only thing I can: I lock myself up. And in doing so, I keep myself, and everyone else, safe.

It is, in simple terms, a shitload of money. Money that I have no earthly idea what to do with. I can spend only so much on sex toys and lube. But thinking about the money makes me think about life outside of this apartment, so I don't. The funds go in my account and are ignored. Maybe they will be used one day, maybe they won't. But I'd rather have the cash than not. I feel protected having it there. I feel like at least one part of my life is going right.

I try to sleep at least eight hours a night. Nighttime is when I typically struggle the most. It is when I thirst for blood, for gore. So Simon Evans and I have an agreement. Simon lives three doors down from me in this shithole that we all call an apartment complex. Over the last three years, he has developed a strong addiction to prescription painkillers. I keep his medicine bottle filled, and he locks me up at night. Without a doubt, my door is the only one in the complex without a dead-bolt switch on the inside.

I used to have Marilyn do it. She's a grandmotherly type who struggles by on the pittance that is her Social Security. She lives across from Simon. But Marilyn stressed out too much; she was always worried that I would have some personal emergency, or fire, or something, and would need to get out. I had to find someone else. Because I knew what was coming. At night, my fingers would start to itch, and I would come close to picking up that phone, to asking her to unlock my door. And then I would wait beside it, wait for the tumblers to move and my door to be unlocked. And when I opened it, when I saw Marilyn's lined and tired face, I would kill her. Not immediately. I would stab her a few times, leaving some life in her, and wait for her to run, to scream. I like the sound of screams—real screams, not the pathetic excuse that most movies try to pass off as the sound of terror. Then I would chase her down and finish the job, as slowly as I could. Dragging out her pain, her agony, her realization that she had caused her own death. I had gotten to the point where I had picked out a knife, started to keep it in the cardboard box that sits by the door and holds my outgoing mail and various crap. That was when I knew I was getting too close. That was when I picked Simon instead. Simon's addiction supersedes any concern he has for my well-being.

I know what you think. That I'm being dramatic. That I saw a Stephen King movie once and got excited at the thought of blood. But you don't know the depravity of my mind. You don't know the thoughts I struggle with, what I fight to contain. Simon certainly doesn't know. He thinks I'm a hermit with night terrors—that I sleepwalk. I'm sure he thinks my steadfast dedication to the lock is ridiculous, the unyielding nature of my strict demands extreme. My threats always heighten when he is late, but that doesn't happen often. It takes only a mention of cutting his supply and he snaps to attention. The most reliable thing on earth is a druggie's cravings. I think they are worse than mine. But the only person Simon is hurting with his addiction is himself. I have a whole world of victims outside these walls.

Chapter 2

HIS FANTASIES ARE getting stronger. It has been almost three years since the last girl, and his need has overtaken the rational part of his mind. The invitation didn't help. The announcement, like a huge glowing sign, that she is turning six. It had come in the mail, pink construction paper with handwritten details in a childish script that could only be hers.

He had hoped that a scratch wouldn't be needed, that the itch could be minimized and held at a level that was bearable, controllable. But he can feel himself weakening, feel a break in his streak coming. He hopes role-playing will be enough to satisfy his itch, his enjoyment of the sessions giving him hope.

But just in case, he needs to prepare. If he is going to stumble, if he is going to fall, things must be in place. This time he will keep the girl around longer. Create enough memories to tide him over for a longer period. His hands shake and he stuffs them in his pockets, moving through the grass to the front of the trailer, pulling out the creased envelope that holds the key. He glances around the empty yard, the wind rustling through quiet brush, isolation surrounding him. Ripping the paper, he ignores the landlord's letter and palms the key.

Preparation. Just to be safe. Maybe he won't need this place. But just in case, better make sure that everything is ready. Preparation has always paid off in the past.

CPSIA information can be obtained
at www.ICGtesting.com
Printed in the USA
FFOW04n1323010915
16452FF

9 780316 343602